THE
ICARUS
TWIN

BAEN BOOKS by TIMOTHY ZAHN

THE ICARUS SAGA
The Icarus Plot
The Icarus Twin
The Icarus Job (forthcoming)

Battle Luna (with Travis S. Taylor,
Michael Z. Williamson, Kacey Ezell & Josh Hayes)
Blackcollar: The Judas Solution
Blackcollar (contains *The Blackcollar*
and *Blackcollar: The Backlash Mission*)
The Cobra Trilogy (contains *Cobra,*
Cobra Strike, and *Cobra Bargain*)

COBRA WAR
Cobra Alliance
Cobra Guardian
Cobra Gamble

COBRA REBELLION
Cobra Slave
Cobra Outlaw
Cobra Traitor

MANTICORE ASCENDANT
A Call to Duty by David Weber & Timothy Zahn
A Call to Arms by David Weber &
Timothy Zahn with Thomas Pope
A Call to Vengeance by David Weber &
Timothy Zahn with Thomas Pope
A Call to Insurrection by David Weber &
Timothy Zahn with Thomas Pope

For a complete listing of Baen titles by Timothy Zahn,
and to purchase any of these titles in e-book form,
please go to www.baen.com.

THE ICARUS TWIN

TIMOTHY ZAHN

BAEN

A Baen Books Original

Baen Publishing Enterprises
P.O. Box 1403
Riverdale, NY 10471
www.baen.com

ISBN: 978-1-9821-9305-8

Cover art by Dave Seeley

First printing, December 2023

Distributed by Simon & Schuster
1230 Avenue of the Americas
New York, NY 10020

Library of Congress Cataloging-in-Publication Data

Names: Zahn, Timothy, author.
Title: The Icarus twin / Timothy Zahn.
Description: Riverdale, NY : Baen Publishing Enterprises, 2023. | Series: The Icarus saga ; 2
Identifiers: LCCN 2023036754 (print) | LCCN 2023036755 (ebook) | ISBN 9781982193058 (hardcover) | ISBN 9781625799395 (ebook)
Subjects: LCGFT: Science fiction. | Novels.
Classification: LCC PS3576.A33 I296 2023 (print) | LCC PS3576.A33 (ebook) | DDC 813/.54—dc23/eng/20230817
LC record available at https://lccn.loc.gov/2023036754
LC ebook record available at https://lccn.loc.gov/2023036755

Printed in the United States of America
10 9 8 7 6 5 4 3 2 1

THE
ICARUS
TWIN

CHAPTER ONE

The popular image of Trailblazers, when the populace thinks about us at all, is one of rugged, solitary figures flying among the stars, searching square-jawedly among the Spiral's thousands of uninhabited worlds, braving tedium, pirates, and claim-jumpers, searching for places with the climate and resources to offer hope to the weary masses, triumphing in the end as they guide those same masses to their new worlds and their new lives. We're probably assumed to sing hearty wayfarer shanties along the way, too.

As usual, popular culture has it completely wrong. Crocketts are almost never alone, given that the upper atmospheric launch and retrieval of bioprobes is nearly impossible for a single person to pull off. We aren't any more square-jawed than the rest of the Spiral's population, we certainly don't find promising new worlds every episode, the pirates know we don't have anything worth stealing, and the claim-jumpers don't show up until a report and claim have actually been filed.

And as for the tedium—

The *Ruth* gave another violent lurch, this one throwing me hard enough against my straps to leave bruises and jolting me out of the tangent line of thought the previous lurch had jolted me into. "Selene!" I shouted toward the intercom.

"I know," she called back, her normally soft and delicate

1

Kadolian voice strained almost beyond recognition. "I don't know where this turbulence came from. There was nothing showing until it was right on top of us."

"Never mind how it got here," I called back, setting my teeth as another gust of wind sent the *Ruth* skittering a few degrees to portside. Our two bioprobes were on their way up, and unless we did something fast they were going to run smack damn into this mass of swirling air. The little torpedo-shaped gadgets weren't all that delicate, and while the air at this altitude wasn't dense enough for even the mightiest gusts to damage them it was more than powerful enough to blow them way and hell off their preprogrammed courses. With their fuel tanks running toward dry, it wouldn't take much of a delay to send them angling away and then plunging them and their hard-won samples to the surface far below.

But as my father used to say, *Teaching the dog to fetch usually takes longer than just getting the darn thing yourself.* "I need you to run us a sixty-degree down-pitch," I told Selene, eyeing the status board and doing a quick mental calculation. "Keep us on that vector for eighty seconds, then pull up level again. Got that?"

"Yes."

"Good," I said. "How's the ship doing?"

There was a brief pause, and I could visualize her nostrils working and her eyelashes fluttering as she sampled the ship's air with her incredibly hypersensitive sense of smell. All of my displays and gauges were assuring me that the *Ruth* was holding up just fine, but systems that were about to go gunnybags often gave off a subtly altered scent that Selene could pick up, usually before the monitor programs figured it out. "We're all right," she said. "The starboard grav beam generator is running a little hot, but I don't think it's going to be trouble."

I mouthed a curse. As if we weren't going to have enough trouble getting the bioprobes back aboard without having to deal with a possibly balky grav generator. "If that changes, let me know," I said. "We may have to try a grapevine."

"All right," she said, her voice suddenly cautious.

"Yeah, me too," I agreed. Using a single grav beam to sequentially snatch both bioprobes was hard enough in calm air. It would be exponentially trickier with the *Ruth* bouncing around like a water droplet on a hot griddle. "But if it comes to that, we won't have a choice. Ready?"

"Yes."

"Okay." Gazing at the status board, I counted out three more seconds. "*Go.*"

The deck dropped out from under me as the *Ruth*'s gravity plates took a fraction of a second to adjust to Selene's sudden maneuver. I watched the displays, focusing on the bioprobes rising up toward us, bracing myself for even more turbulence as we dipped deeper into the atmosphere. A small part of my mind noted the oddity that the buffeting we were receiving seemed to be easing up a little as we descended into thicker air.

And then the bioprobes lurched into sight, and I had no attention to spare for anything else. I watched as the *Ruth*'s computer pinged the probes' transponders and locked on the tight-core grav beams. The starboard grav generator was still holding on, with no indication of imminent failure. Both bioprobes were angling up toward the *Ruth* now—

Without warning, the portside probe gave a violent twitch, twisted out of the grav beam's focal point, and disappeared back into the swirling air below us.

"Gregory!" Selene snapped.

"I see it," I shouted back from between clenched teeth. My first impulse was to tell her to go into another dive and chase after it.

But if we did that, we would lose the other bioprobe, still a few seconds from being reeled into its bay.

As my father used to say, *A bird in the hand is worth a thousand up in a tree two towns over.* "Just hold us steady until we've got the first one aboard," I told her. "After that, if I can track the other one, we'll go after it."

"All right."

The sensors were set for narrow beam; great if you were looking for bioprobes that were where they were supposed to be, less great if one of them had gone walkies. I switched over to a wider beam, boosted the power, and aimed them downward.

There, far below us, was the last thing I would ever have expected to see, out here in the middle of nowhere, in the atmosphere of an unnamed and—so far, at least—unwanted world.

Another ship.

It was already right at the edge of the sensors' atmospheric range, dropping rapidly through the atmosphere, and I got only a glimpse before it disappeared from sight.

But that glimpse was enough. It was another Trailblazer ship, all right, poking around the same planet we were.

And if the signal from our wayward transponder was accurate, they'd just poached our bioprobe and its samples.

"What in the—? Gregory!"

"I see it," I gritted out. But there was nothing we could do. With the single bioprobe we were still reeling in all we had left, it was more vital than ever that we bring it safely aboard. If we lost it, too, this whole trip would have been for nothing.

Of course, it had probably been for nothing anyway. But it was important to stay positive in these things. At least we were on salary now instead of doing our crockett trips at piecework rates.

Which didn't make it any easier to swallow the fact that the poachers down there were going to get away with their crime and their prize.

But as my father used to say, *Being angry doesn't do you any good, or the other guy any harm.* So I took a deep breath, ran through the whole list of expletives I wanted to say, and focused on getting our remaining bioprobe back home.

For once, the universe smiled in our favor. Or, more likely, it got distracted and forgot we were here. As the poacher and our lost property vanished, so did the sudden turbulence that had plagued us for the past few minutes. The bioprobe was pulled in and locked in its bay exactly like it was supposed to, and a few minutes after that Selene had us pulling for space.

Thirty minutes later, once again in hyperspace, we suited up and headed to the *Ruth*'s clean room to see what exactly our most recent atmospheric jaunt had scored for us.

Once again, what it had scored for us was a big fat zero.

"I believe that makes seventeen in a row," I growled as Selene finished packing away the ampules, now loaded with the seeds, spores, and other biological whatnot the bioprobe had scooped from the planet's atmosphere. "Not exactly batting a thousand here."

"It's not *that* bad," Selene soothed as she took off her exam smock and folded it into the laundry hamper. "There were at least three samples in this group that showed medicinal potential."

"I suppose," I conceded.

And really, up until recently that would have been more

than enough to justify the trip. Most of the crocketts plying the spacelanes out there would be doing cartwheels, or at least cautious somersaults, over a haul like that.

But we weren't looking for interesting biochemicals or even habitable planets anymore. Six months ago, we'd been handed a new charter: to begin a quiet search for more of the alien star portals that had first been found and identified by the ultrasecret Icarus Group.

No one knew who'd created the things or where they came from, and after almost seven years of trying the Icarus researchers had only barely scratched the surface of learning how exactly they worked. What we *did* know was that they were the biggest potential game-changer in the field of interstellar commerce and travel since the Patthaaunutth unleashed their fancy Talariac Drive on the Spiral two decades ago. With the Talariac four times faster and three times cheaper than any other stardrive on the market, it had quickly risen to dominate all the major trade routes and many of the smaller ones, a lofty position the drive and the Patth still held.

The only thing that had kept the Talariac from forcing every other drive into oblivion was the fact that the Patth were completely paranoid about their trade secrets leaking out. They'd set things up so that only their own pilots could fly the damn things, and only because they'd had critical parts of the access circuitry and visual display feedback systems surgically implanted into their faces and bodies. Since there were only so many Patth pilots available for other people to hire, there was at least a little breathing space for everyone else who wanted to make a living flying between the stars.

But the Patth dominance would crash and burn if anyone could locate enough Icarus portals to create even a limited transport network. So far there were only three of them known, and all three were under the control—more or less—of the Icarus Group.

Unfortunately, the Patth had had a taste of the portals' potential, and were hell-bent on starting a collection of their own. Their agents were out there, hunting quietly but furiously for hints or rumors, probably focusing on the portals' unique double-sphere shape. The Patth Director General had the people, he had the resources, and he had the burning desire to keep his species on top.

What he *didn't* have was Selene.

Portal hull metal gave off a faint but distinctive odor, a scent that even the Icarus Group's best sensors couldn't sift out of an olfactory background. But Selene could. She could sniff out even the most minute hint of the stuff.

Which was what we were doing out here. In theory, if there was a portal lying around on a given Planet X, sending a probe down to bring up a biosphere sample might also include a few of those hull-metal molecules, which Selene might then be able to sniff out.

There were a lot of *ifs* and *mights* in that theory, enough to make a reasonable person wonder if the approach was worth the effort and money. But the Icarus Group had been poking around alien artifacts for a long time, and they apparently had money to burn.

Still, seventeen failures in a row was bound to eventually attract the attention of whoever was handling Admiral Sir Graym-Barker's budget. Sooner or later they would conclude that the *Ruth* was a money sink, and we'd be back to scrambling for clients who were just looking for habitable worlds and possible medical biomolecules instead of exotic alien technology.

"What is it?" Selene asked.

At the beginning of our relationship, her steadily improving ability to pick up on my mood shifts via the corresponding changes in my scent had struck me as rather creepy. Now, I just considered it a convenient conversational time-saver. "I was just thinking about how it used to be," I said. "Us hustling for clients and fending off poachers trying to underbid us for contracts. That got me thinking about our other poachers back there."

"I've been thinking about them, too," she said, the pupils of her deep-set gray cats' eyes showing puzzled thought. "I only got a glimpse of the ship, but it looked like it had four large bulges, one at each corner."

"It did indeed," I said, rather surprised she'd spotted even that much with most of her attention on keeping the *Ruth* flying straight. "Pretty sure they were tiltrotors."

"Yes, that's what I thought," she said, her confusion deepening. "But I thought tiltrotor ships were designed for deeper atmosphere studies."

"They are," I said. "Which means either they were minding

their own business, heading up through atmo, and just happened to come up right beneath us and close enough to steal our probe—"

"Which seems unlikely," Selene murmured.

"Which seems extremely unlikely," I agreed. "Especially since we now know they were running a particularly delicate lift balance, probably using the center rotors spinning one direction to give them lift while the peripherals blew that wonderful windstorm in our figurative face to keep us busy."

"All of which I assume takes a certain amount of preparation."

"Preparation and foresight both," I said. "Which takes us to Option Two: They were deliberately stalking us."

A shiver ran through Selene's body. "They know we're working for Icarus."

"Not necessarily," I said in my most calming voice, knowing full well that fudging the issue was probably a waste of effort. "They could just be normal poachers. They could have tracked our vector from Billingsgate, waited out at a distance until we were in atmo and our attention focused below us, then slipped in somewhere else and moved underneath us. It could have nothing to do with Icarus."

"Why would anyone have followed us from Billingsgate in the first place?" she countered. "We're not important enough for anyone to keep tabs on." Her pupils gave a little wince. "Anyone except Nask."

I felt my throat tighten. She was right on that one, anyway. Sub-Director Nask, former head of the Patth Firefall project, had more than enough reason to keep us on his radar.

It was unlikely that he knew about the special portal scent we were searching for. But we *were* licensed crocketts, and it wouldn't take a huge leap of logic on his part to guess Graym-Barker might have hired us. A quick search of the records to see how many samples we'd submitted to the Association of Planetary Trailblazers in the past six months—that number being zero—and he'd have a pretty good idea what we were up to.

Or he might not care about what we were doing at all, but was merely looking for a chance to extract a pound of flesh from each of us. We'd been instrumental in ruining his hoped-for moment of triumph and glory, and I was pretty sure Patth weren't the forgive-and-forget types.

Of course, he *did* owe us for pointing out our former employer

Luko Varsi's private arrangement with someone high up in the Patth hierarchy. Still, given everything else, I doubted that would shift the balance scales much.

"I highly doubt it was Nask himself," I soothed. "He must surely have better things to do than personally follow us around the Spiral."

"Even if he knows we're working for Icarus?"

"Working *with* Icarus," I corrected reflexively. I still refused to think of us as anything but independent contractors, no matter how big a monthly stipend Graym-Barker dropped into our account on Xathru.

"Working *with* Icarus," Selene corrected, her pupils showing exaggerated patience. "I note you're not answering the question."

I sighed. "Yes, that might make a difference," I conceded. "But whoever it was, there's not a lot we can do about it. You put us on a course for Reichsbach, right?"

"Yes," she said. "Do you want to change that?"

"I think we need to," I said, popping the clean room's hatch and stepping out into the corridor. "Finish up here and meet me on the bridge."

I was poring over the maps on the navigation console when she arrived. "Where are we going?" she asked.

I gave the maps one more look and came to a decision. "Marjolaine," I said, keying it into the navigational console. "It's close, it's got a sparse enough traffic flow that we should be able to spot anyone following us, but it also has six StarrComm centers we can choose from. Even Nask can't cover that many, at least not seriously."

Selene didn't answer. Probably thinking that a Patth subdirector could surely whistle up the resources to do damn near anything he wanted. "What about this?" she asked, holding out one of the ampules from the clean room.

"Is that one of the promising samples?" I asked.

"It's *the* most promising sample, yes."

I scowled. With visions of angry Patth and their nasty, corona-weapon-wielding Iykam lackeys drifting across my mind's eye, I really didn't have much interest in playing biomolecule roulette, no matter how promising the sample was.

But there *were* Icarus's accountants to think of, plus whatever limits might be on Graym-Barker's patience. Six months was already a long time for a single gig, and I'd be stupid to assume it would last forever.

And Nask's hopes notwithstanding, it was still possible Selene and I would live to a ripe old age. Tucking away a little financial insurance would be only prudent.

"I guess we should take it along," I said, pushing up my left sleeve.

The plasmic blast that had burned away my left arm below the elbow and simultaneously ended our bounty hunter careers still occasionally resonated in my nightmares. Still, the artificial replacement I'd been wearing for the past five and a half years was comfortable enough, and it did most everything the original flesh-and-blood model could do.

Along with one or two handy additions.

The smaller of the two hidden compartments, the one I'd carved out by pushing aside some of the internal wires and sensor clusters on the inner part of the wrist, was just big enough for a half dozen pills. Back when I'd first been fitted with the arm I mostly kept painkillers in there, but since then I'd switched over to a set of potent knockout pills. With a good deal of practice, I was now able to pop the covering, pluck out a pill with the first two fingers of my right hand, and drop it in someone's drink, all without being noticed.

But the larger compartment, the one situated in the inner forearm just below the elbow, was the real key. That one was the perfect size to hold a standard Trailblazer ampule, where it would be hidden from the prying eyes of customs agents, clients I wasn't ready to share with, or just nosey bystanders. I popped it open, took the ampule from Selene and tucked it inside, and closed it up again.

"I assume you're planning to call the admiral?" Selene asked as I pulled the sleeve back into place.

"First on our list of things to do," I confirmed. "We need to warn him that someone may be on to us. Because if they're on to *us*, they're probably on to Icarus, too."

"Nask is already on to Icarus."

"That assumes he was our recent playmate," I reminded her. "It still could have been a random poacher. At any rate, we need to keep our options open."

She pondered while I double-checked our course and confirmed we were on the way to Marjolaine. "And second on our list of things to do?" she asked.

"We give him the rest of the good news," I said. "As my father used to say, *If your cloud has a silver lining, odds are someone else owns the mineral rights.*"

"And the lining in the admiral's particular cloud is...?"

"That he gets to buy us a new bioprobe."

CHAPTER TWO

I'd never been to Marjolaine, but the place had a fair reputation for cultural refinement, an above-average one for restaurants, and an excellent one for tavernos and local whiskeys.

For a people who prided themselves on their weekly challenges as to who could remain conscious the longest during a drinking contest, their customs officials were unexpectedly alert and efficient. I transmitted our names and the *Ruth*'s ID as we approached and got a cheerful greeting and a landing slot assignment that was within a fifteen-minute drive of our chosen StarrComm center. Arriving along with the landing slot's coordinates and approach vector was a colorful brochure with business and tourism highlights, top-rated places to eat and drink, and helpful tips on how to converse with the planet's human, Drilie, and Saffi residents.

I had no intention of staying long enough to take advantage of any of those recommendations or advice, of course. But I appreciated the thought.

No one suddenly popped into space-normal behind us as we headed inward toward the surface. But that didn't completely eliminate the possibility that we'd been followed. Luckily, as I'd pointed out to Selene, there were six StarrComm facilities to choose from, which we'd chosen among using a random toss of a die. Unless our hypothetical tail was very careful, following us to the right one without being spotted would be well-nigh impossible. If Nask or someone else was trying to chase us down, it seemed only sporting to make him work for it.

We'd ended up picking one of the busier centers, and as a result had to wait nearly an hour before we got a booth. But finally we were inside, secure from prying eyes and ears. I fed in the required number of bills—Graym-Barker preferred we use cash for our communications rather than something more convenient but also more traceable—and punched in the proper number.

I'd never figured out if Icarus had their own private StarrComm transmitter or if they were just playing some multi-transfer game that bounced the signals around beyond anyone's ability to track. That system was hardly new—the Spiral's biggest criminal bosses had been using something similar for decades. But given Icarus's ultra-top-secret status, and with some of the best computer people presumably on payroll, I was guessing Graym-Barker's system was likely the most protected one ever.

Unless the Patth had something better. Now that I thought about it, they probably did.

Usually our calls went through a receptionist who confirmed we were who the signal ID said we were and then routed us directly to the admiral. Today, though, things played out a bit differently. We were greeted by the usual neutral-faced young receptionist; but the face that replaced hers wasn't Graym-Barker's. It was, in fact—

"Finally," Tera C said. Her expression and tone were a nicely balanced mix of relief and tension. "We've been trying to get in touch with you for over two weeks."

"In case you'd forgotten, we were out in the middle of nowhere in the lovely CR-207-T system," I reminded her. "Not many Starr-Comm centers out—"

"Yes, yes, I know," Tera cut me off. "Never mind that. Do you know a man named Easton Dent?"

I frowned. "I don't think so. Should I?"

"That's the question," Tera countered. "See if he looks familiar."

Her image vanished and was replaced by a picture of a man in his thirties with tousled hair, a three-day beard stubble, and an irritated expression. "Don't know the name *or* the face," I said. "Why do we care about him?"

Dent's face disappeared and Tera came back, her eyes boring into mine. "Because for the past four months he's been doing identity and location searches for the names *Gregory Roarke* and *Icarus*."

I sat up a little straighter, noting as I did so the little catch in Selene's voice that usually meant surprise or uneasiness. "Combined or separate?"

"Some of both," Tera said. "None of the searches has gotten him very far, though. *Icarus* has too many mythological and cultural connections, and I was frankly surprised at how common the name *Roarke* is."

"And you're just noticing all this activity *now*?"

"Of course not," Tera said patiently. "We noticed it when he first started poking around. We've just left him alone until now because he wasn't making any headway and no one else seemed to have picked up on him."

I felt my stomach tighten. "Only now someone has," I said as the pieces started falling together. "Let me guess: the Patth?"

"Probably," she said, her eyes narrowing slightly. "You don't sound surprised."

"We had a brief game of capture the flag on our last scoop," I told her. "Someone sneaked up on us and snatched one of our bioprobes. Speaking of which, you need to get us a replacement—"

"They stole a *bioprobe?*"

"It's all right," Selene spoke up. "We retrieved the other one, and there was nothing of interest in it."

"I see," Tera said, her brief moment of heightened concern fading away. Though how she thought anyone other than Selene would be able to glean portal clues from a bioprobe I couldn't guess. "And you think it was the Patth?"

I shrugged. "The Patth, or some random poacher."

"Or perhaps Easton Dent?" Selene suggested quietly.

"That's kind of a jump," I said, frowning. "Or does he have a habit of walking off with things that aren't his?"

"Actually, he does," Tera said, peering at something offscreen. "Though nothing on that scale. Up to now he's mostly been a fairly petty thief, though there are indications he's moving up into smuggling."

"Which he would need a ship for," Selene pointed out.

"Yeah, but crockett ships come with some pretty specialized gear," I countered. "You wouldn't fork over the money for all of that if you didn't need it."

"Unless you were trying to deflect attention away from you," Selene said.

That was a good point, actually. "What about it, Tera? Is Dent running enough high-end stuff to have extra money to burn on fancying up his ship?"

"Possibly," Tera said. "But so far the packages he's transporting are pretty small. He could get by with a midsize ship."

"How big exactly are these packages?"

"Gems or other compact items from a thief or sometimes from a fence."

"Small enough for him to carry in a travel bag?" I asked. "Because in that case, he wouldn't need to bother with his own ship. He could just go with commercial transport."

"Sounds risky," Selene persisted. Clearly, she wasn't ready to give up on her theory about our mysterious Mr. Dent being the bioprobe poacher. "What happens if customs or the liner's own security catches him?"

"Actually, so far nobody's security has been able to even spot him in the act, let alone tag him with any stolen goods," Tera said. "He's been involved in a few questionable incidents in the past, but lately nothing."

"How questionable?"

"Differences of opinion with buyers or fences," Tera said. "A handful of them have ended with dead bodies."

"And no one's been able to tag him with those, either, I suppose?"

"The postmortem witness pools have been understandably small," Tera said grimly. "And in the last couple he's had unshakable alibis ready."

"I hope whoever's he's got on retainer is reliable," I said. "You screw up a goods transport and you get to make two entirely different groups of bad people mad at you at the same time."

"It's still marginally better than breaking into someone's safe and getting shot at," Tera pointed out. "You should probably make a note to ask about his alibis when you meet him."

"You're bringing him in?"

"No, you're meeting him for a drink," Tera said. "The Red Poppy taverno near the—"

"Excuse me?" I interrupted, staring at her. "We're *meeting* him?"

"*You're* meeting him, anyway," Tera said. "He's not looking for Selene, so she can sit this one out aboard the *Ruth* if she wants. The Red Poppy near the—"

"That's not the part I was asking about," I again interrupted. "Why am I meeting him at all? I don't even know the guy."

"And this will be your big chance to rectify that omission," Tera said. "The Red Poppy—"

"Tera—"

I stopped, waiting for her to keep going. She also stopped, waiting for me to continue with my complaint, and for a moment we just looked at each other in silence. "You want to hear this, or not?" she asked at last.

I clenched my teeth uselessly. "Sure."

"He's looking for you, Gregory," Tera said quietly. "*And* he's looking for us. More to the point, the Patth have finally noticed him and his searches."

"Are they actively hunting him?"

"If they aren't yet, they soon will be," Tera said. "We need to find out what he knows and what he wants. Unfortunately, you're the best person to do that."

I looked at Selene. She was watching me, her pupils showing only calmness as she waited for me to make my decision. Probably hoping that meeting Dent would prove he was the one who'd poached us. "We only signed up to hunt for portals, you know," I reminded Tera.

"I know," Tera said. "Welcome to the world of improvisation."

"Like I don't already live there," I growled. "Fine. The Red Poppy near the...?"

"Near the Glazunov Spaceport Annex on New Kyiv," she said. "Your meeting is at eight o'clock, local time, in five days. Oh, and we were messaging him as you, so you'll probably want to know exactly what was said. Plug in and I'll copy you the conversation."

I motioned to Selene, who produced a data stick from her pocket. "Can we get a copy of that picture you showed us, too?"

"Of course," Tera said as Selene plugged the stick into the console's data slot. I watched as the indicator flickered briefly with the incoming data and then switched to a steady glow. "I assume you didn't send my picture to him," I added as Selene removed the stick and put it away.

"He didn't ask, and we didn't offer," Tera said. "Apparently, he wants you to do the approaching."

Which was exactly backward from how I would have set it up. That alone was enough to raise a couple of unpleasant red flags. "I suppose backup is out of the question?"

"We're trying to get someone there before the meeting," Tera said. "But our people are spread pretty thin. Better assume you'll be on your own."

"Kind of thought that's where we were heading," I grumbled. "Anything in particular you want me to ask him?"

"We want to know what, if anything, he knows about Icarus," Tera said. "Aside from that, just play it by ear and find out as much as you can."

"Got it," I said. "I don't suppose we get hazard pay for this?"

"I'll look into that."

"Thanks," I said, scowling. As my father used to say, *Telling someone you'll look into it is just a polite way of saying* not a chance.

Maybe Tera hadn't heard that one. Or maybe she'd just never known anyone like my father.

"I'll let you go now," she continued. "Good luck, and let us know if you learn anything." With a final nod, she keyed off.

For a moment Selene and I sat together in silence. "It shouldn't be *that* bad," Selene said.

"Do I smell that worried?" I asked.

"A little," she admitted. "But really, it's not like he's a hired gun or contract killer. He's just a thief and smuggler. They're mostly nonviolent, aren't they?"

"Except when they're involved in shooting incidents where people end up dead," I reminded her. "But you're missing a key point. Back when Geri and Freki were poking their stick into our lives they reinstated our bounty hunter licenses. Remember?"

The reaction of her pupils showed that she had indeed forgotten that. "You think Dent might assume you're after him?"

"*I* would if I were him," I said. "If we're lucky, we'll be able to convince him otherwise before he rabbits. Or gets involved in another of Tera's incidents, this one with us at the wrong end of the shooting gallery."

"Hopefully, it won't come to that."

"Hopefully," I agreed. "Because if it does, Tera and the admiral are *definitely* going to pop for some hazard pay."

❖   ❖   ❖

Tavernos across the Spiral, at least those that catered predominately to humans, were all basically the same. Some were roomier than others, some were better lit, and some had a larger diversity of alcohol blends, but ultimately they all boiled down to places where people could get buzzed or numbed or drunk in comfort and relative safety.

Relative being the key word. The Red Poppy's clientele seemed to be composed of equal parts shady types and desperate types. There was a good scattering of aliens mixed in, and a lot of them seemed shady, too.

If Easton Dent didn't worry about my bounty hunting credentials, there were an ample number of customers in here who probably would.

"He's late," Selene murmured.

I took a sip of my drink and gave the taverno another casual sweep. The picture Tera had sent wasn't great, but it was good enough to confirm he wasn't here yet.

And at a quarter to nine, he was definitely late.

"He may just be the cautious type," I said. "Making sure I don't have a partner lurking outside or something. As my father used to say, *If paranoia is your full-time job, it's probably also your hobby.* In Dent's case—"

I broke off as Selene tensed, her pupils suddenly apprehensive, her nostrils and eyelashes working full speed. "Gregory, I think—yes. Some Iykams have just come in."

"Where?" I murmured, feeling my back suddenly tingling.

"Behind me and to my right."

And since they hadn't crossed my sight lines, they hadn't come in the main door. Casually, I half turned toward the other exit, the door that led past the bar into the kitchen area and then out onto the service alley to the rear.

They were there, all right: three human-sized, lumpy-faced aliens, their hooded robes hiding their shortened torsos and extra-long arms. The robes were too loose to show any sign of concealed weapons, but I'd never yet met an Iykam who wasn't armed with one of their short-range but thoroughly nasty corona guns.

And if Iykams were here, there were bound to be one or more of their Path masters lurking in the shadows, as well.

"I'd say that's our exit cue," I said, dropping payment for our drinks on the table and getting casually to my feet. "Come on, let's get out of here."

"You think Dent's working with the Patth?" Selene asked as we headed for the door.

"Or else they've been watching him, or else they're watching us, or else they just dropped in for a drink," I said. "I really don't care which. The point is that I'm not having a semisecret meeting with Patth and Iykams looking over my shoulder."

I pushed open the door, half expecting to find a semicircle of armed Iykams facing us down with Sub-Director Nask in full gloat mode behind them. But there was nothing but a heavy flow of pedestrians and vehicles. Heavier than it had been an hour ago, I noted, and I wondered if some special event was going on tonight. That was usually something I checked on before landing, but this time I hadn't bothered.

"Where are we going?" Selene asked as I turned us in the direction of the spaceport annex and started weaving us through the boisterous crowd.

"Back to the *Ruth*," I said. "Whatever Dent wanted, he apparently decided he didn't want it that badly."

"Or else he decided it was too crowded in there," a gruff voice came from behind me. "Just keep walking, Roarke."

"Oh, hello, Dent," I said, taking it in stride. Over the years I'd had my fair share of being snuck up on, to the point where I'd mostly gotten used to it. Mostly. "It *is* Easton Dent, right?" I craned my neck to look at the grim face crowding up behind us. There was barely even a passing resemblance to the picture Tera had sent. "Got to say you don't look much like your picture."

"You didn't think I'd give you my *real* face, did you?" he countered. "That wouldn't have been a smart thing to send a bounty hunter."

"Right—the red carnation in the lapel is so much more classic." I dropped my eyes to his chest as if checking for a flower, trying to see if I could spot his weapon.

There it was, tucked into a belt holster on his right hip, mostly hidden beneath his gray jacket: a Golden 4mm, perfect for perforating a target at close range. More to the point, given our current geometry, a quick draw right now would leave the muzzle pointing squarely at the small of my back.

But at least it wouldn't be pointing at Selene. A small but vital point, at least for me.

"No carnation, either," I said, turning back to face front. "I'm disappointed. Incidentally, if it matters, I'm not a bounty hunter anymore. Selene and I are licensed Trailblazers."

"Oh, it matters," Dent assured me. "It matters enough for me to have checked out your hunter profile before I came here. Funny thing—it says your credentials are still active. Some bureaucratic glitch, right?"

"Actually, I was re-credentialed without my knowledge or permission," I said. "If it matters."

"Not really," Dent said. "Nice picture of you, by the way."

"Thanks." So that was why he hadn't bothered to ask for one when he set up this meeting. "So what can I do for you?"

"For now, just keep walking," he said. "I gotta say, your playmates back there are really slow on the uptake."

I threw Selene a look. Had Tera sent some backup after all? "What playmates would those be?"

"Don't play cute, Roarke," Dent growled. "I saw them sneak in through the back door. Probably thought they'd missed me coming in and wanted to see if I was already—"

"Wait a second," I said. "Are you talking about the *Iykams*?"

"Who?"

"The lumpy-faced clowns in the medieval monk robes," I said. "Because that bunch isn't even close to being my friends."

"Meaning?"

"Exactly what it sounds like," I growled. "And their weapon of choice does *not* make for a pleasant way to die."

"Didn't think there *was* such a thing," Dent muttered. "I guess we'd better speed things up. You know this guy?"

There was movement at the corner of my eye, and Dent's hand reached over my shoulder and waved a picture a few centimeters in front of my face. I plucked it from his fingers and held it out to a more reasonable distance.

The image was that of a middle-aged man with a lined face, a fringe of white hair, and a sprinkle of equally white beard stubble. He looked professional, intelligent, and strangely peaceful.

He also looked extremely dead.

"Never seen him before," I said, frowning as I shifted my focus to the picture's edging. It was a real analog-type photo, taken on classic photo stock, not just a print of a dij image. "What happened to him?"

There was no answer. I half turned around again.

To find that Dent had disappeared into the crowd.

"Selene?" I asked.

"That way," she said, pointing to the right as she sniffed the air. "He's moving fast, too."

"For all the good that'll do him." I turned in that direction and looked for an opening in the pedestrian stream.

And came up short as Selene suddenly clutched my arm. "Iykams!" she hissed. "There are three Iykams in that direction."

The three we'd left behind in the Red Poppy? Or was it a fresh bunch?

Not that it mattered. Dent's sudden disappearing act strongly suggested he thought they were after Selene and me and didn't want to be hanging around when they caught up with us.

Unfortunately, the fact that the Iykams in the taverno hadn't immediately opened fire on us also strongly suggested we weren't, in fact, their targets. By process of elimination, Dent was the one who was actually in their sights.

And if they got to him first we were unlikely to ever get the answers Tera wanted. "Understood," I said, taking Selene's arm and ducking between a pair of Ihmisits as we moved across the prevailing travel direction. In a crowd this size, and with no walls or fences nearby that could capture and hold Dent's scent, even Kadolian olfactory magic wouldn't let us keep his trail for long.

We had to get to him before that happened. We especially had to get to him before the Iykams did.

Time to boost our odds a little.

Artificial limbs like my left arm could be customized in an astonishing number of ways. Some people went with additional strength or dexterity; others went with implanted phones or info pads; some, particularly those in the darker professions, added a concealed knife or two-shot plasmic.

By the time my elbow had healed enough for me to be fitted with my new prosthetic I'd already decided that the direction of my life was going to shift away from the latter to something a whole lot safer. I'd therefore skipped the fancy stuff, and contented myself with just the two hidden compartments I'd created in the wrist and elbow area.

Plus one other minor indulgence. A lot of bounty hunter casualties came from walking unwarily around corners, and the loss of my arm had given me a strong aversion to being shot at. Ergo...

I gave the left thumbnail the gentle double stroke that turned it into a mirror, then lifted the arm toward the sky, fingers curled into a loose fist with the thumb resting along the forefinger.

The mirror was designed to be held closer to the eye, either stuck around a corner to give me a view of the blind side or else right beside my face so I could look over my shoulder. But I'd practiced with it enough over the years to have learned how to get at least a limited view over the heads and hats of a crowd of people like this while at arm's length.

Sure enough— "Got him," I said, pulling the thumbnail a little closer to my eye for confirmation. "He's passing the pawn shop at the corner." I grinned at Selene as I lowered my arm and turned the thumbnail opaque again. "Looks very chic in that checkered blue jacket, too."

"Checkered *blue?*" Selene's pupils gave a brief frown, then cleared as she got it. "Oh. Reversible coat?"

"All the best-dressed criminals have one." I looked at my right hand, suddenly realizing I was still holding the picture Dent had given me. Folding it lengthwise, I slid it into my wallet. There were cultures and religions in the Spiral that forbade the use of digital imagery, I knew, but Dent didn't seem the type to be involved with such things. I made a mental note to ask him about it once we'd tracked him down as I stuffed the wallet back in my pocket. "Come on."

We kept at it for the next half hour, weaving in and out of the crowd, turning corners and once going through the front door of a taverno and then straight out the back when Selene caught Dent's scent on the door handle. But in the end it came to nothing. After hovering right on the edge for the final five minutes, the scent finally faded beyond even Selene's tracking ability.

"I'm sorry, Gregory," she apologized as we turned back toward the spaceport annex.

"It's okay," I said, keeping an eye out for a cab or quick-rent runaround. Whatever festival or holiday had filled the area with enthusiastic citizenry, it had apparently sucked all the rental vehicles off the streets, too. "I see now why Dent specified this place and this night. All the cover you could want for ditching an unwanted date."

Selene was silent another few steps. I watched as a cab pulled to the curb ahead, watched it pull away with a customer before I could even start to find a way through the crowd toward it. "I didn't get a chance to tell you earlier," Selene continued. "Just as Dent came up behind us, as he first spoke, I caught Jordan McKell's scent."

I frowned. "It was on *Dent?*"

"No, was in the air." She made as if to say something else, then changed her mind. "He was somewhere behind us."

"Interesting," I said as I pulled out my phone. McKell was one of the Icarus Group's top troubleshooters. Apparently, Tera *had* been able to get some backup to New Kyiv.

It would have been nice if McKell had called or messaged to let me know he was in town. But of course, here at a potentially critical juncture, he wouldn't have done so. Even encrypted phones could give up location and tracking information, particularly if the person asking was also handing out large numbers of certified bank checks.

And if the asking party was a Patth, he could probably even skip the whole bribe scenario. During the twenty years they'd been working their domination of Spiral commerce and transport, they'd wormed little back doors into a surprising range of electronic equipment. Knowing I was here, they could probably do anything they wanted with my phone short of making it sit up and bark.

"You getting anything from him now?" I asked, putting the phone away. I'd had a couple of useful tweaks installed on our phones, but the devices were still a long way from being completely track- or tamper-proof. Someday I needed to see if the Icarus Group had any such truly invisible models, and if so try to talk the admiral out of a couple of them.

"Sorry," she said. "I lost him when we headed off after Dent."

"Yeah." So no Dent, no McKell, and no way back to the *Ruth* except on foot. This was about as wasted an evening as I could remember.

Still, as my father used to say, *If you never had a dull day, you'd never recognize the bright ones.*

I just hoped whoever was in charge of passing out days would find us a bright one soon.

❖   ❖   ❖

The crowds and hilarity choking the main part of the city had thankfully thinned out in the area immediately surrounding the annex. It was one of the more modern spaceports on New Kyiv, with half-cylinder landing cradles instead of just the flat pads that used to be the norm. The cradle design meant that the *Ruth*'s entryway hatch was mostly directly across from the service pathways instead of looming above them, which meant all Selene and I had to do was negotiate a flat walkway instead of making a weary climb up the ramp's alternative zigzag configuration. I punched in the access code, we went inside, and I locked the hatch behind us.

"You want to eat or shower first?" I asked Selene as I headed forward toward the compact living area that included the dayroom, bathroom, and our two small cabins.

"Food sounds best," Selene said. "First, I need to tell you something. When Dent put his arm between us..." She braced herself. "I smelled portal metal."

I stared at her. "Are you sure?"

She nodded. "The scent was faint, but it was definitely there."

"Interesting," I murmured. Was that why Dent was searching for Icarus and me? Had he stumbled on a portal and somehow figured out my connection to it?

But if so, why had he left so abruptly and without warning? It couldn't have been the Iykams that Selene smelled nearby—they hadn't been close enough for me to spot them in the crowd, which made it unlikely Dent had, either.

Did it have something to do with the picture he'd showed us? Was that supposed to confirm we were the people he wanted to deal with? If so, had my lack of recognition scared him away?

Or had he just done a quick fade because he needed time to figure out his next move? "How long since he was near it?" I asked.

"Not too recently," Selene said. "Or maybe it wasn't too long ago but was just a single touch. As I said, it was faint."

"I suppose I'd better go look for him," I said with a sigh as I turned and started back toward the entryway. Heading out into the crowds when I was already dead on my feet wasn't exactly the way I'd planned to spend what was left of the night.

"Are you sure?" Selene asked. "You look tired."

And undoubtedly smelled tired, too. Everything about me

was pretty much an open book to her. "I'm at least an hour past tired," I said over my shoulder. "But there are Iykams out there, and I doubt the Patth are far behind. If they catch up with him before we do—let's just say Tera won't be happy about it."

"Neither will Mr. Dent, probably," she said, and I heard her footsteps on the deck plates as she moved up behind me. "All right. Let's give it another try."

And right on cue came the triple tone that announced someone was at our door.

I stopped, frowning. Had Dent circled around and followed us back to the *Ruth*? "Dent?" I asked Selene.

"I didn't smell him on our way in," she said. "Or McKell, either."

The triple tone came again. "I guess we'd better answer," I decided, starting up again. Maybe it was some late-working dockworker come to tell us the shiny new bioprobe we'd asked Tera for had arrived.

I wasn't really expecting that to be the case. Which was just as well, because the three uniformed humans I saw when I turned on the hatch display were definitely not delivery folk.

They were badgemen.

Badgemen, moreover, wearing city rather than port authority insignia. That immediately marked them as having a wider scope of jurisdiction, as well as raising the question of why they were here in the port in the first place.

The more crucial question being whether they were genuinely working for the city, or whether they'd been co-opted by someone else. Like, for example, a Patth sub-director with a vendetta against a certain ship and its crew. "Stay here," I said, guiding Selene to a spot beside the hatch where she'd be out of our visitors' view when I opened it. "If you smell Patth, Iykam, or anyone else we don't want to see, snap your fingers and I'll try to close up before they can get in."

She nodded, her pupils showing her usual level of tension whenever I trotted out one of my impromptu plans. Confirming that my Fafnir 4 plasmic was ready in its holster, I keyed the hatch.

The display had showed three badgemen. Now, with a more complete view of the world, I saw that they were actually a group of five, their expressions as stiff and tired as I would expect from people on festival patrol duty. Definitely not folks delivering a bioprobe. "Good evening, officers," I greeted them, doing a quick visual sweep of the area behind them and listening for Selene's warning. But no Iykams or Patth were visible, and Selene's fingers remained unsnapped. "What can I do for you?"

"Gregory Roarke, captain of the Trailblazer ship *Ruth*?" a woman wearing sergeant's stripes asked.

"I am," I said. Still nothing from Selene.

"Is this your wallet?" she asked, producing an all-too-familiar bifold.

I winced, touching the pocket where I'd put it earlier. It was missing, all right. "Looks like it," I confirmed, holding out my hand. "May I see it?"

"It has your ID in it," the sergeant said.

"May I see it?" I repeated, taking a step toward her onto the walkway, my hand still extended.

She hesitated, then handed it over.

It didn't take more than a glance to confirm that it was, indeed, my wayward wallet, clearly lifted earlier while we were passing through the crowds out there. Just the same, I took my time leafing through the contents, checking the ID, cash, credit vouchers, and other odds and ends. Everything seemed to still be there.

I felt my stomach tighten. No; not everything. The picture Dent had given me—the old, distinguished, dead man—was gone.

"Yes, it's mine," I said, starting to pocket it. "Where did you—?" I broke off as one of the other badgemen reached over and plucked it out of my hand.

"Where did we find it?" the sergeant finished my question for me. Her voice was grim, but somehow also oddly satisfied. "Where you presumably lost it. Beside the body."

"The body?" I echoed carefully.

"Yes," she said. She drew herself up. "Gregory Roarke, I hereby place you under arrest for the murder of Easton Dent."

CHAPTER THREE

"Wait a second," I protested as one of the badgemen stepped up on either side of me and took hold of my upper arms. The one on my right pulled my Fafnir from its holster with his free hand and handed it to the sergeant. "Wait a damned second. My plasmic hasn't been fired in months. Go ahead—check it for yourself."

"No need," the sergeant said, her eyes boring into mine. "Dent conveniently had his own weapon right there for you to use. I don't know why you thought cremating his face would help you any—we *do* have up-to-date DNA and chondrial tests on New Kyiv, you know."

I winced at the mental image of a corpse with its face burned beyond recognition. A single plasmic shot in a vital organ was usually enough to do someone in. Wasting time with additional mutilation was the mark of a psychotic. "I didn't kill him."

"We'll let the judge decide that," she said. "Where's your partner?"

"She's out shopping," I said. Bad enough that I was about to suffer the noise and squalor—not to mention the pungent aromas—of a police holding cell. There was no need to drag Selene through that, too.

"Is she, now," the sergeant said, clearly not believing it for a minute as she gestured to the remaining two badgemen. "Maybe she came back early."

"Whoa," I said, taking a step backward. Half a step, anyway; the two badgemen attached to my arms brought me to a halt before I could get any further. But I made it far enough to block the hatchway. "You have a warrant to search my ship?"

"Absolutely," the sergeant said.

"Let me see it."

Her eyes narrowed. "I have a warrant for your arrest," she said, her voice now showing just a hint of reluctance. "That includes whatever searching and entering are required."

"Only neither of them is," I pointed out. "Once you've accomplished the main warrant, the secondary powers evaporate."

Her eyes narrowed a little more. "Well, aren't *you* the legal scholar."

"I used to be a bounty hunter," I said. "You learn a lot about Spiral law in that job."

"I'll just bet you do." She glared at me another couple of seconds, then gave a short nod. "Fine. Go ahead and lock up. Jareek, stay here and wait for Roarke's partner."

"Do I bring her in?" one of the badgemen asked.

"Let's see how fast I can get you a warrant for her as a material witness," the sergeant said. "Either way, you can at least offer her a ride to come visit her partner. Don't just stand there, Roarke. Lock it up, and let's go."

Whatever I might think of the Glazunov badgemen's skills at crime analysis and deduction—and neither of those skills was very high on my list right now—at least their processing procedure was quick and efficient.

First on their list of things to do was to take away my phone, multitool, and flashlight—they already had my wallet and plasmic—and put them in a lockbox in the evidence room. After that came fingerprint and retina scans, a sampling of my epidermal skin cells for DNA and chondrial profile, and lots of photos from all sides. Finally, they started a search of bounty hunter licenses to make sure I was who they thought I was. That one, given the Spiral's population and the sheer number of professional bounty hunters, would probably take the rest of the night.

Presumably they were doing the same on Easton Dent's remains elsewhere in the building.

The processing was especially impressive given how short-staffed the station seemed to be. Clearly, the festival out there was absorbing a lot of their resources. Midway through the booking, with my stomach starting to growl, I wondered if the lack of duty personnel would mean a delay in any meals they typically offered their guests. My reluctant conclusion was that, yes, it probably would.

There were fifteen other prisoners in the two wire-mesh cages of the holding tank when they finally brought me down there. The heavy alcohol aroma pervading the atmosphere suggested that most of them had been picked up while drunk and presumably disorderly, with the rest doing the distinctive twitching I'd often seen in short-tempered people coming down from the emotional frenzy of a fight. A few had been in here long enough for facial bruises to materialize, and I made a mental note to steer clear of them.

The guard at the duty desk facing the cages logged me in, and a minute later I found myself in the right-hand cage, the one closest to the room's exit. Not that I expected that proximity to do me any good in the short term, but being closer to escape than the alternative still carried a certain psychological comfort.

I spent the next hour wandering around the cage, avoiding contact with my fellow detainees and acting bored while I surreptitiously looked for weaknesses in the wire mesh holding us in. But as near as I could tell the barrier was solid. The guard at the duty station didn't seem all that excited about his assigned duty, but even with most of his attention focused on his info pad and his coffee cup he found time to take a good look at his charges every minute or two.

During that hour other badgemen brought in three more customers, two human and one Narchner, all of them clearly intoxicated beyond the point of public or personal safety. The Narchner launched into song the second the cage door closed behind him, pitching his voice loud enough to be annoying but not loud enough to earn himself a reprimand or removal to a private cell somewhere else.

Each time the outer door swung open I braced myself for the possibility it would be Selene I saw being marched across the room. But apparently the overeager sergeant hadn't been able to get the search warrant she wanted.

Or else she had and it hadn't done her any good. The *Ruth* had a carefully disguised secret exit near the bow, and I knew Selene would be out through it the minute someone tried using a badgeman override on the entryway lock.

As my father used to say, *Keeping that bird in the hand is usually a lot harder than it looks.* Hopefully, that would also apply to my own current situation.

I was still working on a plan toward that end when the outer door opened and all that mental activity came to a screeching halt.

First through was a Kalix, squat and broad-shouldered, his squashed lizard face holding a brooding expression, his wrists manacled in front of him. Herding him into the room was a uniformed badgeman lugging a mesh animal carrier containing two ferret-sized creatures. So normal and matter-of-fact did the procession look that they were halfway to the duty desk before the faces registered.

The Kalix was none other than Jordan McKell's partner Ixil. The ferrets in the carrier were Ixil's outriders, Pix and Pax, symbiotic animals who could receive uploaded mental orders from their master and send download memories the other direction whenever their long claws were dug into his shoulders and connected to his neural system.

The badgeman, inevitably, was McKell himself.

"What the hell is this?" the guard asked as he eyed the procession.

"Bloodsport," McKell said tartly. He sent a quick visual sweep across the holding cells, his eyes moving past me without visible reaction, before returning his attention to the guard. "Caught this Kalix setting it up. Here's the evidence." He lifted the carrier a few centimeters.

"Whoa—hold it," the guard warned, frowning at the outriders. "What are you bringing them in here for? Evidence locker's upstairs."

"You don't put animals in the locker," McKell said with strained patience. "Don't worry, they're caged, and they'll only be here a couple of hours. Just get them some water and they'll be fine."

The guard gave a huff. "Do I *look* like a food truck? I'm on duty."

"Yeah, well, so are all the rest of us," McKell said tiredly. "Come on, be a brother and go get a soup bowl and bottle of water from the break room. And be thankful you're in here instead of out there wearing out your feet." He nodded sideways toward Ixil. "Give me your key and I'll lock him up."

The guard glanced behind him at one of the wall-mounted video cameras in the room's rear corners, presumably reminding himself that they were focused on the holding cells and not on the desk or its occupant. A quick visit to the break room wouldn't be recorded, and probably not even noticed. "Fine," he grumped.

He walked around to the front of the desk, took a moment to make sure the cuffs on Ixil's wrists were secure, then handed McKell the key card. "You're leaving those on, right?" he asked, eying Ixil closely as he stepped back.

"After all the trouble he caused out there?" McKell said. "Believe it, brother."

"You want help caging him?"

"No, I've got him," McKell said, giving the stunner in his side holster a reassuring pat as he set the outriders' carrier on the floor in front of the desk. "Just go get the water, will you? I can't leave until the animals are settled."

"Sure." Giving Ixil one final look, the guard turned and headed toward the exit. McKell drew the stunner, pressed it into Ixil's side, and nudged the Kalix toward the other holding tank.

And as they started toward the mesh door, with both their backs to the cameras, Ixil looked at me and casually tapped his inner left-hand wrist.

The spot in my artificial arm where I kept my knockout pills.

This part I'd already figured out. Holding my arms casually across my waist, I popped open the hidden compartment with my right hand and pulled out one of the pills. The guard continued to the exit and disappeared; and as the door closed behind him Pax nosed open a hidden door in the side of the carrier. I flicked my pill out through the mesh, sending it to a spot right in front of the desk. Pax picked up the pill delicately with his teeth and disappeared under the desk with it.

I held my breath, waiting for the startled cry that would mean one of my fellow prisoners had spotted the outrider or the pill handoff. One shout or pointed finger in view of the security cameras and we'd be finished.

But McKell had set the carrier below the level of the security cameras, and the pill was really too small to see unless you were looking for it. Besides, every eye in the holding tanks was glued to the entertainment that had suddenly erupted in front of them.

As prison dramas went, it was one of the better ones I'd seen. Ixil was perfection itself as the annoyed prisoner who didn't want to be locked up, while McKell was equally memorable as the badgeman who had no intention of taking guff from him or anyone else. They played the conflict back and forth, keeping things just rowdy enough to hold the prisoners' attention while not letting it escalate to the point where whoever was monitoring the cameras decided it was time to send in backup. The prisoners added in their own bits to the presentation, banging on the mesh and shouting encouragement to Ixil. The Narchner even got interested enough to stop singing.

There was a movement at the corner of my eye: Pax hopping up onto the desk from the far side. He scampered to the duty badgeman's coffee cup, dropped in the pill, then spun around and hopped back down onto the chair and out of sight. Two seconds later he reappeared under the front edge of the desk and let himself back into the carrier.

A second after that, with a loud and authoritative slamming of the holding tank door, Ixil was inside, and the show was over.

Just in time. McKell was still backing toward the desk, ostensibly watching Ixil for trouble, more likely making sure to keep his face turned away from the cameras as much as he could when the duty guard returned carrying a small bowl and bottle of water for the outriders, plus a couple of snack bars for himself.

"Thanks," McKell said, taking the bowl and water. As the guard watched, he opened a door in the top of the carrier, worked the bowl through and set it on the bottom, and poured in half of the water. "There we go," he said, sealing the door and setting the bottle on the desk. "That should keep them happy and healthy until the judge gets to the case and figures out what to do with them."

"By which time you'll be long gone?" the duty officer suggested as he sat back down.

"So will you, probably," McKell assured him, glancing at his watch. "Judge Packerson's on the bench tonight, and he's never been accused of being fast."

"No joke," the officer said. "Have fun out there."

"Oh, yeah," McKell said with just the right touch of sarcastic grumpiness. "Enjoy the"—he looked pointedly at the drunks and rowdies—"quiet."

With a final nod, he strode to the exit and left.

The rumble of desultory conversation resumed, along with the Narchner's low-key singing. The guard gave the tanks a slow visual scan, his eyes pausing briefly on Ixil, then leaned back in his chair and picked up his info pad. He scrolled a page, took a sip of his coffee, and settled back to read.

I looked sideways at Ixil. He was staring intently at the guard. Pix and Pax, in contrast, were staring at Ixil. The guard took another sip and set down his cup. His eyelids drooped...

Abruptly, he sagged in his seat, his info pad dropping into his lap, his head falling forward onto his chest. Out like the proverbial light. I looked back at Ixil, waiting for him to make his move.

Only he didn't.

I frowned. The guard was asleep, but Ixil was still holding the same pose. So far the rest of the prisoners didn't seem to have noticed the unplanned nap, but I knew that wouldn't last long. The minute the inevitable uproar started, whoever was watching the security cameras would hit the alarm button.

The cameras.

I focused on them, noting the little red lights that indicated they were active. Just for fun I started a mental countdown.

I'd reached seventeen when the indicator lights went out. Ixil snapped his fingers, and Pix and Pax sprang into action.

They nosed their way out of their carrier, Pax heading under the desk again, Pix running across to Ixil's cell. He stopped there and stretched upward with his front paws on the mesh, revealing the cuff key taped to his belly. By the time Ixil pulled it free and unlocked his cuffs Pax had joined Pix with the guard's key card clutched between his teeth. Ixil worked the card through the mesh, pushed his way to the holding tank door through a frozen mass of astonished and probably disbelieving prisoners, worked it back through the mesh, and keyed the lock. He slipped through the open door and hurried over to my cage. As he used the card to open the door, Pix and Pax scurried up his legs and repositioned themselves in their usual places on his shoulders.

"Thanks," I said as I stepped out into free air again. "How much time do we have?"

"More than enough," Ixil assured me, looking over at the other holding tank. He'd left the door wide open, but the occupants were still dithering around inside, clearly wondering if this was some trick or a genuine invitation to make a run for it. "Jordan shut down all their security cameras, including the ones on the building perimeter. Right now they're probably focused on defending the station against an assumed external threat, with the drunks and disorderlies in here very low on their priority list."

"Good," I said as we headed toward the door. "Because we're not leaving just yet."

Ixil gave me an odd look. "Why not?"

"We're going to the morgue," I told him. "I need to look at the guy they've accused me of murdering."

"Easton Dent," Ixil said, nodding heavily. "Yes, we heard. That's why we're getting you and Selene out of here and off New Kyiv."

"And we appreciate the effort," I said. "Only two small problems. First: I didn't kill anyone. And second—"

I gestured in the general direction of the rest of the station. "The dead man in there isn't Easton Dent."

CHAPTER FOUR

The morgue was locked, but not all that seriously. If my picks hadn't been confiscated I could have had it open in twenty seconds. Pix, with nothing but a set of long outrider claws and some mental instructions from Ixil, still managed to do it in under a minute.

I'd been prepared for whatever violence was necessary in order get a close look at the body. Fortunately, the morgue was deserted, the examiner and his team apparently gone to shelter elsewhere from the presumed imminent attack.

"What makes you think it's not Dent?" Ixil asked as we checked the log.

"The arresting sergeant told me," I said. "Not in so many words, of course, but—here we go. Drawer eight."

We headed across the room to the neat array of body drawers. "Not in so many words?" Ixil prompted as we opened the door and slid out the rack.

After the sergeant's description of the body's state I'd been prepared for the worst. To my relief it wasn't quite as bad as I'd expected. The face had been badly burned, as she'd said, but it was more strategic spot damage than full-on skullification. The actual killing shot, I also noted, was a dead-center chest burn.

Someone had wanted him dead, and that same someone had apparently wanted him hard to identify.

"She said I'd used Dent's own weapon to kill him and burn his face," I continued. "Problem is, these are plasmic burns. Dent was carrying a Golden four mil."

"You're sure?"

"I saw it," I said. "If the badgemen are convinced his own weapon was used, this has to be someone else."

"That's fairly thin evidence," Ixil pointed out. "Someone else could have brought a plasmic to the party."

"True," I agreed. "But there's more. The last time I saw Dent he'd reversed his jacket from gray to a blue check. This guy's jacket is the right shade of gray, but it doesn't have a reversible side. That a bit more solid?"

"Considerably," Ixil said. "Unless they switched out his jacket."

"Which would have to have happened before he was shot," I pointed out. "The chest burn marks line up perfectly."

"Agreed," Ixil said. "Anything else?"

"Oh, I saved the best for last," I assured him. "Our killer was smart enough to destroy his victim's face, but he missed a bet." I pointed to the undamaged side of the charred head. "Those aren't Dent's ears."

"Really." Ixil gave me an odd look. "You make a habit of memorizing people's ears?"

"It's more a hobby than a habit," I told him. "But it's a useful one. With all the face-changing plastic tech around for the bad guys to take advantage of, you'd be surprised how few of them bother with their ears. They're not quite as distinctive as fingerprints or DNA, but normally they're distinctive enough for at least a first tag."

"Interesting," Ixil murmured. "So you're thinking this is—?" He broke off, as if suddenly realizing he'd been about to say something he wasn't supposed to.

"All I'm saying is that it's not Dent," I said, frowning. "Why? Do you know something I don't?"

"As a matter of fact, I do," Ixil said, sounding thoughtful. "But this isn't the place for that conversation. Anything else?"

I shrugged, running my gaze over the body. "Aside from the jacket, the rest of the clothing is similar to Dent's. The mutilation was done at close range; so was the kill shot. In the chest, too, which means he wasn't running away at the time."

"What about this?" Ixil pushed the jacket cuff up a couple of centimeters.

I leaned a little closer. There were smooth pressure marks on the man's wrist. "He was tied up," I said slowly. "Tied up before he was shot, and not untied until at least a few minutes afterward."

I looked up again to find Ixil's eyes boring into mine. "So he was someone's prisoner," the Kalix said, his voice flat. "Which suggests he wasn't just randomly or accidentally killed."

"And if he was tied up instead of just being tossed into a locked room, there's a good chance he was being interrogated when he was shot." I nodded at the body. "The question is whether he was mistaken for Dent, or whether his similarity to Dent is purely coincidental and he was being interrogated in his own right."

"In which case you also have to explain why they had Dent's wallet and ID to plant on him," Ixil pointed out. "That seems a lot to pile onto coincidence's shoulders."

"Especially when you throw in the fact that they also had *my* wallet to leave beside the body," I agreed.

"Yes," Ixil said. "Speaking of your wallet, I hope you're not going to want to raid the evidence room next."

"No, I think that would be pushing things beyond even my wobbly boundaries," I agreed regretfully. There hadn't been a lot of money in the wallet—and most of it had been the Icarus Group's anyway—but I was a bit annoyed about losing my ID. The set of forgeries tucked away aboard the *Ruth* were reasonable enough, but I'd really liked the photo on that particular one. "Anyway, I've got replacements for everything back at the ship. You said something about getting out of here?"

"I did," Ixil said. He slid the body tray back into its receptacle and closed the door. "Come. Jordan and Selene are waiting."

I'd expected our rendezvous to be in McKell's ship, the *Stormy Banks*, or possibly in the private back room of some seedy, beneath-the-radar bar where badgemen were reluctant to intrude. Instead, we met him and Selene in a far less dramatic but far more logical place: the local StarrComm center.

Because if there was one thing that was consistent across the Spiral, it was that the lifeblood of organizations was timely field reports.

On rare occasions I'd seen Admiral Sir Graym-Barker relaxed and almost genial, a far cry from his usual hard, intimidating self. Unfortunately, this wasn't one of those times.

". . . so once Dent and Roarke made contact, I figured that what they needed most was a bit of privacy," McKell said.

"You were ordered to watch over their meeting," Graym-Barker said stiffly.

I winced. As my father used to say, *A man's face is not a reliable indicator of how angry he is. No matter how mad he looks, he's usually even madder.*

Unfortunately, it did appear that this *was* one of *those* times.

"I was ordered to make sure it came off safely," McKell corrected calmly. I didn't know how much practice he'd had standing up to Graym-Barker, but apparently it had been enough to build up some immunity to the admiral's megawatt glare. "I'd seen a group of Iykams slip into the Red Poppy just before Roarke and Selene left, and it seemed reasonable that they would continue their tailing efforts. So I turned back—"

"Wait a minute," I spoke up. "You're sure they were after us and not Dent?"

"Pretty sure," McKell said. "Dent had already left and had picked a doorway to loiter in where he could wait for you to come out. If the Iykams had been following him, there would have been no reason for them to go inside."

"Why does it matter?" Graym-Barker rumbled.

I looked back at him, forcing myself not to wilt under his glare. "Because after our last little run-in with them, I figure most Iykams out there are after my blood," I said. "Being identified and followed, but not attacked, suggests a new subtlety to the situation."

Graym-Barker looked back at McKell. "Does it?"

"Could be," McKell said thoughtfully. "The Iykams I deflected away from the meeting didn't seem interested in killing anyone. At least not right away."

"And we *do* know one Patth who understands subtlety," Ixil added.

"Sub-Director Nask," McKell agreed, his eyes going dark. He disliked Nask even more than I did, though to be fair his association with that particular Patth went back a lot farther than mine did. "On the other hand, we also know Iykams aren't great at differentiating between human faces," McKell continued, looking back at me. "Maybe they were just out enjoying the New Moon Festival and didn't recognize you."

I raised my eyebrows. "And also didn't recognize Selene?"

McKell's lip twitched as he looked at her flowing, pure-white hair and delicate Kadolian features. "Point," he conceded. "Okay. The other possibility is that Nask has figured out you're working for us and is dropping Iykams along your backtrail hoping you'll lead them to the mother lode."

"He may not be far off," I said grimly. "Selene? I assume you haven't told them?"

"There wasn't a clear opportunity," Selene said. She focused on Graym-Barker, her pupils showing freshly increased nervousness. Normally, she wasn't as intimidated by people as I was; but then, normally she could tell from a person's scent if he was actually angry or just looked scary. Here, viewing Graym-Barker on a StarrComm display, she didn't have that advantage. "I smelled portal metal on Dent's arm."

McKell's jaw dropped a couple of millimeters, Ixil's outriders stiffened in perfect unison, and even Graym-Barker seemed to forget for a moment that widened eyes didn't exactly add to his usual authoritative look. "Are you sure?" he demanded.

"Of course she's sure," I jumped in as Selene winced back from his intensity.

"He means is she sure it was on Dent and not someone else in the crowd," McKell jumped in right behind me, rising to the defense of his boss in the exact same way I'd just come to the defense of my partner.

"It was on Dent," Selene murmured, her voice quiet but firm.

"Interesting," Graym-Barker said, his eyes and face back to normal. "We assumed he'd just heard rumors about Icarus, possibly from Nask or some other Patth. But if he's actually touched one..." He pursed his lips. "How long since he touched it?"

"I don't know," Selene said. "The scent was very faint."

"But it *was* there?" the admiral pressed.

"Yes."

"All the more reason to get on top of this," McKell said grimly. "*And* on him. Okay. First step—"

"Hold it," I interrupted him. "Before we get to steps and flow-charts, there's a dangling thread I want to clear up. Ixil, back in the morgue you said you knew something I didn't. How about sharing with the rest of the class?"

"The rest of the class already knows," Ixil said, an odd look on his squashed lizard face. "We think—we *think*—Easton Dent has a twin brother."

It was my jaw's turn to drop a little. Dent had a *twin?* "What do you mean, you *think?* That sounds like it should be pretty easy to figure out."

"You'd think so, wouldn't you?" Graym-Barker said. "Jordan, you can take this one."

"As much as *anyone* can take it," McKell said, scowling. "Okay. When Dent first popped up on our radar Tera and I started poking into his background. Along the way, we noticed a few anomalies. For one thing, while he seemed to work alone, there were a few times when a deal gone bad ended up with the other party shot, usually in the back."

"Yes, Tera mentioned the various stray bodies," I said. "I have to say Dent didn't seem the type to go out of his way to be that irritating."

"Not sure if he instigated the conflicts or just had the bad luck to deal himself into high-risk agreements," McKell said. "Obviously, the other parties involved weren't available afterward to give their side of it."

"It may not be simple happenstance," Graym-Barker put in. "Tera noted that he walked away from each of those confrontations with whatever it was he'd originally stolen *plus* the other party's planned payoff."

"*When* the other party actually brought payment," McKell amended. "We know that on at least two of those occasions they came to the meet empty-handed, probably with the intent of stealing Dent's goods outright."

I nodded. Selene and I had occasionally been on the short end of that kind of deal. As far as I was concerned, shooting such blatant swindlers in the back was completely justifiable. "As my father used to say, *If he looks like he's going to hit you, don't hit him back first. Hit him back* only. So Dent's got a silent partner with good aim. How does that make the partner a twin?"

"We sent Jennifer to check his background," Graym-Barker said. "You remember Jennifer, I assume?"

"She's a bit hard to forget," I assured him. Jennifer—like Tera, I'd never heard her last name—was one of the Icarus Group's operatives, handling everything from quiet diversions to facing down armed Iykams.

She'd also threatened Selene and me once or twice, but I didn't take that personally.

"She is that," McKell agreed. "Anyway, we sent her to the province on Gremon where Dent grew up and had her check his original birth documents. It turns out that sometime in the past fifteen years they were hacked into."

"Fifteen years," I repeated, thinking back over the slim file on Dent that Tera had sent us. "So just about the time Dent left the planet."

"Right," McKell said. "The record only lists one live birth, of course, but Jennifer found indications that there'd been a link to another record with the same date and place. That file had unfortunately been deleted."

"A good hacker should be able to reconstruct it."

"Jennifer had an excellent hacker with her," McKell said. "Dent's hacker was better."

"I understand that it had also been too long for some of the more subtle techniques to be useful," Ixil added.

"Correct," McKell said. "All they could pull up from the deleted file was a name: Weston Dent."

I raised my eyebrows. "*Weston* Dent?"

"I know," McKell said dryly. "Easton and Weston Dent. Sounds like a comedy team."

"Not if you're the one being shot in the back."

"Point."

"What about people who knew the family?" Selene asked. "Could Jennifer have talked to one of them?"

"She tried," McKell said. "But it was a rural area that had gone through a lot of economic upheaval over the past decade, and there was no one there who remembered the Dents."

"And you couldn't track them?" I persisted. "Come on. The government tracks *everyone*."

"Except those who hire hackers to clear them out of those databases," McKell said.

"I decided it would be dangerous to continue," Graym-Barker said. "Wide-ranging probes like that inevitably draw unwanted attention. If the Patth hadn't already noticed Dent, we didn't want to accidentally put them on his scent."

"Right." Like the Patth needed an excuse to go poking around Commonwealth data listings.

"But there are a few other indicators," McKell said. "Dent's first ship was named the *Southern Cross*, while his current one is named the *Northern Lights*. Add it to Easton and Weston and he's got the whole compass boxed."

"Of course," I said. "Since cutesy clues are something professional thieves really like scattering around for badgemen to zero in on. Just to make it clear: No one on our side has actually seen this mystery twin. Right?"

McKell's lip twitched. "Right."

"Unless," Ixil added quietly, "you and I just saw him in the morgue."

A hard knot settled into my stomach. "You think that was Weston Dent?"

"I don't know," Ixil said. "He was a bit taller than Easton, and his skin seemed a bit lighter."

"Then again, there's no indication whether Weston was identical or fraternal," McKell pointed out.

"*If* he existed at all," I said.

"If he existed at all," McKell again conceded.

For a moment no one spoke. I counted off the seconds, idly calculating how much this thoughtful hush was costing the Icarus Group in StarrComm fees. Fortunately, it was Graym-Barker who was paying that bill, not me.

It was McKell who finally broke the silence. "All right," he said. "Now that that's out in the open, let's get back to the steps and flowcharts Roarke mentioned. If that body is indeed Weston Dent, Easton may try to retrieve it."

"And will be royally pissed at whoever killed him," I warned, flipping a mental coin. They'd told me what they knew about Weston Dent. Should I tell them what *I* knew, or not?

Not, I decided.

"Which may put him in the mood to take stupid chances," McKell continued. "Unfortunately, none of us can hang around long enough to do anything about that."

"Why not?" I asked. "You got somewhere else you're supposed to be?"

"As a matter of fact, we do," McKell said. "And after your extraordinarily brilliant jailbreak, you need to get off New Kyiv, too."

"I suppose," I said reluctantly. I really hated being chased off planets. "I guess we'll just have to wave him off some other way."

"Any idea on how to do that?" McKell asked.

"Apart from alerting the local badgemen," Graym-Barker added. "Getting him arrested won't do us much good."

"Not to mention pinpointing his location for anyone who might still be gunning for him," I agreed. "No, I was thinking more along the lines of telling him what he's up against. Assuming he's smart enough not to just charge in at dawn with his Golden blasting divots in the station's walls, he may pause long enough to drop into a StarrComm center and check his messages. If we give him some reasonable options, he might be willing to surface again."

"Not sure how receptive he'll be, given how fast he bailed on you," McKell said doubtfully. "But it can't hurt to try."

"At least until we come up with something better," Graym-Barker said. "Jordan?"

"Yes, sir," McKell said, nodding. "I'll set it up for him as soon as we're finished here."

"Thanks," I said. "So I guess my only other question, Admiral, is who was the dead guy in the picture Dent showed us?"

They were good, all right. There was barely a flicker of reaction from either McKell or Ixil, and nothing at all from Graym-Barker. It was only Pix and Pax who gave noticeable twitches. Luckily, with my eyes focused on the screen and the admiral, I could pretend I hadn't seen that. "He was middle-aged and balding," I continued, "with a kind of professorial air about him."

"Any idea how he died?" McKell asked.

"The photo only showed his face," I told him, "and I didn't see any signs of trauma there. It was also an analog photo, on old-style film, not a dij copy."

"Interesting," Ixil said thoughtfully. "It sounds like Dent didn't want to be caught carrying around a dij of the victim."

"That was what I thought, too," I agreed. "Which not only adds another layer of suspicion but also raises the question of where he got his hands on an analog camera to begin with."

"Lots of places he *could* have gotten a camera," McKell said, his forehead furrowed as if he was genuinely concentrating on the problem. "But *why* he would have one is less obvious. We'll look into it."

"Into which one?" I asked. "The victim or the camera?"

"The victim, of course," Graym-Barker said stiffly. "I'll start that inquiry. You and Selene will meanwhile concentrate your efforts on finding out where Dent touched a portal." He raised his eyebrows. "If and when you do, you *will* contact me immediately. No going off and playing detective on your own."

"Of course," I said, as if such a thing had been the furthest thing from my mind. "You're the professionals here, not Selene and me."

"And try not to forget that." He gave me a brisk nod. "Good luck." He reached somewhere off camera and the display went blank.

"And good-bye to you, too," I muttered as McKell started working the board. "Let me know when you're ready."

McKell made a final adjustment and nodded. "Go."

I recorded a short message for Dent, loosely based on the speeches I used to give targets I was trying to persuade to surrender peacefully, though in this case I made it clear he was merely an information source and not in any sort of trouble. When I finished McKell keyed the message to Dent's mail drop, and we were done.

"I hope that works," McKell commented as he collected his change from the slot. "If it doesn't, he's going to be doing his vengeance charge alone."

"I still think Selene and I should stay here a day or two and watch for him," I said. "After tonight, the badgemen will be pretty well beat."

"No," McKell said firmly. "You need to get off New Kyiv as soon as possible."

"Which may present a problem," Ixil warned. "By now the *Ruth* is certainly being watched." He looked at McKell. "We *could* fly them out in the *Stormy Banks*."

"Only if they hurry," McKell said. "We need to get back to the job."

"I thought *we* were your job," I said, putting some disillusionment into my voice. "I'm crushed."

"You're not our sole reason for living, either," McKell assured me. "Just be thankful we were close enough to help out. So do you want a ride or not?"

"Not if it means leaving the *Ruth* here," I said. "Thanks for the offer, but we can get out on our own."

"Do remember that you're running from a murder charge," Ixil said. As if I might have forgotten. "Surveillance is likely to be hotter than you're used to."

"Right," I agreed. "And of course badgemen are usually cool with people who break fugitives out of lockup."

"Not saying they won't be all over us, too," McKell said with a shrug. "But we know a few tricks."

"Likewise," I said. "You might be surprised how often the person offering the bounty isn't on the same planet as the target."

"And the locals sometimes want their own crack at him?" McKell suggested.

"Pretty much always," I said.

"They must love to see you land," he said philosophically. "Anything we can do to assist before we go?"

"If you have time, you could get an order logged into the Port Authority for the *Ruth* to be impounded tomorrow morning," I said. "It would save me the trouble of doing it myself."

"No problem," McKell said. "Any time in particular?"

"Let's make it around seven. That's when a lot of big-shot ships are starting to head out."

"Sounds intriguing," McKell said. "I almost wish we could stay around and watch this one. You want a side order of diversion or distraction with that?"

"No, thanks," I said. "Well, actually, it would be convenient if you could get all the low-orbit patrol ships moved somewhere else other than directly overhead. If not, don't worry about it. We can work around them."

"I'll see what we can do," McKell said. "Good luck, and watch your backs."

"Ditto," I said, nodding in turn to each of them. "Come on, Selene. Let's go home."

The badgemen were still roaming the streets out there, of course. But I wasn't much worried. We'd been out of sight long enough that their logical conclusion should be that we'd either gone back to the *Ruth* or else headed for the tall grass. Since they were certainly keeping an eye on the ship, that left the tall grass. If I were them, I'd be monitoring the city's various transit lines, cabs, and runaround rentals.

Given the crowds still filling the streets, all of whom would eventually be taking those same cabs and transits to get home, I wished them luck with their search.

"You don't think it was Easton Dent's brother who was killed, do you?" Selene asked quietly as we wended our way through the merrymakers toward the spaceport annex.

"I don't just think it, I'm a hundred percent sure it wasn't," I said. "Put yourself in their place. You're Weston Dent, and you've been quietly working with your brother for the past fifteen years. Not just working with him, but successfully staying invisible that whole time. Would you *really* wear an outfit that could let you be mistaken for him?"

"Unlikely," Selene conceded. "So who was he?"

I shook my head. "My guess is he was just some poor sap who turned up at the wrong place at the wrong time."

"And in the wrong clothing," Selene murmured. "And they didn't realize he wasn't Dent?"

"Not quickly enough," I said. "Maybe not until after they'd shot him. After that, of course, they had to destroy his face to hide the fact they'd grabbed the wrong man."

"But why kill him at all? Why not just let him go?"

"No idea," I said. "I assume he saw or heard something he shouldn't."

Selene was silent a few more steps. The crowds were starting to thin out, I noted uneasily, with the last determined holdouts finally starting to call it a night. If the landscape opened up too much before we got back to the *Ruth* we would be painfully easy for the badgemen to spot.

"In that case, why didn't they hide the body instead of leaving it where it could be quickly found?" she asked. "And why steal your wallet and leave it there with him?"

"Obviously, to frame me."

"But that wouldn't hold up to a real investigation." She looked sideways at me, her pupils showing dread. "Dent was just the bait and hook, wasn't he? You and I were their real targets."

I sighed. "Yeah, I think so," I conceded. I'd been hoping she wouldn't reach that disturbing conclusion, or at least not this quickly. "In which case, a dead nobody everyone thinks is Dent works just as well as the real thing. They were probably working on a plan to have the badgemen hand us over to them, only McKell and Ixil got there first."

"I don't know," she said doubtfully. "It seems very inefficient. Why not just take us when they stole your wallet?"

"Too public or too crowded, maybe," I said. "Or they knew they'd never be able to sneak up on us and that super nose of yours. Hiring a local pickpocket who you'd never smelled before would be safer."

"If they were worried we'd spot them, they must be someone we already know," she pointed out.

"Or a group of such someones," I agreed. "Any Iykam, for instance."

Selene inhaled sharply. "A pickpocket. *That's* why Dent ran off the way he did. He realized he'd been robbed and was chasing the thief."

"Could be," I said, remembering back to what I'd seen of him moving through the crowds. He hadn't been rushing, but he'd definitely looked like a man with a purpose. "I hadn't thought of that, but it makes sense. It would also explain why he reversed his jacket. Easier to tackle someone if they don't instantly recognize who it is who's bearing down on them."

"And the path of him following someone would look very much like him trying to get away from us," Selene said. "If that's true, then we didn't frighten Dent away. That should make him more likely to answer the message you just sent."

"Let's hope so," I said, refusing to let my hopes get too high on that one. As my father used to say, *Hope may spring eternal, but jumping up out of the weeds is a good way to get shot.* "Unless he thinks we're the ones who had him robbed. Either way, he may not be willing to surface again until he knows who did."

"Which we don't know, either."

"Not yet," I said, a plan slowly forming in the back of my mind. "Though maybe we can find out." I took her arm and picked up our pace a little. "Come on, let's get back to the *Ruth*. We've got places to go and people to see."

"Which people?" Selene asked, fluttering her long eyelashes as she tried to read my sudden change of mood. "The pickpocket, or Easton Dent?"

"Who says we have to choose?" I countered, giving her a tight smile. "Let's see if we can find both."

CHAPTER FIVE

Given the festival's ongoing security needs, I hadn't expected the badgemen to have the personnel to spare to post a guard at the *Ruth*'s hatch, even given the heinousness of my supposed crime. I *had* expected them to set up a monitor camera on the ramp, though, and probably another one or two hidden off to the side somewhere in case I disabled the obvious one.

I was right on all counts. There were four cameras in all, pointed at the hatch and the walkways leading up to it. There was also probably a good chance that the badgeman tasked with watching the monitors all night was the hapless officer I'd drugged during my holding tank escape.

Unfortunately for the hounds, the hares had another way into their burrow.

Getting to the far side of the ship unseen was straightforward enough, involving just a couple of other ramps, a small maze of cargo pallets, and one short section of crawling to avoid one of the port annex's permanent security cameras. It was the same route Selene had taken in reverse when she'd sneaked out of the ship earlier that evening, and certainly no worse than we'd done many times during our bounty hunter days.

Once we were there, it was simply a matter of sliding down the curved surface of the cradle to the Number Two equipment bay near the *Ruth*'s bow. That particular bay held electronics for the hyperspace cutter array, equipment that was only supposed to be accessible from the outside while the ship was on the ground. I reached past the neat rows of wires and modules, unfastened the hidden catches on the inner hull plate behind it, and swung open the panel.

Selene went in first, climbing through the opening and into the service crawlway, from which she could get back to the midship hatch where she could climb up into the *Ruth*'s main deck. I followed, sealing the outer equipment access panel and the hidden inner door behind me. Every bounty hunter occasionally needed to get a prize past official scrutiny; this was our way of dealing with that particular obstruction.

Selene was running the pre-check when I arrived on the bridge. "Any news?" I asked, going to the nav table and starting to set up our course.

"The ship seems all right," she said. "No locks or barriers, and everything reads green. I also found the seven o'clock impound order McKell set up."

"Good," I said, finishing the nav details and then looking over Selene's shoulder to make sure she hadn't missed anything in her review. She hadn't. "That gives us five hours. I'm thinking we grab four hours of sleep, then get back here for the big moment."

"All right," she said, her pupils troubled. "Gregory . . . that body you found in the morgue. Is it possible that was the same person as the one in the photo Easton showed us?"

I shook my head. "That man was already dead, remember?"

"Are you sure?" she countered. "We really don't know when either of them died. What if Easton had already killed him, showed us his picture to see if we could identify him, then went back and destroyed his face?"

"Or it could have been someone else who did that last bit," I said reluctantly. The hell of it was, she could be right. Easton's photo had been physical, without the time stamp a dij would have had. And with the photo having been stolen from my wallet, there was no way to do a facial reconstruction. On top of that, with the photo only showing the dead man's head a body profile was out of the question. "Like maybe the Iykams. I get the feeling they would enjoy doing something like that."·

"They don't usually carry plasmics," Selene pointed out. "Would their corona guns create the same pattern of damage?"

"Not from what I've seen of them," I conceded with a shiver. "But just because they don't normally carry plasmics doesn't mean they couldn't use one for special occasions." I frowned as her pupils suddenly showed fresh consternation. "You disagree?"

"No. I just..." She winced. "We know the Iykams don't usually carry plasmics. But we do know someone who does."

"We know lots of people who do," I reminded her. "Including me."

"And McKell."

I stared at her. "You're not serious."

"Aren't I?" she asked. "He and the others lied about the dead man."

"Yeah, I know," I said, still eyeing her. But really, McKell as a murderer was a ridiculous and outrageous suggestion if I'd ever heard one.

Or was it?

We knew the lengths Graym-Barker and the rest of the Icarus Group went to to keep their secrets. If someone threatened those secrets, would the admiral hesitate even a minute before ordering him dealt with?

And if McKell got that order, would he hesitate to carry it out?

I liked to think both of them had a little more moral integrity than that. But then, I'd never seen either of them pushed all the way against the wall.

"Though it doesn't make much sense for McKell to get me hauled in for murder just to send Ixil in to haul me back out," I pointed out.

"The frame-up might not have been his idea," Selene said. "McKell could have killed the man, then the Iykams or Patth found the body and used it to set you up."

I glowered at the universe at large. "I wish to hell I had that photo back," I muttered. "I'm pretty sure he and the guy in the morgue had different facial shapes, but I only got a quick look at the photo and don't remember enough detail to make that call."

"The plasmic burning could also have affected that."

"I know," I said. "Still, I'm leery of a scenario that requires one party to kill someone while another party steals my wallet—and Easton's—on the off chance they'll be able to use them. You start making things too complicated, and they start collapsing under their own weight."

"I don't really believe it, if that helps," Selene said. "The possibility occurred to me, that's all, and I thought I should mention it."

"And you were absolutely right," I assured her. "I don't believe it, either; but I also don't necessarily *disbelieve* it. We've also got a lot of unidentified players in this game, and we need to start slapping name tags on them."

"How do we do that?"

I gestured back to the nav table. "We start by going back to the CR-207-T system. If we're lucky, our mystery friends will realize we're heading there and follow."

"And we're going to confront them?"

"In a manner of speaking," I said. "They stole our probe, remember?"

"You're going to ask for it back?"

"Not at all," I said. "I'm going to give them the other one."

The scheduled seven o'clock impound order didn't get underway until nearly seven fifteen, long enough for me to wonder if the badgemen had figured out the listing was bogus but not long enough for me to come up with a backup plan.

Still, once it was actually going, the operation went smoothly enough. The landing cradle repulsors activated, nudging the *Ruth* off the ground and into range of two of the annex's perimeter grav beams. Normally, the beams raised a departing ship to an altitude where its thrusters could be kicked in without damaging the surrounding terrain, at which point the spaceport figuratively waved good-bye and the ship handled the rest of its journey up and out into space on its own.

Impound situations, though, were handled a bit differently. Instead of lifting the *Ruth* up and out to altitude, the grav beams raised us only about a hundred meters off the pad and then guided us sideways toward the impound lot at the edge of the field, each pair of beams handing us off to the next pair as we glided over the rest of the parked ships below.

Some of the Spiral's fancier fields had designated heavy-lift vehicles, modeled after orbital tugs, that could come together in whatever size group was necessary and use their own grav beams to transport the tagged ship to impound without having to tie up the perimeter system. But smaller spaceports like Glazunov

Annex usually didn't have much call for such specialized equipment, and the bosses had apparently decided an upgrade wasn't worth the money.

If things went according to plan, they would soon regret that decision. Hunched over the monitors at the pilot station, splitting my attention between the view of the field and the slowly rising rumble coming from the *Ruth*'s thrusters—a sound that the supervising badgemen would never notice amid the cacophony of other nearby ships also powering up—I waited for the right opportunity.

There it was, on the traditional silver platter: a fancy trimaran-style yacht, a good three times the size and ten times the mass of the *Ruth*, rising slowly from its cradle about six landing slots directly ahead. Probably loaded to the cutter array with celebrants from last night's festival, the majority of them asleep or badly hung over, none of them expecting anything out of the ordinary to happen. It finished rising as high as the cradle could send it, and my displays showed the perimeter grav beams in the process of locking onto its hull.

As my father used to say, *Never run away from your troubles. Flying is faster, and you present a smaller target.* Keying the *Ruth*'s bioprobe grav beams, I aimed them at the trimaran and fired.

Firing a grav beam at a relatively miniscule bioprobe meant the probe came to you. Firing at something that seriously outmassed you, on the other hand, meant instead that you went to it.

Mostly went to it, anyway. Newton's Laws being what they were, yanking on the trimaran meant we both started moving toward our common center of mass. Adding in the contributions of the perimeter grav beams, all of which were trying very hard to keep both ships where they were, and you had a neat problem in undergrad theoretical physics.

The real universe didn't need to bother with pedantic calculations. In less time than it would take the undergrad's professor to even define the problem, the mix of forces and masses shook out with the *Ruth* pulling itself straight out of the focus of the beams carrying it across the field and nudging the trimaran halfway out of its own set of beams.

The Glazunov Annex executives might have scrimped on equipment for their impound yard, but they were solidly up-to-date on safety protocols. The trimaran, bigger and way more expensive than the *Ruth*, would have been assigned a higher spot in the computerized priority stack, which meant that when my maneuver suddenly put both ships at risk of a tumble it was the trimaran that got immediate attention. Even as its own assigned perimeter grav beams scrambled to reestablish a solid lock, the next nearest beams shifted over to the bigger ship to bolster their effort.

Unfortunately for the impound crew, the next nearest beams were the ones currently trying to reestablish a lock on the *Ruth*.

We actually dropped about ten meters before I got the thrusters kicked in at sufficient power to start us blasting upward. There was a brief window where the perimeter beams could have grabbed us again, but they were too busy rescuing the trimaran. Before any of the human controllers could wake up to what was happening and override the auto system, we were too far out of range for them to do anything about it.

There was another layer of security, of course: the cadre of patrol ships tracing lazy orbital paths around New Kyiv. Unfortunately for them, while McKell was faking the *Ruth*'s impound order he'd also somehow gotten the majority of the patrol ships reassigned to watch other parts of the planet. Only one of the patrollers was in position to chase us, and we were able to stay ahead of him long enough to activate the *Ruth*'s cutter array and launch us into hyperspace.

I just hoped that the people who'd been poking fingers into our lives had taken note of the vector we'd escaped on and had drawn the correct conclusions. That is, the conclusions I wanted them to draw.

The CR-207-T system hadn't changed much in the few days we'd been away from it. Hardly surprising, really.

What *had* changed was my ability to do more than one thing at a time. This time around, as I drove us toward the upper atmosphere and the area where we would release our remaining bioprobe, I also kept a close watch on the space behind us.

We were just entering the outer reaches of the stratosphere when I spotted the other ship pop out of hyperspace in the distance.

"They're here," I told Selene.

"Yes, I saw," she said. "Are you sure you want to go through with this?"

"Of course," I said, frowning. "I didn't spend the past two

days tearing apart the probe and putting it back together just for the fun of it. Why, are *you* having second thoughts?"

"I'm not sure I ever had any first thoughts," she said, her pupils showing a hint of nervous humor. "I'm just wondering if they'll see this as an attack."

"They might," I conceded. "But it's not like they'll think their lives are in danger. And if they wanted us dead they had lots of chances the last time we were all here together. Not to mention whatever shots they might have been able to line up on New Kyiv."

Her pupils winced. "Not a good choice of words."

"Yeah," I said wincing a little myself. *Shots.* "Sorry. Look, if you're really uncomfortable with this I'm willing to abort. We can just lose them here and head back to civilization. Go see if Easton Dent has surfaced yet."

Her pupils hardened. "No," she said firmly. "We can't go back to Dent without some idea who's coming after him. *And* after us."

"Okay, then," I said, standing up. "You get set here while I go get the probe ready."

Because as my father used to say, *Fool me once, shame on you. Fool me twice, and you've shown a pattern I can work with.*

I stuck with the flight pattern I'd laid down on our first trip here, except that now I was working with only one bioprobe instead of two. Once again, as the probe started to rise from the lower atmosphere, the *Ruth* began to experience the same buffeting we'd gone through the last time as the poachers once again went all creative with their tiltrotors.

I wasn't sure whether the primary goal was to keep us busy holding the ship steady or to hide themselves a bit better in the turbulent air. But it didn't really matter. All I needed to know was what they were planning.

One of the warning lights on my board flashed: the probe was nearing grav beam range. I resettled my hands on the controls, my eyes flicking over the displays as I searched for the poacher. He had to be at the far end of the incoming winds...

"I have him," Selene's voice came from the bridge intercom. "Eight o'clock nadir, ten kilometers."

"I see him," I confirmed as I spotted the dim shape through a cloudy layer of air that was strangely translucent.

As well as also being completely artificial. They weren't just playing games with their tiltrotors, but were also using some sort of fancy smoke screen to cover their approach.

Which was a good sign. Pulling out all the stops this way meant they'd followed the logical bread crumb trail I'd laid out and concluded that the reason we'd come back so quickly was that there was something here worth a second look.

It was probably killing them that they hadn't been able to figure it out from the first set of samples they'd made off with. But now they had a second chance, and they were determined to do whatever it took to grab it.

Including letting me sucker them into coming too close.

As my father used to say, *Using an opponent's size and weight against him is fine, but his desires and flaws are much better levers.*

Our probe should be visible on the poacher's scanners now, and I saw him shift position slightly in response, rising upward while staying behind the supposed protection of his smokescreen. I watched him closely, trying to anticipate the moment when he would fire his grav beams...

"Now," I called to Selene.

An instant later the deck dropped out from under me as she sent the *Ruth* plunging straight down through the atmosphere. We fell below the poacher's altitude, no doubt startling the hell out of him as we shot past a couple of kilometers away—

And as he fired his grav beams Selene kicked our thrusters back in and brought us to a halt directly between him and the probe.

His beams caught us squarely in our center, just as I'd planned. Even as the *Ruth* jerked in response to the sudden pull, I fired our own beams back at him. There was a second jolt as we grabbed on, and now we were a pair of wrist-roped wrestlers pulling at each other. The poacher's beams belatedly winked off, but by then he was thoroughly in the *Ruth*'s own grip. He twitched violently, trying to break our hold, probably scrambling like crazy to figure out how he was going to handle the boarders he naturally assumed were poised to attack.

Unfortunately, in the midst of all that misdirection and burgeoning panic, he forgot all about our probe.

Even with our beams pinning him mostly in place he might have been able dodge out of its path if he'd spotted it fast enough. But he didn't. By the time it came arrowing straight at his airlock, it was far too late for him to do anything but gape in horror. Even a good string of curses was probably out of the question. The poacher quivered as the probe slammed into the airlock, its momentum driving it through both the outer and the inner doors, its own bow disintegrating along the way.

For about half a second it just sat there, wedged in place, looking strangely like a dog hanging out a runaround's side window. Then, the poacher's emergency systems kicked in, the inner backup airlock seal slamming into place and shoving what was left of the probe back out into the atmosphere. I shifted my grav beams from the poacher to the probe, grabbing it away from the damaged ship and hauling it toward the *Ruth*—

"*Go!*" I shouted.

Unnecessarily, as it turned out. Selene was paying close attention to the drama, and even as I opened my mouth to give the order she had us clawing for space as fast as we could travel without losing my grip on the probe. I watched the poacher, waiting tensely for him to pull himself together and come charging after us.

But he'd apparently had enough for one day. He stayed put, no doubt watching balefully as we drove through the remaining bits of tenuous atmosphere and into the starlit black beyond. I reeled the probe back into its bay, and without missing a beat Selene activated the cutter array and we were once again in hyperspace.

"Gregory?" she called.

I huffed out a breath as I did a quick double check of the displays. That had worked out better even than I'd expected. "We're good," I confirmed. "What course did you put in?"

"Marjolaine," she said. "I thought it would be a good place to find out if Dent has answered your note."

"Sounds like a plan," I said. "Come on back and suit up. Let's see if we can figure out who wants our probes this badly."

The probe was a mess, of course, what was left of the bow a tangle of twisted metal, crushed plastic, and shattered ceramic. But that was okay. The important parts, the samplers and collectors, were tucked safely away toward the rear where my two days of sweat and toil had repositioned them.

Admiral Graym-Barker was now going to have to buy us *two* new bioprobes.

I waited silently while Selene went through each collector, smelling the air and dust and whatever else they'd collected during the probe's half-second visit to the poacher, then taking them and sealing them in official Trailblazer sample containers. Finally, her pupils looking troubled, she handed me the last container and took a cleansing breath of the clean room's air. "There were four men aboard," she said. "Human males. I'm not completely sure, but I think I smelled three of them on New Kyiv."

I nodded. That made sense, since only a ship that was already at the Glazunov Annex could have gotten its people loaded aboard and charged after us as quickly as the poacher had. "Were they in the Red Poppy or on the street?"

"Two were in the Red Poppy," she said, gazing at the sample, her pupils focused in concentration. "The third was outside. The fourth...I don't know, Gregory. I've smelled him before, I think, or at least a trace of him. But not recently."

"Okay," I said cautiously. I'd run into elusive and half-remembered scents with Selene before. Usually it was real, but occasionally she conflated something with something else. "Can you pin it down any better than that? Either by timeframe or location?"

"No," she said, her pupils showing frustration.

"But you'll know him if you smell him again?"

"Of course," she said, as if that was obvious.

"Good," I said. "Well, at least it isn't Nask. Now we just have to figure out—" I broke off as her pupils abruptly gave a little wince. "Don't tell me. Nask?"

"No, not him," she said with clear reluctance. "But there might have been a Patth aboard. Not aboard *now*, but earlier, and only for a little while. Or else one of the humans aboard may have simply spent some time with one. I'm sorry. I wish I could be clearer."

"It's okay," I said, trying to force down my sudden frustration. If the Patth really were involved...

But trace smells were trace smells, and if Selene couldn't track them down any more precisely making her feel guilty about it wouldn't do any good. "Did you smell any Patth on New Kyiv when we were hunting for Dent?"

"No," she said, her pupils narrowed in concentration. "I

remember thinking that was odd, since we knew there were Iykams in the area."

"Yeah, I wondered about that, too," I said as a new thought struck me. "Okay. You said the scent was faint. Could the ship have been built by the Patth, or else owned by one of them, sometime before our four humans took over?"

"I didn't know they ever sold their ships to non-Patth."

"I've never heard of that, either," I conceded. "But just because we haven't heard of it doesn't mean it never happens. Especially when you and I are involved."

"Or when Dent is," Selene said, her pupils going thoughtful. "Remember, he's the one who's been searching for you and Icarus."

And Tera *had* said he might be on the Patth radar. "Well, whatever we're up against, at least we now have a baseline," I said. "When we run into these guys again, we'll know it."

"I just hope they're not pointing plasmics at us when that happens," Selene murmured.

"If they are, it'll make it even clearer," I said. "Come on, let's get everything stowed away. If Dent hasn't sent a message, we can at least have another nice conversation with the admiral."

CHAPTER SIX

Like CR-207-T, Marjolaine hadn't changed much since we'd last been here. We set up a new ID for the *Ruth*, just in case the locals were paying close enough attention to InterSpiral Law Enforcement reports to have noticed an angry fugitive-ship report out of New Kyiv. Then, we once again rolled a die to see which StarrComm center we would use, and came up with the one at the southern edge of a city named Khayelitsha. The two closest landing fields were full, but the controller was able to get us into one about an hour's drive away. I put down, set up a refueling, and snagged us a runaround.

We arrived at the StarrComm center half an hour past local noon, apparently an especially busy time of day in this part of Marjolaine. I had to park three blocks from the main entrance, and I could see a steady flow of people going through the wide double doors as we walked toward the building. "This could take a while," I warned Selene. I turned to her, saw a suddenly stricken look in her pupils—

"Not as long as you might think," a quiet voice said from behind me as a hard object the size of a gun muzzle pressed briefly into the small of my back before withdrawing.

I came to a smooth, controlled stop, with none of the jerkiness that might make our assailant think I was about to try something stupid. "This one of them?" I asked Selene casually.

"Yes," she said, her voice low and edged with shame. "I'm sorry, Gregory. I didn't—"

"It's all right," I interrupted her. If our new playmate didn't already know about her extraordinary sense of smell, I didn't want to enlighten him. "I gather we're not supposed to make any StarrComm calls right now?"

"Maybe later," he said. "We'll see what the Pup has to say. Come on—across the street and down that alley over there."

"Which alley?" I asked.

"Just walk." The muzzle touched my back again, this time nudging me in the direction of a service lane a half block away on the other side of the street.

"Oh, *that* alley," I said as I checked both ways for traffic and confirmed we were clear. This area was supposed to be one of Khayelitsha's main tourist centers, but aside from the foot traffic into the StarrComm center this particular couple of blocks seemed pretty empty. "I assume the Pup's waiting for us?" I asked as I started angling across the street.

"He's supposedly on his way," the other said, his tone strongly suggesting he wasn't all that thrilled about being kept waiting, either. "He thought you might show up at one of the other Starr-Comm centers."

"Only you're the one who pulled the lucky straw," I said, nodding. "Congratulations."

"Yeah, I'm thrilled," he said sourly. "Come on, pick it up."

"You parked over here somewhere?" I asked as we passed the street's center line. "I just ask because we had trouble finding a space, too. Hope it's not too far. Leg's been bothering me."

"It's just a couple of blocks," he said. "We'll get a room and you can put your leg up or whatever you need."

"Sounds good," I said. "Hope the room's nice."

"They're all nice there," he said, starting to sound a little testy. Maybe he'd expected more fear and groveling on my part.

"Don't suppose you can upgrade us to a swirl tub," I went on as we neared the walkway on the other side. "It's all on the Pup's tab, right?"

Again, the gun jabbed into my back, a little harder this time. "*Look*, Roarke—"

"Hey," I complained, looking partway over my left shoulder as if to give him an irritated look. I let my eyes suddenly refocus on the street behind him and widen in shock— "Watch it!" I snapped. I swung my left arm up and back, pointing at the oncoming vehicle supposedly barreling down on us.

And as he reflexively looked that direction I just kept the arm moving, slamming my forearm hard against the side of his neck as I simultaneously pivoted on my left foot to rotate myself out of his line of fire. He was just starting to turn back when I completed my spin, my left hand getting a grip on the back of his head as my right hand swung into position to grab the barrel of his gun. A quick pull downward with my left hand, an equally quick pull upward with my right, and I slammed his gun hard into his face.

He was too tough to go down quite that easily. But the blow was strong enough to loosen his grip on his weapon. I twisted it out of his grip, shoved his head a little closer to the ground, and smashed the barrel against the side of his head.

This time he went down and stayed there.

I handed his gun to Selene—it was a Skripka 4mm, I noted—and got a grip under his arms. "Gregory, they're all watching," Selene warned tensely, nodding behind me at the people heading into the StarrComm building.

"I know," I said. "I'm just getting him off the street." I pulled him onto the walkway, then knelt beside him as if I was checking to make sure he was all right. He had the look of an experienced street tough, I saw, but was far older than I'd expected. Somewhere in his midfifties, I estimated, possibly even crowding sixty, at least twenty years past the prime age for this kind of work.

Still, whatever his story, the same response applied. As I leaned close, I slid one of my knockout pills from its left wrist cubby and pushed it between his lips and into his mouth. The pills were designed to be dissolved in someone's drink, but I saw no reason it couldn't do so in someone's residual saliva as well.

At any rate, it was worth a try. The last thing we wanted was for him to wake up and start screaming to someone on his phone. Speaking of which...

His phone was snugged away in the leftmost of his jacket's inner pockets. I slipped it out, hoping he'd been careless enough or rushed enough to have left it unlocked since its last use. If we could find out who he'd called to announce our arrival, we might be able to figure out who he was working for.

No such luck. It was locked down solid.

"Is that an extra emergency call button?" Selene asked, pointing.

"Sure looks like one," I agreed, looking closely at the display. Emergency call buttons were standard on every phone sold in the Spiral, a way of quickly summoning badgemen or medics. They were standard, they were universal, and there was absolutely no reason to install an additional one.

Unless it was to summon a rather different type of assistance. That had all sorts of possible implications, none of them good.

It was also way too tempting a chance to pass up.

Selene must have smelled my sudden change in mood. "What are you doing?" she asked warily.

"A little experiment," I said. With only a slight hesitation I pushed the secondary emergency button, replaced the phone in his pocket, and straightened up. "Time to make ourselves scarce."

"Where are we going?" she asked.

"First job is to get out of sight," I said, taking her arm and steering her into the alley we'd been aiming for. It was pretty much what I'd expected: a narrow lane wide enough for small transport and garbage vehicles but too narrow for full-size run-arounds. There were access doorways and small windows to the street-level stores on either side, with compact ladder lines to the two floors above. No one was visible, but I nevertheless hurried us along. Getting caught on the street had been bad enough. Getting caught in here would be worse.

"Second job is to park you somewhere out of sight," I continued, picking up our pace a bit. "Third job is for me to come back and watch what happens to our playmate back there."

"Gregory—"

"Because your lovely face and white hair are a little too distinctive to blend into the background," I continued. "Don't worry, I'll find you some place that's safe."

"What if I wear my head scarf?" she offered. "I could draw up the sides to cover my face."

I hesitated. Hiding her face that way would certainly help protect her from prying eyes.

The problem was that the scarf also unavoidably blocked off some of the airflow to her nose and eyelashes, which was the equivalent of a human wearing extra-dark sunglasses indoors. It seriously restricted her senses, and I knew that always made her feel vulnerable.

"I appreciate the offer," I said. "And you *will* need to use the scarf, at least over your hair. But you'll be using it in there." I pointed to the nearest of the hotels, and the impressive slip-luminescent sign over the grand entrance that identified it as the Golden Pyramid. "Find a spot in the lobby where you can watch the street, wait for whoever comes to collect Sleeping Beauty to show up, and see where he goes."

"What if he doesn't come here at all?"

"Then we're out of luck," I said. "But he said he'd called for a room, so I'm hoping his backups are already here. Speak of the devil..."

A black eight-passenger van had just emerged from the side street between two of the hotels, keeping up with the rest of the traffic but displaying the impatience and twitchy sense of urgency I'd seen a hundred times back when I was a bounty hunter. "I'm guessing that's them now," I said, nodding her toward the hotel. "As soon as they're out of sight, go."

"All right," she said. She still sounded a little uncertain, but was ready to trust me. "You're not going back through the alley, are you?"

"Walking straight into their arms would probably save time," I said, "but overall it would be a tad counterproductive. No, I'll head over to the street at the end of the block and approach the crime scene from the other end. Stay out of sight as best you can, and call or text if there's any trouble."

"I will. Be careful."

"Count on it."

I headed to the street and joined with the pedestrian flow heading from the busy entertainment hub to the slightly less garish—and probably slightly less expensive—neighborhood where StarrComm had chosen to set up its facility. I kept pace with the general mass of humans and aliens strolling along, wanting to hurry but knowing better than to make myself stand out in any way, until we reached the corner.

A lot of the people who talked about sparking a reaction— and I'd known my share of them—didn't really understand how much of an acquired skill it was. Push too gently and nothing happened; push too hard and you could wind up in the middle of a firestorm. Or as my father used to say, *The difference between a cozy fire and arson is how much kerosene you dump on it.* Staying close to my fellow pedestrians, I headed across the street and sent a casual look to the side.

For once, it appeared I'd hit the sweet spot dead center.

There were three vehicles grouped together by the walkway: a medvan, a badgeman patrol car, and the black van I'd seen scorching the pavement one block over. Our playmate was lying on a rolling stretcher in the middle of the group, still sound asleep, while two medics, two badgemen, and three men in gray suits stood gathered around him. All of them were paying their full attention to each other and ignoring the knots of gawking onlookers.

And while their conversation was too faint for me to hear over the distance and the city noises, it was pretty clear that they were arguing about which of them got to keep Sleeping Beauty.

Turning down the street toward the StarrComm entrance would get me into eavesdropping range of the discussion, and for a moment I was tempted. But there might still be people in the vicinity who'd witnessed the brief altercation and would remember me. Instead, I finished crossing to the corner, then stepped into the nearest shop. A bakery, as it turned out, with a nice selection inside the display window that I could pretend to be studying as I watched the drama half a block away.

I had assumed from Sleeping Beauty's manner of accosting us that he wasn't anyone official, either a badgeman or some government rep, and that whoever showed up in response to the emergency call would be similarly unconnected. The fact that everyone was still arguing supported that theory, since someone with higher rank than the locals would have already flashed their credentials and bundled the unconscious man into their vehicle.

But the fact they were still arguing also meant that the Gray Suits had a fair amount of informal clout, else the badgemen would have already told them to get lost and let the medics get on with their jobs.

Meanwhile, a couple of other bakery customers were wandering into my vicinity. I pulled out my phone and keyed for Selene.

"It's me," I said when she answered. "You there?"

"Yes. No sign of the car yet."

"I know," I said. "Okay. They have lemon and raspberry tarts, rhubarb and apple and bigglebern strudel, horns, dragon claws, and a whole bunch of different breads and cookies."

"You're in the bakery at the corner?"

"That's right," I confirmed. "Don't know exactly what would be best for everyone."

"The badgemen are arguing with the van people?"

"Yep," I said. "What do you think?"

"I don't smell our attacker anywhere in here," she said. "That would suggest he was on the ship that followed us."

"Agreed," I said. I'd already tentatively concluded that from our brief conversation about the mysterious Pup. "Which raises the question of timing."

"You mean how he got to the StarrComm center ahead of us?"

"Right." The browsing customers had now wandered back out of earshot. "He's clearly got friends in high places. Wait a second. Looks like . . . yes. The Gray Suits have won," I told her as one of them began unstrapping Sleeping Beauty from his stretcher. "They're getting him ready to put in the van—looks like the badgemen have confiscated his gun, though."

"How do the badgemen look?"

"Not happy," I said. "Okay, he's in. Badgemen glaring at them . . . and there they go. Down the street . . . turning the corner . . . headed your way."

"I'm ready," she said. "What are you going to do?"

"Get back to you," I said, frowning. "What else would I do?"

"It might be a good time to call the admiral," she said. "You're already there."

"He can wait," I said firmly, heading for the shop door. "This is more important."

"Gregory, I can watch and see where the car goes all by myself," Selene said, her tone mildly chiding. "You need to let the admiral know what's happened, and get him started on tracking down our attacker."

I winced. With my thoughts distracted by the fancy emergency button on the man's phone, I'd completely forgotten to get his picture. "Yeah. Unfortunately, I didn't think to get his picture."

"I did," Selene said. "Here."

I looked at my phone as a dij of my sparring partner appeared. "Got it," I said, pushing open the shop door. "You sure you'll be okay?"

"Of course. Call me when you're done."

The crowd lined up at the StarrComm entrance had thinned

a bit during the street drama. Some of the people had probably needed to get back to work, others had decided it was taking too long, while others had perhaps been unwilling to stand there with their faces hanging out all visible with a couple of badgemen standing a dozen meters away. I didn't recognize any of the remaining group; more importantly, none of them seemed to recognize me.

Even with the reduced clientele it was still nearly twenty minutes before I got a booth. I fed in the bills, punched in the Icarus Group's number, and waited for Admiral Graym-Barker's perennially glaring visage to grace the screen.

Once again, those expectations were dashed.

"Good to see you," Tera said briskly. "I presume this call means you've talked to Dent?"

"Not yet," I said. "We had a couple of side trips to make first. Where's the admiral? On vacation again?"

"He *does* have duties other than answering your calls," Tera pointed out archly. "I trust these side trips were at least relevant to the task at hand?"

"Aren't they always?"

"Mmm," she said in a noncommittal tone. She settled back in her chair. "Okay. Impress me."

I gave her a detailed summary of our trip to CR-207-T and our second encounter with the mysterious poacher, adding Selene's analysis of the aromas we'd captured, and then described the attack here outside the Khayelitsha StarrComm center and the interesting tug-of-war between the badgemen and our assailant's friends. "Here's what he looks like," I finished, transmitting the dij Selene had taken. "He was carrying a Skripka 4mm, incidentally. Decent weapon, and pricey enough to suggest he's with someone important."

"Russian for *violin*," Tera commented thoughtfully as she gazed at the dij. "Okay, I'll get this to the analysis section and see if anyone can tag it. What's your next move?"

"Selene's watching for the car and Sleeping Beauty to go to ground," I said. "Once it does, I'll see if I can get a handle on who he's working for. What's funny?"

"Sorry," she said, smoothing away her brief twitch of a smile. "Jordan once used the name *Sleeping Beauty* on a fake ship's ID for his *Stormy Banks*. He might still have that ID lying around, actually."

"He should probably leave it where it is," I warned. "Freki and

Geri had the same name on a fake ID they used for the *Ruth* at Pinnkus. Interesting coincidence."

"Or not so much coincidence as a not-so-subtle throwback to when the Patth were first hunting us."

"Or a way to make sure McKell doesn't use the ID again," I said, thinking back to the circumstances of that temporary name change. Now that Tera pointed that out, I was pretty sure she was right. "Our old playmates *do* have a warped sense of humor, don't they?"

"If you want to call it that."

"*Warped sense of humor* is easier to pronounce than *petty vicious vindictiveness*," I said. "But getting back to our current playmates and that comment about seeing what the Pup has to say. You don't happen to know any shady characters who use that title, do you?"

"Sounds more like a name someone else would give an unliked colleague," Tera said. "Or an unliked boss, given the subservience implied in the phrasing."

"Camaraderie at its finest," I said. "Though if it comes to that, I can't see the Pup being all that thrilled with his man's performance today, either."

"*I* certainly wouldn't be," Tera agreed. "All right. Go ahead and check your mail drop and see whether or not Dent has responded to your message. Either way, call me right back."

"Got it. Back in a minute." I signed off, fed in more bills, and called my mail drop on Xathru.

Dent had indeed responded, though with a text and not a voice message.

Last chance. Roastmeat Bar, South Joapa, Gremon, ten days from now, seven o'clock pm local time. Don't be late.

I scowled as I copied the note onto a data stick. As Tera herself had underscored with the setup preceding my first meeting with Dent, if you had someone's coding information and access to his or her mail drop you could send all the fake messages you wanted without anyone at the other end being the wiser.

Which meant this was either genuinely from Dent, or else someone was setting a trap. Or possibly both.

But the only two options were to bail on the whole thing or else continue following the bread crumbs, and I was pretty sure Tera wouldn't let us bail. Pumping in a few more bills, making a mental note to restock my cash supply as soon as we were back aboard the *Ruth*, I again punched in the Icarus Group's number. The intricate StarrComm logo appeared and began swirling in its "contacting" indicator, and I settled back to wait.

And kept waiting. The logo finished its usual ten-second loop, then started up again. And again. And again.

By the time it started its fifth repetition a cold feeling was starting to settle between my shoulder blades. Tera had been right there at the comm station, and she'd known I'd be calling back as soon as I finished checking my messages. She wouldn't have just wandered off to do something else.

Not unless she had a hell of a good reason to do so.

As my father used to say, *Stalling is an art form. Don't try it unless you can—you know, that reminds me of an interesting story.*

Finally, the logo cleared and Tera was back. "Was it something I said?" I asked, filtering most of the sarcasm out of my voice.

"It was something you sent," she corrected, her face and voice even more serious than usual. "We found your friend in the ISLE listings."

I sat up a little straighter. Among its other duties, InterSpiral Law Enforcement was tasked with keeping tabs on the Spiral's most notorious criminals. But even badgemen with ISLE's resources had to prioritize, and for Tera to have found him this fast meant he must be pretty high up in their stack of Bad Guys To Keep An Eye On. "And?"

"His name's Eziji Mottola," she said, her eyes steady on me. "He's a senior enforcer for Luko Varsi."

I had learned curses for every occasion from my father, though it hadn't exactly been a formal course on the subject. For this particular situation, none of them seemed quite adequate. "You're sure?"

"Very sure," Tera said. "The ISLE data suggest that he basically grew up in the Varsi organization."

"So what's he doing on Marjolaine chasing down crocketts?"

"No idea," Tera said. "But if Varsi sent him, he must *really* want to see you."

"Do we know where Varsi is right now?"

"As far as we can tell, he dropped off the edge of the map about three months ago." Tera raised her eyebrows. "I don't suppose he might be the forgiving type?"

I huffed out a breath. The forgiving type. Forgiving the man who'd caught on to his private little deal with the Patth and called him on it. Forgiving the man who'd apparently shined enough official light on his organization that he'd been forced to scurry underground for the past few months. Forgiving the man who'd ruined his plan to kidnap and kill Tera. "In general, I doubt it," I told her. "In my case, not a chance in hell."

"I assumed as much," she said. "Okay, you're officially off the case. Grab Selene—"

"Whoa," I cut her off. "What do you mean, off the case? Whatever happened to *we're the only ones who can deal with Dent*?"

"That was before Varsi popped up on your tail," Tera said. "You and Selene are too valuable to risk."

"The admiral might disagree," I said, thinking back to our spotless zero-zero record over the past six months. "Anyway, pulling us means handing Dent to the wolves. The Patth are on to him, and if he really *does* know something..." I left the sentence unfinished.

I'd expected Tera to be able to fill in the blank, and from the expression on her face I saw she'd had no trouble doing so. "It's still too dangerous," she said.

"I don't think so," I said. "It didn't sound like Mottola bothered to call it in before our little fight, and I gave him a knockout pill afterward to make sure he stayed down. It'll be a few more hours before he can tell them what happened. We've got at least that long to retreat to the *Ruth* and get back on Dent's trail before they're even on the same page."

"But they must know you're here," Tera pointed out. "They followed you in, right?"

"Probably," I said. "But there's a fair amount of traffic in and out, and we came in under one of your handy little fake IDs. If we're out before they figure out who we are, they'll have lost us and we can go to Gremon without Mottola or Varsi the wiser."

Tera's eyes narrowed. "To *Gremon*? As in—?"

"As in Dent's home planet, yes," I confirmed. "That's where he wants to meet ten days from now."

"He *said* that?"

"Well, no, it was a text," I admitted. "And yes, I know that means it could be a fraud."

"Or a trap," she said bluntly. "Or both."

"Probably," I said. "But we have to at least try. If we get to Gremon and Varsi's thugs are still on our tail, I promise we'll bail and Dent will be officially on his own. If not, I think we should give this one last shot."

Tera stared at me, little muscles of uncertainty working under her skin. "All right," she said at last. "But watch your backs. And if you have any doubts—*any* doubts—you run and we find another way to lasso Dent. Clear?"

"Clear," I said. "We'll call you again from Gremon."

"All right," she said. "Just bear in mind that if there's trouble, I can't get you any backup. I believe Jordan and Ixil told you they were on assignment, and I can't get anyone else to Gremon ahead of you."

"We've been on our own before," I soothed. "We'll manage."

I could see in her face that she wanted to remind me how well we'd managed on New Kyiv before McKell and Ixil arrived. But she passed over the obvious and simply nodded. "All right," she said. "Good luck."

"Thanks," I said. "Give the admiral our best, will you? And remind him he needs to sign off on a new pair of bioprobes."

There was a message waiting on my phone when I left the StarrComm building and headed back up the cross street toward the hotel where I'd left Selene. I looked around as I walked, confirmed that no one seemed to be particularly interested in me, then keyed for it.

Golden Pyramid Suite 2005.

I frowned. Selene was only supposed to have watched to see where Mottola and his new friends went. She wasn't supposed to have tracked them all the way to a room. *Talked to Tera,* I messaged back. *Is 2005 them, or you?*

Them. Wait.

I got another half block before my phone signaled her incoming call. I ducked into an unoccupied doorway and keyed it on. "You all right?"

"Yes," she murmured, her voice barely loud enough for me to make out. "For the moment."

"For the *moment?* What does that mean?"

She gave a soft, frustrated sigh. "I'm sorry, Gregory. I think I'm trapped."

CHAPTER SEVEN

I'd been planning to settle down in my newly chosen doorway while I checked on Selene's progress. Now, instead, I lurched back into the pedestrian flow and hurried toward the Golden Pyramid as fast as I could without drawing attention. "Where are you?" I asked.

"Room 2007," she murmured. "It's the next room over, the one beside the suite's bedroom. I'm in the far back corner right now, the farthest I could get away from them. They used a freight elevator in the back of the hotel to get Sleeping Beauty up here—"

"His name's Eziji Mottola, by the way."

"Oh. That was fast. Did Tera recognize him?"

"No, but the ISLE database did," I said. "Seems he's one of Luko Varsi's chief thugs."

There was a moment of silence. "I see," she said. "Varsi must have smoothed things over with the Patth."

I frowned at that comment, then remembered the Patth scent she'd picked up from the poacher ship. "Could be," I said. "Never mind that now. What happened with you?"

"I saw where the car went and moved from the lobby to one of the private dining rooms," she said. "Through the window I watched them park and then carry Mottola in through an employee entrance. I searched through the hallways until I found that entrance, which had a freight elevator nearby. I took it up and found out which floor they'd gone to, then went back down and took one of the guest elevators to that floor. I found out which room they'd gone into, and snicked the lock into the room beside it."

I nodded. It was a trick she'd pulled many times back when we were bounty hunters: Travel to each floor until she picked up the target's scent, then walk down the hallway until she spotted that same scent drifting out from under their door.

At which point she should have gone straight back to the lobby to wait for me. "What went wrong?"

"It wasn't anything I did," she said, some defensiveness in her tone. "I took off one of the outlet plates on the adjoining wall and was listening in through the gap when one of the men told two of the others that Mottola's boss was on his way and to go outside and wait for him. Before I could get out, they were already in the hallway."

And if they saw a stranger leave an adjoining room—especially if the organization owned the whole floor and knew that room was empty—she'd be worse than just trapped. "No chance they'll go down to the lobby and meet the Pup there, I suppose?"

"They haven't moved yet."

"How many men total?"

"Counting the two in the hallway, there are six," she said. "But one of them is Mottola, and he's still asleep."

I looked up at the Golden Pyramid now looming over me as I crossed toward its main entrance. So if I had to take them on, it would be at five-to-one odds. Terrific. "We have to find a way to make them move," I said. "Did you hear anything else interesting?"

"They seemed amused that Mottola had been taken out so easily," she said. "From that I assume he's reasonably well known."

"According to Tera, he's one of Varsi's senior enforcers," I said. "Assuming the other guys are high enough in the local branch, they'd almost certainly have heard of him. Any mention of us?"

"Not by name," Selene said. "They also don't seem to know why Mottola is here, though one of them suggested they could call Brandywine and ask. I don't know if there was something Mottola was carrying that indicated he'd come from there or whether that's just Varsi's current headquarters. I had a sense it was the latter, but it's just a sense. Oh, and I haven't heard them use the name *Pup*, so maybe that's something private between him and Mottola."

"Or between Mottola and the rest of the team," I said. "All right, let's think this through. Mottola and the guys you smelled on the poaching ship have been chasing us, first from CR-207-T to New Kyiv, then back to CR-207-T, and now here to Marjolaine."

"They may also have been following us before CR-207-T."

"And we just never spotted them," I agreed, nodding. "Okay— good point. So. Mottola's high up in Varsi's organization, and since he apparently answers to the Pup that suggests the Pup is even higher up."

"And from what Mottola said earlier it sounds like the Pup's on his way from one of Marjolaine's other StarrComm centers," Selene reminded me. "Even if he was at the one closest to Khay- elitsha, we should have another hour or two before he gets here."

"That depends on what kind of air vehicle he's got," I warned. "And where exactly he was when he was alerted."

"So you're saying he could be here any time?"

"Basically," I said. "Hopefully, once he gets here they'll all go back inside. But I don't think we can count on that."

"I agree," she said. "Do you have a plan?"

I looked up at the hotel again, trying to think. Strolling out of the elevator, pretending to be confused or drunk, and hoping I could get and hold the thugs' attention long enough for Selene to slip out and make it to the far end of the corridor was too risky to seriously consider. Trying to bluff them by claiming I was another of Varsi's people was only marginally better. Charg- ing out of the elevator with plasmic blazing was completely out of the question.

On the other hand...

Varsi was mad at me. That part was undeniable, though the amount of actual blame I deserved for what had happened was debatable. He was the head of a criminal organization, and his reputation for how he dealt with his enemies was important to him, if for no other reason than to make sure the heads of similar organizations didn't start thinking he'd lost his edge.

But he was also a businessman. If I could convince him that Selene and I were more valuable alive than we were as object lessons he might go for it.

"Of course I have a plan," I said. "I'm going to go up there, tell your two loiterers that I want to talk to Mottola, and get them to take me inside. As soon as—"

"Mottola is still asleep."

"Right, but since I wasn't the one who decked him I don't know that," I said. "As soon as the hallway is clear, get out of the room and the hotel. Get to the StarrComm center, call Tera, and bring her up to date."

"With the information that you're now their prisoner?" Selene protested. "That won't be at all well received. Let's just wait until they leave and I'll get out then."

"That could be hours," I said. "And if we wait too long they may be able to drill through our fake ID and tag the *Ruth*. If that happens, we'll be trapped here."

"Like you'll be if you go in there?"

"But I've got something to trade for my freedom," I said. "I'll identify myself, hand over the ampule I've got up my sleeve, and tell them to ask Varsi if he wants to deal for our other CR-207-T samples."

"We don't *have* any other samples."

"Right, but he doesn't know that," I said. "And it doesn't matter, because somewhere down the line we *will* find something useful to give him. He surely knows that by now."

"It's crazy," Selene repeated. "Please, Gregory. Just let me wait it out here."

"I wish we could," I said. "But the fact that the Gray Suits' response was so quick suggests that the Golden Pyramid is Varsi's local headquarters, which means they probably own the whole floor. If the Pup or the locals have called in any additional thugs along the way, the rooms flanking the main suite are the first ones where they'll put them. I've got a bargaining chip I can wave under their noses. You don't."

There was a short pause, and I could visualize the play of emotions flowing across her pupils. "What do you want me to say to Tera?" she asked at last.

"Start by telling her the new plan," I said. "If I can make peace with Varsi, that should go a long way toward clearing out our path to Dent. She might also want to alert the local badge-men that Mottola's in town, in case there are any outstanding warrants against him."

"You think getting one of Varsi's people arrested will endear you to him?"

"I'm thinking we could hold that gambit in reserve," I said. I'd reached the hotel's outer door, and strode into a large and elaborately decorated foyer. I looked around for the elevator bank, spotted it off to my right. "If the locals are reluctant to deal, having badgemen show up to grab Mottola ought to distract him, hopefully long enough to let us slip out under his radar. Alternatively, if Mottola seems interested in repairing bridges, I can maybe cement that by being the hero who gets him out from under the authorities' noses."

"I still don't like it," Selene said with a sigh. "But if you're really determined to go ahead with this, I can't stop you."

"I don't much like it, either," I conceded. "But it's that or I leap out of the elevator with plasmic blazing. I think our odds are better if we make sure everyone's guns stay in their holsters. Varsi's mad enough without me gunning down a couple of his thugs."

"I suppose that makes sense," Selene said. "Let me know when."

I reached the elevator bank and pressed the *up* button. "On my way now," I told her. "Wait by the door, and when all of us go inside get going."

"All right. Be careful, Gregory."

"You too." The car arrived and I stepped inside. The doors closed, and I was on my way up.

I took a deep breath. As my father used to say, *In for a penny, in for a pound, provided the pounding isn't coming in your direction.* Varsi had probably never really liked me, but I'd made him occasional piles of money during our rather one-sided relationship. I could only hope he was smart enough to let greed trump anger. The elevator hummed its way upward...

My phone signaled a message. I pulled it out—

The other three men from the poacher ship are here! Don't come up!

I took a quick step toward the control panel. The elevator was just passing thirteen on its way to twenty; quickly, I jabbed the buttons for fourteen and fifteen. I'd get off at a lower floor, then head back to the lobby and rework my strategy. The car reached fourteen—

And kept going.

I swore again and hit the buttons for sixteen, seventeen, eighteen, and nineteen. The car breezed through those as well.

I yanked out my plasmic, knowing even as I did so it was a useless gesture. Elevators in fancy hotels didn't malfunction, at least not like this. Someone must have spotted and identified me as I crossed the lobby.

And I'd even saved them the trouble of getting me out of the public eye by walking into one of their elevators under my own steam.

As my father used to say, *When you're a fly, and your potential host is gesturing you into their parlor with more than six hands, run like hell.*

Only I couldn't. Selene was still trapped, and I still had to get her out of there.

The car glided to a stop, and the doors slid open to reveal three men waiting for me. Two of them were standing shoulder to shoulder just outside the elevator doors, their handguns leveled and ready, the eyes and faces above those guns hard and cold. Like Mottola, they seemed way too old to be pointing weapons into elevators. Half visible behind them was a third man, his eyes just as hard as the others', but the rest of his face wearing a malicious grin.

"Hello," I said cheerfully, nodding to the group as if I walked out of elevators into a pair of Skripka 4mms all the time. "I suppose you're going to want this." Shifting my grip to my plasmic's barrel, I turned it around and held it out politely toward them. "You don't know me, but I used to work for Mr. Varsi—"

"Don't be so modest, Roarke," the man in back growled as one of the others took my gun. "We know all about you."

"I'm flattered," I said, frowning at him. The face was vaguely familiar, but I couldn't place it. "Have we met?"

"You've forgotten already?" the man retorted, his mocking tone going suddenly dark. "Havershem City? Pinnkus? That nice little private park?"

I felt my eyes narrow as the prompting and the face suddenly clicked together in my memory. "*Fulbright?*"

"See? You *do* remember," he said, his voice going a little meaner. "You remember pounding my face into the sand?"

"I think so," I said, feeling a hard knot settle into my stomach. Varsi I could maybe trust to put profit over revenge. I had no such expectations with Fulbright. "There've been so many others over the years."

"Yeah, and it's about time someone did that back to you," Fulbright said.

"Well, you and your friends certainly tried," I said, focusing on the two still pointing their guns at me. Whoever they were, they weren't the friends Fulbright had been running with during that earlier incident. "I see you've picked up a couple of new ones."

"Come on," Fulbright said, ignoring my comment and nodding to his right. "Let's grab ourselves a little privacy."

He turned and headed down the hallway. The two aging thugs stepped back out of my way, and as I left the elevator one of them holstered his gun and got a firm grip on my upper left arm. Marching along together, we headed off in Fulbright's wake. The two men Selene had mentioned were still flanking the suite door. Locals, presumably, and much closer to the appropriate age for this job than the two men walking me toward them. They were eyeing our procession with a sort of subdued interest, and maybe even a hint of respect.

Did that make my two guards more of Varsi's upper-level elite?

"So I take it you're the Pup?" I called past them to Fulbright.

Fulbright didn't turn around, but the sudden stiffness in his back was as expressive as a glare would have been. "That's a yes, then," I concluded. "A term of endearment from your colleagues, no doubt."

"Shut him up," Fulbright ordered over his shoulder.

"You heard him," the man holding my arm growled. "Can it."

"Sure, no problem," I said. So Fulbright was definitely the boss of this little group.

On the other hand, I couldn't help noticing that while the thug's demand to me had been harsh enough, the hand gripping my arm hadn't given it the warning squeeze I would have expected from a man who really meant what he'd been told to say.

So Tera had been right. *Pup* was an epithet that had been assigned to Fulbright by associates who were less than enthusiastic about their current subservient roles.

Which made Fulbright . . . what?

I had no idea. But for the moment I didn't care. All I cared about was clearing all of us out of the hallway so Selene could get free.

Fulbright pointed toward the two men loitering beside the suite door. "Open it," he ordered. One of them nodded and gave the door an oddly syncopated knock, clearly a prearranged signal to the men inside.

But as he did so, I noticed a slight smile twitch briefly at his lips, the kind of smile that might appear behind someone's back. At a guess, he'd overheard my Pup comment, and was just as unimpressed by Fulbright as Fulbright's own cadre were.

Fulbright either missed the smile or else didn't care. "Cole, you wait out here," he said, looking back at the man walking on my right. "I don't want to be disturbed."

"Sure," the thug said.

I felt my stomach tighten. If anyone stayed in the hall, this whole thing would be for nothing. But it wasn't like I could tell Fulbright that.

Or maybe I could. I didn't know the depths of Fulbright's personality, but from our brief encounter in Havershem City I *did* know he could be counted on to react properly if the cues were presented in the right way.

And so, as he started to turn back toward the door, I smiled.

Not a big smile. Hardly a smile at all, really. Just enough of a lip curl to indicate that I was pleased about something and trying hard not to show it. Hopefully, he would notice.

He did. His head snapped back toward me as I quickly wiped away the smile. "What?" he demanded.

"What what?" I countered.

For a second he just stared, his eyes narrowed. The door opened—

"Never mind," he said. "Roarke looks like the type who enjoys company. Everyone inside." He gestured to the other two men. "*Everyone.* Floyd?"

"Sure," the man holding my arm said, giving me a nudge.

Obediently, I followed Fulbright into the suite. Floyd and Cole continued at my sides, with the two younger thugs following the parade and sealing the door behind us.

I gave a quiet sigh of relief. Whatever Fulbright planned for me, at least now Selene was clear.

And whatever he planned, he certainly had the resources for it. Aside from the two men he'd brought and the two who'd been in the hallway, there were the other three Selene had tagged hanging around the suite's conversation area. One of them was standing by the door he'd just opened for us, one was lounging in a chair across from a low coffee table, and the third was sitting at the suite's desk, staring at a monitor split-screened into a dozen different vid images. The hotel's security cameras, I saw, probably how they'd spotted my otherwise surreptitious entrance into the lobby.

Fleetingly, I wondered if he would spot Selene's exit, then put it out of my mind. Selene wasn't nearly as recognizable with her scarf covering her distinctive hair as she was otherwise. Anyway, even if they spotted her there was a good chance most of Khayelitsha's local thug contingent was up here with me right now. At the very least she would have a good head start.

There was no sign of Mottola, but there was a door off to the right that presumably led into the bedroom Selene had also mentioned. He was probably in there, snoozing off the pill I'd given him.

Hopefully he wouldn't wake up any time soon. Everyone probably already suspected I was the one who'd taken him out, and Fulbright's current mood was bad enough without Mottola confirming that.

"Sit," Fulbright ordered, jabbing a finger at the chair at the far side of the coffee table. "Everything on the table. Cole, get his phone. Where's your partner?"

"Who, Selene?" I asked, handing Cole my phone and starting around the table toward the indicated chair. Out of the corner of my eye I saw my other guard, Floyd, make a beeline for the bedroom, presumably to check on Mottola. "She's out shopping."

"Right," Fulbright said sarcastically. "So tell me about the other guy."

"What other guy?" I asked as I sat down and began emptying my pockets onto the table.

"Don't play stupid," Fulbright growled. "The guy on New Kyiv."

"No idea what you're talking about," I told him. I'd figured that Fulbright would know about Dent, given Tera's warning that the Patth were on Dent's trail and that there'd been Patth odor aboard the poacher ship.

What I *hadn't* expected was that Fulbright's men weren't similarly up to speed. Out of the corner of my eye I saw Cole give Fulbright an obviously puzzled look. I understood the concept of need-to-know, but when that group didn't include your own team something was seriously wrong.

"Yeah, sure you don't," Fulbright said. "That everything?"

I focused on the small collection of items I'd set out on the table: wallet, notebook, flashlight, card holder, multitool, and two spare charge mags for my plasmic. "Yes," I said.

"You travel pretty light."

"I'm on a budget."

Someone snickered. Fulbright sent a brief look around the room, sent me a more focused glare, then turned to Cole. "Well?"

While I'd been cleaning out my pockets Cole had hooked up my phone to one of the gadgets on the desk. "Nothing much here," he told Fulbright. "Lots of calls to one number—probably his partner—plus small clusters of others. Probably fueling and maintenance numbers when he's on the ground."

"What about the partner?" Fulbright asked. "Has her phone got a locator?"

"You're wasting your time," I put in. "Selene's a master of disguise. You could have her location down to ten square meters and you still wouldn't see her."

"Cole?" Fulbright pressed.

"Yeah, I got her," Cole confirmed. He keyed the device, and the display that had been showing the hotel cameras changed to a map of Khayelitsha. Another adjustment, and he'd zoomed in on the section centered around the Golden Pyramid. "There," he said, pointing to a red triangle. "That's her. Six blocks due west of us. Looks like she's on foot and moving south."

I tightened my throat briefly, just enough to show the apprehension a man in my position ought to feel at the revelation that his partner was a sitting duck. I sent a hooded look at Fulbright, partly to play up my supposed concern, partly to make sure he was watching my performance.

His twitch of a smile showed that he was. "Good," he said briskly. "Get someone over there and bring her back."

"I thought you wanted all of us to stay here and protect you," the man at the desk said with just a hint of sarcasm.

"Don't play stupid," Fulbright growled, glaring at him. "Mr. Draelon told me you had over a thousand people on Marjolaine."

"Eleven hundred, actually," the man at the desk countered stiffly. "But they're not all in Khayelitsha, and they're not all enforcers."

"So get me the ones who *are* enforcers."

"You're looking at us," one of the others retorted. "And I suggest your tongue watch how it wags unless it wants a steak knife stuck in it."

For a second Fulbright seemed to draw back. But only for a second. "It's not *my* tongue that needs to watch itself," he said. "Cole, you want to remind him what Mr. Draelon said about full cooperation?"

Cole's lip twitched. "Mr. Fulbright—"

"I said *tell him!*"

Cole clamped his mouth shut...and suddenly the room was rigid with tension.

I winced. I'd already figured out that none of them particularly liked Fulbright. But I hadn't realized how *much* they didn't like him. And if he pushed that animosity too far, there could be serious and immediate consequences.

"Fine," I spoke up into the brittle silence. "*I'll* go get her."

It would be too much to say that the scowls that turned in my direction had any genuine relief mixed into them. But I could feel the easing of the tension as I gave all of them someone else to be mad at instead of each other.

In fact, I could almost imagine I saw a brief and very small smile cross Cole's face.

Fulbright again either didn't notice or didn't care. "Cute," he growled. "Fine. You two"—he pointed to the men who'd been guarding the hallway when we first arrived—"go get her. Roarke isn't going to make any trouble, are you, Roarke?"

"Of course not," I said. "But really, you're wasting your time going after Selene. You won't find her."

"We'll see," Fulbright said. He looked at the two thugs as if he wanted to give them further instructions, apparently thought better of it, and merely nodded toward the door. They nodded back just as silently and left the suite.

"While we wait, let's talk about Mottola," Fulbright said, turning back to me. "What exactly did you do to him?"

"I don't know any Mottola, and I haven't been doing anything to anyone," I assured him. "I just came to Khayelitsha to make a StarrComm call."

"A call to...?"

"To the person at the other end," I said patiently. "Come on,

Fulbright, you're a bounty hunter. Employer confidentiality works the same way with Trailblazers."

He snorted. "Trailblazer. Right. Nice cover. So who paid you to kill Easton Dent on New Kyiv?"

I felt my stomach knot up. Somehow, it had never occurred to me that he would know about that.

But then, I didn't know until an hour ago that he was with Varsi, and Varsi's organization had fingers and ears everywhere. "Still comes under the confidentiality clause," I said.

"What if there's a gun pointed at your head?" he countered, slipping a Balgren 5mm from under his jacket and waving it idly around.

"Interesting question," I said consideringly. "Given that you've been stalking me at least since CR-207-T, I'm guessing that this Mr. Draelon you mentioned is probably hoping to talk to me personally sometime in the near future. I doubt he'd be thrilled if you delivered me in damaged condition."

Fulbright's face darkened. "Maybe you tried to get away."

"Maybe these other gentlemen would rather be on Mr. Draelon's good side than on yours," I countered. "Certainly when it comes to lying for you."

For a moment Fulbright just stared at me. Behind him, Floyd emerged silently from the bedroom, his own face carved in stone, his eyes on the back of Fulbright's head. His hand wasn't *quite* reaching for his jacket opening, but I had the feeling it wouldn't take much effort for him to get to whatever was concealed there.

Maybe Fulbright sensed that, or maybe he just knew when to walk back from the edge. Trying to make it look casual, he put away the Balgren. "Come to think of it, Mr. Draelon *would* probably like you delivered in working condition. Well. As soon as we have your partner, we'll be off."

"Mm," I said, looking at the map and the track of Selene's phone. Actually, despite what I'd said about her being able to disappear into crowds, her white hair and distinctive Kadolian facial features made that virtually impossible.

Which was why Admiral Graym-Barker and his Icarus Group techs had gimmicked Selene's phone to always show her tracking marker as being exactly one point nine kilometers due west of where the phone actually was.

And right now, subtracting that skewing, I could see she was in the StarrComm center, hopefully talking to Tera or Graym-Barker and figuring out our next move. Tera had said she didn't have any backup that could get to us on Gremon, but maybe she had something close enough to Marjolaine—

"So you made a StarrComm call and then came *here?*" Fulbright asked suddenly. "Why?"

As my father used to say, *When in doubt, a half-truth is always better than a lie, provided you pick the right half.* "I was told Mr. Varsi's organization worked out of the Golden Pyramid," I told him. "He and I didn't part on the best of terms, and since I had a few hours to spare I was hoping I could touch base with him and see if we could clear the air."

"Who told you Mr. Varsi's people were here?"

"The person I talked to," I said patiently. "I hope he was right. I never heard of your Mr. Draelon—I assume he's one of Mr. Varsi's top people?"

"You could say that," Fulbright said. "You could also say he's *the* top person."

"Ah," I said. So whatever Varsi wanted with me, this was being handled at a very high level. I hoped that was a good sign.

The room fell silent, Fulbright apparently uninterested in responding to my brilliant riposte, me not having anything of interest to add. Cole walked over to Floyd, and I caught enough of their whispered conversation to learn that Mottola was still sleeping, but that his breathing was steady and he didn't seem to be too badly beat up. Floyd sent me a speculative look; I gave him an innocent one in return and he lapsed back into silence.

I watched the display and the little triangle that was Selene, wondering when the thugs Fulbright had sent would reach that location and realize they'd been had. I'd assumed they'd taken a car instead of walking, so that outraged revelation could come at any time. At that point, if Fulbright was smart, he would figure out what had happened and check the locator on my phone for comparison.

Not that it would do him any good. Mine was gimmicked with an entirely different skew, marking it as half a kilometer northeast of where it really was.

I frowned at the display. That triangle hadn't moved for a long time. Was Selene still waiting for a booth? Or had she gotten through to Tera and they were still working to find a way out of this mess?

From behind Fulbright came the snick of an opening lock. I looked over as the door swung open—

"Look who we found trying to sneak back into the hotel," one of the thugs said cheerfully as he strode in. Walking right behind him—

Selene.

"I'm sorry, Gregory," she said softly. Her head was bowed in shame, her face half hidden beneath the front edge of her scarf, her eyes focused on the floor in front of her. "I know you told me to leave. But I couldn't."

I took a careful breath. "Selene—"

"It's different with humans," she went on, her voice almost pleading now. "You can leave someone without even thinking. But for me, I had to come back. I couldn't tear away, you see. Asked to do so..." She trailed off and raised her head to look me in the eye.

And now, finally, I got a clear look at her pupils.

"That was fast," Fulbright commented, standing up and giving Selene a once-over. "You get her phone?"

"No, she didn't have it on her," the thug said.

"We barely got out of the hotel," the other one added as he came in behind Selene and closed the door. "She was trying to find a way in back where we parked the van."

"She must have figured we were tracking her phone and ditched it," the first thug said.

"No loss," Fulbright said. "Well, that was easy. Floyd, call the aircar and tell them to fire up—we'll be heading to the field where Roarke parked. You don't mind if we all ride with you, do you?"

"Why not?" I said sourly. "The more the merrier."

"Good," he said. "Because some idiot rammed my ship and the airlock needs fixing. Cole, get some restraints on them—we'll go back down the freight elevator."

"What about Mottola?" Floyd asked as Cole produced a set of plastic restraints and motioned me to my feet.

"He can stay here until he wakes up."

"He comes with us," Floyd said.

"He can follow once he's better," Fulbright said. "Right now he's just dead weight."

"He comes with us," Floyd repeated, and this time there was something in his voice that warned against further argument.

For a wonder, Fulbright got the message. "Fine," he growled. "Your men can help get him in the van."

Ten minutes later we were in the black van, maneuvering our way down the busy Khayelitsha streets. One of the local thugs was at the wheel, with Cole seated beside him in shotgun position. Selene and Fulbright occupied the two seats directly behind them, while Floyd and I were in the next pair of seats back. The still snoozing Mottola was all the way in the back, laid out across the rear bench seat.

"I hope we're not planning to go very far," I warned. "The *Ruth* is pretty cramped, even for just Selene and me. Adding in four more will make it a hell of a lot tighter. *And* it only sleeps three, so we're all going to have to do that in shifts."

"Sorry to disappoint you," Fulbright said, craning his neck to look over his shoulder at me. He was seated between Selene and the sliding door, of course, just in case she had a sudden urge to leap out into city traffic. Floyd had thoughtfully set himself to guard against the same impulse on my part. "You know, in case you were hoping for a chance to escape while everyone's asleep. But we're just hopping over to Brandywine."

"Ah," I said. So Selene's pickup of Brandywine's name and her sense of the planet's significance to this group had been right on the money. "That's, what, forty hours away?"

"About that," Fulbright said. "Why?"

"Just wondering," I said. Forty hours there and back, plus whatever time we spent on the ground, should still give us time to get to Gremon for Dent's meeting. Providing I was still in shape to travel at that point. "Still a little long to go without sleep."

"You can sleep all you want," Fulbright said. "You won't have anything else to do. My team and I can handle a trip that short just fine."

"Ah," I said again. "You should probably be careful about that. Stim drinks eventually catch up with you if you use too many of them."

His eyes hardened, just slightly. He gave Selene a quick look, then without another word turned back to face forward.

I focused on the back of Selene's head. She hadn't spoken since her broken-voiced apology back in the suite, not to me or anyone else. And if Fulbright was smart, he'd make sure that lack of private communication continued once we were aboard the *Ruth*.

Which was fine by me. I'd already seen he was the suspicious type, and doing anything to inflame those qualms would only make things worse.

Besides, I'd already gotten Selene's message. Both through the words, and through the calmness and resolve I'd seen in her pupils.

But for me, I had to come back, she'd said. *I couldn't tear away, you see. Asked to do so. Tear away, you see. Tear away. See.*

Tera C.

Selene hadn't come back out of panic or some misguided hope of rescuing me. She'd come back because Tera had told her to. Clearly, the two of them had cooked up a plan.

I was looking forward to finding out what the hell it was.

CHAPTER EIGHT

We arrived to find the *Ruth* freshly fueled and ready to go. I fully expected Fulbright to take over the bridge duties, but instead he waved me to the pilot's chair and took the nav station for himself. Given that he held his Balgren on me the whole time, I was less than overwhelmed by his trust. I ran the launch checklists, signaled the tower, and half an hour later we were boosted up off the ground and headed for space.

Sometime along in there Mottola finally woke up. I wasn't exactly sure what was said, but even from the bridge I could tell that his part of the conversation was louder than it had to be, while Floyd's was calm and barely audible. Fortunately, the discussion was over and Mottola had stomped off someplace by the time I finished slicing us into hyperspace and returned to the ship's living areas.

Floyd told me later that the injured man had been sent back to my cabin to rest and continue healing. More than once I wondered if I would find the place trashed when I was finally allowed back in.

I'd been right about Fulbright keeping Selene and me apart. From the cockpit I was taken straight to the dayroom, where Fulbright settled me onto the couch and left me there under Cole's watchful eye. From snatches of conversation I heard from the corridor I gathered Selene had asked to do some work in the clean room, and had been allowed to do so, but was otherwise restricted to her own cabin and the bathroom.

With nothing useful or even interesting to do, I settled in for a long, boring trip. I made myself a meal from the dayroom's larder, traveled to the bathroom as needed, and took a couple of short naps. I awoke from the first to find Floyd carrying a pair of meal trays from the dayroom and Fulbright chomping down on his own meal from one of the fold-down seats across the way. Awakening from my second, I found Cole back on watchdog duty.

Thirty-nine and a half hours after lifting from Marjolaine, I put us down in a small landing field on the southern edge of West Pontus on Brandywine.

I'd been to the planet exactly once in my life, a brief visit to one of the northern hemisphere regions. West Pontus was in the southern hemisphere, and profiled in as one of the planet's more compact trading and manufacturing hubs. In some ways it reminded me of Varsi's old headquarters on Xathru, where he would sit in his lofty high-rise overlooking the city, an urbane and rot-hearted spider spinning his invisible webs around the oblivious citizens below.

But while Brandywine's population and culture were similar to those of Xathru, the planet's more out-of-the-way location made it somewhat less suitable for some of Varsi's quieter and more unsavory activities. My best guess was that his trouble with the Patth had convinced him to get off Xathru for a while.

There was a van waiting beside the *Ruth*'s landing cradle when we emerged. We piled in, Cole taking the wheel this time, and headed out.

I'd assumed we would be going into the center of the city and the urban environment Varsi had preferred on Xathru. Instead, Cole turned us south, heading out through the suburbs and into the industrial region that formed a half ring around West Pontus on the south and east edges. After a forty-minute trip we pulled off onto a private drive leading toward a large, two-story manufacturing-type building set into an open area a kilometer back from the road. From what I could see the building had a single line of windows just below the roof and two heavy-paneled freight doors and a single person-sized door on our side. Everything else looked to be solid reinforced concrete and steel.

A high-rise might be nice for the view and prestige, but when push came to punch there was nothing like a nondescript fortress to offer a man a good night's sleep.

Especially a well-guarded fortress. Two hundred meters from the road we were stopped at a checkpoint consisting of two armored cars and four combat-suited men hefting Rolfkin over/ under plasmic/10mm assault rifles. As we were passed through I spotted the slender strands of fiberwire leading away in both directions from the checkpoint lintels, forming an almost invisible fence around the building and grounds. A second checkpoint awaited us outside the building itself, this one involving four soldiers and a pair of disguised ground-pit sniper nests. As we filed out of the van, I spotted three more armored cars patrolling the open area around the building.

As my father used to say, *Beware of anyone who lives in a bunker. If that many people are gunning for him, there's generally no place nearby where it's safe to stand.*

I'd been in many manufacturing plants over the years, once even having to chase a target through one, and was prepared for bright lights, equipment clusters, overhead cable-trays loaded with power lines and coolant conduits, and lots of busy people. Instead, Selene and I were escorted through the door into what was effectively an indoor ghost town.

The big open floor stretching out in front of us was all but empty, with mountings and concrete slabs showing where equipment used to stand. The cable trays were still in place, and some still had cables lying in them, but they didn't seem to connect to anything. To the right, a pair of what looked like freshly built walls sectioned off a cube enclosing maybe a tenth of the overall floor space, with a single door leading into it. Possibly storage for Varsi's special records or merchandise; possibly a heavily armored last-ditch safe room. Off to the left, built against the outer wall, was another rectangular room with large tinted windows looking out onto the empty floor. Unlike the new walls to our right, this structure looked like it had been an original part of the building. There were two doors into it, their positioning suggesting that the room was divided into two separate offices. Crisscrossing the space above us were catwalks and the rails for hoists and rolling cranes, though the equipment that had been suspended there was gone. All in all, the place looked like it had been abandoned for years, making it an ideal place for a private meeting.

"Come on, come on," Fulbright growled, nudging me toward the structure to our left. There was a fresh tension in his voice that suggested he wasn't looking forward to this meeting any more than I was. "You don't want to keep him waiting."

"Definitely not," I agreed, looking sideways at Selene. Her nostrils were flaring rhythmically, her long eyelashes fluttering as she sampled the air. I had no idea what she was smelling, but it was apparently pretty interesting.

The right-hand office door opened as we approached, and a large, dead-eyed man stepped out. He looked each of us up and down, made lingering eye contact with Floyd, then moved to the side and gestured us in. Fulbright nudged me again; bracing myself, I walked through the doorway.

At the back of the room, seated behind a desk, was a husky, dark-haired man I'd never seen before. He was dressed in an expensive suit and equally impressive collar pins in much the same style Varsi had usually worn.

The desk, in stark contrast, was boxy and functional, without any extravagance whatsoever, the sort of item that Varsi would have ordered to be dropped into the nearest convenient undersea trench. If this was Varsi's new headquarters, he was clearly still in the middle of the move.

"This him?" the man at the desk asked as Selene and the others filed in behind me.

"Yes, Mr. Draelon," Fulbright confirmed. "This is Gregory Roarke."

"Taller than I expected," Draelon commented, focusing on me. His eyes, I noted with a shiver, looked somehow even deader than those of the bodyguard he'd sent out of the office to meet us. "I'm told you used to work for Mr. Varsi, Mr. Roarke."

"Yes, sir, I did," I confirmed. "As far as I know, I still do."

"Really," Draelon said. "It's been over six months since you contacted him or anyone else in the organization." He raised his eyebrows. "One might wonder if you've been avoiding us."

"Not at all, sir," I hastened to assure him. What the *hell* was going on? "Our agreement with Mr. Varsi was always that when Selene and I found something useful in one of our planetary sweeps we would contact him. Sometimes those discoveries are few and far between."

"So you've found *nothing?*"

I thought about the ampule hidden inside my artificial arm.

"No, sir, unfortunately," I said. "But you can ask Mr. Varsi about our agreement."

Something seemed to flicker across his eyes. "Perhaps later," he said. "Tell me, how would you respond to the charge that you betrayed him to the Patth?"

And with that, this whole conversation had gone completely sideways.

"I would say, sir," I said, picking my words carefully, "that the person who told you that was either wrong or a liar. Mr. Varsi's generosity was what kept us flying for several years. Why would I do such a thing?"

"Maybe a better offer came along," Draelon said. "Maybe part of the price of that offer was that you help your new employer clear away some of the less respectable parts of your past."

"I can't imagine an offer I would find compelling enough for such a thing," I protested, a fresh tingle running up my back. In fact, that scenario was uncomfortably close to what had actually happened with our recruitment into the Icarus Group. "Again, all I can say is that you can ask Mr. Varsi about that. Is he here?"

"He won't be back until the end of next week," Draelon said. "The question is whether he'll wish to talk to you, or whether he'll just leave your punishment to me."

Behind me, Fulbright cleared his throat. "If I may suggest, Mr. Draelon," he said hesitantly, "if Roarke has new friends who are out to get us, we might not want them connecting him to this place. If you want, I could—"

"To get *us*?" Draelon cut him off, his voice glacially calm. "Who is this *us*, Mr. Fulbright?"

"I'm sorry, sir," Fulbright said, the words stumbling over themselves. "I thought—when Mr. Varsi hired me back on Pinnkus I thought—"

"Mr. Varsi hired you on Pinnkus for a specific job," Draelon again interrupted. "Did you succeed in that task?"

I didn't dare turn to look, but I could hear a soft, uncomfortable rumble in Fulbright's throat. "Not . . . completely, sir," he admitted. "But I *did* bring Roarke here just now."

"Yes, though you required considerable assistance from Mr. Floyd and his men to succeed in that effort," Draelon said pointedly. "Why are you suggesting you take him elsewhere before he and I have finished our conversation?"

"I was just thinking that we—that you—might not want him connected to—"

"Yes, you said that already," Draelon said. "Tell me, Mr. Fulbright: Do you think him worth additional money? Would you say he's worth, say, ten thousand commarks a minute?"

"Uh . . ." Fulbright floundered, clearly trying to come up with an answer.

I could sympathize, given that I was feeling as confused by the question as he was. Ten thousand commarks a *minute?*

"I . . . don't understand, sir," Fulbright managed at last. "What—?"

Draelon silenced him with a gesture, his eyes flicking over my shoulder. "Bring him in," he ordered.

"Yes, sir," the dead-eyed guard said from behind me. There was the sound of heavy footsteps, then the creak of hinges as the office door opened and closed.

"Excuse me, Mr. Draelon," Floyd spoke up, his voice respectful but with a hint of perplexity to it. "I was under the impression we were bringing Roarke here for discussion of his Trailblazer work—"

"You were ordered to assist Fulbright in his hunt," Draelon cut him off. "If my plans for him have changed, that's none of your business."

"No, sir," Floyd said quickly. "My apologies, sir."

"Accepted." Draelon looked back at me. "What about you, Roarke? Do *you* have any idea why you might command such a price?"

"No, sir, not really," I said, trying to sound sincere even as my heart started thudding like a panicked deer.

Because there was indeed one person who would probably pay that kind of money to get me alone. Especially if he had a few specialized instruments of pain at his disposal.

I'd hoped that sticking with obscure planets in less-desirable parts of the Spiral would keep me off Sub-Director Nask's radar. Apparently, my luck had run out.

"I *am* very good at finding useful worlds," I continued. If Nask was here, it wouldn't hurt to remind Draelon how much money I'd made for Varsi's organization over the years. "Maybe someone needs an especially good crockett to find a new development locale."

"Or possibly a new street drug?" Draelon countered, his eyes flicking to Floyd.

"Yes, I've also had some successes in that area," I confirmed. If that fact had been part of Floyd's pre-hunt briefing, it would help explain why he'd treated Selene and me with restraint on the flight here, including not letting Mottola take a poke at me. "Both of those make my services invaluable." The door behind me opened and closed again—

"Excellent. You found him."

I didn't recognize the voice. But there was a cold anticipation in those four words that sent a fresh chill up my back. Some bounty hunter I'd pilfered a target from who still held a grudge? A target I'd brought to justice, now out of prison and looking for payback?

Out of the corner of my eye I saw a flicker of reaction in Selene's stance. I turned my head slightly, hoping for a better look at her pupils, but her head was bowed, her eyes focused on the floor.

"Obviously," Draelon said. "I brought you in to tell you the deal's off."

He looked back at me. "I've decided to finish with him myself. Right here, right now.

"For his betrayal of Mr. Varsi, he's going to die."

"Really," the newcomer said, the coldness I'd heard there going darker. "A rather drastic reversal of your plans of a few days ago. May I ask what's changed?"

"Nothing's changed, Mr. Niles," Draelon said. "I've simply decided I really don't need his services, and think he'll be more useful as an object lesson for anyone else who might think about betraying our organization's trust."

I opened my mouth to protest, to tell him that I'd never betrayed Varsi or anyone else—

"Such object lessons can be useful," Niles said, finishing his walk from the door and stopping beside me. He was about as stereotypical a bounty hunter as ever graced a star-thriller drama: medium height, curly pirate-black hair and unkempt beard, prominent nose and cheekbones, and three scars digging through the skin of forehead and cheeks. "Still, you're at heart a businessman," he continued, "and it seems wasteful to kill someone who someone else is willing to pay for." He sent me a glance that seemed both intrigued and contemptuous. "Especially since I'll be happy to hand him back to you as soon as I'm finished with him."

"Allowing me to have my cake *and* eat it, as the saying goes," Draelon said. "Except that you haven't explained why you're offering far more money than Mr. Roarke is worth."

"In my experience, Mr. Draelon, a target is worth whatever someone is willing to pay for him," Niles countered. "If my client is offering ten thousand commarks a minute for me to talk with him, I should think that would settle the matter." He looked at me again, running his eyes up and down. "As for the full payment that will be involved, I don't anticipate the conversation lasting very long. I'm guessing ten minutes will be all I need. A negligible delay in your program, and you'll be a hundred thousand commarks richer."

"And what are you expecting to learn during those ten minutes?"

Niles shook his head. "I'm afraid that comes under bounty hunter confidentiality. Of course, as I've already stipulated, the conversation would need to be a private one."

"Someplace outside this facility, no doubt?" Draelon suggested with deceptive casualness. "Out in the open where you could suddenly call in an aircar and spirit him away?"

"Not at all," Niles assured him. "An unoccupied corner of this building would do nicely." He gave a slightly derisive snort. "Really, Mr. Draelon. While I'm committed to completing the job I've been hired for, I have no desire to leave a trail of enemies in my wake."

"Very wise of you," Draelon said. "Why is Roarke worth that much?"

"As I said, that's confidential."

Draelon shook his head. "I'm afraid I must insist."

And suddenly the room was bristling with guns, one each in the hands of Draelon's men. All of the weapons pointed at Niles.

The room went silent, and for a moment Niles stood motionless. Then, slowly, he turned his head to the left, then to the right, observing and assessing. Finally, he turned forward to face Draelon again. "What I just said about not leaving a trail of enemies works in both directions, Mr. Draelon," he said quietly. "I'm not to be trifled with. My client is *certainly* not to be trifled with."

"Your client needs to learn the art of compromise, Mr. Niles."

"And what exactly would this compromise consist of?"

"You tell me why Roarke is so valuable," Draelon said. "I give you my assistance in accomplishing whatever the job consists of, and we divide the proceeds evenly."

"We don't need your help."

"Every job goes easier when you have help," Draelon said. "Besides, now that I know Roarke is hiding something, I could ask him about it myself and cut you out completely."

"Interesting thought," Niles said. "However, you assume Roarke knows what makes him valuable. He may not, and without that knowledge you could ask questions for days without finding the right one."

"Mr. Niles—"

"On the other hand, you make some valid points," Niles went on. "But an even split is out of the question. We could, perhaps, go with an eighty-twenty split. The eighty to us, of course."

Draelon looked speculatively at me, then turned back to Niles. "Seventy-thirty," he said. "Along with supplying all the necessary personnel and equipment, I'll also get you through the various official roadblocks in our way."

Niles paused, then shook his head. "I'm afraid I can't authorize that high a percentage."

"Thirty percent is hardly unreasonable," Draelon said. "Considering that it includes your life."

For a moment the two men locked eyes. Then, Niles inclined his head. "Let me transmit the offer to my client," he said, pulling out his phone. "If he agrees—" He broke off, frowning at the phone. "A jamming lock? Really?"

Draelon waved a casual hand. "Outside communication is forbidden right now."

"I can't make any deals on behalf of my client without contacting him."

"Then don't," Draelon said, his tone and expression changing subtly. "Make a deal on behalf of yourself. How much is your client paying you to bring in Roarke?"

"Sixty thousand commarks," Niles said. "Another hundred thousand if Roarke's information leads him to whatever he's looking for."

"I'll pay you two hundred thousand right here and now," Draelon said. "Plus thirty percent of whatever pot is at the end of Mr. Roarke's rainbow."

"And Roarke?"

Draelon shrugged. "Sadly, you were unable to find him. Not that unusual—bounty hunters miss their targets all the time."

"That won't be good for my reputation," Niles warned. "Especially when he pops up again later."

"I doubt he'll be popping up anywhere after we're done with him," Draelon assured him. "As I said, Roarke's going to be an object lesson."

I cleared my throat. It was about time I joined this conversation. "Before we get too far into the pie-cutting exercise," I said, "I hope no one's assuming I'm going to cooperate for free."

"You think you have a choice?" Draelon asked calmly. "There are lots of ways of prying information out of a person."

"But all of them take time," I pointed out. "*And* they're vulnerable to lies and misdirection. I'm not sure what Mr. Niles thinks I've got to sell, but most things in life come with an expiration date. If I hold out long enough, you may find the pie plate empty."

Draelon smiled thinly. "What we'll find is that my people are *very* persuasive."

"But since you don't know the expiration date, you don't know how much time you have to play with," I said. "Neither do I, and I doubt Mr. Niles does, either."

Draelon's eyes shifted to Selene. "What if we worked on your partner instead?"

My stomach turned into a hard knot. If they tortured Selene— "Actually, that would be the worst of all worlds," I said, forcing as much indifference into my voice as I could. "She's a Kadolian. A rare and delicate creature whose tolerance for pain you have no clue about. If you kill her, intentionally or otherwise, not only do you no longer have anything to hold over me, but you'll have wasted valuable time."

"So you wouldn't care if she was tortured to death?"

"Of course I'd care," I said. "But I also don't want her starving to death in poverty. All I want is a fair share of the pie you expect me to serve up to you."

"What would you consider a fair share?" Niles put in.

"Let's make it fifty thousand up front and twenty percent of the back end," I said. "And this thing about me dying goes away."

"No," Draelon said flatly.

I shrugged. "Then enjoy your thirty percent of nothing."

"Let's not be too hasty, Mr. Draelon," Niles put in. "Mr. Fulbright, you seem concerned."

I looked over at Fulbright just in time to see him try to erase whatever expression Niles had spotted. "No, no, not at all," Fulbright said, just a bit too quickly. "I'm just thinking...there's something about all this that seems off to me, Mr. Draelon. What do we really know about Niles? He could be a badgeman, he could be from the people who attacked Mr. Varsi—"

I never saw Draelon's signal, but suddenly Cole stepped up beside Fulbright and slapped him hard across the back of his head. Fulbright gasped, breaking off in mid-sentence, and the room went silent.

Draelon gave it five more seconds. Then, very deliberately, he turned to face Fulbright. "Mr. Varsi's current situation is not to be mentioned," he said, his voice as dead as his eyes. "At all. To anyone. Under any circumstances. Do I make myself clear?"

"Yes, sir," Fulbright said, his breath coming in short bursts. "I'm sorry, sir. I'm just worried. If this is a setup, you could be in danger. Maybe I could...I could go with Mr. Niles when he takes Roarke to his ship. Once you've made your agreement, I mean. That way there'd be nothing to connect either of them to you."

"Roarke and his friend won't be traveling on Mr. Niles's ship," Draelon said. "They'll be traveling with Cole and Floyd on one of mine."

"Actually, Mr. Draelon, that won't work," Niles spoke up. "The man Roarke is meeting probably knows about the *Ruth*. If Roarke arrives on any other ship—mine *or* yours—he may be suspicious and call it off."

"So he's meeting someone, is he?" Draelon asked. "Who?"

Niles gave a small sigh. "As Mr. Roarke suggested, we have a limited window of opportunity. Very well, I accept your offer. The person of interest is a human male named Easton Dent. Roarke is going to be meeting him on...?" He raised his eyebrows invitingly.

"On a planet I'll name once Selene and I are back aboard the *Ruth*," I said. "You're welcome to follow us in your own ship if you'd like."

Draelon seemed to measure me with his eyes. He looked at Niles, then gave a twitch of a smile. "We may do that," he said.

"Floyd, I assume you and your associates can keep Mr. Roarke in line?"

"No problem, sir," Floyd assured him. "What about Fulbright?"

"Before you say anything, Mr. Draelon," Fulbright spoke up, "remember that I was the one you hired to bring Roarke in."

"At *your* suggestion," Draelon said.

"Regardless, sir, I'm the bounty hunter of record here," Fulbright said doggedly. "I have a responsibility to see it through to the end. If Roarke's going somewhere, I should be along."

Draelon eyed him a moment, then looked back at Floyd. "Floyd?"

"He *did* guess that Roarke would go back to Marjolaine," Floyd said reluctantly. "I suppose he might still be useful."

"Very well," Draelon said. "But understand, Mr. Fulbright, that this is Floyd's mission now, not yours. He's in charge, and you'll take orders from him."

"Yes, Mr. Draelon," Fulbright said with Floyd's same lack of enthusiasm.

Not really surprising, on either side. The quiet nickname *the Pup* was ample indication of what Floyd and the others had thought about Fulbright's authority over them, and the tense confrontation in the Golden Pyramid showed the animosity worked the other direction as well. Under the circumstances, especially with the now reversed chain of command, if I was Fulbright I'd have taken my payment and waved good-bye.

But then, Fulbright seemed a lot more stubborn and a lot less pragmatic than I was.

"What about you, Mottola?" Draelon continued. "Are you up to continuing?"

"Yes, sir," Mottola said. His voice was grim, and I could visualize his eyes boring into the back of my head. "I'm ready to see this through."

"Yes, well, if I may?" I again spoke up, lifting a finger. "The *Ruth*'s only designed for two people, three at the most. And this will be a much longer trip than the one from Marjolaine, several days at least."

"Don't worry about it," Floyd said with a sort of malicious humor. "I had a good look at the ship, Mr. Draelon. We can easily sleep five."

"What about the sixth?" I asked.

"I hardly think four men escorting two prisoners will all choose to sleep at the same time," Niles pointed out.

"Exactly," Floyd said.

"Then I think that does it," Draelon said. "Floyd, you and your men escort Roarke and his partner to their ship. You, Mr. Niles, will wait with me until we hear their destination. At that point, we'll decide on our own course of action."

"I really should be with them," Niles said, giving me another brief, speculative look. "But I suppose your men and Fulbright will be an adequate guard."

"More than adequate." Draelon smiled faintly, his eyes glittering as he gazed at Niles. "And while we wait, you'll tell me exactly what Easton Dent has that's worth this much of my time and effort."

"As you wish," Niles said. "Safe travels, Roarke. I'm sure we'll see you again very soon."

"Thank you, Mr. Niles," I managed. The look in his eye... "I'll look forward to it."

CHAPTER NINE

I'd wondered where Floyd thought there was enough floor space inside the *Ruth* to bring our bed count from three to five. The last time we'd hosted this much company we'd had to remove the examination table from the clean room, and I *really* hoped that wasn't what he had in mind.

It wasn't.

"You're joking," I said flatly, staring at the narrow opening into the equally narrow portside bioprobe bay. "It's like a coffin in there."

"Don't be so dramatic," Floyd chided. "The bay's inner hatch will be open. Plenty of air. You can even have a nightlight if you want."

"Thanks," I said, eyeing the bay's low ceiling. "What happens if I need to roll over?"

"You'll do it very carefully." He considered. "At least you will after the first time."

"It's that or you sleep in the corridor," Cole warned from off to the side where he and a silent Selene were standing.

"'Course, if someone has to get from the bridge back to the engine room, you'll probably get stepped on," Mottola added as he appeared in the hatchway. "I'll bet that would hurt."

"Pretty much a given," Floyd agreed. "Everything set up there?"

"We're on our way to Gremon," Mottola confirmed. "I also got confirmation from West Pontus before we sliced that they got my message and would pass it on to Mr. Draelon."

"Confirmation *with* passcodes?"

"Of course," Mottola growled. "You think I've forgotten field procedure?"

"Just checking," Floyd said, giving me a hard-eyed look. "We don't know how much he scrambled your brains when he hit you."

"It wasn't me," I insisted. From the lack of actual murderousness in Mottola's eyes I'd tentatively concluded that the head trauma of our brief fight had deleted his memory of the incident, including the identity of his attacker. But everyone aboard—including him—clearly thought it was me, and I doubted that senior enforcers in Varsi's organization needed the same level of proof as the typical badgeman.

Fortunately, right now they needed me alive and mostly unharmed. Once they had Dent, though, those bets were probably off.

I had until we reached Gremon to figure out what I was going to do about that.

"Sure it wasn't," Floyd said, almost as if he actually believed it. "Where's Fulbright?"

"In the dayroom," Mottola said. "He said he was hungry, and I told him he could make himself some dinner."

"Just make sure it's *his* dinner and not ours," Floyd said. "Cole, you're in charge of our meals. *And* theirs," he added, gesturing to Selene and me. "So you taking these berths, Roarke? Or do we set you up in the corridor?"

"Where Mottola might step on you," Cole added.

I looked back at Mottola. He was standing beside the hatch into the starboard bioprobe prep room, presumably where Selene would be bunking down, directly across the corridor from where the rest of us were standing. Forward along the corridor were the clean room and the *Ruth*'s living areas, with the bridge all the way at the bow, while aft were the engine room and storage areas.

I could work with this.

"Fine, I'll take it," I said with the kind of exaggerated sigh they were probably expecting. "Mottola, what speed did you give us?"

"Normal," Mottola said, his eyes narrowing. "Why? You going to tell me this slop bucket has a top marginal of minus-ten?"

"No, just the opposite," I said. "If we're going to make Gremon in time for my meeting with Dent we need to boost it to plus-twenty."

"Forget it," Mottola said firmly. "That'd burn forty-five percent more fuel. We'd need to stop at least once to refuel."

"Dent said not to be late," I warned. "If I miss my window, he may go underground where we'll never find him. If that happens, Mr. Draelon will *not* be happy."

"Awfully convenient that we're just hearing about this now," Floyd said suspiciously. "Why didn't you say something earlier?"

"I *did* say something earlier," I countered. "I gave you the location and the time, and assumed you'd be able to do the math."

"You never gave us the time," Floyd insisted.

"I most certainly did," I insisted right back. "I told Niles and Mr. Draelon before we left."

Which was a complete and total lie, of course. I'd had no intention of giving Draelon any details that might let him figure out where we were going and possibly get someone there ahead of us.

But Floyd didn't know that. And now that we were in hyperspace and out of communication with the rest of the universe there was no way for him to check on that part of my story.

"Listen, Roarke—" Mottola began.

"No, that's all right, Mottola," Floyd interrupted. He was eyeing me closely, his voice suddenly gone all thoughtful. "Go check and see if boosting our speed like Roarke wants will let us make a fuel stop on Huihuang."

"What's on Huihuang?" I asked.

"Fuel," Floyd said.

"There's fuel in a lot of other places, too," I pointed out. "I know at least three planets that have better—"

"I don't recall asking you, Roarke."

I focused on Selene, saw puzzlement in her pupils. So she had no clue why Floyd would suddenly want to go to Huihuang, either. "Just trying to be helpful," I said. "So when's dinner?"

"Couple of hours," Floyd said. "I'll have Cole bring it in. You need anything from your cabin before you settle down in here?"

"A few things, yeah."

"Okay," Floyd said. "Cole, put Selene in her new sleeping room. I'll take Roarke to get his things, then you can do the same for her. Let's go, Roarke."

❖   ❖   ❖

Dinner that night was a bit on the meager side. Part of that was that I hadn't had a chance to restock the *Ruth*'s larder, as I'd planned to do at Marjolaine. Mostly, though, it was probably Floyd and the others being disinclined to do Selene and me any favors.

Hardly surprising. Draelon had accused me of betraying Varsi, Floyd's ultimate boss and the man he'd likely been with for years if not decades. He might need me alive and well, but he didn't have to make sure I was comfortable or well-fed.

The problem was that I hadn't done what Draelon claimed. Or at least, I hadn't done it on purpose.

True, I'd told Sub-Director Nask about Varsi's quiet and probably forbidden deal with someone in the Patth hierarchy to get his hands on the tech required to fly Talariac-equipped ships. But my intent had been to help Nask get back in the Director General's good graces by exposing a traitor within their own ranks. Unfortunately, Draelon's accusation strongly suggested that Nask had also gone after Varsi.

Only there shouldn't have been any way to track any of that back to me. Nask would hardly have announced that a Patth traitor had been fingered by a human, especially a human who'd just helped freeze Nask himself out of a career-defining victory. The less Nask needed to think about me, the better he probably liked it. The only other person in that conversation had been McKell, and he also wouldn't have told anyone.

Or would he?

Selene and I were in this mess because Tera had apparently told her to rejoin me after their StarrComm conversation on Marjolaine. Floyd and Fulbright had then taken us to Brandywine where, lo and behold, a complete stranger had popped up out of nowhere who apparently knew all about Easton Dent.

Or at least knew *something* about him. The question was what did he know, where had he gotten that information from, and what exactly had he told Draelon after Selene and I left.

Normally, I would assume Niles had been briefed by Nask or someone working for him, with an eye toward keeping Selene and me on a short leash. But adding Tera into the mix opened the possibility that Niles's tip-off had come from her instead.

Whatever was going on, the next thing on my to-do list was to get Selene alone for an update on her side of our current game. Maybe a look at her cards would give me the handle I needed on this mess.

Fortunately, I had a plan for doing exactly that.

My supervised trip to my cabin earlier had allowed me to collect everything I needed: my toiletry kit, an oversized bath towel, and a loose-fitting, knee-length white nightshirt. It wasn't something I ever actually used as a nightshirt, though it was sometimes useful when I was leaving the ship and needed something to temporarily cover the skulking outfit I was wearing underneath. But our current guests wouldn't know any of that.

I undressed and put on the nightshirt, then went to the bio-probe workbench and the supply drawers beneath it. Floyd and Cole had already cleared out all the larger tools and anything else that could be used as a weapon, but they hadn't bothered with any of the smaller items. Arming myself with a half dozen small black washers, I went over to the hatch and turned off the room light.

The automatic hatch release made a small but distinctive swooshing sound. It was probably not loud enough to be audible to anyone more than a couple of meters away, but this was no time to take chances. Instead, I opened the access panel to the manual crank and slid the hatch open a couple of centimeters. Stroking my left-hand thumbnail to activate the mirror, I eased it through the opening.

As expected, Floyd had left a guard on duty: Cole, lounging in one of our collapsible camp chairs in the center of the corridor a dozen meters away from me and a couple meters past the bathroom hatch. He was nursing a steaming cup of something as he gazed at an info pad propped up on one knee.

I took a moment to study the setup. He was facing toward me, but seemed pretty well engrossed in whatever he was watching or reading. More importantly, one of the overhead ceiling lights was about a meter in front of him. Not directly in his eyes, but nicely illuminating that section of deck.

With a little luck, this would work.

I eased my thumb back in and stroked the nail back to normal, then cranked the hatch open another few centimeters and knelt down by the opening. Picking out one of my collection of washers, I tossed it gently across the corridor to bounce off Selene's hatch.

The impact wasn't very loud, especially against the *Ruth*'s general background engine noises. But I knew Selene would be expecting some kind of signal from me. Hopefully she would spot the subtle clink.

I'd thrown four washers and was preparing a fifth when her hatch began to slowly open as she also cranked it on manual, with her room light also off.

After hours of forced isolation, we were finally face-to-face again.

Face-to-face across an empty corridor, anyway, with an armed man seated nearby. But sometimes you had to take what you could get.

Are you all right? I mouthed silently.

Yes, she mouthed back. *I need to talk to you.*

Likewise, I replied. *I'm going to head to the bathroom. Get ready to do a shadow sneak.*

She nodded, and set to work silently opening her hatch the rest of the way. I opened my toiletry kit, pulled out my shaving mirror and the white plastic razor case, and set them on top of the other items, half closing the kit's seal so that both items were peeking out. Draping my towel over my right shoulder like half a serape, I picked up the toiletry kit in my left hand and stood up.

Selene had her hatch open far enough for her to slip through. Leaving it open would be risky, but there was no way to close it without sparking the swooshing sound we'd both worked so hard to avoid. Still, as long as the room's light was off and Cole didn't decide to wander back this way he shouldn't notice. Selene and I exchanged confirmation nods, and I cranked my door closed again. Mentally preparing myself, I turned my light back on and keyed the hatch.

Either Cole did indeed catch the subtle sound of the hatch opening or was alerted by the sudden swath of soft light washing into the corridor. Regardless, he was gazing down the corridor at me as I stepped out of the room, his info pad tucked down along his side, his hand gripping the Skripka resting on his lap. "Where do you think you're going?" he growled as I started walking toward him.

"I need a shower," I said, hefting the towel a little for emphasis. As I did so, I shifted my toiletry kit a couple of degrees, angling the half-hidden mirror and razor case so that they caught some of the light from the overhead fixture and bounced it across Cole's face.

Not directly into his eyes, of course, at least not for more than a fraction of a second at a time. I needed him to think the reflections were just a random occurrence and not a deliberate effort to obscure his vision. The minute he thought I was trying to distract him, the whole thing would blow up.

Especially since the subtle movement of air against the back of my neck told me that, right on cue, Selene had slipped out of her own room and was flitting silently along behind me.

It wasn't a trick she and I had used very often. But when the geometry was right, it could be surprisingly successful. Marching in step with me a pace back, her head scrunched down and her arms tucked close to her sides, she was completely invisible from Cole's point of view. Add in the brief flickering from my mirror and the softer but broader reflected light coming off my white nightshirt, and he had very little hope of spotting her.

"Unless you don't think that's necessary," I added. "What do you think?" I tapped the bathroom hatch release as I passed it and took another two steps toward Cole.

Who naturally wasn't having any of it. "One more step and I'll shoot you," he warned, tightening his grip on his Skripka.

"I was just making a point," I said mildly, coming to a halt a step past the bathroom hatch and leaning against the wall on that side. Again, the brush of air against the back of my neck told me that Selene had slipped inside. "Don't worry, I'll be out soon."

I retraced my last step and followed Selene into the bathroom, flicking on the light as I did so. Another touch of the release, and the hatch slid closed.

Selene had moved as far away from the entrance as possible, which in the *Ruth*'s bathroom meant standing at the back of the shower alcove. "You okay?" I murmured, crossing over to her.

"Yes," she said, pressing close to me, her lips up against my ear. "I don't think he saw anything."

"Didn't seem like it," I agreed. "First things first. Get out of there—Cole's expecting to hear water running."

She stepped out of the alcove. I turned on the water—cold; no point wasting hot water if I wasn't actually going to get in—then returned to her side. "Okay," I said. "Now. Back on Brandywine—"

"No, wait," she interrupted. "Two things. First: Ixil is aboard."

I felt my eyes widen. "Aboard where? *Here?*"

She nodded. "Tera told me he and Jordan were going to try to sneak him aboard, but they weren't sure they'd be able to. But I smelled him when we came in."

I huffed out a breath. In through our secret hatch in the Number Two equipment bay, no doubt, and into concealment in the service crawlway. As long as no one found a reason to go down there, he should be fine. "About time we got some good news," I said. "You said there were two things?"

"Yes," she said. "That bounty hunter, Niles? That was Jordan."

I stared at her. "You're kidding."

"No, I'm not," she assured me. "I know he didn't look like him or sound like him. But it was."

"That's insane," I insisted. "Even his ears looked different. Why the hell—?"

"Are you going to argue with me?" Selene cut me off impatiently.

"No, of course not," I said from between clenched teeth. It was still insane, but there was no way I could doubt her conclusion. No matter how carefully someone altered his face or voice—or ears—there was nothing he could do to hide his scent. "He knew you knew, right?"

"I assume so," she said. "I don't know why he was in such a heavy disguise."

"McKell said the two of them were on a job," I reminded her. "Why they were on Brandywine does strain credibility a little, though."

"Maybe they were tracking us all along, but couldn't say anything."

"That *does* sound like the admiral." I huffed out a breath, trying to clear my brain. "So what's the plan? I assume there *is* a plan?"

"I assume so, too," Selene said. "But Tera and I didn't have much time to talk about it. I also had the feeling that Jordan didn't have it fully worked out."

"That sounds like *him*, too," I growled. "Can't say I think much of any plan that sends us after Dent with four of Varsi's thugs hanging around our necks."

"Yes," Selene said hesitantly. "That's something else. Didn't Draelon say that Varsi would be back at the end of next week?"

I thought back to that conversation. "Yes, he did. Is that a problem?"

"I don't know," she said. "When people say someone is coming back it usually means they've been there before. But there's no scent of Varsi in that building. Not in the big room, not on the desk or doors, not in the vehicle, not on Draelon himself. Nowhere."

I frowned. "How long?"

"Since he was there?" Selene shook her head. "I don't think he ever was." She paused. "One more thing. There was no scent of Varsi; but there *was* scent of Patth."

"Interesting," I murmured, pulling up a mental image of that building. Big and open, with only two places where one of the aliens could be hiding. "Did you get a fresh puff when McKell came out of the other office and into ours?"

"No."

"So he must have been in that closed-off area."

"That's my assumption, yes," Selene said. "But why would Draelon have a Patth in there?"

"*And* why would he lie about Varsi?" I added. "So Draelon and his people are playing some sort of game. Surprise, surprise."

"Or it could be just Draelon," Selene said. "Do you remember when Floyd started talking about why we'd been brought there and Draelon interrupted him? Floyd was very confused by that."

"Was he, now," I said, thinking back. "*How* confused?"

"Very," Selene said. "Cole and Mottola also seemed confused, but not as much."

"Not unreasonable," I said. "The team leader usually gets more details and notices more quickly when something goes off track. That means Floyd's the top dog."

"Top dog?"

"A human slang term for boss." I snorted. "Hence, their nickname *the Pup* for Fulbright."

Selene seemed to consider that. "Not very respectful," she pointed out.

"Wasn't meant to be," I said. "Tera said Mottola was one of Varsi's senior enforcers, and Floyd's above him, which means Floyd must be near the top of Varsi's organization. If he was taken by surprise by Draelon's sudden change of plan, it must have just happened."

"You think the Patth I smelled is involved?"

"Could be," I said. "A Patth nosing around Varsi's little country home while Draelon loudly declares that Varsi will be back soon could mean the Patth are still hunting him."

"All right," she said slowly. "But how does Draelon declaring his intention of killing you help Varsi?"

I shook my head. "Not a clue. Maybe Varsi's gone stir crazy and wants to kill someone, and I was the nearest convenient target."

"Until Jordan came and bailed you out."

Which was, I had to admit, the thing that rankled the most about this. McKell and his cohorts had spent a lot of time a few months back playing puppeteer with Selene and me, and I wasn't at all happy to be back at the other end of their strings.

"He *did* save your life, you know," Selene reminded me. "And he didn't need to send Ixil to watch over us."

"I know," I grumped. "But don't assume Ixil is here purely on our behalf. I've seen enough of this group to know they've probably got six different plays going right now."

"Maybe," Selene said. "But he *did* seem mostly pleased with the way the meeting went. That's a good sign."

I shrugged reluctantly. "I suppose."

"So what do we do next?" she asked.

"We're in a ship with a bounty hunter and three men who think their boss wants me dead," I said with a sigh. "Not much we can do but go along and watch for options to present themselves. Step back there by the sink, will you?"

I waited until she was out of the way, then leaned my head into the shower just far enough and long enough to get my hair wet. I backed out again and shut off the water. "Anything else we need to talk about?" I asked as I toweled my hair partially dry.

"I don't think so." Selene hesitated. "Gregory...assuming we find Easton Dent, what do we do with him?"

"We start by getting him away from Floyd and the others, I suppose," I said. "Hopefully, get *us* away from them at the same time. And no, I don't know how we're going to do that. Probably depends on how this Roastmeat Bar is set up. Ready for a reverse shadow sneak?"

"Yes." She gestured. "Since they may assume you've done everything here you need to for the evening...?"

"Oh. Right." I gave a twirling motion with my finger. "Turn around, will you?"

A minute later we were finally ready. I draped the towel over the rack, then picked up my toiletry kit and stepped to the hatch. Confirming that Selene was ready, I hit the release and turned off the light, and as the hatch opened I walked out into the corridor.

And stopped short. Cole was where I'd left him, still lounging in the camp chair.

But he'd picked up some company. Fulbright was standing in the corridor beside him, leaning with a sort of fake nonchalance against the opposite wall.

And with that, the shadow sneak was suddenly off the table. I could block one person's point of view as Selene hunched her way down the corridor in my visual shadow, but there was no way I could block two of them.

Which left me only one option. Instead of turning left toward the *Ruth*'s stern and my temporary quarters, I turned right toward the ship's bow. "Excuse me," I said as I walked between the two of them and continued forward. "I need to check something on the bridge."

The move was so unexpected that I got three more steps before they broke out of their stunned paralysis and scrambled after me. Fulbright, coming from a standing start, got there first, grabbing my left upper arm and yanking backward hard enough to nearly pull me off my feet. "Where the hell do you think *you're* going?" he demanded.

"I told you: the bridge," I said, letting him spin me around to face him. Cole had made it out of his camp chair now and was about a step behind Fulbright, an even darker glare on his face, his gun clutched in his hand.

Behind them, completely unnoticed, Selene was hurrying silently back to her pod maintenance room.

I let out a quiet sigh of relief. Perfect. Now all I had to do was stall Fulbright and Cole another ten seconds so that she could get out of sight, then extricate myself from the confrontation with as much dignity as I could and head back to my own room.

"Is that Roarke?" Floyd's voice wafted into the corridor from the open dayroom hatch behind me.

"Yeah, boss," Cole called back.

"Bring him."

Once again, Fulbright spun me around. "Go," he said. He started to shove me toward the dayroom hatch—

"I've got him," Cole said. He brushed Fulbright back, inserting himself between us, and got a grip on my left arm. "Come on."

Floyd and Mottola were both in the dayroom as Cole and I entered, Floyd seated on the foldout couch, Mottola on one of the fold-down seats across from him. Both had drinks in their hands, and both were gazing at me as Cole guided me to the center of the room. "Out and about, are we?" Floyd asked.

"Just wanted to hit the shower before I settled down for the night," I told him.

"The shower *and* the bridge?" Floyd asked pointedly. "Or did I mishear you just now?"

"No, you heard right," I confirmed. "I was in the shower when I had a feeling that one of the engines was off-synch by a couple of degrees. I wanted to give it a quick check."

Floyd's eyes shifted to Mottola. "Mottola?"

"I don't feel anything," Mottola said. His eyes were still on me, but there was a slight unfocusing of his gaze.

"Me, neither," Cole added.

"Likewise," Floyd said, looking back at me. "But I'm told every ship has its quirks. Interesting outfit."

"It's a nightshirt," I explained. "We're not used to having company aboard."

"I suppose not," Floyd said. "Speaking of *we:* Cole, go check on Ms. Selene. See if she also needs the bathroom before bedtime."

"Okay." Behind me I heard footsteps as Cole headed back out into the corridor.

"And while he does that," Floyd continued, looking again at Mottola, "go see what Fulbright needs before he beds down. I want everyone settled in their compartments within the next half hour."

"Right." Mottola stood up, hesitated. "Uh, boss—?"

"It's all right," Floyd assured him. "Mr. Roarke is smart enough not to make any trouble." He raised his eyebrows slightly. "You *are* smart enough, aren't you?"

"I like to think so," I said.

"Good," Floyd said, pointing to Mottola's vacated fold-down seat. "Over there."

I walked over to the seat and sat down, throwing a casual look around the dayroom as I did so. I knew Pix and Pax could travel through the *Ruth*'s air ducts, and I assumed Ixil was routinely using them to keep an eye on things. But if something nasty was about to happen, there was no way the hidden Kalix could get himself out of his hidey hole and up onto the main deck in time to do anything about it.

Floyd waited until Mottola had left, then readjusted himself comfortably on the foldout's cushions. "In three days we're going to hit Huihuang for the fueling stop you suggested," he said. "I wanted to let you know what's going to happen there."

"All right," I said cautiously.

"Mottola will handle the refueling," he continued. "You, Fulbright, and Ms. Selene will also remain aboard. Cole and I have an errand to do ashore."

"Anything I can do to help?" I offered.

"You *want* to help?"

"I'd like to show I'm still a team player," I said. "No matter what Mr. Draelon heard or thinks he heard about me."

"Very commendable," Floyd said. "What sort of work can you do?"

"I have all the usual bounty hunter skills," I said. "Along with those I've picked up as a crockett—"

"We're going to kill someone."

My tongue froze in midword. "Oh," I said lamely.

"Mr. Gaheen was once one of Mr. Varsi's most trusted men," Floyd continued, watching me closely. "Unfortunately, with Mr. Varsi currently in seclusion, he apparently thought this was a good time to go rogue and take as much of the Huihuang organization with him as possible. Mr. Varsi has decided that an object lesson must be delivered. We're that lesson."

"I see," I said. The organization was apparently very big on object lessons these days. "Must be terrible for someone you trusted to turn on you that way."

"Terrible and sad both," Floyd said, still eyeing me. "Especially someone like Mr. Gaheen. I've always had a high regard for his talents and dedication. Still, greed and opportunity sometimes combine to lead people into self-destructive behavior."

"Well, you don't have to worry about me," I assured him. "I don't have much greed, and I doubt I'm going to get any opportunities, not with you and your men aboard. Mr. Varsi was quite angry at Mr. Gaheen's treachery, no doubt?"

"I assume so," Floyd said. "Mr. Gaheen's been with the organization a long time."

"You *assume* so?" I asked, putting puzzlement into my voice.

"If I were given a job this important and irreversible, I'd kind of want to hear it from the boss directly. You know, just to make sure there were no misunderstandings."

"The order was delivered through Mr. Draelon," Floyd said, an odd edge to his voice. "There were no misunderstandings."

"Mr. Draelon was himself angry, I suppose?"

"Actually, Mr. Draelon was quite impassive."

"That's good, too," I said. "As my father used to say, *The only decision you should make when you're angry is to stop being angry.*"

"Interesting way to put it," Floyd said. "Now that you know what the job is, you still want to help?"

"Under the circumstances, I think I should sit this one out," I said. "Not really my business, and hardly my forte."

"A wise decision." Floyd cocked his head slightly to the side. "Tell me, Mr. Roarke: Have you ever killed anyone?"

"Once or twice," I admitted. Funny how a chill could produce a fresh burst of sweat. "But always in self-defense. Not like..."

"Not like cold-blooded murder?" Floyd shrugged. "To be honest, I don't go in for that sort of thing, either. Maybe you could think of this as self-defense, or rather defense of Mr. Varsi and the organization."

I thought about Draelon's thinly veiled threat on my own life. Did he consider my supposed betrayal something that Floyd should defend the organization against? "Why are you telling me all this?" I asked, for lack of anything better to say.

"I wanted to see what sort of person you are," he said. "You seem too smart to have gotten yourself into this situation."

"I appreciate the compliment," I said ruefully. "Unfortunately, sometimes the situations I find myself in aren't my fault."

Floyd shrugged. "*As you make your bed, so shall you lie in it.*"

"So I've heard," I said. "But you have to remember that it works in both directions."

"Meaning?"

This probably wouldn't do any good, I knew. Floyd was a loyal minion of Varsi, and he firmly believed his orders were coming from on high. Still, even a slim chance was better than none. "Meaning Mr. Varsi is partially why I'm sitting here with you. He made an under-the-table deal with some Patth—"

"Mr. Varsi doesn't deal with the Patth."

"Well, actually—"

"If he was talking to them, it was because he was setting them up for something," he continued in a tone that didn't offer room for debate.

"Yes, that makes sense," I said, thinking fast. "Naturally, I don't know what his ultimate plan was. All I know is that the setup was something the rest of the Patth hierarchy wouldn't approve of. One of them apparently picked up on the scheme and went after Mr. Varsi, trying the whole time to pin it on me. As my father used to say, *When the going gets tough, the tough look for a scapegoat.*"

"Why didn't you warn Mr. Varsi?"

"I tried," I said. "But by then I was with some people who were doing their best to isolate me from the rest of the Spiral. They also told me the Director General's plan was to go after the people at the Patth end of the deal." I held out my hands, palms upward. "Looking back, I figure sowing trouble among them was part of Mr. Varsi's plan."

For another few heartbeats Floyd's eyes bored like plasma torches into mine. Then, almost reluctantly, the glare softened a bit. "Only they went after Mr. Varsi instead."

"Or after him and the other Patth both. I never heard how any of that came out."

"It came out with Mr. Varsi in seclusion," Floyd said bluntly. "Who was this Patth who gave the alarm? A friend of yours?"

I snorted. "Hardly. Let's just say the last time I saw him he was *very* angry with me."

"When did you see him last?"

"Quite a while ago," I said. "Really, if you've been tracking me you know I haven't been in touch with the rest of the Spiral lately."

"*Fulbright's* the one who's been tracking you," Floyd corrected, his thoughts clearly still back with the Patth. "We're just along to make sure he doesn't lose you."

"Probably a wise move on Mr. Draelon's part," I said, "given that Fulbright has already lost me at least twice."

"I get the feeling he does that a lot." Abruptly, Floyd stood up. "Come on."

"Where are we going?" I asked, getting to my feet.

"Time for you and Ms. Selene to settle down for the night," he said, gesturing toward the dayroom hatchway. "But let's first go to the bridge and see if you were right about the engines."

"Sure," I said, my heart picking up its pace. The only reason I'd brought up the engines in the first place was to get Cole and Fulbright to turn their backs so that Selene could sneak back to her quarters.

Still, I'd only said I *thought* the engines were off-synch. Hopefully, that would cover any suspicions Floyd might have.

Mottola was in the pilot's chair when we arrived. "Any problems with Fulbright?" Floyd asked.

"Nope," Mottola said.

"Any problems with the engines?"

"Nothing I noticed," Mottola said, throwing a glower at me. "But I couldn't find the micro data in the full status list, so I don't know for sure."

"Those numbers are on their own page," I said, stepping up behind him. "Let me pull them up."

I leaned over his shoulder and punched for the engineering status listings, getting my excuses ready. *I only* thought *the engines were off-synch*... The listing came up, and I scrolled down to the engine timing entries.

"Son of a toad," Mottola muttered.

"What?" Floyd demanded, leaning over his other shoulder.

"There," Mottola said, turning a baleful eye up at me. "Starboard's two and a half percent off-synch."

"Well, as Mr. Floyd said, every ship has its quirks," I reminded him, trying to hide my own bewilderment. I was good, but I wasn't *that* good. How in the world—?

Of course. Ixil. He'd gotten the word from one of his outriders that I'd said there was engine flickering and somehow managed to tweak the timing from down there in his hiding place.

As my dad used to say, *The easiest way to keep them from looking behind the curtain is to keep them from noticing the curtain in the first place.*

"The *Ruth*'s not as quirky as some ships I've been on," I continued. "But it does have its moods. If you'll let me have the seat for a minute, I can bring it back into line."

"Boss?" Mottola asked.

Floyd nodded. "Go ahead."

Five minutes later, the engines were once again in synch. "That should do it for now," I said, standing up again. "But you might want to check it whenever you're running a diagnostic.

It'll have to drift at least eight percent before it starts being a problem, but it's better to catch these things early."

"*Thank* you," Mottola growled, giving me one final glare as he slid back into the chair. "I *do* know a thing or two about starships."

"It was just a suggestion," I said mildly. It never hurt to remind people that the ones who owned the ship were usually the ones best qualified to pilot it.

"Easy, Mottola," Floyd said. "Your professional expertise isn't on the line here. Come on, Roarke. Time to shut down for the night."

"I can find my own way, if you'd rather not bother," I offered. "It's not like there's anyplace I can run."

"I don't mind," Floyd said. "Besides, I want to see if there's a set of repeater displays in there."

"There isn't."

"I'll see for myself." He gestured to the hatch. "After you."

We left the bridge and headed down the corridor, where Cole was back on duty in his camp chair. He looked over his shoulder as we approached and exchanged nods with Floyd as we sidled past him. "If that engine acts up again, we may want to have a mechanic take a look at it while we're being refueled," Floyd commented. "I understand some of the more delicate equipment can only be accessed from the outside?"

"That's right," I said. "I don't know anything about Huihuang, but any major spaceport should have the techs and equipment we'd need." I frowned as a sudden thought struck me. "By the way, what would you have done about this other job if I hadn't suggested a fuel stop? Detour and land us there anyway?"

"We'd just have gone back after we delivered Dent to Brandy-wine," Floyd said. "That was Mr. Draelon's original plan, actually, when the word came from Mr. Varsi about Mr. Gaheen. But Mr. Varsi appreciates efficiency from his people. Switching the order of the jobs works better, so we do that."

"Makes sense," I said, nodding. So Floyd had at least a little wiggle room in his orders. That could be useful down the road. Especially when it came to whatever Draelon's orders were regarding Selene and me. "Well, if the *Ruth* throws us any more curves, I should be able to calm her down. Selene and I have been with her a long time."

"I imagine so." We stopped by my new quarters and he keyed the hatch. "After you."

I walked in. He paused just inside and gave the room a quick visual sweep, then nodded in apparent satisfaction. "Good night, Mr. Roarke. Hopefully, we won't need any more of your expertise tonight."

"Fingers crossed," I agreed. "Good night, Mr. Floyd."

The hatch slid closed, and I was alone.

With a sigh, I shut off the light, pulled off the ridiculous nightshirt, and maneuvered my way into my cramped bunk. Actually, I rather hoped Ixil would find something else to tweak a couple of hours down the line.

As my father used to say, *Always try to make yourself indispensable to people. Especially people who are thinking about shooting you in the back.*

CHAPTER TEN

Three days of boredom later, we landed at Poccoro Spaceport on Huihuang.

Floyd had already told me that Mottola would be handling the details of the *Ruth*'s refueling and equipment check. I stayed in my room that whole time, listening to the soft thunks as people connected hoses or opened and closed access panels on the various equipment bays, itching at the thought of people messing with my ship without being able to see what they were doing.

Once, I poked my head out into the corridor to ask our seemingly ever-present guard Cole if they wanted my help with anything. He assured me that they were fine, and that if he saw my face again before we were back in space he would do his best to shoot off one of my ears.

The ship had been quiet for a couple of hours, and I was dozing in the bioprobe bay, when I was jolted awake by tense voices and rapid footsteps approaching along the corridor. I'd just managed to blink the sleep out of my eyes when the hatch slid open to reveal Mottola, his Skripka 4mm gripped tightly in his hand. "Get up," he ordered, half turning to slap the release on Selene's hatch. "Both of you—get up. *Now.*"

"What's the matter?" I asked, sliding out of the bay onto the deck. Luckily, I hadn't gotten undressed, but had just taken my shoes off. "Where are we going?"

"Dayroom," Mottola said, half turning again to peer into Selene's room. "You hear me?"

"Yes," Selene's voice came back. "Just let me get my shoes."

"You don't need to do this," Fulbright's voice came from somewhere forward of where Mottola was standing. "I can stay—"

"*Yes*, I need to do this," Mottola bit out, turning a brief glare that direction before looking back to me. "The foldout only has two sets of restraints, right?"

"Yes," I said, finishing with the shoes and crossing to him.

"I can stay and watch them," Fulbright insisted. "You can just go."

"Another word out of you and you'll stay here with two slugs in your legs," Mottola said. "You two—dayroom."

He took a step aft to let Selene and me into the corridor. Fulbright was standing in our way, his face working with frustration and annoyance. "You heard the man," he said. Spinning around, he headed forward.

The dayroom looked the way it usually did, except that the two sets of hack-proof magnetic shackles and their chains had been pulled from their compartments behind the foldout. "Sit," Mottola said tartly, gesturing with his Skripka.

"What's going on?" I asked as Selene and I did as ordered. "Where are Floyd and Cole?"

"In trouble," Mottola growled, gesturing at the restraints. "Lock yourselves in."

"Did something happen with the job?" I persisted as we fastened the shackles around our wrists. "Because I was a bounty hunter—"

"You want the slug in the leg I just offered Fulbright?" Mottola demanded.

"And I was probably better at it than he was," I added as the look on Fulbright's face suddenly made sense. "If you need him, you need me more."

"I don't *need* him at all," Mottola said glowering at Fulbright. "Just isn't any safe way to leave him here. Anyway, he's on Mr. Varsi's payroll. You're not."

"You need someone here to watch them," Fulbright insisted. "I don't trust them."

"They'll keep until we get back," Mottola said. He confirmed that our restraints were properly locked, then waved Fulbright toward the hatch. "Let's go."

"What about my gun?" Fulbright asked.

"You'll get it when we get to the square," Mottola said. "Go."

"Good luck," I called after them.

Fulbright sent a last frustrated look in my direction. Mottola didn't bother with even that much of an acknowledgment. I listened as their steps faded down the corridor, heard the main hatch open and close.

And Selene and I were alone.

I took a deep breath and turned to face her. "What do you think?"

"It's bad," she said, her pupils simmering with concern. "I don't know what's happened, but Mottola's very worried."

"I'm not surprised," I said sourly. "Floyd talked about him and Cole going up against this Gaheen fellow like it would be a run to the local market."

"You think Gaheen knew they were coming?"

"If *I* was poking Varsi with a stick, I'd sure expect trouble," I said. "Are they gone?"

Her nostrils flared and her eyelashes fluttered. "Yes," she said. "Both of them. Do you want me to get the key, or shall we wait a little longer in case they come back?"

"If they come back, we'll hear them," I said. "Get it now."

She nodded and pulled the vacuum toilet from its hiding place in the wall. As she busied herself with the maintenance panel, I reached to the upper end of my artificial left arm with my right hand, pressing my thumb and first two fingers into the flesh at the three quick-release points. A squeeze and twist, and the forearm came free, the artificial skin unweaving from the real skin of the elbow and upper arm. "I'll be on the bridge," I told Selene, standing up and laying the arm on the cushion. "Bring the arm when you come."

I looked toward the nearest air vent. "Ixil, come on up and join the party," I called.

I was sitting in the pilot's seat, staring at nothing in particular, when Selene arrived with my arm. "What's the matter?" she asked anxiously. "Why haven't you started the prelaunch?"

I waved tiredly at the control board. "Because Mottola was smarter than I am," I said. "He's locked down the whole piloting board."

"Actually, it was Fulbright, not Mottola," a new voice came from behind her.

I turned to see Ixil step into the hatchway, Pix and Pax riding his shoulders. "Fulbright, huh?" I said.

"Yes," Ixil said. "A seven-digit code. Unfortunately, Pax wasn't in position to read the numbers."

"He also put a cascading repetition delay on top of it," I told him. "No way we're going to clear it without him."

"Interesting," Ixil said. "He hadn't struck me as being that clever."

"Even the least clever occasionally have their moments," I said. "I suppose I could try an overcat. But if it bursts, it'll be locked down even tighter."

"Will that make a noticeable difference?"

"Point," I conceded. "Okay, here goes."

I keyed in the overcat program, a hack system I'd picked up during my bounty hunter days. "So what was going on back there with Draelon?" I asked as the thing started chugging its way through the *Ruth*'s computer system. "What were you and McKell even doing on Brandywine?"

"We had returned to the job we interrupted to come to New Kyiv," Ixil said. "I'm afraid the details are still classified."

"Even from us?"

Ixil shrugged. "I'm sorry. Still, our presence there, even if coincidental, turned out to be highly useful. When Selene told Tera that your captors had talked about Brandywine and that she thought there was a strong possibility you'd be taken there, we decided to see what we could do to help."

"And to see if our presence shook anything loose?"

He shrugged again. "You know how this business works."

"Not as well as I'd like to," I said pointedly. "So what's this Jordan McKell, famous bounty hunter thing?"

"You laugh," Ixil said. "But the admiral and Jordan have been developing and nurturing the Algernon Niles identity for several years now, precisely for this sort of situation."

"So what, he pops out in disguise a couple of times a year, parades around the Spiral and then disappears again?"

"Actually, this is the first time he's shown up with a visible face," Ixil said. "All his other appearances have been masked or otherwise shrouded."

"Well, he certainly went to the nines on it here," I commented. I'd used my fair share of aliases over the years, but I'd never carried the prosthetics or makeup to nearly that extreme. "So why did he butt in? If Varsi had wanted me dead, Floyd could have shot me anywhere along the line."

"That was our initial assumption as well," Ixil said, his voice going dark. "In fact, Draelon seemed almost casual when he first ordered Floyd to help Fulbright track you down a few weeks ago. But sometime in the hours before you arrived his mood changed." He cocked his head. "Did you do anything during that time that might have upset him?"

I winced. "Aside from just being hard to catch, I sort of clobbered Mottola with his own gun,"

"And then drugged him," Selene murmured.

"That, too," I said, a chill running up my back. "I guess he takes employer-employee loyalty very seriously."

"So it would seem." Ixil gestured. "Anything?"

I looked back at the board. The overcat had run its course, with no results. "No," I said. "The only other approach would be to replace several components, which we don't have, or dig *very* deeply into the programming, which I can't do. Looks like we're here until Floyd says we're not."

"It would seem he *really* wants to find Easton Dent," Selene added.

"Or at least doesn't want us finding him by ourselves." I frowned back at Ixil. "So what exactly is going on out there?"

"As Mottola said, Floyd and Cole are in trouble," Ixil said. "From what Pix was able to overhear, there's a secret tunnel entrance leading from Two Degree Square into the Varsi organization's operations center, which is located in Gaheen's personal mansion. They were going to use the tunnel to bypass Gaheen's security."

"Convenient for someone," I said. "Sloppy for everyone else. So what's the plan?"

"If we can't get the *Ruth* out, we'll have to find another way off Huihuang," Ixil said. "We'll start with a runaround to the aircraft side of the port and put some distance between us and Poccoro Spaceport. We'll then need to find a ship that will to take us to—"

"No," I said, turning back to the frozen pilot board. "We're not leaving. Not yet."

"Gregory?" Selene asked, her pupils gone wary.

"We're not leaving," I repeated. "We're going to get Floyd and the others out of whatever mess they're in, and then we're all flying out of here together."

"Why?" Ixil asked calmly.

I chewed at the inside of my cheek, trying to pin down the sudden rush of thoughts swirling around my brain. So far it wasn't even close to coming together.

But it would. Deep down, I knew it would.

The only question was whether it would come together in time. As my father used to say, *An important part of being right is being right* fast.

"Fulbright wanted to stay behind and guard us just now," I said. "You heard him. Mottola was just as adamant that they both go and told him that we'd be fine here on our own." I looked back at Selene and Ixil. "So why didn't either of them remind the other that the pilot board was locked? Or even just tell us about it so we would know it was useless to try to escape?"

For a moment both of them were silent. "Mottola doesn't know about the lock," Selene said at last. "And Fulbright doesn't *want* him to know."

"That's what I'm thinking," I said, shifting my eyes to Ixil. "Was Fulbright alone in here when he locked down the board?"

"Yes," Ixil said, eyeing me closely. "What do•you think he's up to?"

"Damned if I know," I said frankly. "But I can't shake the feeling he's playing an entirely different game than the rest of us. *And* I don't like the idea of him being alone with men who are supposed to be guarding me. If something happens to Floyd and the others... well, Fulbright's story will be the only one Varsi and Draelon hear."

"Which could be awkward," Ixil agreed thoughtfully. "You realize that if Fulbright's planning to pin something on you and you're seen off the *Ruth* you'll be playing directly into his game."

"I know," I said. "But even if he never says a word, the fact that I disappeared after Floyd ran into a buzzsaw will have Varsi on my tail forever. The only way to keep that from happening is to wade in on Floyd's side."

"You think helping Floyd will persuade Varsi to back off on your death sentence?" Ixil asked.

"No idea," I admitted. "But it can't hurt."

There was another short silence. "All right," Selene said, handing me my arm. "Where do we start?"

"We retrace Floyd's steps," I said, lining up the arm and starting to reattach it. Like most things in life, it was harder to put back together than to take apart. "Ixil, you said there was a tunnel from Two Degree Square?"

"Yes," Ixil said. "Floyd had a map marking its location, but he and Cole took it with them. Floyd called Mottola from inside Gaheen's mansion, but before he could give him the location his phone call was jammed."

"Jammed, or the call broken off?" I asked.

"From the sound, I'd say it was jammed," Ixil said. "It sounded like the two of them were trapped somewhere inside the building, but hadn't been captured."

"Let's hope they can keep it that way," I said, wincing at the unpleasant tingle as the arm's artificial nerves and motor systems linked back up with the flesh-and-blood ones. "How far away is this square?"

"A little over half a kilometer from the edge of the landing field," Ixil said. "I gather the mansion itself is only another two hundred meters away."

"Sounds about right," I said. "Your typical criminal mastermind wants his emergency exit tunnel long enough to put him outside whatever cordon his enemies have set up, but not so long that it takes him forever to get through it and snag a runaround or aircar. Do you know where Floyd stashed our stuff?"

"Top left-hand cabinet in the dayroom."

"Selene, get your info pad and check on the traffic and terrain between us and the square," I told her. "Find us the best runaround route in."

"Right," she said, and hurried from the bridge.

"You'll need a weapon," Ixil said, reaching into his tunic and pulling out a little four-shot derringer-style DubTrub 2mm. "Your Fafnir is still on New Kyiv."

"And my first backup is with Varsi's people on Marjolaine," I said, eyeing the weapon. DubTrubs were far more sophisticated than they looked, their projectiles not simple chemical-driven slugs but tiny missiles that vented from the back and gave the gun no more recoil than a plasmic.

But that very sophistication carried with it a hidden risk. DubTrubs and their ammo were expensive, which suggested the person carrying one was either wealthy or else sponsored by someone with cash to spare.

For badgemen, that logic train would mark the carrier as well above the level of a street criminal. For street criminals, that same train pointed straight back at an undercover badgeman. Neither of those was a profile I especially wanted to fit into at the moment.

Fortunately, I didn't need to. "You'd better keep it," I said, waving the weapon away. Shaking off the last of the tingling from my left arm, I reached up beneath the pilot's board to the hidden compartment and retrieved my second and last backup plasmic, a weapon I'd invested in after the last time someone took all my guns away from me. "You'll need it if someone decides to take a shot at you while we're out."

"He's not staying here?" Selene asked as she reemerged from the corridor, working her pad. "What if they see him?"

"If they figure out we're together, there'll be trouble," I agreed. "Ditto if he doesn't make it back before we do and gets left behind. But I want backup handy if Mottola needs convincing that we're on his side."

"I agree," Ixil said. "If for no other reason than that Tera will be furious if I let you get killed. She's quite fond of you, you know."

"Hadn't really noticed." I stood up, checked the Fafnir's charge, and tucked the weapon into my belt at the small of my back. "Selene?"

"There's plenty of traffic out there, but there are a couple of mostly clear routes," she said. "There are also four runarounds listed as being available two landing cradles east of here."

"Good." I flexed my left-hand fingers one final time and nodded. "Let me get my jacket, and we'll go play white knight."

From the name, I'd envisioned Two Degree Square as something out of old Earth history: an open area in the middle of the city, bounded on all sides by quaint, probably ancient-looking stone buildings.

But as my father used to say, *Those who don't know history usually don't know much about anything else, either.* Two Degree Square turned out to be more like a combination park and flea market, with benches, paths, a couple of play areas, and a whole bunch of small vending carts and stalls lined up along the edges.

The carts were clearly moveable, which eliminated them from consideration as the entrance to Gaheen's bolthole. But the larger stalls were more permanent, built on solid foundations, and a couple of them were big enough to have two or three separate rooms inside. "We'll start with the big stalls," I said, pointing Selene toward the closest one. "Ixil, go back and find someplace near where we came in where you can stay out of sight. We'll call if we need you."

"Be careful," Ixil said. "And keep an eye out for Pix and Pax. If they spot anything, they'll point it out to you."

"You may not want to send them in," I warned, eyeing the people milling around. "Those booths are a little far for them to jump between, and I don't want them to get stepped on."

"On Kali they hunt tusked animals twenty times their size through forests and rough terrain," he said mildly. "I think they're nimble enough to avoid human feet."

"Be it on your own head," I said doubtfully. "Come on, Selene."

We headed in. "You getting anything?" I asked quietly as we maneuvered our way around a knot of people who'd decided to have a conversation in the middle of the path.

"They're here," she said, turning her head back and forth as she sampled the air. "Mottola and Fulbright. Somewhere to the north or northwest."

"How far?" I asked. The next path heading that direction, I saw, angled off past a jewelry cart a few meters ahead of us.

"Not too far," she said. "Thirty to fifty meters, I think."

I frowned. Fifty meters would put them right at the edge of the square, back in the wooded areas beyond all the vending stalls. "You sure?"

"Yes."

"Okay." We reached the jewelry cart and turned onto the other path.

And I felt a smile quirk at my lips. In the distance, beyond two more rows of booths and carts at the edge of the square, were three dilapidated stone buildings. Their roofs were partially caved in, their walls discolored and pitted with age and erosion, their doors and windows boarded up. Relics of an earlier age, presumably, the sort of place historical societies try to maintain and local kids make up scary stories about.

Bingo.

"I'm guessing they're in one of those," I said. "Let's go find out which one."

One of the many advantages of a partner like Selene was that we knew the location almost to the square meter of the person we were trying to sneak up on. No need to depend on luck for a glimpse of the target; no need for a muttered word or unwary footstep on the target's part to give away the game.

Which meant that we were able to pinpoint the house on the right, find the hidden entrance through the supposedly solid wall, figure which of the three rooms Mottola and Fulbright were in, and come up directly behind them as they poked with growing frustration at the walls and tiled floor.

Back in our bounty hunter days, I'd enjoyed milking such moments. But this wasn't the time or place. "Afternoon, gentlemen," I said in a conversational tone. "Just leave your guns where they are—we're here to help."

Mottola obeyed me halfway, his hand snapping up onto the grip of his Skripka but leaving the weapon holstered. Fulbright's hand managed to get halfway to his own holster before he remembered that Mottola still had his gun. "It's okay, you can turn around," I went on. "Like I said, we're on your side."

"I *told* you I needed to stay with them," Fulbright bit out as they both turned slowly to face us.

"I guess you were right," Mottola said, his eyes flicking to my Fafnir before settling on my face. "Nice trick, Roarke. How'd you manage it?"

"What, getting out of my own shackles on my own ship?" I countered. "Just because I'm mostly retired doesn't mean I've gone stupid. But never mind that. I take it you haven't found Floyd's back door yet?"

"No," Mottola said, still studying my face. "I don't suppose you have any ideas."

"I've got the best idea of them all," I assured him. "Selene?"

"That wall," she said, pointing to the wall to the left of the one Mottola had just been searching.

"I've already looked at that one," Fulbright growled. Unlike Mottola, his expression as he glared at me was one of pure hatred. "The wall's not thick enough to hide a secret door."

"You're absolutely right," I agreed. "If the two of you would just step back a bit...?"

Mottola complied, his gaze now shifted to Selene. It took a small twitch of my Fafnir, and a less subtle prompting poke from Mottola, for Fulbright to reluctantly do likewise.

Selene walked over to the wall, her eyelashes fluttering double time. She moved along it, stopped right at the center and crouched down, sniffing the whole way. A moment bent over with her face close to the floor, then back up the wall. She paused about waist high... moved over and paused again shoulder high, then straightened and looked back at me. "Here," she said, pointing to the two spots she'd been sniffing. "The releases are here."

Fulbright snorted. "What kind of *crap*—"

"Shut up," Mottola said quietly. "Roarke? Your idea. You do the honors."

As my father used to say, *Don't worry about people who think they're a good judge of character. Worry about those who also think they're the jury and executioner.*

But I had to risk it. Mottola couldn't go charging into a rescue mission with one eye on his back, and neither could I. If we couldn't trust each other for at least the next hour, we might as well go home now.

And so, with only the barest hesitation, I returned my Fafnir to its spot behind my belt and walked over to the wall.

As I passed him, out of the corner of my eye I saw him take his hand off the grip of his Skripka.

There was nothing obvious I could see about the two patches of wall that Selene had identified. But she'd smelled Floyd or Cole there, and that was good enough for me. I settled the heels of my palms on the spots, braced myself, and pushed.

Silently, the wall's base swung up, swiveling on hidden hinges in the ceiling. It pulled a thin layer of flooring tile along with it, the layer sliding up over the top of the flooring in the room behind the wall.

And as the tile layer receded, it exposed a recessed handle in the floor.

"Hold it there," Mottola said, stepping over and dropping to one knee beside me. As I held the wall in place he angled the handle up and twisted it. There was a soft click; with a grunt, he resettled his grip on the handle and pulled upward.

Across the room, a meter-square section of tile popped up, rising about five centimeters up from floor level.

"I'll be damned," Mottola breathed. "Keep holding."

He stood up and hurried over to the risen section. For a moment his fingers explored the edges; then, with a barely audible creak, it swung up from one edge. "Selene?" I prompted.

"Yes," she once again confirmed. "They went down there."

"Big surprise," Fulbright grumbled. "Where *else* would they have gone?"

"Good point," Mottola said briskly. "Okay. Roarke, you go first. Fulbright next, then me."

"Where's my gun?" Fulbright demanded.

In answer, Mottola pulled Fulbright's Balgren from behind his jacket and tossed it over. "Don't use it unless I tell you to," he warned. "Selene, will you be able to find Floyd and Cole once we're out the other end?"

"Yes," Selene said.

Mottola eyed her for a moment, and I could tell he was wondering how in the world she was pulling this off. But he'd seen her magic once and was apparently ready to take her on faith. "Good," he said. "You're up front with Roarke. Okay—let's go."

CHAPTER ELEVEN

The trapdoor opened onto a steep stairway that headed down about seven meters to what looked in the faint glow from my flashlight to be a dirt floor. I headed down, Selene and Fulbright behind me, Mottola bringing up the rear.

The tunnel floor was indeed plain dirt, I saw as I reached it, but the walls and ceiling were a dull gray ceramic. I puzzled at that for a moment until I realized that footsteps on dirt were a lot quieter than the same footsteps on metal or ceramic. The tunnel was narrow, about one and a half people wide, which meant we would be traveling in single file.

Something about it also felt very old.

"Mottola?" I called softly as Mottola's head cleared the floor above and he got a grip on a strap on the trapdoor's underside. "Did Gaheen put in this tunnel himself?"

"No," Mottola replied, pulling the trapdoor shut. As he did so, I heard what sounded like a faint scraping sound in the distance.

"The wall's gone back into place," Selene murmured in my ear.

I nodded. With the wall back to its normal vertical position, and the attached section of flooring hiding the release handle, this end of the escape route was once again closed to anyone who didn't know its secret.

"It was already in place when Mr. Varsi bought the mansion

and made it the local operations center," Mottola continued as he walked carefully the rest of the way down the stairway. "Gaheen probably doesn't even know it's here."

Fulbright grunted. "That could be handy."

"We think so." Mottola reached the tunnel floor and drew his Skripka. "Let's go. Roarke, watch for traps or marking triggers."

"Any idea what we're walking into?" I whispered over my shoulder. "How big this place is, how many guards there are, where Gaheen is likely to be."

"Four stories tall," Mottola whispered back. "Gaheen's office and living area are on the third. At least twenty guards, five to fifteen of them inside, most of them probably on the bottom two floors. This time of day, Gaheen's probably in his office."

I nodded. Unless, of course, Floyd and Cole had flushed him out into the arms of his guards or some kind of safe room.

Come to think of it, if Gaheen had been alerted, those twenty guards had probably swelled to fifty by now, most of them crowded around their boss. "So what went wrong?" I asked.

"We don't have time for that now," Mottola said. "And be quiet—"

I caught Selene's arm and brought both of us to a sudden stop. I turned around, to find Mottola's Skripka pointed at my face over Fulbright's shoulder. "*Make* time," I said flatly. "We're going into an armed camp. We need to know everything we can about the situation."

For a moment the gun held steady. Then, reluctantly, Mottola lowered it. "Fine," he said. "Floyd and Cole were getting ready to breach Gaheen's office when some big-time Najik and his entourage arrived. They made it to the office across the hallway without being seen and are currently stuck there. Gaheen and the Najik are still in Gaheen's office, the hallway is filthy with Gaheen's guards, and someone could walk in on Floyd and Cole any minute and blow the whole thing into the clouds. That enough to get you moving?"

It was almost enough to get me moving in the other direction, actually. As my father used to say, *Two's company, three's a crowd, fifty is probably someplace you don't want to be.* "How many guards are in the office with Gaheen and the Najik?"

"Probably none," Mottola said. "Floyd said the Najiki guards delivered their boss and then went down to the second floor.

That's Mr. Varsi's standard protocol: visitor security has to be somewhere else during negotiations. That's what the phone jamming is about, too—no calls in or out once talks have started."

I nodded. I'd seen those rules in play once or twice when I happened to be in Varsi's office at the same time some business associate came calling. "So Gaheen's working a deal with the Najik?"

"Like Floyd said, he's gone rogue," Mottola growled. "If you want details, you'll have to ask him. *After* any guns have stopped waving in our direction."

"Got it," I said. Turning around, I resumed my walk down the tunnel. It all seemed pretty clear now.

And yet...

I sidled a bit closer to Selene. "That plant sporete we picked up on NK-177-D a couple of years ago," I murmured. "You remember that?"

"Of course," she murmured back.

"Didn't Varsi say something the next time we saw him about how that drug looked like it would work especially well with Najiki biochemistry?"

"Yes," Selene confirmed. "He also said it might be effective on Narchners."

I thought back to the singing Narchner who'd annoyed everyone in the cells back on New Kyiv. Personally, anything that could shut up that species for a while was fine with me. "But his primary focus was pitching it to the Najik?"

"That's how I remember it, yes."

"And he was telling the truth?"

Selene paused, presumably thinking back to the conversation. The subtle changes in a person's scent when they were lying or under strong emotion were like a transit map for someone of her abilities. "Yes, as far as I could tell."

"Interesting," I said.

"Didn't I say to be quiet up there?" Mottola warned sharply.

I lifted a hand in acknowledgment and apology, and we continued on in silence.

A hundred or so meters later, we came around a corner and ran squarely into a dead end.

"What the *hell?*" Fulbright snarled.

"Relax," I said, playing my flashlight around the short alcove the tunnel had become. It was the same gray ceramic as the rest of the walls, and looked just as old. But it was smoother, and its floor was also ceramic instead of the dirt of the rest of the tunnel.

And at chest height on the left-hand side were six slightly discolored spots.

"There's an edge here," Selene said.

I turned my light to where she was pointing. Sure enough, there was a hint of a vertical crack from floor to ceiling right where the tunnel turned into the alcove.

A crack that went across the ceiling and then down to the floor on the other side.

"It's not a dead end," I said. "It's an elevator."

"Ridiculous," Fulbright insisted. "There's no door. There's not even any room for one."

"I don't think it has a door," I said. "It's an open-sided car. You stay in because the shaft wall keeps you from falling out." I focused my light on the discolored spots. "Here are the controls."

"So why is the car down here?" Mottola asked suspiciously. "If Floyd and Cole took it up, why isn't it still waiting for them on the third floor?"

"I don't know," I said. "Maybe after it sits for a while it comes down on its own."

"It didn't just come down," Selene said. "It arrived soon after we entered the tunnel. I think it was triggered when we closed the other end."

I raised my eyebrows in silent question. *The scents of Floyd and Cole increased,* she mouthed.

I gave her a microscopic nod of understanding. Yes; a brief puff as the scent they'd left in the car flowed into the tunnel would be something she would catch. "So it's not just an escape hatch," I concluded. "The original builder probably designed it as his own private entrance and exit."

"Or designed it for someone else to use," Mottola muttered thoughtfully. "Who knows who lived in that house a hundred years ago?"

"Yeah, thrilling stuff," Fulbright growled. "We doing this or not?"

"Yeah, we're doing this," Mottola growled back, playing his own light up and down the elevator car. "Problem is, it won't take more than two at a time. Okay. Roarke and I will go up first, find Floyd or someplace where we can go to ground, then send the car back down."

I looked at Selene, saw the sudden apprehension in her pupils. "I don't think so," I said quickly. I didn't have to wonder at her reaction; I didn't want her left alone with Fulbright, either. "Selene needs to be in the first group so she can pinpoint the others."

"Yeah, how is she doing that, exactly?" Mottola asked suspiciously. "You've been pretty vague on how this is supposed to work. Is it some kind of telepathy or something?"

"It's difficult to explain," I deflected. "It's also not important. The point is that she *can* do it, so she needs to go up first."

"Oh, it's important, all right," Mottola retorted. "But I suppose it can keep for now. Fine. She and I will go first, then you and Fulbright."

"No," Selene said quickly. "I need Gregory with me. He provides a sort of..." She looked at me helplessly.

"It's called a para-cognitive baseline," I told Mottola, picking the first set of vaguely impressive words that popped into my head. I didn't know why Selene didn't want to be alone with Mottola, but I was more than willing to back her up on it. "We need to be close together for it to work."

Mottola was looking at me like I was trying to spin him a dish of whipped soap. "Yeah, *that's* convenient."

"What's convenient is that she can do this in the first place," I countered. "Look, what's the problem? It's not like we'll be wandering around all alone up there. Floyd and Cole are waiting in the wings, remember?"

"Fine," Mottola ground out. "But you send that car back down *damn* fast. Got it?"

"Got it," I promised, stepping into the car and pressing my right shoulder against the back, facing the spots Selene had identified as the controls. "Which ones do we push?"

"That one's the release," she said, pointing to the lowest spot. "That's the floor the others went to," she added, pointing at the fourth spot above it. "You hold down the first and then press the second."

"You got that, Mottola?" I asked. "Good. See you soon."

Selene squeezed herself into the cramped space in front of me, her back pressed against my chest, her hair brushing my face. I reached over her shoulders and pushed the spots she'd indicated. Without even a creak, the car started upward, moving at a slow, deliberate, and silent pace. Through the opening I watched Mottola's and Fulbright's upturned faces disappear beneath a wall of more gray ceramic as we rose into the elevator shaft.

And now that they were out of sight, I was finally able to huff out a sigh of relief. "I thought they'd *never* leave," I murmured into Selene's ear. "Thanks for tipping me off about Mottola. So you don't trust him either?"

"No, I actually think Mottola's all right," she said. "At least for now. He needs our help. I just didn't want you being alone with Fulbright."

I frowned. Granted that Fulbright had so far proved to be lousy company, I hadn't felt any particular threat from him. "Something I missed?"

"I don't know," Selene said. "There's something about the way his scent keeps changing that worries me." She paused, and I could visualize a bit of humor touching her pupils. "Para-cognitive baselines are hard to explain."

"Absolutely," I agreed. "And don't forget those words, because that's the story we'll be camping on from now on. Speaking of stories, what do you think about Mottola's theory that Gaheen is meeting with some Najik?"

"He may be right," Selene said. "There's a faint scent of Najik in here that could have come in when Floyd and Cole got out."

"Great," I muttered. Najik were tall, spindly things whose hairy arms and legs—and multiple eyes—always made me think of giant tarantulas. As a species, they tended to be good bargainers, and they really, *really* liked creating wealth. The jury was still out on whether they liked the wealth itself or just enjoyed the challenges involved in the amassing process. Either way, if Gaheen was dealing with one of them, he had his work cut out for him.

The car made its slow way upward, passing doors that I assumed opened up onto the first and second floors. Finally, its leisurely pace slowed even more. "All right, get ready," I said, turning off my flashlight and putting it in my pocket. "I doubt the door will open automatically—secret entrance and all that. So I'll open it a crack and you can see what's out there."

I felt her nod. "Ready."

The car stopped. I felt around the panel, found a handle, and gave it a tentative turn. There was a soft *snick* and I eased the door open a couple of millimeters.

I'd expected a blaze of light from whatever was outside. Instead, we got a very muted glow, like from an unlit room that had a door open somewhere.

"No people nearby," Selene whispered. "There's cleaner, air freshener, and the smell of the local water."

"A bathroom?"

"Yes, I think so," Selene said. "Farther away but inside the air-flow . . . three Najik and two humans. The Najik were in the bath-room for a while, but they're gone now. One of them smells . . . odd."

"How odd?" I asked. So we had five people hanging out in whatever room was connected to the bathroom? Still, the more crucial question— "Is that door the bathroom's only exit?"

There was more sniffing, longer and deeper this time. "No," she said. "There's another room the other direction. The door's closed, but there's air coming in from beneath it. I think Floyd and Cole are in there."

"Good," I said. At least we wouldn't have to go hunting for them.

All right. First job would be to figure out how to send the car back down to Mottola and Fulbright. After that, we could link up with Floyd and Cole and hopefully figure out how to get their distasteful job done quickly and get us all back to the *Ruth* and off this planet. "Okay. First thing—"

"Wait," Selene said, pressing her nose up against the open crack. "There's something else."

"What?" I asked, trying to get to the plasmic tucked away behind my back. My hand made it about halfway before the constraints of the elevator car stopped it.

"Another scent," she said, and in the faint light I saw puzzle-ment and growing alarm in her pupils. "Coming from the room with the Najik. I think . . ." She turned stunned eyes to me. "Gregory, that's the sporete you were just talking about. The one we found on NK-177-D."

I frowned. The sporete we'd dug out of the *Ruth*'s bioprobe two years ago was *here*?

And then, I got it. The sporete—a group of Najik—

"I'll be damned," I muttered. "Varsi did it. He actually got a drug out of the thing. So what, Gaheen's trying to sell it to the Najik?"

"Not just selling it," Selene said, her eyelashes fluttering. "I think they're testing it in here."

"Really," I said. "Let's take a look."

"*What?*" Her pupils went full-on astonished. "Gregory, we can't do that. We're not even supposed to *be* here."

"Just a quick look through the doorway," I assured her. "I want to see what they're doing." I cocked an eyebrow. "Don't you?"

Her pupils were still troubled, but she gave a reluctant nod. "All right. But just a look."

I nodded and pushed the door all the way open.

We were in a bathroom, all right. Nicely appointed, with lots of gold filigree and artistic curlicues on the walls. The room itself was long and narrow, boasting a toilet, dual sinks, and a shower and swirl tub against the wall opposite to us. To our right was a large enclosed box that was probably either a steam chamber or sauna, while to our left was a matching bulge. I puzzled at that one for a moment until I realized it was the building's main elevator, opening out into the hallway behind us, which our secret one had been·built up against. Probably why no one had realized it was here—the empty space and machinery would naturally be assumed to be associated with the main elevator system. The bathroom door at the far right end was closed; the one to the left was cracked open a few centimeters. Now that we were out of the car, I could hear a low murmuring of voices coming through the gap, human and the distinctive scratching rumble of Najik.

I stepped out and looked behind me. Our hidden door was plastered with the same sort of decoration as the rest of the room, perfect camouflage for the cracks that marked the edges. "Come on."

Selene stepped out of the car, and together we crossed toward the open door. She was sniffing rapidly, getting more nuances as we approached the opening and the swirl of scents coming at us grew stronger. We reached the door—

Abruptly, she clutched my arm. "Wait," she whispered, a sudden urgency in her voice. "The strange-smelling Najik in there," she said. "He's ill. No. He's . . . Gregory, I think he may be *dying.*"

I stared at her. The drug we'd found was going to kill someone? "Can you tell what's wrong? Is it our sporete, or something else? No—skip that. Do you know how to fix it?"

She had her info pad out and was scrolling rapidly through the Najiki biochemistry section. "Not from here," she said, her pupils showing a turmoil of emotions. "All right. Yes, I see what

I might be smelling. But the mix is too faint to be sure. I have to get closer."

"Like inside the room?"

She winced. "I know," she said. "We can't."

I looked over at the partially open door. Selene was right—we had no business sticking our necks out this far. Especially if whatever was happening in the next room was about to go sideways.

But if there was a sick Najik in there, that implied the sporete chemical was something medicinal, not a street-level drug. That was strange all by itself—I'd always assumed from Varsi's statements and gloatings that his primary interest in our discoveries was the latter.

I'd already been interested in taking a look at what was going on in there. Now, I was even more intrigued to find out what Gaheen was up to.

Besides, aside from a physical appearance that sort of creeped me out, I'd never really had any problems with the Najik. It seemed a little callous to just walk out and let one of them die if we could do something about it.

On the other hand, we were running critical timing here, and Floyd and the others were waiting on us.

I squared my shoulders. And they could just keep waiting.

"I know we can't," I told Selene. "But we're going to anyway."

"Gregory, they're not just going to let us walk into a top-secret facility where they're testing a top-secret drug," she said tensely. "They'll ask for ID or they'll call someone. At the very least they'll know we don't belong here."

"And if we don't go, the Najik might die?"

She closed her eyes briefly, cutting off the turmoil in her pupils. "Yes."

Selene had had a reputation for cool ruthlessness among the other bounty hunters we'd known, but most of them had missed the fact that she made a sharp distinction between criminal targets who deserved ruthlessness and innocent bystanders who didn't. Her fears notwithstanding, she'd clearly decided the ailing Najik was in the latter category.

As my father used to say, *The milk of human kindness tends to curdle if it's left corked in the bottle too long.*

"Then we go," I said. "You ready?"

She lifted a finger and turned her attention back to her info pad. For another half minute she continued to read through the files. Then, with a decisive tap she shut it down and slipped it back into its pouch. "Yes."

"Okay," I said, giving her hand a quick squeeze. "I'll do the talking. You do the sniffing." Setting my face into my best authority expression, I pushed open the door.

The room was large and well furnished with low tables and comfortable chairs, the wall decorations more tasteful and low-key than the slightly garish ones in the adjoining bathroom. Not the bedroom that I'd expected, but a business-style conversation room designed for casual discussion or negotiation.

My mind flicked back to the steam chamber/sauna in the bathroom, which I'd assumed was for the use of overnight guests. Gaheen must hold some very interesting meetings.

Only not today. Today, all the furniture had been moved out of the center of the room and a plain white medical table moved in. It was set at human waist height, and had a group of sensors and monitors arrayed around the head end. Stretched out on the table was a Najik, and even with my exceptionally limited knowledge of the species I could tell something wasn't right with him. Two other Najik and a white-jacketed woman were working at his sides, their low voices and rapid hand movements as they checked monitors and prepared hypos indicating a rising anxiety. A few meters back from everyone else, a hard-faced thug type was silently watching the drama.

"*There* you are," I said in my most imposing voice as Selene and I strode toward the table. "I thought you were going to be in the other room. You were supposed to call us before you started."

"Who are you?" the human female demanded, her eyes narrowing as she took in our street clothing. Her eyes lingered a split second on Selene's Kadolian features, then returned to me. "What are you doing here?"

"I'm Dr. Moriarty," I said. "This is Dr. Watson. We came in from Brandywine to observe the test."

"Thank you, but we're doing just fine," the woman growled.

"Are you?" I countered. "Let me lay it out for you: Dr. Watson and I are the ones who developed the drug you're playing with, and I don't—"

"*Playing* with?"

"We do not play," the taller of the two Najik said in his species' typical scratching rumble.

"—*and* it looks to me like you're not playing with it very well," I finished, raising my voice over their objections. "Which of you is in charge?"

"I am Physician Livicby," the Najik said. "I am to test Patron Gaheen's serum for my superior, Patron Yolorist. You said you have come from Brandywine?"

"I did," I said looking at the woman. "And you?"

"Dr. McDermott," she said tartly as she turned back to the table. "And we don't have time for this."

"You got some ID?" the thug demanded, his eyes narrowed as he looked at me.

I winced. Exactly as Selene had warned he would. All I could do now was pile on the bluster and hope I could brush him back long enough for us to get this done and do a quick fade into the sunset. "As Dr. McDermott said—"

"There is no need," Physician Livicby cut me off, gesturing to the thug. "I am familiar with Dr. Moriarty and his work. Do you understand the problem?"

"I think so," I said, trying not to show my surprise at Livicby's unexpected support. I had no idea why he would vouch for a total stranger, but right now I would take anything I could get. Maybe he was as worried about his patient as Selene was. "Let's take a look."

I took a step to McDermott's left. She caught a glimpse of me out of the corner of her eye and moved sharply sideways to block my path. "*Excuse* me," she bit out, throwing an elbow into my ribs to further hinder my approach and giving me a glare that could peel paint.

Which was fine with me, since I'd only crowded her in the first place in order to draw her attention while Selene slipped past on her other side.

As my father used to say, *The hand doesn't have to be quicker than the eye if the eye is busy elsewhere.*

"Look, Doctor," I growled back, trying to stretch the distraction a little more if I could. "I don't mean to pull rank—"

"What do you?" Livicby demanded.

McDermott spun back around. Selene was standing at the table beside the shorter Najik, leaning over the invalid's face. From everyone else's point of view, I knew, it looked like she was just staring into his eyes. From my more knowledgeable perspective,

it was simply her need to get close enough to zero in on the
nuances of his breath and skin secretions as she tried to match
them up with the medical tutorial she'd just read.

"Get away from there!" McDermott snapped, reaching for
Selene's arm.

"He needs more," Selene said, straightening up and twitching
her arm away from McDermott's clutching fingers. "He needs
another dose."

"No," McDermott snapped again, still trying to grab Selene's
arm. "He's already had two doses—"

"Listen to me," Selene said firmly, again evading McDermott's
hand. "The patient has Tro-Figree Syndrome. The first dose of
the drug has taken him to perisyn. He needs a second to bring
him through perisyn and back up to metastasis."

I had no idea whether the tech talk Selene was spouting
made any sense at all. But from the look on McDermott's face
as she broke off her efforts to chase Selene away I gathered it
was spot on. "He's already had two doses," McDermott insisted.
"Two six-cc injections, as prescribed. Physician Livicby delivered
them himself."

I looked over at the tall Najik. He was staring back at me,
his short neck hairs standing up with an unnatural stiffness.

It was a reaction I'd seen only once before on any of his species. In that instance, it had been a bounty hunter facing down
a target who he fully expected to kill him. For whatever reason,
it seemed Dr. Livicby was suddenly concerned for his life. And
not just because of the limb he'd just climbed out on for Selene
and me.

I looked down at the invalid, focusing on the arm lying
stretched out in front of Livicby. There were two injection marks
there, all right, one beside the other. Two doses, just like McDermott said.

Only now that I had a suspicion of what he was up to I
could see that one of the punctures wasn't *quite* inside the line
of hairless skin that marked the path of the Najik's vein.

And surrounding that injection mark was the barely visible
outline of a subcutaneous receiver capsule.

Livicby had delivered two doses, all right. But only one of
them had been delivered to the patient. The other had been quietly tucked away for clandestine delivery elsewhere.

I looked back up at Livicby. "I understand you've done as you were instructed," I said, keeping my voice even. "But perhaps this is an extreme case of the disease that will require three doses. One more, if you please."

For a couple of seconds we stared at each other. Then, his stiffened neck hairs smoothed back to their normal fluffiness. I knew what was going on, he knew I knew, and we both recognized that I wasn't going to rat on him. "As you suggest," he rumbled. He picked up one of the hypos the other Najik had laid out and injected the contents into the patient's arm.

This time, he hit the vein properly.

"Done," I said briskly.

"Good," Selene said. She stepped past McDermott—this time, the woman made no attempt to stop her—and again leaned over the patient. "Yes, he's coming back to metastasis. He should recover fully."

"We thank you," Livicby rumbled.

"Glad we got here in time," I said. "I trust your patron will be satisfied."

"He will," Livicby confirmed.

"Good," I said. "So will my patron on Brandywine."

The neck hairs stiffened again for a second, then settled back down.

"Well, then," I said, taking Selene's arm and backing toward the bathroom. "We're going back to our lab to start writing up our report."

"Yeah, hang on," the thug spoke up. "I'll walk you there."

"There's no need for that," I assured him, my carefully crafted mild expression in sharp contrast with my suddenly racing heart. My plasmic was reasonably well hidden beneath my jacket, but the minute I turned my back on a fellow professional he was bound to spot the subtle bulge. "Anyway, aren't you already on duty here?"

"They don't need me anymore," the thug said, starting toward us with deceptive nonchalance. "No, no—don't bother going through the bathroom. There's a door right here."

"Yes, that would be quicker," I agreed.

Except that Floyd and Cole were presumably still waiting in the room on the bathroom's other side. If we left by a different door, they might never realize we were even here.

Worse, I realized belatedly, I'd never found the trick to sending the secret elevator car back down. Unless Mottola and Fulbright had figured it out at their end, they were presumably also waiting, and getting madder at me by the minute.

I was still trying to come up with an excuse to go through the bathroom when Livicby once again came to my rescue. "I fear you are mistaken, Master Kovon," the Najik spoke up suddenly. "We will require your assistance soon to move the table and the patient outside to our vehicle. Dr. Moriarty and Dr. Watson need not wait here to observe the transference."

"Your patient doesn't move until after Mr. Gaheen and your patron have seen him," Kovon countered, his eyes still laser-focused on me. "This way, Dr. Moriarty."

"Certainly," I said, angling toward the room's door and flipping a mental coin. Heads, I take Kovon out right here and now, before he spotted my plasmic, and figure out afterward how to keep everyone else quiet. Tails, I try to keep him on the hook until I find someplace more private to deal with him.

"My patron will accept my word regarding the test," Livicby countered right back again. "As your patron will presumably also accept the word of Dr. Moriarty and Dr. Watson." He looked at me. "Is that not so?"

As my father used to say, *Sometimes when you flip a coin, it lands on the edge.* "I don't see why not," I said. "I believe Mr. Gaheen's office is right down the hall. Let's ask him." I gestured to Kovon. "I presume you'll want to escort us?"

Kovon made as if to say something, apparently changed his mind. "Sure, fine," he said. "Out the door to the left."

"Thank you." He would follow close behind us, I knew, where he'd be in position to spot any suspicious move any of us might make, not to mention having a clear view of my hidden weapon.

But now, with both Selene and a tall hairy Najik to run visual interference, I should be able to keep him from seeing anything.

Sure enough, as we headed toward the door Selene moved in close behind me, in perfect position for her right arm to block Kovon's view of my back. For my part, I made sure to keep both of my hands visible, just in case he was the nervous type.

Gaheen's office was directly across from the room where Floyd and Cole were holed up, with the doors to the building elevator about midway between our room and his. Four more thugs flanked the office door, watching as our group approached but not making any effort to draw any weapons. Probably the fact that Kovon was with us was a big part of that restraint.

But I doubted his pull went far enough to get us past them and into Gaheen's office. Unless Livicby had an additional trick up his sleeve, we were going to end up standing around awkwardly with five armed men who were maybe ten seconds away from spotting my concealed weapon and raining trouble down on us. I eyed the guards as we kept walking, trying to come up with a way to take them down before they could react. Floyd and Cole were lurking right across the hall, presumably ready to assist, and their presence would certainly go a long way toward evening the odds. But without a prearranged signal I had no way to summon them.

We were two steps away when all four guards stiffened simultaneously, as if they'd just received a silent message. A second later the door between them swung open and a hard-faced, elderly man strode out of the office, followed by a slightly graying Najik. The man spotted our group and nodded toward Livicby. "Dr. Livicby," he said briskly, sparing a brief glance at Selene and me. "Dr. McDermott tells us the test was successful."

I felt some of the compression in my chest easing. No need to get in to see Gaheen; Gaheen had come out to see us. Livicby must have known McDermott would signal her boss as soon as the patient had started his recovery and decided to come along and meet his patron when he and Gaheen emerged.

Maybe he was hoping to expedite the patient's transfer so that he could get to the hidden vial of medicine as quickly as possible. Trying to move things along might explain why he'd been willing to run interference for me.

"Yes, Patron Gaheen, he is," Livicby confirmed. "If you wish to see him, he is now out of danger."

"That's where we're going." Gaheen's eyes shifted back to me. "Who are you?"

"He is Dr. Moriarty," Livicby said before I could answer. "He came to observe and assist."

"He *says* his name is Moriarty, Boss," Kovon corrected. "Hasn't proved it. He also says he and the female developed the drug."

"Does he," Gaheen said. His expression hadn't changed, but out of the corner of my eye I saw Selene shift uncomfortably.

"Interesting. Have them wait in my office while I take a look at the patient and we finalize payment." He turned to look at one of the door guards, his eyebrows raised slightly, then turned again and brushed past me without another look.

"You heard Mr. Gaheen," the guard said, beckoning to me. "In here."

Ten seconds later the door closed behind us, and Selene and I were alone in Gaheen's office.

All alone. With no one watching us.

Sure we were.

CHAPTER TWELVE

———— ❖ ————

"How many?" I murmured to Selene as we paused just inside the door.

"Two," she murmured back.

I nodded, looking around at the paintings and art shelves adorning the rare-wood paneling on the walls. A man who would design his mansion with a secret tunnel to someone else's house would certainly not pass up the chance to put in hidden observation boxes to make sure his visitors behaved themselves. Whether or not Gaheen had found the tunnel, he'd certainly found the boxes. "Where?"

"I can't tell from here," she said. "I'd need to walk the perimeter."

"Don't bother," I said. It had been obvious from the outset that Gaheen wouldn't put us in his office without someone watching to see if we'd come here in search of mischief. Where exactly in the room those watchers were located wasn't important. "I just wanted to make sure I wasn't playing my acts of goodwill to an empty room."

Flanking the door were a pair of small display tables holding vases of cut-crystal flowers. Casually, I drew my plasmic and laid it beside the vase on my side of the door, then took Selene's arm and steered us toward the ornate desk and the cushy chairs facing it. "On second thought, go ahead and do a circle or two. See if you can get a baseline."

"All right," she said. "Do you have a plan for getting out of here?"

"Depends on how knowledgeable and cooperative Mr. Gaheen is," I said. "Maybe we can also get some answers before we leave." I nodded toward the lines of wall art and the carved liquor stand set against the wall behind the desk. "Baseline, please."

She nodded, her pupils nervous, and started looking and sniffing her way around the room. I picked one of the guest chairs and sat down, doing some art-appreciation looking of my own but mostly keeping an eye on the walls where the two guards were hidden. Hopefully, my voluntary disarming would encourage them to stay put.

Selene had finished her sweep and taken the other guest chair, and we'd been sitting in silence another five minutes when the door behind us opened and Gaheen walked in. I looked over my shoulder as he walked past the crystal flowers, casually scooping up my plasmic without even breaking stride. He circled around the desk to his chair and sat down, setting the weapon on the desktop in front of him. "So," he said calmly. "Dr. Moriarty, is it?"

"Not really," I said in the same tone. "But I *did* help with the drug Dr. Livicby was testing in there."

"Did you, now," he said. "Since when do bounty hunters have medical degrees, Mr. Roarke?"

So Gaheen was indeed clever, or at least the people he'd put in charge of digging through official data bases were. Good. "We're retired as bounty hunters, sir," I told him. "We're crocketts now. Trailblazers," I added, in case he wasn't familiar with the more colloquial term. "Selene and I are the team who found the sporete that was the basis for the drug you were just testing."

"Where?"

"A planet in the NK-177-D system," I said. "I assume Mr. Varsi mentioned the drug's origin when he gave it to you to pitch to the Najik."

Gaheen's expression didn't change. But I wasn't expecting it to. Faces did what their owners wanted; body aroma, not so much. "Actually, Selene's the real expert at picking out these things," I added, turning my head to smile at her.

And in her pupils I saw the complete lack of reaction that I'd expected. Like Gaheen's face, his scent had also remained unchanged when I dropped Varsi's name.

For me, that was the final confirmation. Time to grab Floyd and Cole and get out of here.

"I'm gratified the drug was so successful," I said, standing up. "With your permission we'll call Mr. Varsi with the good news. Thank you for your time, Mr. Gaheen—"

"Sit down," Gaheen said flatly.

Fighting back a grimace, I did so. "Tell me something, Mr. Roarke," Gaheen said, his voice cooling a few degrees. "Certainly I know your part in the drug's development. Mr. Varsi told me about you, and at any rate I know everything that passes through Huihuang. So tell me this: If you're here to check on the drug, why didn't Mr. Varsi tell me you were coming?" He waved a hand around the office. "Perhaps you'll start by telling me how you got into my mansion without my guards seeing you."

I huffed out a dramatic sigh, mentally crossing my fingers. I'd hoped I wouldn't have to play this card. "My apologies for the deception, sir," I said. "I should have said Selene and I were *mostly* retired from the bounty hunter business."

"Not exactly startling news," Gaheen said, giving my plasmic a sharp tap with his finger for emphasis. "Your target had damn well better not be someone in my house."

"No, sir, not at all," I assured him quickly. "It's a Najik named Villivink who's loosely connected with Dr. Livicby. When we found out Livicby was going to be working the drug test, I thought we might be able to make contact with him and worm out some information. The fact that we also had a unique connection with the drug gave us a tag we could play off of. He and the others haven't left yet, have they?"

"Not yet," Gaheen said. "Not until Yolorist's payment has been fully transferred. You still haven't explained why Mr. Varsi didn't tell me."

"Again, my apologies, sir, but that was at my request," I said. "There were questions about some of the others involved in this test, and I didn't want to take a chance on alerting Livicby."

"And you thought my people might spill information to them?" Gaheen asked, a fresh undertone darkening his words.

"No, sir, not at all," I assured him. "But if they knew Livicby was under special watch someone might have given him a look or made some odd gesture that would have warned him. The person we're after is very astute, and we have to assume he's trained his people to the same standard."

Gaheen rumbled something in the back of his throat. "What's Mr. Varsi's interest in this situation?"

"As far as I know, he's not directly connected," I said, keeping it vague. "But he clearly has a strong interest in the case. Enough interest to give me the back door into your mansion."

Gaheen's eyes narrowed. "Where is it?"

"First floor, southeast corner," I said. "It's a bit hard to describe; I'll show you before we leave. In the meantime, we'd very much like a private word with Dr. Livicby before he and his patron take off. Is there a room nearby where we could talk?"

For a moment Gaheen just gazed at me. I held his eyes, feeling fresh sweat breaking out on the back of my neck. He didn't believe me, at least not fully. But there was nothing in my story he could point an accusing finger at. It would take some long-distance conversations before he could either confirm or unravel it.

As my father used to say, *If you can't get someone to buy your story, at least try to get him to rent it.*

"The room they're in right now would work," I suggested into the silence. "You could clear everyone else out, we could have our talk, and your people could go back to rearrange the furnishings afterward. Or we could let them finish that task and I could talk to Livicby later."

In Gaheen's eyes I caught the subtle flash I'd been hoping for. Some people had a strong aversion to the excuse word *later,* and I'd correctly tagged him as one of them. "You can talk to him now," he said. "There's another meeting room connected to the test room—door's across from my office. You'll use that."

"Thank you," I said, standing up. I paused, waiting for him to order me down again. But apparently this time we were being allowed to go. I gestured to Selene to also stand and held out my hand. "May I . . . ?"

"When you give me your report on Livicby," Gaheen said, laying his hand on my plasmic. "*And* after you show me where you broke into my house."

"Of course, Mr. Gaheen," I said. "I'll go get Dr. Livicby."

"Just go to the room," Gaheen said. "I'll have him delivered to you."

"Excellent," I said, giving him a slightly malicious smile. "Always useful to see someone's reaction when he goes into a room and sees someone he isn't expecting. This shouldn't take long."

"It had better not," Gaheen warned. "I'll speak with you later, Mr. Roarke."

I'd hoped Gaheen had bought into my story enough to let Selene and me go into the other room without an escort. No such luck. As we stepped out into the hall, one of the door guards detached himself from his section of wall and joined us, moving ahead of me to take the knob and open the door. "After you, Mr. Roarke," he said, stepping to the side and gesturing us in.

"Thank you," I said, walking past him. "You can return to your post now."

"Mr. Gaheen wants me to keep an eye on things while you talk to the Najik," he said.

"I asked to speak with the doctor alone."

"Mr. Gaheen decided otherwise."

I felt my lip twist. At least Gaheen wouldn't miss him. While we'd been inside the office the hallway had sprouted another dozen guards, probably summoned to this part of the mansion in preparation for the Najik group's imminent departure. Just one more reason to collect Floyd and Cole and get the hell out of here.

"I understand," I said as Selene and I walked into the room. "But it's a matter of getting Livicby to speak freely."

"I won't say a word," the guard assured me as he walked in behind us and flipped the door closed behind him. "I'll be practically invis—"

I had just a glimpse of Cole stepping into view from his hiding place behind the door, his right arm snaking around the guard's throat, his left hand slapping a gray patch onto his neck on top of the carotid artery. The guard got in about two seconds of useless struggle before sagging abruptly in Cole's arms.

"What the *hell* are you two doing here?" Floyd snapped in a stage whisper from behind me as Cole lowered the guard silently to the floor.

I turned to see him rising from concealment behind one of the chairs. "Mottola and Fulbright needed our help to get the other end of the tunnel door open," I explained.

"So where are they?"

"Still down there," I said. "We came to find you, and then I couldn't figure out how to send the car back down to them."

"Then you're an idiot," Floyd growled. "And now you're stuck here, too. The damn Najik locked the bathroom door on us."

"Not a problem," I assured him. Squatting beside the unconscious guard, I pulled out his keycard and handed it to Floyd.

"Unlock it, then get in the car and get out of here. You too, Cole."

"Like hell," Floyd said, starting toward the bathroom door. "We've got a job to do."

"The job's gone bust," I said, moving to catch up with him. "The hallway out there is full of guards. You won't get two steps."

"Don't worry, we'll make it," Floyd said grimly, not slowing down.

"It's also not necessary," I added. "Gaheen hasn't gone rogue."

That one finally got through. He slowed and turned halfway around to frown at me. "Mr. Draelon said he was."

"Mr. Draelon was wrong," I said.

"Or maybe *you* are," Cole said.

"Fine—assume I'm wrong," I said irritably. We didn't have time for this. "In that case, you're welcome to come back after we collect Dent, the way you were supposed to. Right now, you can't do anything except leave or get yourselves killed. Your choice."

Floyd's eyes flicked over my shoulder to Cole, then lowered to the unconscious guard. Whether he believed me or not, he was smart enough to recognize that with one of Gaheen's people down for the count our clock was ticking. "Fine," he growled. "You two, then us."

"No, *you* first," I said. "Mottola may not be happy if we pop in without you. Anyway, Selene and I have another way out. We'll meet you at the *Ruth*."

Floyd's eyes narrowed. "You're not thinking about running out on us, are you?" he asked, his voice deceptively smooth.

"With Fulbright's lock on the pilot board?" I retorted. "Not a chance."

Floyd's eyes narrowed a little more. "Fulbright put on a *lock*?"

"You didn't know?" I asked. "I assumed you told him to."

"You assumed wrong." Floyd's lip twisted briefly, then he gave a quick nod. "Fine. Come on, Cole."

Floyd unlocked the bathroom door, and we all filed through. The place was still empty, but with Livicby presumably on his way it wouldn't be empty much longer. Floyd popped open the elevator door and he and Cole squeezed into the car. "We'll see you back at the ship," he said, the words as much of a threat as they were an order. "Watch yourselves."

"You too," I said.

Floyd nodded and pushed the proper buttons, and the car started its slow descent. I took Selene's arm. "Get ready," I whispered. The car continued down, cutting off our view of its occupants.

And as their faces finally disappeared Selene and I stepped silently onto the car's roof. I pulled the hidden door closed, and we were once again in darkness.

I felt the brush of Selene's hair on my cheek as she moved her lips close to my ear. "What now?" she whispered.

"We get off at the first floor," I whispered back, touching my left-hand fingertips lightly against the wall moving past us. "It'll be on the fly, but we should have enough time for you to scope it out before we get off. Certainly at the speed this thing makes."

"And then?"

"We walk out the closest door."

I couldn't see her pupils in the dark, but I could imagine the surprise and concern that were undoubtedly there. "You're joking."

"Not at all," I said. "Mottola told us there were around twenty guards, most of them inside. You saw the hallway we just left— there have to be at least fifteen of them already up there, with probably more down the hall watching Livicby and the Najik pack up their gear. Add in a couple more to bolster Gaheen's personal guard, because he still doesn't trust us, and that's most of them. There'll be a few still watching the grounds, but if we get out before anyone finds the one Cole clobbered they shouldn't have any reason to stop us."

"*Shouldn't?*"

"I know, it's a bit risky," I conceded. The texture of the wall changed, and I flicked on my flashlight at its lowest setting. Sure enough, we were passing the second-floor exit. I watched the door move slowly past, counting down the seconds to myself. It would be tight, but we should have enough time to make our exit. "Alternatively, if there are too many people around but there's a place to go to ground we'll see if we can get the car back before anyone comes by."

"I like that one better," Selene said. "Especially since when the alarm goes off the search will probably start near Gaheen's office and work its way outward."

"Rippling its way down here last," I agreed, nodding. As my father used to say, *If you can't duck the grenades completely, at least try to pick a spot between them.* "You know how to call the car?"

"Yes, I think so."

"Okay," I said. "Plan B it is. Coming up on the first floor now. Get your sniffers ready."

I watched the wall; and there it was, the first-floor exit. I crouched down, waiting...and as the door handle came into reach I got a grip on it and gave it a twist. It gave a snick, and I eased it open a couple of centimeters. "You're on."

I looked up to see her face stiff with concentration, her nostrils and eyelashes beating their familiar pattern. The door and handle slowly rose, and I rose from my crouch along with it, wondering what the holdup was. If Selene didn't give me an okay in the next few seconds there wouldn't be time for us to both get out before the literal window of opportunity was gone.

And then, she gave a sharp nod. I shoved open the door with one hand, giving her a push at the small of her back with the other. She stepped up and out of my way through the exit; with literally centimeters to spare, I joined her.

A minute ago I'd wondered what the holdup was. Now, I understood. We'd emerged into a large walk-in pantry, the subdued smells of fruits, vegetables, and spices filling the air around us. No wonder it had taken her a minute to sort through all of it.

I was checking the pantry for exits when Selene stepped behind me, reached into the empty elevator shaft, and pressed her fingers against two spots on the side wall. "It should come back up as soon as Floyd and Cole get off," she said.

"Good," I said, reaching for my plasmic before remembering it was still in Gaheen's office. "Probably be another minute at the least. Feel like a snack?"

Selene's gaze flicked around the room. "No, thank you."

"Because raw rice is a lot tastier than you might think," I said. There were two exits from the pantry, I saw, one into the rest of the mansion—probably the kitchen—the other an armored door that probably led outside.

"I'll take your word for it," she said, her pupils puzzled as she continued sniffing. "Gregory, there's something else in here. Something that smells...I think it's a form of explosive."

I felt a shiver run up my back. "There may be heating tray fuel in here," I reminded her, starting a second visual sweep of the room. "Or stuff for flambé blowtorches."

"This isn't fuel," she said, turning her head slowly. "It's definitely something faster-burning."

I scowled. No wonder Floyd hadn't kicked up too much of a fuss about leaving the job unfinished. He'd stopped in here on his way up and arranged a little backup plan. "Can you tell where it is?"

She pointed toward the armored exit door. "Somewhere over there."

I headed off through the narrow aisles between the shelves. A bomb that was designed to blow the door, maybe? In which case, it might not be so much a backup plan as a diversion. Not designed to bring down the house and kill everyone in it, but something to get the guards looking for an outside threat while the real danger was already inside.

And if *I* was setting such a charge...

There it was, right where I would have put it: a wide, flat blast ribbon slid into the gap under the door, largely unnoticeable until the door was opened, and even then visible only if someone was looking down. I didn't know how big the charge was—there were several different formulas out there—but Floyd was undoubtedly experienced enough to pick one capable of blowing the door off its hinges.

I crouched down, focusing my flashlight on it. The detonator was at one end—a remote, I saw, instead of timer or vibrational. That explained why it was still here: Gaheen's phone blanket would block any activation signals. Carefully, I unplugged the trigger and tossed it behind one of the shelves where it couldn't do any damage, then started pulling the strip itself out. There were a couple of small tears in the protective wrap, I noticed as it came free, which was where the smell had come from that Selene had picked up.

"It's here," Selene stage-whispered. "Gregory? The elevator's here."

"Keep it there, will you?" The strip was wedged pretty tightly, and I didn't dare open the door to make it easier to move. I tugged at it, alternating between one end and the other.

"Gregory!"

All at once, it came free. Rolling it into a bundle, I sprinted back to the elevator. Selene was already inside, her fingers on the controls. I ducked in behind her, pulled the outer door closed, and we started down.

"What are you going to do with that?" she asked in the darkness.

"Well, for starters, make sure Floyd doesn't know I untrapped his booby," I told her, unfastening my left shirt cuff and pushing up my sleeve. There were any number of places where a blast ribbon could be hidden for smuggling purposes, but one of the most common was on the bomber's arm. Smoothing it out, I began wrapping it around my forearm.

"Are you putting it around your *arm*?" Selene asked.

"It's as good a place as any," I said. "And it's safer for me than it would be for most people. Artificial arm, and all that."

"Only if you're holding the arm straight out," she reminded me. "Otherwise, the blast would seriously damage your hip, thigh, and ribs."

"Well, yes, there's that," I conceded as I finished with the wrap and pulled my sleeve back down. "You should probably also make sure to walk on my right side until we get back to the *Ruth* and I can get rid of this."

"Gregory—"

She broke off as light suddenly appeared at our feet. We'd reached the bottom of the shaft and the tunnel. "Don't shoot," I called softly toward the sweeping flashlights. "It's us."

"No kidding," Floyd growled. "What the *hell* was that all about, Roarke?"

"Can we get to the *Ruth* before we have this talk?" I asked, squinting into the glare as the car came to a halt. "And will you get those lights out of my face?"

"Yeah," Floyd said. "About that." One of the lights intensified; and suddenly there was a gun muzzle pressed against my chest. "Whether you two even *get* to the ship is up for grabs right now," he continued, his voice gone deadly. "I want to know why you kept us from doing our job."

"I already told you," I said. "Your job was to take out a rogue member of Mr. Varsi's organization. Mr. Gaheen isn't a rogue."

"And what makes you think so?"

"Point one: He's following all of Mr. Varsi's protocols," I said. "You pointed that out yourself: extra guards, no one present during negotiations except him and the other person, phone shielding that whole time. You don't bother toeing the line when you don't care anymore what your boss thinks."

"He's following those protocols because they make sense," Cole put in.

"Maybe," I said. "Point two: He knew who I was. He recognized that—"

"Wait a minute," Floyd cut me off. "You *talked* to him?"

"Yes," I said. "He recognized my name—"

"How the *hell* did you get to talk to him?"

"He invited me into his office," I said. "You want me to tell this, or not? Thank you. He recognized me as the person who'd found the biochemical basis for the drug that he was selling the Najik. That's probably why he wanted to meet me."

"*You* came up with a drug?" Cole asked skeptically.

"Selene and I are crocketts, remember?" I said. "Finding promising spores and seeds is part of our job. But Mr. Gaheen also knew I was a bounty hunter. More than that, I made sure during our chat to drop a couple of vague hints about working with Mr. Varsi to root out a target involved with this drug sale."

"Though you told him the person of interest was one of the Najik," Selene murmured.

"Which I did deliberately," I said, "because that kind of obvious deflection wouldn't fool anyone. Not someone with a guilty conscience, anyway. The point is that he doesn't have one."

"One what?" Floyd asked.

"Guilty conscience," I said. "I defy anyone who's betraying his boss to sit in a room with a bounty hunter who's on a job and not wonder if that boss is onto him."

Floyd snorted. "Like you could tell? Come on. I've seen Gaheen play poker—his face doesn't give anything away."

"No, *I* couldn't tell," I agreed. "But Selene could. And she did. Selene?"

"There was no reaction from him," Selene said. "No fear, no guilt, not even any concern. Gregory is right. If he'd gone rogue, there's no way he wouldn't have shown *something*."

"And there's one other point," I said. "The drug he was selling was a medicinal one, something for treating a Najiki disease. Yet when Selene and I brought back the sporete Mr. Varsi said that it could possibly be made into a street drug for Narchners. If Mr. Gaheen was looking to maximize his profits—and I figure financing a mutiny is majorly expensive—he would have tweaked the formula and approached a Narchner buyer."

For a moment Floyd was silent. "That it?" he asked.

"That's it," I said, feeling my chest trying to shrink back from the muzzle still pressed against it.

"And we should all just take it on your word?" Cole asked.

"I guess that's up to you," I said.

"I guess it is," Floyd said. "Mottola, you're being awfully quiet."

"Yeah," Mottola said, his voice thoughtful. "Here's the thing. I've seen Selene at work, back when she found the way into this tunnel. I don't know how she does this stuff, but if she says Gaheen didn't react... I think we can believe her."

"And one way or another, we're running out of time," I said. "Gaheen will have found the drugged guard by now, and he *won't* have found Selene and me, and I'm guessing he'll be a mite perturbed. If we need to discuss this further, can we please do it in hyperspace?"

Floyd was silent another couple of seconds. Then, to my relief, the pressure was removed from my chest and his flashlight angled downward out of my eyes. "Fine," he said. "Let's go. But this isn't over." He pointed his light down the tunnel. "You and Selene are in front."

Given how neatly the tunnel access system had reset itself after we were all underground, I'd worried a bit that getting the trapdoor open from this end might be a problem. But the designers had that covered. There was a release handle on the door's underside that unlocked that section of floor and let me push it up out of our way. We all filed out into the ruined building and Cole pushed the door back into place. There was a soft click, and it was once again locked against casual entry.

I'd expected Two Degree Square to be swarming with Gaheen's people by the time we were once again out in public. But either he'd missed a bet or else was slower on the uptake than anyone high up in Varsi's organization had any business being. We made our way through the square to the runaround parking area, grabbed ourselves one, and headed back toward the *Ruth*.

It was as Mottola was guiding us through the outer archway that I spotted a pair of crumpled human figures at the edge of the square, partially concealed by a line of bushes.

Apparently, Gaheen had been every bit as fast and smart as I'd expected. He just hadn't been as fast and as smart as a quietly determined Kalix.

I'd been concerned that clearing out our path might seriously delay Ixil's return to the ship. Fortunately, it took Fulbright a few minutes to unlock the pilot board, after which I had to help

Mottola coax the engines back to full life. By the time we were finally ready to lift, I could see Pax's nose as he lay watching us from behind one of the bridge ventilation grilles. Ixil was aboard, and all was well. Or at least as well as anything could be under the circumstances.

Especially since one of those circumstances was bound to be a fresh search of my clothing and person. I managed to preempt that with a quick trip to the bathroom, where I stripped the blast ribbon off my arm and stuffed it behind one of the ventilation grilles. By the time Floyd had finished his pat-down and sent Mottola to make sure I hadn't hidden any contraband in the bathroom, the ribbon was long gone.

Fifteen minutes later, we were once again safely back in hyperspace.

I'd hoped Floyd would reconsider or even forget his threat to drag me over a few additional coals after the Gaheen debacle. But no such luck. One day into our trip to Gremon, just as I was starting to breathe a little easier, he suddenly hauled me into the dayroom, and with Cole and Mottola sitting silently by he made me run through everything that had happened from the moment Mottola and Fulbright left the *Ruth* on their impromptu rescue mission.

Fulbright himself, I noted, was conspicuous by his absence.

I did as requested, tracing my steps from the *Ruth* to our final reunion in the tunnel. I described everything I saw and everything I did, added in Selene's own observations, and reconstructed conversations verbatim to the best of my recollection.

I did, of course, omit all mention of Ixil and the blast ribbon, which Pix had returned to me in the middle of the night, and which was currently hidden beneath a couple of coils of tubing in my bioprobe prep room prison.

For a few seconds after I finished Floyd just stared at me in that unreadable way of his. I sat quietly, waiting him out, and at last his lip quirked. "I spent part of yesterday looking up what the Spiral data lists have on Kadolians," he said. "You know how much is there?"

"Very little?" I suggested.

"Very damn little," he said. "Where the hell did she come from?"

I waved a hand vaguely. "Around."

"That's not an answer."

"It's all I've got," I said. "I know she's part of a small colony, and that her people move around a lot."

"And can figure out stuff no one else can," he said sourly. "What is it, some kind of telepathy?"

"Mottola already asked me that," I said, nodding at Mottola. "All I know is that I have to be with her for it to work properly."

"It's a para-cohesive baseline," Mottola spoke up.

"A para-*cognitive* baseline," I corrected. "Whether it's true mind-reading or a consolidation of a hundred small factors that most people don't even notice—" I shook my head. "All I know is that it works. If Selene says someone's gone this way or that way, or is calm or nervous, that's the reality of it."

"Yeah," Floyd said. "Still sounds like bull to me."

"Agreed," I said. "But as my father used to say, *One man's bull is another man's grilled dinner.* So are we finally done with this? And don't say *for the moment.*"

"For the moment," Floyd said. "Who is Easton Dent?"

"I really don't know," I admitted. "He found my name somewhere and messaged me a few times wanting to talk about some project or other."

"Something called *Icarus*, maybe?"

"Yeah, that was one of the names he dropped," I said, long practice enabling me to keep my face and voice nonchalant. McKell hadn't *really* given Draelon that name, had he?

No, of course he hadn't. Floyd must have gotten it from someone else.

Nask, maybe? Selene *had* said there'd been a Patth aboard Floyd's ship at one point.

Of course, she'd also said that Patth wasn't Nask. Still, it could presumably be one of Nask's associates.

Assuming sub-directors even *had* associates. The Patth were pathologically secret about their internal politics, but enough details had leaked out over the years that we knew they were nearly as cut-throat with each other as they were with everyone else in the Spiral.

Still, even if Nask didn't have allies at his same level he presumably had subordinates and minions. After all, he was a sub-director. Surely that meant he was sub-director of *something*.

"So what is it?" Floyd persisted.

"What is what? Icarus?" I shook my head. "He didn't go into details."

Floyd grunted. "You don't know a hell of a lot, do you?"

"Not a damn thing, really," I agreed. "That's why I need to meet with him. Something big is on the horizon, and I want to find out what it is."

"Like everyone else, it seems," Floyd said. "Where are you meeting him?"

"A place called the Roastmeat Bar in South Joapa," I said. "Seven o'clock in the evening, local time. I assume you'll all be coming with me?"

"Any objections?" Floyd asked.

"Aside from the likelihood that you'll spook him?"

"We'll be very discreet," Cole promised.

"Not sure how well that's going to work on a paranoid like Dent."

"It's not up for discussion," Floyd said firmly.

"Fine," I said. "Just remember that if he rabbits, you'll be the ones who have to tell Mr. Draelon."

"We'll get him," Floyd said. "All right. It's four days to Gremon. Mottola, you'll look into this Roastmeat Bar place; Cole, you scope out the area around it and find us some good vantage points. You, Roarke, will figure out how you're going to approach him. We'll have another talk the day before we land. Any questions?"

"It's more a requirement than a question," I said. "Selene and I will be approaching Dent together, which means we need to work together to sort out a plan and discuss variants. That means we'll need to do a lot of talking, which means not keeping us apart like you've been doing since Marjolaine."

"Sounds reasonable," Floyd said. "Also sounds wrong. You don't need to talk, because she won't be going."

I felt my eyes narrow. "What are you talking about? I need her there to read Dent."

"No, because you're not reading Dent," Floyd corrected. "All you're doing is picking him up and hauling him aboard the *Ruth*."

I looked at Cole and Mottola. Neither looked surprised by Floyd's announcement. "What if he's got some underhanded trick planned?" I persisted. "We won't know until it's too late."

"In that case, I'm sure Mr. Varsi will give you a nice funeral," Cole said.

"Yes, he's very good at that," Floyd agreed.

"Floyd—"

"Let me make it clearer," Floyd cut me off, his voice gone stiff. "I don't trust you to behave yourself out there. So we're keeping Selene aboard to make sure you don't wander off."

"We could both have wandered off on Huihuang," I reminded him. "We didn't."

"No, and we appreciate that," Floyd said. "But the *Ruth* was locked down, and you told Mr. Draelon that you couldn't approach Dent without it. On Gremon you'll have all your little eggs in the same little basket."

Again, I looked at the other two. But it was clear their minds were made up. "Fine," I growled. "Can I at least ask you not to leave her with Fulbright? I don't trust him."

"No, she can stay alone," Floyd agreed. "Properly restrained, of course. With *our* restraints this time."

"And with the *Ruth* locked down, I assume?"

"Goes without saying," Floyd assured me. "But this time I'll have Mottola handle it. Anything else?"

I sighed. "No, that should do it."

"Good," Floyd said briskly. "Then it's back to your quarters. Cole, keep him company. Dinner's in two hours—Cole will bring it to you."

Three minutes later I was in my bioprobe prep room cell, the hatch closed behind me. Leaving me silence, solitude, and a shredded plan.

Floyd was right. The idea had been for Selene to be with me when we contacted Dent, and for all three of us to then fade rapidly into the sunset. Now, that scenario was off the table.

Or at least, it was going to be a whole lot trickier.

I waited until I was sure Cole wasn't coming back. Then, I settled down beside the floor vent of the *Ruth*'s air system. "Pix?" I murmured. "Pax? One of you tell Ixil that he and I need to talk."

CHAPTER THIRTEEN

———— ❖ ————

South Joapa was the regional capital of Gremon's Midland Township, as well as being the largest city in an otherwise rural and small-town part of the planet. The Roastmeat Bar was near the center of town, in an area that Cole's research laid out as one part government workers, one part government influencers and hoping-to-be influencers, and three parts small-business types cashing in on the presence of groups one and two. Seven o'clock on a Thursday evening was apparently the ideal time to find all three groups running at full bore as the government folks looked for one last chance to indulge themselves before heading out for their three-day weekend, and the influencers and restauranteurs stood eagerly by to provide the necessary indulgements.

I wondered if we might also find some kind of festival going on, as we had on New Kyiv, just to make things louder and more chaotic. But nothing had shown up on Cole's calendar listings. Either Dent had missed a bet or else there just wasn't anything interesting happening in the area right now.

Of course, any large mix of people, money, and liquor also attracted thieves, pickpockets, and outright armed robbers. That was the thought uppermost in my mind as I pulled open the Roastmeat's decorated front door and walked into the dim lighting, buzzing conversation, and alcohol-scented atmosphere. Thieves and robbers; and with my main plasmic in police holding on New Kyiv, my backup weapon with Varsi's people on Marjolaine, and my backup-backup in Gaheen's office on Huihuang, all I had were Floyd's blast ribbon, my flashlight, my info pad, and my phone. Clearly, I needed to invest in a backup-backup-backup.

My phone, especially, I didn't want to lose, given that it was now very much a one-of-a-kind device. Floyd had kept it locked away with our other equipment until we reached Gremon, but Ixil had worked up a specialized plug-in, delivered by Pax a few hours before our arrival, with some exotic programming that I'd now installed into the phone's location interface.

Unfortunately, we hadn't had a chance to test it, which meant we would have to do this without rehearsal. Hopefully, Dent would be willing to cooperate.

Hopefully, he also wouldn't shoot me on sight.

It was still early evening, but the place was already pretty crowded. Most of the tables seemed to be occupied, though not necessarily to full capacity: a lot of couples were sitting at four-person tables, while several singles had laid claim to two-seaters. Floyd, Cole, and Mottola were among the latter group of table hogs, seated at widely spaced positions that together gave them interlocking views of the room, the three official exits, and the bar with its less official doorways into the back. For a minute I thought Fulbright had missed the party, then spotted him sitting at yet another two-seater beside one of the side doors, being even more unobtrusive than the others.

Which made sense. Floyd and his buddies were senior enforcers, their days in the field presumably far behind them. Being a—mostly—former bounty hunter myself, I was painfully aware of how quickly those skills and that mindset could fade.

So why had Varsi sent them on this job in the first place?

Earlier, when I'd assumed I was a person of some value to the organization, it had made sense to send a high-level person like Floyd to hold Fulbright's leash, especially given how relatively low a physical threat I was likely to present. But based on my conversation with Draelon, it sounded like Varsi had now decided that my future would be more along the lines of graveyard filler.

Maybe Varsi had thought that, harmless though I might be, I was sufficiently clever to run rings around any of his usual thugs. Certainly I could do that with Fulbright.

But that was speculation for another time. Right now, my focus was on finding Dent and learning what he knew, if anything, about Icarus.

And before I did that, I needed to find somewhere to sit down so I wouldn't be so conspicuous.

Fortunately, there was still a lone unoccupied table available, tucked near the back between a pair of curtained alcoves set into the wall across the room from the bar. It was a four-seater, but unless I wanted to join Floyd or one of the others it was my only option. I maneuvered my way through the tables and chairs, dodging the various waiters and waitresses scurrying around on their appointed rounds, and finally reached my goal.

Only to discover a flat RESERVED plate lying defiantly in the center.

I came to a scowling halt. So much for that. My best chance now was to see if some group looked like they were packing up and try to get to their abandoned table fast enough—

"No, you're in the right place," came a quiet voice from behind me. "Go ahead—sit down."

"Oh, hello, Dent," I said as cheerfully as I could. This was the second time he'd sneaked up behind me, and I was starting to get tired of it. "I'm rather surprised you actually showed up."

"Ditto," he said. "Did you hear me tell you to sit down?"

"Yes, I did, thanks." I took the last two steps to the table, pulled out one of the chairs, and lowered myself into it. "So what exactly—oh. Nice."

"Thanks," he said, looking down at his outfit. Instead of the classy reversible jacket he'd been wearing the last time we met he was now dressed in black shirt and slacks with a dark blue pocket apron cinched around his waist and a round serving tray tucked under his left arm. The same ensemble currently being worn by the Roastmeat's waiters and waitresses. "A little over the top, you think?" he asked.

"Not at all," I assured him. "It's always good to have a second career lined up in case the first one falls through."

"Actually, this *was* my first career," he said as he set the tray on the table and pulled out a small info pad. "I worked here for two years slinging drinks and veg sticks before I decided I could do better elsewhere. You bring just the three friends?"

So he'd spotted Floyd and the others. "They're more millstones than friends," I told him, wondering if he'd actually missed Fulbright or if undercounting my entourage was a test. The latter, I decided. "The fourth is over by the east exit, by the way."

His lip twitched, just enough to show I'd read him correctly. "So what now?" he asked, making notes on his pad as if he was taking an order.

"Ideally, we shake the watchdogs and get out of here," I said. "The plan is to—"

"Don't bother," he cut me off. "My world; my plan. See that talent tank over there?"

"Talent tank?"

"That curtained alcove thing. Not that one," he added as I started to turn toward the curtain a few meters back from my table. "The other one, over there."

"Ah," I said, shifting my attention to the farther alcove. "You called them *talent tanks*?"

"They're for the bar's entertainers," he said. "Singers, comedians, spiral dancers, whatever. They come on, and if the crowd likes them they push the *up* buttons to keep them at stage level. If they don't, they push the *down* buttons and they get lowered into the basement and their turn's over. Majority rules."

"Interesting," I said. I'd been wondering about the small red and green buttons in the center of the table. "Democracy at its finest."

"Something like that," he said. "Here's the question. Is there one of your babysitters you dislike more than the others?"

"Excuse me?" I asked, frowning. I focused again on the alcove.

And felt my stomach tighten. Visible now, poking a couple of centimeters out from the edge of the curtain, was a thick black cylinder.

The barrel of a gun.

I looked up at Dent. He was watching me closely, still holding his info pad. "You don't want to do that," I said, keeping my voice steady. "Neither does your brother."

His expression didn't change. "My brother?"

"Weston Dent," I said. "Yes, we know about him. The point is that all four of my escorts are former criminal enforcers, they're all armed, and they're too spread out for him to get all of them before they nail him."

"You weren't listening," Dent said, his voice just as steady as mine. "A single shot—one babysitter down—and the others can waste all the ammo or plasma charges they want while he drops into the basement." He gave a small twitch of his head toward the talent tank behind me. "Then, while everyone is screaming and falling all over each other trying to get out, we get into the other tank and leave by the basement door."

"What about the people who'll be hurt or killed in the stampede?"

He shrugged. "Bars are dangerous. So is life. People who want to be safe can stay home."

"Just because life carries risks doesn't mean we should go out of our way to exacerbate them," I said, fighting back the sudden urge to stand up and give this jerk my best gut punch. Of all the callous, sociopathic—

"Uh-oh," he muttered, frowning to my right. "I assume these aren't your friends, either?"

I turned to look. Striding through the west entrance like they owned the place were six Iykams draped in their usual hooded robes. As they cleared the entrance, they split into three pairs, one twosome each angling off toward Floyd, Cole, and Mottola. I looked in the other direction in time to see four more Iykams come in through the east door. One headed toward Fulbright, while the other three made a beeline for Dent and me.

"Damn right they aren't," I gritted out, a sinking feeling in my stomach.

And as of right now, it was no longer a question of whether or not we could risk starting a panic. If we didn't create a diversion, and fast, we would quickly end up dead or Patth prisoners. "We're going to have to—"

"Thanks; I've got this," Dent interrupted. There was a muffled *crack* from the direction of the hidden gunman—

One of the two Iykams who'd been heading toward Floyd jerked and collapsed. There was another *crack*, and his partner joined him on the floor. A third shot, and one of the pair targeting Cole was also out of the game.

But with that, the gunman's luck ran out. The last Iykam's partner had his corona gun out and ready, and from the angle of his hood I could tell he'd spotted the barrel. With a hoarse cry, he leveled his weapon and sent a sizzling blue-white blast into the alcove, turning the curtain into a wall of flame. Someone screamed.

And as if that was the signal everyone had been waiting for, the entire crowd rose to their feet and charged for the exits in a flurry of screams, panicked shouts, and crashing chairs.

"Come on," Dent snapped, starting toward the alcove behind me.

He got one step before I grabbed his arm and pulled both of us under the table. "The *hell?*" he snarled, trying to pull free. "Come on, we've got to get out of here."

"Not yet," I said, tightening my grip. Our table had been near the edge of the crowd, but even so there were plenty of feet thundering past us. "Iykams may be nasty and hateful, but they're not stupid. They saw the first tank, they saw the second, and they saw us. They're going to be watching for us to make a move that direction. *And* with the tank above floor level they'll have a clear view of us over the crowd."

"We can't just sit here," Dent insisted.

"We aren't," I assured him. "Ixil: *go.*"

"*What?*"

"Code word," I told him, pulling out my phone and showing it to him. "See this phone? It's got a locator that my other four non-friends have figured out how to hack into. They know exactly where we are, and they have a whole barrel full of reasons to get to us before the Iykams do."

"So what, you're expecting them to walk us out past them?"

"Not at all," I assured him. "At this very moment, they're scrambling like maniacs through the crowd trying to catch up with us."

Dent's face had turned into a roiling mass of confusion. "What are you talking about?"

"See, we're not hiding under a table," I said. "We're already outside, and we're heading north at a high rate of speed."

For a long moment he just stared at me. The running feet from our vicinity had mostly passed by, but there was still a lot of noise and chaos coming from the directions of the exits. I listened, watching the moving feet, trying to gauge the right moment to make our move.

And then, Dent's lip curled in a wry smile. "You've hacked their hack, haven't you?"

"Exactly," I said. "My partner is currently manipulating my phone's signal to show us charging back toward our ship, exactly the direction everyone will expect us to run." I lifted a finger for emphasis. "But in about a hundred meters we're suddenly going to veer off toward one of the runaround stands and head toward the government field where the *Northern Lights* is parked."

"How did you know about that?" Dent asked, sending me an odd look.

"Your ship, or its parking place?" I shook my head. "Never mind; doesn't matter. The point is that when the Iykams see my babysitters heading that direction...?" I paused, raising my eyebrows in silent invitation.

"They'll all head that same way together," Dent said sourly. "I don't suppose it occurred to you that you've just burned my ship."

"Probably," I conceded. "Sorry about that."

"Never mind the sorry," he growled. "You could have just let them think we were going to your ship and instead left in mine."

"Wouldn't have worked," I said. "For one thing, my partner's still stuck on my ship, and we have to get her off. More importantly, your ship only has two fake IDs and you've already burned both of them. I, on the other hand, have three that haven't been touched."

"Yeah, and how do you know these things about me?" he demanded, his scowl turning into heavy suspicion. "Who *are* you, anyway?"

"You already know that," I reminded him. "I'm Gregory Roarke. No one of consequence, but I have friends."

"A friend named Icarus, maybe?"

"No idea what that means," I said in the distracted tone of someone who doesn't have time for irrelevant conversation. It was easy enough to pull off—I'd been expecting a version of that question since Dent first came up behind me. "You certainly have your share of friends, too."

"What, you mean *them*?" he growled, nodding back toward the noisy chaos. "They're looking for you, not me."

"Actually, they're looking for both of us," I told him. "See, your searches for me managed to catch the attention of the Patth. Iykams are their weapon of choice when they decide to stop being subtle. Stay put while I take a look."

I eased to the edge of the table and cautiously raised my head. There were still a lot of people visible at the exits, but the earlier panic seemed to have faded. A few people were still seated at their various tables, some of them looking dazed while others clutched arms or legs where they'd apparently been injured. But at least there wasn't anyone lying trampled on the floor. With the center area finally clear, two of the bar staff were hurrying toward the still burning curtain with fire extinguishers in hand. Floyd and my other three handlers had vanished, as had the remaining Iykams.

"Looks clear," I said, dropping back down. "You said the talent tank had a secret exit?"

"Not all that secret, but at least no one else should be using it."

"Good enough." I hesitated, but it had to be asked. "What about your brother?"

"Like I told you, he's already long gone."

"Headed to the *Northern Lights*?"

"Headed to wherever I need him," Dent said. "So down the rabbit hole, out the basement, and then a runaround trip to your ship and we're out of here?"

"Basically," I said. "It'll probably be a *little* more complicated, but basically. As my father used to say, *If they think you're stupid, be smart. If they think you're smart, be smarter.*"

"Which of those do they think you are?"

"Not entirely sure," I admitted. "So let's go with the *being smarter* option." I gestured toward the curtain. "After you."

Much of the crowd that had been inside the Roastmeat was still hanging around outside, possibly waiting to see if they were going to be allowed back in. They'd been joined by a fair number of other passersby, some of whom I suspected were hoping to see a major fire or maybe even a few bodies.

At least the Dent brothers had delivered on half of that wish.

We found a runaround and headed toward the *Ruth*. I'd hoped that Ixil's little phone gambit would mean the ship would be clear by the time Dent and I arrived, but I wasn't really expecting it. Accordingly, I made sure to overshoot the *Ruth* by a couple of ships before pulling the runaround to a halt and covering the last leg of the trip on foot.

Sure enough, as we made our way through the shadows toward the *Ruth*'s stern we found a pair of Iykams pacing the walkway in front of the *Ruth*'s main hatch.

"So much for being smarter," Dent muttered as we backed up

into positions behind a pair of shipping crates. "I don't suppose you're armed."

"I've got a blast ribbon wrapped around my arm," I told him. "Not the most versatile weapon in a firefight, unfortunately."

"I'm not even going to ask," he said, drawing a ChasArms 4mm. "Well, at least there's only two of them. Let me give you—"

"Hold it," I said, putting a restraining hand on his arm and pulling out my phone. "Let's see if it really *is* only two." I cranked down the phone's volume, keyed for Selene, and pressed the device to my ear.

"Are you all right?" her anxious voice came back promptly.

"We're fine," I assured her. "I've got Dent with me, and we're about fifty meters down the walkway from the stern and the two Iykams watchdogging the *Ruth*'s hatch. Any idea how many other players are in the game?"

"There are three more," she said. "One between you and the ship, and two hiding near the bow. And one of them is in position to see down the starboard side."

I scowled. So much for my plan to sneak in via our secret rabbit hole. Even if the Iykam wasn't actively watching that side of the ship, we couldn't risk some sound or movement drawing his attention. "What about ship prep?"

"All set," she said. "It's all set."

I nodded to myself, feeling a trickle of relief at the pre-established code phrase. This time, knowing that Mottola would put in another pilot board lock, Ixil had made sure Pix and Pax were in position to witness the code. The *Ruth* was now fully ours again. "When's our lift slot?"

"Twenty minutes," Selene said. "But we can bounce that back if we need to."

I eyed the ship and the loitering Iykams. "Can you bounce it forward any?" I asked.

"*Forward?*"

"Our Pied Piper routine isn't going to fool Floyd and company forever," I pointed out. "The minute they realize they're chasing a ghost they'll be on us like a Texas hurricane. I'd kind of like to be off the ground when that happens."

"How are you going to get to the hatch?"

"We're not."

I gave her a terse rundown of what I wanted her to do.

Watching the change in Dent's expression out of the corner of my eye, I could see he was starting to seriously wonder what kind of lunatics he'd fallen in with. "Can you do it?" I asked when I finished.

"Yes," Selene said. Her voice was calmer than Dent's face; but then, she already knew what kind of lunatic I was.

"How soon?"

"Three minutes?"

"Three minutes it is," I acknowledged. I put away the phone and eased my head up, trying to spot the hidden guard Selene had warned me about.

"There," Dent murmured, pointing along the side of his crate. "By the herringbone-patterned container."

"I see him," I said, nodding. The Iykam was crouched in the shadow of the crate Dent had tagged, corona gun in hand, his hooded face sweeping methodically back and forth as he watched the aft approaches to the ship. "You clear on the plan?"

Dent grunted. "If you call that nonsense you just spouted *a plan*."

"One of my finest," I assured him.

"Somehow, I'm not surprised. Let me know when you want him taken out."

"Yeah," I said hesitantly. I certainly had no more reason than anyone else to be nice to Iykams. But it the plan played out as I hoped, Dent taking out this particular guard would mean shooting him in the back. Not a pattern I really wanted to get used to. "Tell you what. Once the show starts, I'll do whatever taking out is necessary. You stay here, watch for the opening, and when it happens run like hell."

"What about you?"

"Don't worry, I'll be right behind you," I promised. In the near distance, I heard the faint sound of a generator ramping up. "Get ready," I warned, bracing myself.

Five seconds later, the *Ruth*'s portside grav beam erupted into the night.

I'd seen plenty of spaceport perimeter grav beams blast their way through atmosphere. But they were more powerful and with a much wider focus, and they mostly just lifted their target ship and maybe stirred up a little dust.

Not so the *Ruth*'s tighter beam. Suddenly, the air around

the otherwise invisible line was writhing and twisting, grabbing dust and dirt from the ground and adding it to the whirlwind that blasted toward the projector and then splashed outward as the wind roaring in behind it forced the earlier waves out of the beam. It was awesome and mesmerizing, and even though I'd had at least an inkling of what was coming I was still all but paralyzed by the spectacle. God only knew how the Iykams were reacting. A heartbeat later came a loud and high-pitched creaking.

And from a spot a dozen meters past the *Ruth*'s bow a large maintenance cart began rolling along the walkway toward the ship.

"Go," I muttered to Dent. Without waiting for an answer I ducked around the side of my crate and headed toward the Iykam sentry.

I was halfway there when all five aliens opened fire.

I winced as the electrical display joined the windstorm, creating what was essentially our own private mini-thunderstorm. Fortunately, the Iykams weren't shooting at us but at the cart inexplicably bearing down on the *Ruth* and, not coincidentally, bearing down on them.

If I'd given them a moment to think, they might have figured it out. Or maybe they wouldn't have. After all, most civilian ships didn't come with their own grav beams, and the Iykams had no way of knowing that the cart wasn't just a normal collection of machinery and parts but might be a deliberate and targeted attack.

Either way, I had no intention of giving them any more thinking time than I had to. They were still firing uselessly at the cart when I reached the sentry and slammed the edge of my hand against the side of his neck. His knees buckled, and he dropped to the ground.

I turned back toward the ship, scooping up his corona gun as I did so and stuffing it into my belt. I didn't particularly want the damn thing, but I also didn't want to leave it where it could be pointed at me if the sentry recovered faster than expected.

The maintenance cart was still moving, the remaining Iykams blasting at it for all they were worth. One of the shots struck something critical, and a sudden burst of sparks joined in the rest of the visual chaos. Along the *Ruth*'s side, about midway between the hatch and the stern, a narrow ovoid opening had now appeared. Even as I ran toward it, a faint haze of light appeared in the gap, indicating that the inner hatch was now also open.

Around the edge of our earlier vantage point Dent appeared, running madly toward the ship and the opening.

And as I picked up my own pace he leaped from the edge of the walkway, grabbed the edge of the hatch and pulled himself through into the bioprobe prep room.

Someone shouted, and abruptly the corona attack on the sizzling cart faltered. Clenching my teeth, I covered the last steps toward the ship and launched myself toward the opening.

I damn near didn't make it. My right hand caught the hatch edge solidly, but my left only got a partial grip. But even as I scrambled for better purchase, Dent was there, grabbing my wrists and pulling me up and in. I glanced to the side as my feet tried for a foothold on the hull, swore under my breath as I saw the Iykams charging toward me. Dent lost his grip on my left wrist, and for a moment I was hanging by one hand. My left hand scrabbled to regain its grip, and I felt my borrowed corona gun pop out of my belt and disappear into the cradle below me.

And from the spot where we'd been hiding came the barks of two quick gunshots.

One of the Iykams running toward us twisted half around with the impacts and dropped to the walkway. The remaining three abandoned their attack in favor of diving for cover. A third shot rang out—

And then Dent was back, leaning out and reestablishing his grip on my wrist. He fell back into the room, his momentum hauling me bodily through the opening. I fell headfirst through the hatch—

"Selene—go!" I shouted.

I was scrambling to get back to my feet when the *Ruth* lurched upward, the twin bioprobe hatches closing. A moment later the port's perimeter grav beams kicked in, and I once again sprawled on the floor as the ship lurched toward the stars.

"Shouldn't we strap in?" Dent called over the sudden roar of the *Ruth*'s thrusters as he grabbed my arm and hauled me to my feet.

"No straps in here," I called back, brushing past him and dodging out the hatch. "This way!"

Selene was in the pilot's chair when we reached the bridge, her fingers stiff as they worked the controls. "Strap in," I ordered Dent, pointing him to the nav station. "Selene?"

"Trouble," she said, glancing a tense look at me. "An alarm's been triggered. We've been ordered back, and patrol ships are scrambling to intercept."

"Wow," Dent muttered. "Your non-friends are persistent."

"We can compliment them later," I said tartly, my eyes flicking over the board as I searched for inspiration. Selene already had the thrusters running all the way to redline, and the incoming patrol ship formation was rapidly weaving an impenetrable web around us. Unless Ixil could come up with some tweak of the thrusters or cutter array, we were finished.

"Do you think invoking Mr. Varsi's name would do any good?" Selene asked quietly.

"I doubt it," I said. "That would require the badgemen to know who he was, and he's always tried to keep a low profile. Can you angle us back downward and try to lose them that way?"

"It'll cost us too much speed."

"Yeah," I growled. She was right, unfortunately. Besides, the badgemen probably already knew that one. "Well, then..."

"Are you two done?" Dent spoke up impatiently. "Give me comm and I'll get us out of here."

Selene looked at me, and in her pupils I saw that she was as fresh out of ideas as I was. "Fine," I said, reaching over and keying comm to the nav station. "You're on."

"Don't come any closer," Dent snarled.

I twitched. The sudden strength, anger, and intensity in his voice was completely unexpected.

"You hear me?" he continued in the same vicious voice. "Don't come any closer. I have John Foster Brighthunter's daughter Alicia here. You come any closer and I'll start cutting off parts of her. You hear me?"

Selene again looked at me, confusion and question in her pupils. I shrugged and lifted my hands in mute agreement.

Still, if she and I had no idea who Alicia Brighthunter and her father were, whoever was in charge of the pursuit apparently recognized the name. "Take it easy, friend," a soothing voice came back. "No one's going to hurt you."

"Don't give me that," Dent spat. "You say you're not going to hurt me? Well, I *will* hurt Alicia if you don't back off." He gestured urgently toward the pilot board. *How soon?* he mouthed silently.

Twenty seconds, I mouthed back.

He nodded. "Here's what I want. I'll send the Honorable Mr. Brighthunter the details, but you might as well get things started. I want five million commarks in certified bank checks, ten thousand commarks each. They're to be delivered—"

He broke off as a muffled *thump* came from somewhere near the *Ruth*'s stern. "What the *hell*?" Dent shouted. "What the living livid *hell*—?"

The cutter array indicators went green. Selene hit the control, and Gremon vanished behind us as the *Ruth* blasted into hyperspace. "That's it," I announced.

"Yeah." Dent slumped in his seat. "Oh, yeah. That's it, all right."

"If you're worried about the tracer they threw at us, don't be," I assured him. "We stop somewhere, I spacewalk out and pry it off—"

"It wasn't a tracer, you idiot," Dent bit out. "It was glitterpaint. A whole freaking load of *glitterpaint*."

I looked at Selene, feeling my stomach tighten. "I didn't know anyone still used that stuff."

"Welcome to Gremon," Dent muttered.

I looked past him at the nav table, feeling like we'd just been attacked by a volley of blunderbusses. Glitterpaint had been all the rage among badgemen fifty years ago, who saw the ability to permanently tag a ship as the ultimate time-delay weapon against fleeing criminals. The paint itself couldn't be easily removed or covered up, and if the mere sight of it didn't attract a spaceport's official attention it also blazed a low-level radiation that the proper detectors could pick up a hundred meters away.

For a while it had worked just fine. But as was always the case in the struggle between order and chaos, the criminals figured out a way around it. Chemicals that could remove the paint were developed, and some shady entrepreneurs set up dark space stations in the outer parts of key systems where fugitives could come and for a hefty fee be scrubbed clean. The glitterpaint fad lasted maybe fifteen years, then slowly faded away.

At least it had in the main parts of the Spiral. Apparently in places like Gremon, it was still alive and well.

Or maybe it was just poised for a revival. After all, with the private cleaning stations long since abandoned or repurposed and the specialized cleaners all but forgotten, glitterpaint could start serving its original purpose again.

In the meantime, the *Ruth* was now the ultimate in hot potatoes. And if the criminals had forgotten about this gambit, you could bet the badgemen hadn't.

"We need to find a place where we can hide for a while," Selene said. "Do you think we could make it to Bonvere Seven?"

I shook my head. "Not without at least one fueling stop. Maybe two."

"Someplace off the common track, then?" she pressed. "If we can park the *Ruth* somewhere and get to a StarrComm center we can contact"—her eyes flicked to the side—"our friends and see if they have a solution."

"Only if no one sees us come in," I said. "Even if the port command doesn't recognize glitterpaint, you can bet they'll still call it in to the badgemen."

"Fine," Dent growled.

We both looked at him. "What?" I asked.

"I said *fine*," he repeated. "If you two clowns can't—never mind. Can you make it to Popanilla?"

"No idea," I said, reaching past him to punch up the name on the nav table. The location came up—

"Fifty-three hours away," I told Selene, running a quick calculation. "Fuel shouldn't be a problem." I raised my eyebrows at Dent. "Landing, on the other hand, might be."

"It won't," he said, looking distinctly unhappy. "Fine. Set course for Popanilla."

"What's on Popanilla?" I asked.

"I left a stash of stuff there I need to retrieve," he said. "Money, equipment, some—" He paused, eyeing me warily. "Well, nothing that concerns you."

"Things you contracted to smuggle, maybe?" I suggested.

His lip twisted. "Your friends again?"

"The knowledgeable ones, yes," I confirmed. "Don't worry, none of us care how you make your living."

Dent grunted. "Damn decent of you. Fine. Our landing site on Popanilla will be Shiroyama Island."

His lips compressed briefly. "Also known as the Island of the Dead."

CHAPTER FOURTEEN

———— ❖ ————

It was abundantly clear that Dent didn't completely trust us, enough so that he probably would have preferred to stay awake the entire trip to Popanilla. It was equally clear that, after the long evening and the trip to our destination stretching out over two days he didn't have a hope in Hades of doing so.

Selene put together some food—I'd frankly lost track of what meal it was supposed to be—while I went back to my cabin and moved out all of the stuff Floyd had put in there during his brief residency, piling it all in the portside bioprobe prep room. The three of us ate together, and I escorted Dent back to his new quarters. He thanked us rather unenthusiastically for our hospitality and went out of his way to mention that he usually slept lightly and always had his ChasArms close at hand.

He also made sure to remind us that Weston was still out there, and would take a very dim view of events should something happen to his brother.

Selene and I said our own good nights back and returned to the dayroom. I'd spotted Pax lurking in one of the cabin's air ducts, and figured that Ixil would join us as soon as the outrider reported to him that Dent was asleep.

Fifteen minutes later, he did.

"First things first," Ixil said as he fixed himself an enormous meal. "Were you able to find anything on this John Foster Bright-hunter person Dent was threatening Gremon system patrol with?"

"Unfortunately, he's too small a fish to be in any of our data lists," I told him. "Dent says he's a local big shot whose daughter is a known ditwit—sometimes disappears for days at a time. He said claiming we'd kidnapped her wasn't something they could quickly call bull on and could therefore buy us the extra couple of minutes we needed."

"Do you believe him?" Ixil asked, shifting his attention to Selene.

"Yes," she said. "There was no indication he was lying."

"I hope you're right," Ixil said doubtfully. "I find myself thinking about how sociopaths often show no outward or even deep-biological indications when they're lying and wondering how that might affect your own scent readings."

"We've dealt with some pretty sociopathic characters in the past," I pointed out.

Still, he had a point. Selene's ability to read emotions had been tested a lot less often than her more basic tracking skill. And we really didn't know much about our current passenger.

"I'm aware of that," Ixil said. "I just wanted to remind all of us that no system is perfect."

"I know," Selene said. "I would never want a crucial decision to be based on my abilities alone."

"Which are still better than anything else you'll find out there," I said. "I just hope that nothing has actually happened to Ms. Brighthunter. It would be the height of irony if Dent picked a name out of a hat and happened to hit someone who *had* been kidnapped."

"Agreed, on all counts," Ixil said. "We're drawing enough attention as it is without having a kidnapping charge out in the Spiral."

"He says she'll probably pop up again in the next couple of hours," I said, eyeing the mountain of food as he set it onto the table. "You know, you could have told us you needed food down there."

"And you would have delivered it to me in front of Floyd and Cole?" Ixil said around a massive bite as Pix and Pax likewise attacked the plates he'd loaded for them. "But really, we were quite well equipped down there, with no danger of starvation. Meal bars simply become tiresome after a few days."

"Well, enjoy," I said. "This may be your last chance at real food." I turned to Selene. "So what do we know about Popanilla and this Island of the Dead?"

"Popanilla is a colony world," Selene said, her eyes shifting to her info pad. "Shiroyama Island is mainly a resort area, with skiing, hiking, off-shore boating, and some warmsuit diving. There are a few people scattered around the entire island, but the main population concentrations are on the west and northwest coasts. It's called the Island of the Dead because there appears to have been a battle there thousands of years ago that left numerous alien skeletons behind."

"What species?" I asked, craning my neck to look at her pad.

"An unknown one," Selene said. "Most of the remains have been scattered by animals, erosion, and groundquakes, but various scholars have tried making reconstructions." She turned the pad so we could both see it.

"Uh-huh," I said. *Tried* being the key word. There were no fewer than five different drawings on the page she'd pulled up, all of them bipedal and humanoid but otherwise looking completely different from each other. The only thing they had in common was a colored and patterned arm or shoulder band, and even there the different artists couldn't agree which arm to put it on. "I'm assuming we think they were soldiers because of the armbands? Some kind of rank or insignia markers?"

"A reasonable assumption," Ixil said, his voice oddly hesitant. "I find it disturbing that resorts were built on what is essentially a burial ground. But there are still aspects of the human psyche I don't understand."

"Probably comes under the heading of *out of sight, out of mind*," I said, eyeing the shaded area on the map that showed where the remains had been found. All were in the southeast part of the island, whereas the resort areas were on the west and northwest. "If we're not actually walking or skiing on something, we can usually ignore it. Does the island have a proper spaceport?"

"There's a landing field for smaller ships on the northwest coast between Trailhead and Aerie," Selene said, marking the two spots on the map. "Aerie is where the main resorts are, and where the lifts and trams up the mountains to the ski slopes begin. Trailhead's the starting point for the six major hiking paths below the mountains. Mostly the port handles spacehoppers and private ships. For anything bigger you need to go to the mainland." She tapped the pad. "There's also a small StarrComm office between the spaceport and Trailhead."

I nodded. Even on vacation, the rich, powerful, and compulsive still couldn't bear to be out of touch with the rest of the Spiral for very long. Selene and I had nailed a target that way once. "So Dent's either heading for the spaceport to rent or steal a small ship, or he could be planning to call his brother from the StarrComm center to arrange for a pickup."

I raised my eyebrows at Ixil. "Unless you think the portal Selene smelled on him on New Kyiv is here."

"That would certainly be the most convenient from our point of view," Ixil agreed. "But only time will tell."

Selene stirred in her seat, her pupils uneasy. "Something?" I prompted.

"Dent's brother," she said. "There's something about that whole thing that bothers me. People pick up scent traces from everyone they interact with. But Dent...there's no scent on him that stands out more than any of the others. Yet he supposedly interacts regularly with his brother. Certainly they must have been in close contact in order to coordinate their activities at the Roastmeat Bar and then later outside the *Ruth*."

"It *does* sound a little strange," I agreed, looking at Ixil. "Thoughts?"

"If they don't want to be seen together, they might run all their communication through phone or message," Ixil offered thoughtfully. "But you're right, that would have been hard with an impromptu operation like the one by the *Ruth*."

"There's also the possibility they're identical twins," I said. "I don't think we ever established that one way or the other."

"No, we didn't," Ixil confirmed. "Are you suggesting their scents might be similar enough that they blend into one?"

"Something like that," I said. "Selene?"

"I suppose that's possible," Selene said, still looking troubled.

"Well, *someone* out there was shooting Iykams off my back," I reminded her. "If it wasn't Weston Dent, it was a pretty good imitation. So. I guess we follow along, let Dent call the shots, and play it by ear?"

"I have nothing better to suggest," Ixil said.

"Yeah," I said, scowling at him. "You know, we really *did* only sign up to hunt for portals."

"Isn't that exactly what you're doing?" Ixil countered.

"That's not what I meant," I growled. "Never mind. Selene, can you watch the ship for a couple of hours?"

"Yes, of course," she said.

"And can I use your cabin?" I added, belatedly remembering that Dent was ensconced in mine.

"Also of course."

"Thanks." I pulled myself to my feet. "Enjoy your meal, Ixil. I'm going to get some sleep."

It had been a long night, and it looked like the next few days would be equally wearing. Especially as we would be dancing to Dent's tune the whole way.

As my father used to say, *Live and learn, because at some point you may lose the opportunity to do either.*

I could only hope that, at the end, this would all prove to have been worth it.

CHAPTER FIFTEEN

———— ◆◆◆ ————

"There," Dent said, pointing at the forward visual display. "You see it? That gap right there."

"Yes, I see it," I growled. I saw the narrow opening in the rows of trees, all right. I also saw that it was way smaller than any landing pad I'd ever tried to put the *Ruth* down on. Not to mention that the whole thing was lined with spindly evergreen trees that would be trying to grab and unbalance the ship the whole way down.

But this was the last of the three small clearings Dent had offered, and we couldn't doodle around up here forever. The only other option was to admit defeat, fly up to the Aerie Spaceport, and hope that no one noticed the glitterpaint currently adorning the *Ruth*'s butt.

And I had no intention of admitting defeat. Not in front of Selene and Ixil. Certainly not in front of Dent.

"Go back to the dayroom and strap in," I ordered him. "Selene?"

"No signs of ships or aircraft," she reported from the nav station, where she'd taken over sensor duty. "Popanilla has three multipurpose satellites, but none of them are in position to see us."

And that lack of a full overlap probably didn't occur very often. It was now or never. "Okay," I said, hunching my shoulders and resettling my fingers on the controls. It could be worse, I reminded myself as the forest rushed up toward us. I could be down in the service crawlway like Ixil, blind and deaf to what was happening, and squarely in line to be the first casualty if it all went diagonal. "Here we go."

After all the sweat, prep, and mental drama, the landing itself was actually rather anticlimactic. Between the main thrusters in the stern and the maneuvering jets at the bow, I was able to ease the *Ruth* to a mostly stationary stop over the gap, and a little more fancy footwork and we were down. Not quite as smoothly as I'd liked, but not nearly as crushing as I'd feared.

"Welcome to Shiroyama Island," I said as I shut down the ship's systems to erase our electronic signature and prayed that the thrusters' residual heat would burn away fast enough to keep some wandering IR detector from spotting us. "What now?"

"We head out," Dent said from the bridge hatchway. "It's a good two-and-a-half day march to Trailhead, and most of that will be through virgin forest. The sooner we start, the better."

"What about this stash of yours?" I asked.

"We'll pick it up on the way to Trailhead," he said. "Let's break out the camping gear and get moving."

I made a face. *Camping gear*: the odds and ends from the *Ruth*'s stores that Dent had repurposed. Thin flexible tubing in lieu of rope, clamps in lieu of crampons, spare bracing struts in lieu of walking sticks, mesh bags and tool pouches in lieu of backpacks. But it was better than nothing.

"Phones?" Dent prompted.

"They're in the dayroom," Selene said. "Batteries and data chips removed."

"Good," Dent said. "They won't be any good for most of the trip anyway, and even turned off they could still be tagged by badgeman scanners. Roarke, you're lugging the food. Feel free to grab a mule if we happen across one."

"Funny," I grunted. Dent had planned our food supplies based on his two-and-a-half-day estimate: eight food bars total for each of us. He'd gone light on water, doling out a single liter bottle each, assuring us there were innumerable creeks and streams flowing from the snow-packed mountains at the island's northern end.

But I'd seen the terrain we were passing over as I headed for our landing site, and as my father used to say, *If you're going to err, err on the side that doesn't leave you hungry or shot.* Ignoring

Dent's condescending disdain, I'd packed an extra day's worth of food bars for each of us, plus an extra liter of water.

I also packed all the cash and certified bank checks we had aboard, and made sure Floyd's blast ribbon was secured around my arm under my sleeve. We had no idea what we were heading into, and it was never a bad idea to have a diversion ready at hand.

It was even more useful to be armed. Unfortunately, the only weapon we had left was Dent's ChasArms 4mm. "I can also carry your gun if you want," I offered. "There's a perfect spot for it in with the meal bars."

"I'll bet there is," he said, making a point of snugging the weapon a little more solidly into his holster. "Come on—we're burning minutes."

Three minutes later, we were on our way.

It was still two hours until local sunrise, which meant that for the first hour our route would be lit only by Popanilla's two small moons and whatever starlight could get through the trees, augmented by the microscopic glow levels Dent was willing to allow for our flashlights. I had my night-vision monocular, but out here in the wilderness even its tiny electronic signature might be detectable, and Dent had forbidden me to use it except in case of emergency. That meant a slow pace and a fair amount of stumbling, but he was insistent that we get on our way as soon as possible.

On this one I had to agree with him. No matter how stealthy our approach and landing had been, there was no way it would remain unnoticed forever. The farther away we were when curious badgemen swooped in for a closer look, the better.

Especially since we were heading northwest, roughly in the direction of Trailhead and Aerie. Our hope was that the badgemen would look at a map of the island, note that the surfing and wavewatching resorts directly to the west were only two hours away by foot and the largest boat tour and warmsuit diving center directly east only four, and concentrate their efforts in those directions. The farther and faster we could move out of those search zones, the better.

Like the landing itself, the first stage of the hike turned out to be easier than I expected. There was plenty of underbrush, but there weren't a lot of big stones or other obstacles, and the local trees mostly kept their roots underground where they belonged. About an hour into the trip, with still an hour to go before sunrise, the sky to the east began to lighten, and from that point on the trip became almost easy.

Until, that is, the terrain started to slope upward.

"I swear, you two are in the worst shape of anyone I've ever seen," Dent grumped at us during the third of our rest stops, this one taking advantage of a downed tree that was just the right height for a human butt to park on. "Don't you ever get any exercise in fresh air?"

"We're crocketts," I grumped right back at him, wincing at the aches in my thigh muscles. "Our whole job description is to fly to unexplored planets, collect bio samples from the air, then go on to the next one. Not a lot of call in there for traipsing through alien forests."

"You're still listed as bounty hunters. I'd think that would get physical every now and then."

"Most hunter targets don't hide out in the boonies," I said. "And all your better cities have cabs and runarounds. We also try very hard to get the restraints slapped on *without* chases or running gun battles."

"Was hiding out the reason you were here?" Selene asked.

"Of course not," Dent said. His voice was even, but I could see the sudden wariness in his eyes. "What makes you think that?"

"You seem to know the place quite well."

"Comes of a year of working it," Dent said. "I already told you there were a lot of high-end tourist places on the island. I worked out of Trailhead as a hiking guide."

"Picking out which of those high-end tourists to rob?" I suggested.

He gazed coolly at me. "Considering that you're currently traipsing through an alien forest without a single clue as to what you're doing, I'd be a little less antagonistic toward your trail guide if I were you. There's a hell of a lot about Shiroyama Island that you don't know."

"There's a hell of a lot about Patth and Iykams that *you* don't know," I shot back. "How about we work together toward the goal of all of us walking out of here alive and with all our current limbs intact?"

He snorted a laugh. "Right. Yeah, okay. I guess you've got a point."

There was a sudden soft rustle in the underbrush off to the

side. I started, peering that direction, but Dent just gave another laugh. "Relax, Roarke, there aren't any big predators on the island."

"What about small predators who hunt in packs?" I countered gruffly. I was pretty sure I knew now what the sound had been, but I'd already reacted nervously and it seemed best to keep the act going for the moment.

Sure enough, two meters past the spot where I'd heard the noise, Pax's bright eyes appeared briefly through the weeds before he darted out of sight again. Ixil had followed us, as I'd expected him to, and was using his outriders to monitor our progress and, presumably, record our conversations for playback once they were back on his shoulders and reconnected to his nervous system.

I just hoped he'd warned them to stay out of sight. If Dent really *had* spent a year here, he would certainly know which animals were native to the island and which weren't.

"Oh, don't go all dramatic on me," Dent scoffed. "You want to see the worst packs Shiroyama has to offer? Fine. Pull out one of those pointless meal bars you packed, will you? Make it one of the dark chocolate ones."

I dug out the requested bar, resisting the urge to tell him that they were *not* pointless and that if he got lost or injured he'd be damn glad I'd brought them. "You suddenly need a snack?" I asked sarcastically.

"*I* don't, no," Dent said. "Peel off the wrapper, then shred the top of the bar between your fingers and scatter the crumbs on the ground over there."

I frowned at Selene, got an equally puzzled look in return, and did as requested. "If we end up with short rations, by the way, that was one of yours," I warned him. "What exactly—?"

And with a flurry of flapping wings, the forest around us exploded in birds.

They were small birds, I saw after that first brain-freezing second: brown and sparrow sized, the sort that some people call songbirds. No talons, no sharp beaks, basically harmless to anything that wasn't a seed or a bug. But in that first surge of adrenaline, as they swarmed around and past me, it was like someone had kicked over hell's own birdcage.

A second later the chaotic flow was over, and thirty or more of the things were on the ground, busily scarfing up the crumbs I'd unwittingly tossed to them.

"Fun, aren't they?" Dent asked with a blandness that didn't even try to hide his satisfaction at my reaction. "They're called *sugarbirds.* Love anything and everything that contains earth-based sugars. If you're planning a picnic on Shiroyama Island, make sure to leave the sweet tea and desserts at home."

"Or else bring enough to share," I muttered, watching the birds in fascination. It reminded me of the times when I was a child when a colony of ants had found some melted ice cream or a dead grasshopper and were putting every bit of communal effort into collecting everything their little pincers could carry. Here, though, there was more competition than cooperation. The birds were standing wing to wing, jostling for position as their heads bobbed up and down.

And then, as abruptly as they'd arrived, the whole flock lifted into the air again, splitting apart and darting madly off in all directions. Five seconds later, it was as if the whole thing had never happened.

Except that half my meal bar was now gone.

"You mean like bringing one cake for you and another one for the birds?" Dent shook his head. "Doesn't work. You bring more sugar, you just get more birds."

"And you'd know this how?"

"It was a great way to entertain my trail clients," Dent said. "Good opportunity for pictures, and makes a great story to tell the folks at home afterward."

I felt a sudden tightening of my throat. *Pictures...* "Except that it all happens pretty fast," I said, keeping my tone casual. "By the time they have their phones or cams out, all the fun stuff is over."

"Only half of it is," Dent said, sounding suddenly cautious. "They can catch the eating and the exodus."

"They'll still miss the mad arrival, though," I said. "Or will they? Selene, get your cam out, will you? Let's see how much of it you can get."

"We're wasting time," Dent said, getting abruptly to his feet. "Come on, we need to get moving."

"This'll just take a second," I soothed. The remnant of the meal bar was still clutched in my hand, sheathed in the wrapper I'd reflexively twisted back around it when the birds appeared. I waited until Selene nodded that she was ready, then broke the bar in two pieces, crushed a section in either hand, then tossed the crumbs to my sides.

For a moment nothing happened. I saw Selene's nostrils and eyelashes working as she tried to smell the birds' arrival.

Then, but only because I was listening for it, I heard the faint fluttering sound warning that the scavengers were on their way. The sound ramped up, and two seconds later they were there, the swarm dividing in half to attack the new heaps of crumbs. A minute later they were gone, and all was again quiet. "Did you get it?" I asked, looking at Selene.

"Yes, but not very well," she said, turning her cam around to show me. "They're too fast for the camera's lens speed to handle."

"So I see." She had indeed caught the incoming swarm, but the picture was so blurry you could barely make out what was happening. "So even a second showing isn't going to do most people any good. Not unless they specifically reset the camera's speed."

"Yes." Selene looked up at Dent, who was still standing. "Or unless someone else has good photos from an analog-type camera to sell them."

I saw a subtle movement in Dent's throat. Maybe he was remembering that the photo of the dead man he'd shown us had been taken with precisely that kind of camera. "You make it sound like I'm cheating them," he said, his voice low.

"Not at all," I assured him. "I've worked in the entertainment and service industries. Upselling your customers is how you make the gig worth it. Offering them pictures they didn't know they wanted is a lot cleaner than a lot of angles I've seen people run."

"So glad I've got your approval," he said acidly. "If you're done playing games, we've still got a lot of ground to cover, and we're already behind schedule. Keep up or I'll leave you behind."

"Not a problem." I stood up, suppressing a groan as my legs again took loud exception to the change in position. "We'll just wait for you to open a meal bar and follow the birds."

"Funny," he said with a grunt. "Let's go."

Dent had said it was two and a half days to Trailhead. But at the rate Selene and I were going—certainly at the rate Dent's complaints suggested we were going—it was clear we were falling further and further behind that schedule.

The sun was touching the top of a ridge to the west, and Dent was looking for a place to bed down for the night, when we topped a small rise and he peered back along our route. "Uh-oh," he muttered. "Say good-bye, everyone."

I followed his line of sight. In the distance, midway down the slope we'd been climbing all day, I could see a trio of small aircars slowly circling a section of the forest. "That the *Ruth*?" I asked, a lump forming in my throat.

"Yep," he said, shading his eyes from the glare from some snow-covered peaks on the eastern horizon. "Those are too small to be tugs, and there are too many to be any of Popanilla's small-time crime bosses. Process of elimination leaves the badgemen."

I scowled. Who would of course spot the glitterpaint and send out a flurry of queries to every corner of the Spiral.

We'd already been down two bioprobes, and now we were down a whole Trailblazer ship. I tried to imagine what Admiral Graym-Barker would say, but my weary imagination wasn't up to it.

"What's that?" Selene asked.

"It's your ship," Dent said with exaggerated patience. "Pay a little attention—"

"No," Selene interrupted, pointing toward the ground in front of us. "*That.*"

I looked where she was pointing. In an angled cut of dirt where erosion had sliced away part of a small mound, I could see something metallic glinting in the last light from the setting sun.

"I'll be damned," Dent said, stepping over and digging a short cylindrical object out of the dirt. "Remember all the alien soldiers who supposedly died here?"

"Yes," I said, staring as he held it up. "Is that...?"

"One of their armbands," he confirmed. "Congratulations," he added as he walked back to us and handed it to Selene. "You're now officially a couple thousand commarks richer. These things go like straw in the wind on the collector market."

"Sounds great," I said, watching as Selene gently brushed off the remaining dirt, her eyelashes again fluttering. "Maybe we can use it to get the *Ruth* out of impound."

"You sell it here and you'll only get a fraction of what it's worth," Dent warned. "The real market is with spoiled billionaires who already have one of everything else."

"Even better," Selene said. She admired the armband a moment, then put it away in the tool pouch around her waist. "Would you be able to introduce us to one of them?"

"Possibly," Dent said. "What's in it for me?"

"What do you want?" I asked.

He looked me straight in the eye and visibly braced himself. "I want Icarus."

I looked past him at Selene. Her pupils were wary and warning. "Why?" I asked.

"I'm getting sick of your evasion, Roarke," he growled. "Do you know him, or don't you?"

"Still waiting to hear what your interest is."

"Yeah." He took a deep breath, huffed it out. "Never mind. You keep your secrets, and I'll keep mine." He turned his back and stalked off into the trees. "Let's find a place to camp. The trickiest part of the walk starts tomorrow, and I plan to be asleep by nightfall."

Five minutes later we found a sort of hollow spot in the ground filled with matted leaves and mosses that Dent declared would be adequate for our needs. We'd brought some spare blankets with us from the ship and set about making the best sleeping pads we could. It was quickly clear, though, that we were in for an uncomfortable night.

My suggestion that we name our temporary home Sleepy Hollow went ignored.

Dent was clearly an old hand at this. While Selene and I were experimenting with blankets, jackets, and piles of leaves, he got himself organized, scarfed down his meal bar and a couple of chugs of water and was wrapped up ready to sleep well before the last light left the western sky. I lay down on the other side of Sleepy Hollow and waited, eyes open, for the inevitable.

Sure enough, fifteen minutes after Dent's breathing settled into the slow rhythm of sleep, a small rodent nose prodded insistently into my ribs. I sat up, saw that Selene was still awake, and motioned for her to keep watch on Dent. Stifling the groans that my whole body was urging me to voice, I got up and headed into the forest as quickly and quietly as my stiffened muscles would allow.

This, I told myself blackly, had better be good.

Ixil was sitting in a stand of thick trees, his back resting against the largest of them. "How are you and Selene holding up?" he asked softly as I reached him.

"Tired, aching, and looking forward to a good night's sleep," I said, wincing some more as I eased myself down beside him. "This better not be you asking if I'll swap meal bars with you."

"It isn't," he said. "Three things. One: The badgemen have located the *Ruth*."

"I know," I said. "We saw them circling over it earlier."

"Interesting," he said. "I didn't realize you would be in sight of it. My information came from the official comm channels."

"Didn't know civilians could access those."

"They can't," he agreed. "Two: that armband you found. Is it really as valuable as Dent claims?"

"There was no indication from Selene that he was lying," I told him. "If the history of the island is accurate, I can see that kind of artifact being reasonably rare. What are you getting at?"

"If it's that valuable, I'm wondering why Dent didn't make more of a fuss about ownership," Ixil said. "Just giving it to Selene strikes me as odd."

"Oh, that one's obvious," I told him. "He's planning to steal it."

Pix and Pax, crouching on Ixil's shoulders, gave one of their little synchronized twitches. "You think so?"

"You said yourself he should have made a fuss," I reminded him. "Oh, it won't happen tonight. He won't take it until he's ready to ditch us and get out of here. Probably tomorrow night."

"I hope he's not planning to leave via the Aerie Spaceport," Ixil warned. "Because that's bit of news number three. Floyd and the others are here."

I felt my eyes widen. "You mean here on Popanilla?"

"I mean here on Shiroyama Island," Ixil said grimly. "They put down at Aerie about six hours ago."

"And I doubt they're here for the skiing," I growled. "*Damn* it all. I was hoping we'd lost them."

"Unfortunately not," Ixil said. "Thoughts?"

I scowled into the darkness. It would just be our luck to march out of the wilderness and straight into Floyd's arms. "Any idea where they are now?" I asked. "Dent suggested that the badgemen might start with the warmsuit and surfing areas east and west of the *Ruth*. If he was right, maybe Floyd elected to tag along and see if they would flush us out for him."

"It would certainly be convenient for us if he was looking the wrong way right now," Ixil agreed. "And yes, that appears to be where the badgemen have begun their search. Unfortunately, I don't know about Floyd and his group. It's even possible they've split up."

"That *is* how Fulbright organized the search for us on Marjolaine," I conceded. "Each of them watching one of the likely StarrComm centers."

"And we saw how well that worked for them."

"Only because Mottola wasn't ready for me," I said. "They'll be more on their guard this time. We really need to know where they are before we leave the forest."

"I'm sorry," Ixil said. "I can't access private phones, and there's been nothing about them on official channels since the *Northern Lights* landed."

I frowned through the darkness. "They came in the *Northern Lights*? How do you know it's them?"

"I sent them there when they thought they were chasing you on Gremon, remember?" Ixil said. "Who else could it be in that ship?"

"Maybe Easton's brother Weston?"

"I thought he was guarding your backs outside the *Ruth* when Floyd reached the *Northern Lights*."

"Yes, he was," I conceded. And of course the news of that melee would have been blared all over the official badgeman comm system. If Floyd was monitoring it—and as one of Varsi's senior enforcers I had no doubt he had the same kind of illegal access that Ixil did—he would have known instantly that he'd missed us and started working on a new plan. The *Northern Lights* sitting empty right there in front of him was the obvious solution. "So the *Ruth* is gone, and the *Northern Lights* has been commandeered. Popanilla is starting to feel a little claustrophobic."

"A bit," Ixil conceded. "But there are still options. If I can get to the StarrComm center I can have the admiral send a ship for us. The question then would be whether we can go to ground until it gets here."

"Just as well that I brought extra food," I said. "There is, of course, another possible option. If the portal Dent found is here on Shiroyama, and if we can get to it, we can blink out of here."

"That not only assumes the portal is here, but that it's operational," Ixil warned. "*And* that Dent knows where it is. Remember,

Selene said the scent she detected on him was faint. If he touched it without recognizing its significance, he may genuinely not remember where it is."

"Then why was he searching for the name Icarus?" I countered. "Okay, yes, I know he thinks Icarus is a person, but still. And why is he searching for *me*?"

"That does unfortunately remain a mystery," Ixil agreed.

"And it's got plenty of company," I said. "Anyway, thanks for the heads-ups. I'd better get back before Dent wakes up and notices I'm gone. Keep an eye out, and watch yourself."

"I will," Ixil said. "Though as Dent said, there don't appear to be any dangerous animals on the island."

"Maybe, but something like those sugarbirds could still make life unpleasant," I pointed out. "Dent says we'll have one more night on the road. I'll try to check in with you tomorrow after he's asleep."

"I'll send Pix to guide you to me," Ixil said. "You be careful, as well. Remember that Dent himself might be the biggest danger in this forest."

"That thought had not escaped me," I said. "Sleep well."

Selene was still awake when I got back to camp. She caught my eye as I passed the last line of trees and twitched her fingers to beckon me over. Stepping carefully through the matted leaves, I eased down beside her. The ground on her side of Sleepy Hollow was just as lumpy as on my side. "Dent still asleep?" I whispered.

"Yes," she whispered back. "What did Ixil want?"

I gave her a quick summary of our conversation. "It sounds like he doesn't think the portal is here," she said when I'd finished.

"I really don't know *what* he thinks," I said. "*Or* what he knows. *And*—well, never mind," I interrupted myself, suddenly wondering if I should even bring this up.

"Are you thinking that Ixil or someone at Icarus might have been the one who told Floyd where we'd gone?"

I made a face in the dark. I really needed to stop forgetting she could think as fast and twistedly as I could. "I know it sounds crazy," I said. "But if Graym-Barker wants to force Dent to use the portal—assuming Dent even knows how to do that—closing off all other exits from the island would be one way to do that. *If* the portal is here."

I felt the warm breath of her quiet sigh on my cheek. "It is."

I pulled away far enough to turn my head and stare at her. In the darkness, it was a complete waste of effort. "You sure?"

"Yes," she said. "It was only after you left—after the breeze shifted to the north—that I was sure the scent was coming from the portal and not Dent or something he was carrying."

I pursed my lips, visualizing the map of the island. North... "So somewhere up in the mountainous part? Maybe tucked away at the edge of a glacier or under a snowpack or something?"

"Those areas are fairly well traveled by the skiers," she pointed out. "I think it more likely to be in one of the scree fields between here and there."

"Makes sense," I agreed. There were at least three major rock fields and five minor ones below Shiroyama's ski areas, fields that shifted a bit every time a tremor or groundquake ran through the island's fault lines. "I was wondering how everyone could have missed a big chunk of alien metal sitting out in the open."

"The last groundquake was eight years ago," Selene said. "That may have been when the rock shifted enough to make it accessible."

"Long after the island had been mapped and surveyed," I said. "If it wasn't in any of the areas everyone had decided were worth traveling to, no one would ever notice it was there."

"The question then would be how Dent found it."

I thought about the picture of the dead man he'd shown us on New Kyiv. "Maybe he had help," I said. "But that's a question for another day. Better get some sleep—tomorrow's likely to start very early."

"I will. Sleep well, Gregory."

I made my way back to my own spot and eased tired muscles back onto my blankets. Dent didn't really strike me as a killer, and there were a dozen perfectly reasonable explanations as to why he'd been carrying a picture of a dead man.

But I'd been wrong about such things before. So far none of those lapses had gotten me killed, but there was always a first time for everything.

And as my father used to say, *When in doubt, doubt.*

CHAPTER SIXTEEN

———— ❖ ————

Morning did indeed start early. An hour before sunrise, to be exact.

And not just early, but quick. From the time Dent prodded us awake to our departure from Sleepy Hollow was no more than ten minutes.

The day was basically a duplicate of the previous one. We tromped through the grass, avoided trees and the occasional vine tangle, paused whenever our muscles and joints demanded, and endured Dent's complaints about our lack of woodland skills. The ground continued the gradual uphill slope it had started the middle of the day before, but now it had also become more undulating, with lines of small ridges and the occasional hill. We endured the former and, mindful of the possibility of aerial surveillance, avoided the latter.

It was early afternoon when we reached the edge of the first scree field.

"Impressive, isn't it?" Dent commented as we skirted the edge, staying under cover of the trees as much as we could. "The geologists figure a series of groundquakes a few hundred years ago ripped off the side of Mount Traxx and sent it shattering downhill. That big rock pile is the result."

"There are several of them, aren't there?" I asked.

"Eight to ten, depending on how you count them," Dent said, giving me an odd look. "You an amateur geologist?"

"No, just a very amateur hiker," I said. "When you said we were going to be walking from wherever we parked the *Ruth* I made a point of checking out all the places I wanted to avoid. The scree fields were one of them. Or eight to ten of them, depending on who's counting."

"We won't have to cross any of them, will we?" Selene asked, her pupils wary as she gazed at the rock field.

"In those shoes?" Dent asked scornfully. "You'd better hope to hell not. You really need to start carrying some real survival gear in your ship. You have to do a hike like this again without a guide and you'll be toasted wheat."

"Did you see a lot of free space on the *Ruth*?" I countered. "Bedrolls, travel mattresses, and backpacks take up a lot of room."

"You're thinking like a tourist," Dent said. "Do what the professionals do: Skip the bulky stuff and go with some mesh hammocks, collapsible shoulder bags, multitools—that sort of thing."

"I'll keep that in mind," I said, "the next time we bring aboard someone wanted by the Patth."

A flicker of emotion crossed Dent's face. "You think the Patth are after me?"

"You saw all those Iykams," I reminded him. "As far as I know, the Patth are the only ones they work for. So what did you do to them?" I tilted my head. "Or what do you have that they want?"

He locked eyes with me. "I'll talk to Icarus," he said. "No one else."

I hesitated. I could make that happen, of course. All I had to do was take Dent to the Aerie StarrComm center and punch in my Icarus Group contact number. Graym-Barker would be furious, but depending on what Dent could tell him that anger would probably blow over.

Assuming he actually knew anything. That still hadn't been established. "Fine," I said. "But I can't walk you in cold. I need some idea what it is you're sitting on."

For a moment I could see an echo of my own hesitation. He wasn't any more trusting of me than I was of him. I waited, cultivating my patience.

And then the mask went back up. "I'll think about it," he said, turning away and continuing along the edge of the scree field. "And no, we won't have to go across the rocks. Come on—we need to pick up the pace a little."

The second part of the day went pretty much the way the first part had, except that now we had the additional challenge of avoiding the increasingly frequent rocks as we kept close to the edge of the scree field. Finally, as the sky began to darken, Dent found us another more or less comfortable camping site. We made our individual sleeping arrangements, ate our last meal bars of the day, and settled in to sleep.

Or Selene and Dent did. Once again, I instead settled in to wait for Ixil's summons to compare notes and plan for our imminent arrival at Trailhead.

Or so went my plan. Unfortunately, I hadn't counted on two solid days of unaccustomed exercise separated by a too-short night's sleep. One minute I was focused on the sound of Dent's breathing; the next, I was startled awake by a hand shaking my shoulder. "Gregory, wake up," Ixil's voice murmured in my ear.

"I'm awake," I murmured back, blinking my eyes furiously to drive the sleep out of them and propping myself up on one elbow. If Dent woke up and saw Ixil leaning over me—

I muttered a curse. No fear of Dent seeing Ixil, because Dent was no longer here.

"Yes, he's gone," Ixil confirmed. "My fault—I hadn't expected him to leave so soon, and so hadn't instructed Pix to return to me immediately when he did."

"How much of a lead does he have?" I asked, looking over at Selene. She was awake now, too, her nostrils and eyelashes sampling the air.

"Nearly an hour," Ixil said grimly. "I know the direction he took"—he pointed in the direction we'd been going before we bedded down for the night—"and I've sent Pix and Pax after him. But they have to tag-team in order to keep us informed. Depending on how fast he travels we may not be able to catch him."

"Do we *have* to catch him?" Selene asked. "I assumed we were mostly interested in the portal."

"*If* the portal is here," Ixil warned. "We still don't know for sure."

"Yes, we do," Selene said, pointing in a direction a few degrees off the one Ixil had indicated. "It's that way."

I wasn't all that good with Kalixiri expressions. Even so, Ixil's surprise was pretty obvious. "It *is* here?" he asked.

"Yes, and very close," Selene assured him. "No more than a kilometer away. I can take us there right now if you'd like."

"Absolutely," he said. "Pack whatever you need and we'll go." He stepped past me to Dent's former sleeping spot and pulled a slip of paper from beneath a stone. "Oh, and he left you a note. Pix saw him writing it."

"What does it say?" I asked, cinching up the pack with the rest of the meal bars and slinging it over my shoulder.

"*Sorry to cut out on you, but it's obvious you're unwilling or unable to help me,*" Ixil read. "*Head due west from here, and in an hour you'll hit the Scree View trail. Turn left and follow it about a kilometer and you'll reach Trailhead. Sorry about the armband.*"

"The armband?" I asked as Ixil handed me the note.

"The alien armband," Selene said. "He took it from my bag before he left."

"At least he didn't hurt you," I said, wincing. Yet another opportunity missed by my unintended nap. As my father used to say, *The spirit may be willing, but the flesh is usually in charge.*

"Or completely abandon us," Selene said. "He could have just left us here instead of telling us how to get back to Trailhead."

"Assuming the directions aren't a lie," I warned, glancing over the note and then stuffing it into my pocket. "You said the portal's a kilometer away?"

"Yes," Selene said. "Dent's somewhere in that same direction, but the breezes are too variable for me to get a firm location."

"He's got to be heading for the portal," I said, fastening the tool pouch with the water bottles around my waist. "Let's see if we can head him off."

"You two go," Ixil said, drawing the little DubTrub 2mm he'd shown me before and pressing it into my hand. "I need to follow behind Pix and Pax or they'll get lost."

"Okay," I said. "We'll meet you there. Come on, Selene."

With Dent on the loose and undoubtedly watching for signs of pursuit, I was hoping to avoid using my flashlight. But the footing was increasingly treacherous, and after one too many near falls I gave up and made us a small spot of light. Gripping the

DubTrub tightly, hoping Dent wasn't twitchy enough to shoot on sight, we continued on through the darkness.

And then, suddenly, we were there.

"He's moved the stones beneath it," Selene said softly. "You see?"

For those first few seconds I had no idea what she was talking about. Then, across the moonlit scree field I spotted a small but clearly visible section of smooth wall framed by lines of the more jagged stones above it and on both sides. The bottom edge, though, was more of a semicircular dip, indicating that Dent had indeed done some clearing of that area.

"Probably needed to move them to get access to the hatch," Selene continued. "I wonder how he opens it."

"Good question," I said, frowning. We'd seen various open portal hatches, but as far as I could remember we'd never seen one of them actually *being* opened. "I guess we're about to find out."

"No," Selene said. "He's not here anymore. He's either used the portal or continued on to Trailhead."

I scowled. Terrific. "Well, Ixil probably knows how it works. Can you find him?"

"He's fifty meters that way." She pointed. "I think Pix and Pax are with him."

"Okay," I said, turning away from the stones and the half-buried portal. "Let's go."

With no reason to be circumspect now that Dent was gone, I cranked up my flashlight to full power, and in the brighter glow we were able to cover the uneven ground faster and far more safely. With maybe ten meters to go I spotted Ixil's own flickering light, and half a minute later we rounded the last tree and were once again together.

"Any luck?" he asked.

"We found the portal," I said. "But it looks like Dent's already flown the coop. I hope you know how to open the front door."

"You press against the hatch's trigger and it pops open," Ixil said absently, stepping to the side and gesturing. "First, tell me what you think of this."

I frowned. Sitting beside him, pressed against a thick tree trunk and nestled beneath its branches, was probably the last thing I would expect to run across in an alien forest: a meter-tall Brinx-Chakrar safe. "Well, Dent *did* say he'd stashed some stuff out here," I reminded Ixil. "I don't suppose Pix or Pax was in time to see him work the combination."

"Pax did in fact arrive as he approached it," Ixil said. "Unfortunately, there wasn't any combination for him to witness."

I frowned, looking closer. There was the usual rectangular keypad block set into the door beside the handle. But now that I was focusing on it I saw that the spot was empty.

"The door simply popped open as he came within a couple of meters," Ixil continued. "Apparently, he's reconfigured the mechanism for remote control."

"Great," I growled. Remote-trigger codes, even rolling-river ones, could be captured and analyzed, and in a lot of cases successfully hacked. Unfortunately, Pax had apparently neglected to bring the necessary five kilos' worth of equipment with him. "Well, I *do* have Floyd's blast ribbon with me."

"Sadly, I don't believe even that much explosive will do us any good," Ixil warned. "I've dealt with Brinx-Chakrars before, and they're incredibly resistant to everything in a safecracker's arsenal."

"Yeah, I was afraid of that," I said. "Do we know what Dent took out of it?"

"There was a rectangular box that looked like a jewelry container," Ixil said. "Also a couple of small cylinders. Unfortunately Pax wasn't close enough to obtain details on either."

"Okay, so a blast ribbon won't get us in," I said. "What will?"

"Specialized drills and saws," Ixil said. "Heavy ones, requiring power supplies and trained operators."

"None of which are likely to be found in Trailhead or Aerie?"

"I would say not," Ixil agreed. "Even if they did, getting them out here would be a massive and very public undertaking."

I put my hand on the safe's corner and gave it a tentative push. The box didn't even quiver. "And we're not going to lug it somewhere more convenient."

"Not a Brinx-Chakrar, no,"

"I have a question," Selene spoke up. "What's it made of?"

"High-end safes like this are typically compressed titanium," I told her.

"Which this appears to be," Ixil added.

"Right," I agreed. "It may also have a lead-swirl liner to block X-rays."

"Is there any woven nylon in it?" she asked.

"I don't remember seeing anything like that listed in the specs for high-end safes like this," Ixil told her.

"I see," Selene said thoughtfully. "A moment, please." She started off slowly around the safe, circling it and the tree it was backed up to.

Ixil gave me a questioning look; I shrugged and went to catch up with her. I didn't know where she was going with this, but when she got all thoughtful and mysterious it was always worth seeing where she ended up.

In this case, she ended up exactly halfway around the safe. There she stopped, gazing at the back of the tree, her eyelashes fluttering. Then, she stirred. "There," she said, moving her pointing finger to a spot in the center of the trunk. "And there," she added, lowering her finger to point twenty centimeters farther down. I trained my flashlight on the first spot she'd identified.

There, practically invisible amid the whorls of the gnarled bark, was a broad-headed screw, dug into the tree directly behind the safe. Shifting my beam, I found a second screw in the other spot she'd marked.

Both screws made of woven nylon.

"Well, now, isn't *that* cute?" I said, trying to decide if I should be mad at Dent or just impressed.

"I don't understand," Ixil said, sounding confused. "What do those screws mean?"

"They mean that Dent's a fraud," I said. "Or at least his fancy safe is." I tapped the upper screw head.

"Are you saying he bolted it to the *tree*?" Ixil asked, sounding even more confused. "Why?"

"Because it's not a Brinx-Chakra," I told him, allowing a little smugness into my voice. As my father used to say, *People who say virtue is its own reward have probably never tried gloating.* "I've seen this before. It's some cheap tin or aluminum box plated with a thin layer of titanium and with a company logo slapped onto the front. The whole façade is designed to scare off potential thieves before they even try to take a crack at it."

"Only the box's lighter weight would be a dead giveaway if any of those thieves tried nudging it," Ixil said, finally catching on. "So he fastened it to the tree with long bolts to enhance the illusion."

"Right," I said. "Actually, we should have figured it out the minute we saw the damn thing. How could Dent have lugged half a ton of metal out here in the first place? Even if his brother had been on hand to help?"

"How indeed?" Ixil agreed. "Well. Now, I believe, getting a look at what's inside should be fairly straightforward. The blast ribbon, if you please?"

"Not sure this is a good idea," I warned as I unwrapped the ribbon from my arm and handed it over. "There are some tactical advantages to knowing something your target doesn't know you know. Blowing the front off his supposedly secret stash kind of violates that principle."

"Trust me," Ixil said, glancing at the info bar along the ribbon's edge and then pulling out his multitool. "My skills at subtlety aren't limited to hiding in Trailblazer ship crawl spaces."

He started by slicing off razor-thin pieces of the blast ribbon and laying them out neatly along the top of the safe. Once a dozen or so were ready, Pix and Pax hopped off his arms onto the safe, presumably at his silent command, and began taking the strips one by one to the back wall of the safe. There, using their long claws, they delicately tucked the strips into the almost invisible seam where the titanium plating on the top of the safe folded over onto the plating on the back. Ixil continued cutting pieces, and the outriders continued stuffing them into place, until the entire seam was full, with the strips also extending a few centimeters down the rear side seams.

"Good," Ixil said briskly, checking the outriders' handiwork. "Let's see if this works."

Putting his palms on the safe, he snapped his fingers, bringing Pix and Pax scrambling up his arms and back onto his shoulders. To me, they looked rather pleased with themselves, but I was pretty sure that was just my imagination. Motioning me back, he pulled out an igniter and gingerly touched it to the closest strip.

There was a drawn-out, stuttering *pop* as the pieces of ribbon exploded sequentially, each triggered by the explosion immediately beside it. The popping ended, and together Ixil and I stepped in for a closer look.

I'd had my doubts. Not anymore. The multiple mini-explosions had neatly pried up the rear titanium flap, exposing the plain aluminum beneath it.

"Thinner than I thought it would be," Ixil commented, prying experimentally at the titanium with his multitool. "And it's not even plated onto the main box."

"Neither were the other two safes I saw that used this scam," I told him. "I heard once that compressed titanium doesn't really bond with aluminum or other cheap metals. You'd have to do an interlace weave, which would kind of defeat the whole *cheap* part of the *cheap replica* gimmick." I poked experimentally at the loosened flap. "Still thick enough to be trouble, though."

"Only if the plan was to peel it back," Ixil said. "Fortunately, the aluminum beneath it is just as thin and far more malleable. We should be able to bend it far enough to pop it off, or at least far enough to get access to the interior. I'll get started while you go find Selene."

I looked around in surprise. With my full attention on Ixil and the box, I'd completely missed the fact that Selene had disappeared. "And you didn't *say* anything?"

"She'll be all right," Ixil soothed. "No predators, remember? She headed back the way you just came, so I assume she went to open the portal."

I scowled. No predators; except possibly Dent if he happened to come back and caught her snooping around. "Right," I said. Pulling out the DubTrub, I headed into the forest.

"Whistle if there's any trouble," Ixil called after me, his attention already back on the safe.

I expected to find the portal hatch open and Selene either already inside or preparing to go in. But as I reached the edge of the scree field I could see in the starlight that the portal hull was still smooth and solid. "Selene?" I stage-whispered.

"Here," her voice came from my left. The word was calm enough, but there was something in her tone that sent a shiver up my back.

I worked my way through another couple of meters of shrubs and tangled tree branches and found her standing at the edge of a narrow clearing that threaded its way back toward Ixil and the safe in one direction and opened up onto the scree field in the other. "What's up?" I asked as I came up beside her. "Did you get into the portal?"

"No." She nodded toward the clearing. "I saw this and stopped."

I frowned. The clearing was narrow, with a few low undulations like small ocean waves that had been frozen in the dirt and grass. Too low to surf, but high enough to stumble over if you weren't paying attention to your footing. "Anything in particular that caught your eye?"

"I walked it back," she said, her tone edging a little darker. "It goes to within fifteen meters of the safe and all the way to the scree field and the portal. It's a much easier walk than the one we took through the woods."

"Something handy to tuck away for later," I said, trying to get a clear look at her pupils in the faint light.

"Yes." Selene paused. "So why didn't Dent take it?"

"You sure he didn't?"

She nodded. "He followed the path you just took. The path we both took when we left the portal and went to find Ixil."

I looked back at the clearing. So why *didn't* Dent want to take the easy road?

And then, I saw it. Undulations in the ground . . .

"Come on," I said, taking Selene's arm and turning her toward Ixil. "It's time we and our resident Icarus professional had a little talk."

Ixil had said that with the titanium shell breached the safe would be relatively easy to open. It wasn't until we reached him that I discovered just how much of an understatement that had been. In the short time he'd been alone he'd managed to slide the entire aluminum back panel out of its titanium edging, leaving it fastened to the tree behind it. With the rest of the box unattached, he'd swiveled it around, exposing the interior and four shelves' worth of odds and ends. We arrived to find him thumbing intently through a short stack of picture-sized cards, his flashlight tucked between his shoulder and Pax's belly. "That was quick," I commented as we walked up to him. "Are those more pictures?"

"Yes," he said. He seemed to hesitate, then selected one of them and offered it to me. "You said Dent showed you a picture of a dead man. Is this him?"

I took the picture and shined my light on it. It was him, all right. Only instead of just a head shot, this one showed his entire body, stretched out limply on a flat gray surface. But he was just as dead. "That's the guy," I confirmed. "Who is he?"

"That's the question, isn't it?" Ixil said ruefully, taking the picture back. "I'm afraid there's a lot going on here that we don't have a handle on."

"Oh, I doubt it's quite as bad as that," I soothed. "Let's start with our dead man, and the fact that you, McKell, and Graym-Barker all lied about not knowing him."

"Gregory—"

"I know Selene and I aren't exactly at the top of anyone's need-to-know list," I cut him off. "But we're sitting on a portal, and there are at least two groups out there gunning for us, and we need to be brought into the picture. Fast."

Again, Ixil hesitated. "I'm sorry, Gregory," he said. "But I can't simply break protocol."

"How about we work a trade, then?" I suggested. "Something for something. You tell us who the dead man is."

I looked at Selene. "We'll tell you where he's buried."

CHAPTER SEVENTEEN

"His name," Ixil said quietly, "was Dr. Ian Riley."

We were standing beside the clearing, gazing over the small, uniform mounds in the ground. Mounds I'd assumed were natural undulations.

Mounds I knew now were graves.

"He was one of our theoretical researchers," Ixil continued. "Six months ago—closer to seven now—he left on a scheduled vacation. Two months after that, he disappeared."

"I'm guessing it wasn't *just* a vacation?" I asked.

"Apparently not," Ixil conceded. "Sadly, he didn't share those other plans with anyone else."

"What was he working on?" Selene asked.

"He had a theory about portals and portal distribution," Ixil said. "Unfortunately, according to his colleagues, he never thought it had jelled well enough to talk about."

I snorted. "In retrospect, I'd say it jelled just fine."

"So it would seem, but we only learned about it after he disappeared and we went through his private journals. Even then, there wasn't much detail."

"Except that the portal was on Popanilla?"

"Actually, we thought it was on Armorica," Ixil said. "He sent a StarrComm message from there to his private journal log saying he was getting close and sounding quite excited. After that, nothing."

I gazed out over the impromptu graveyard. "So he makes a big show about being on Armorica," I said slowly. "Complete with a StarrComm transmission just in case he's not being obvious enough about it. And then he quietly scoots over to Popanilla?"

"That's my reading, yes," Ixil said. "Armorica's only a two-hour flight away, and it has a couple of weekly shuttle runs to Shiroyama Island and the other recreational areas of Popanilla."

"Trying to throw pursuit off track," I said, gazing again at the graves. "Only whoever was shadowing him wasn't fooled. Are we thinking Dent?"

"He's the obvious candidate," Ixil said. "But as much as I try, I can't get the timeline and logic to work. Dent *was* on Shiroyama at the time Dr. Riley disappeared, but there's no record of him ever going to Armorica. It seems clear that the two of them had at least a brief conversation, though. Otherwise how would Dent have your name and your connection to Icarus?"

"The timing there works, too," I pointed out. "Riley's death is just about the time Dent started his grand search for me."

"Correct." On Ixil's shoulders, his outriders gave a little twitch. "And then, there's this."

He handed me the rest of the pictures from the safe. "Go ahead," he said, waving in invitation. "I'd very much like to hear your take."

I took the stack, my stomach settling into a knot as I leafed through them. There were several head shots of three other dearly departeds, along with more of the full-body-sprawled pictures like the one Ixil had showed us of Dr. Riley.

Except that the other faces and bodies in Dent's visual trophy collection weren't human. Two of them were Iykams.

The third was a Patth.

I looked at Ixil as I passed the pictures to Selene. "So now he's also killed a Patth?"

"So it would seem," Ixil confirmed. "And *that's* likely to cost him."

I nodded heavily. He was right on that one. The Patth were not known to treat the death of one of their own in anything approaching a casual manner. "*If* Dent's the one who actually pulled the trigger," I pointed out. "There's nothing in these photos that really proves that."

"I thought photographic evidence was sufficient protocol for bounty hunters," Ixil said. "Documented proof of a successful mission."

"For bounty hunters, sure," I pointed out. "But Dent isn't one. Besides, that protocol requires the pictures be dij so that there's a time-stamp. Analog photos like this aren't of any official use."

"Then why take them?"

"Probably so he'd have something to show around to get an ID," I said. "Remember he had Riley's picture when he asked if I knew him."

"Or he could simply have been recording the scene," Selene offered. "He was about to bury the bodies, and if he didn't have photographic evidence of how they were originally laid out, there would be little he could tell the badgemen later."

"Not that he seems to have told anyone anything about it to date," I pointed out. "I could also mention that carrying around evidence of four murders isn't usually considered a smart thing to do."

"Three," Selene corrected me. "Dent may have shot the others, but he didn't kill Dr Riley." She handed me one of the photos. "There's blood on the deck beneath the heads of the others. There's none beneath Riley's."

"She's right," Ixil said. "That's something, anyway."

"Not that it'll make the Path feel any better," I said.

"True," Ixil conceded. "I suppose we should go inside and see if he left any clues as to where he went. We can look through the rest of the items in the safe later."

I nodded. Using an Icarus portal left a temporary record of both the destination and home addresses. Unfortunately, those patterns were only held for about fifteen minutes before being erased, and Dent had made it past that threshold long before we came on the scene.

Still, there was a chance he didn't know we were on to him, in which case he might have left some notes in there. It was a slim hope, but right now it was all we had.

We made our way across the rocky terrain to the exposed section of the portal. Selene found the spot where Dent had pressed his hand when he'd opened the hatch earlier, and at Ixil's direction held her own hand there until there was a soft click and a section popped open. Ixil caught the edge of the hatch and pulled it open the rest of the way, swinging it a full one-eighty degrees around invisible hinges until it was up against the main hull. He continued pressing; and to my amazement the entire hatch seemed to melt into the hull, leaving the portal with the familiar rectangular opening but no obvious way of closing it.

"I wondered how Alpha stayed sealed way out there in deep space," I commented as Ixil stooped and shone his light inside. "How do you get the hatch back closed?"

"Same way I opened it, except in reverse," Ixil said. "You can also set it to open inward if you prefer." He eased his way into the hatchway, and disappeared inside. I glanced at the edge of the forest behind me, confirming as best I could that no one was skulking out there, and followed.

Entering a portal was the kind of experience that no one who'd never done it could ever quite be prepared for. The main sphere—the receiver module, the one I was currently climbing into—was about forty meters across, with a gravity field radiating outward from the center with "up" everywhere perpendicular to the curved surface. Walking along the hull was literally like a stroll along a walkway, except that looking anywhere except directly in front of you was an invitation to vertigo and falling flat on your face. The other sphere, the launch module, was about half the diameter of the receiver, with a similar radial grav field of its own. The two spheres were connected by a rectangular opening, with the transition between the two and their associated grav fields even more of a challenge for the uninitiated to navigate.

Fortunately, Selene and I had plenty of practice. I finished getting into the receiver module, confirmed that Selene was climbing in gracefully behind me, and turned toward the launch module interface halfway around the sphere.

And came to a sudden stop. Ixil had taken a few steps toward the hatchway and then suddenly stopped, his head tilted back as he stared straight up across the sphere. "What's the matter?" I asked, following his sight line and seeing absolutely nothing.

"This sphere is much smaller than all the others," he said, gesturing. "It's no more than twenty meters across, half the size of a normal receiver module."

I squinted upward. He was right. "Is that a problem?"

"I don't know," he said. "All of the others have had a uniform diameter of exactly forty point three six meters."

I looked at Selene, got a small shrug in return. "Well, you *do* only have three samples," I reminded him. "Maybe this one was made for people on a budget."

Ixil didn't answer. For another moment he remained standing, then lowered his gaze and continued toward the launch module. "Let's see if there are any other surprises."

He reached the interface and did the lie-down-and-roll maneuver that continued to be the best way to cross the spheres' opposing gravitational fields. I gave him a moment to regain his feet and move away from the opening, then lay down at the edge and did my own roll. I gave my inner ear a moment to adjust, then stood up and stepped away, looking around the sphere. It looked like all the others I'd seen: the inner surface covered by monitors and control boards, lots of cables snaking everywhere, all of it held in place by a flexible mesh that covered the whole inside. Across from us, a slender, black-and-silver-banded extension arm stretched out into the center of the sphere.

"Gregory," Selene murmured from behind me, a sudden tension in her voice.

I looked straight up. Like the half-sized receiver module out there, this sphere was also only about half the usual thirty-meter diameters of the Icarus, Alpha, and Firefall launch modules. "Yes, I see," I said. "Definitely the budget version."

"Not there," Ixil said, his voice suddenly odd. "Look at the control board."

Frowning, I shifted my attention to that section of the surface.

The control board wasn't there.

Not wrecked, or removed, or even just covered up. It simply wasn't there. Not only that, but with other sets of controls and displays taking up that space, there was no indication that one had ever been there.

"He was right," Ixil murmured. "Dr. Riley's theory postulated there could be sets of permanently linked portal dyads. It appears he found one."

"Dyads?" Selene asked.

"A pair of portals permanently linked to each other," Ixil explained. "And *only* to each other."

"But why?" I asked, my brain still trying to catch up. "Why build something this complicated and advanced, and then have it only go one place?"

"I don't know," Ixil said. "But at least we won't have any trouble figuring out where Dent went."

"Won't we?" I asked. "Do we *know* this is one of Dr. Riley's dyads?"

"What else could it be?" Ixil asked.

"What *else* could it be?" I countered. "Oh, come on, Ixil—use your imagination. It could be a trap, something leading directly to the creators' version of hell. It could be their version of a magic mystery tour. Step in, ride the extension arm up, and then figure out where it sent you. Heaps of fun."

"No," Selene said firmly. "Dent's clearly been using this portal. Without a home address indicator in here for him to copy down, there's no way he'd be able to return."

"Unless the addresses only show up at the other end," I shot back.

But she was right, and as my confusion-driven consternation started to fade I could see she had a good handle on the internal logic of the place. Besides, Dent would hardly still be using it if it wasn't safe and reliable. "Fine," I said. "I suppose you're going to want us to go through and see what's at the other end?"

"I could send Pix through first if you'd like," Ixil suggested. "For once, there won't be any tricky key-setting logistics involved in getting him back."

"Thanks for the offer," I said, walking over to the extension arm. "But Dent might still be hanging out in there, and I'd like to keep you and the outriders our little secret for the moment. No, no—hold back a minute," I added as Selene started to join me. "I'll go first. Give me two minutes before you follow."

"All right," Selene said. "Be careful."

I gave her my best shot at a confident smile. "Absolutely."

I reached the extension arm and got a loose grip around it. The gravitational field around me shifted, starting me on my leisurely journey upward and inward toward the center of the launch module. I was nearly to the gray trigger section when it belatedly occurred to me that we had no idea whether there were other controls we had to turn on or off to make this thing go.

Fortunately, the portal's creators really had apparently decided this was to be a simple back-and-forth operation. The end of the arm turned the familiar luminescent gray, and as I arrived I closed my fingers firmly around it. There was the usual low-level electrical-type tingle, and the world around me went black.

Mentally, I counted down the seconds—as with all the other portal trips I'd taken, there were three of them—and then the lights went back on again, and I was somewhere else.

In this case, *somewhere else* being the center of the Popanilla portal's twin's receiver module.

I looked around as I floated downward. Unlike the portal I'd just left, this one definitely had the lived-in look. On one side of the curved surface was a full camping setup, including a folding chair, a hammock stand, and one of the light-weight mesh hammocks Dent had talked about during our hike. A food cabinet and a small cooker were over in another area, while a small chemical toilet sat off by itself. Sitting on the deck near the hammock was a small rectangular box, presumably the jewelry case Pax had seen Dent take from the safe on Popanilla.

As my father used to say, *Home may be where the heart is, but the heart is usually happy enough if it can find a place where no one's shooting at it.*

I reached the deck, coming to the slightly jarring landing that was typical with portals. I walked over to the launch module and checked inside, just in case Dent was hanging out in there—this one didn't have a control board, either—and was sorting through the jewelry case when I felt a subtle movement of air above me that indicated Selene's arrival. "Looks like we're alone," I called up to her. "Can you find the hatch? The whole surface in here looks the same to me."

"Yes, as soon as I land," she said. "Is that the jewelry case Ixil mentioned?"

"Probably," I said, holding it up so she could get a better view. "Very pricey collection of stuff, too."

"You think Dent stole it?"

"I assume *someone* did," I said. "Dent may just be the delivery team. Tera said he was moving into smuggling, remember?"

"He certainly has an interesting setup for that kind of job."

"Oh, it's about as perfect as you can get," I agreed. "You fly your stolen goods to Popanilla, stroll out into the woods and hop down the rabbit hole, hand them over to the recipient here—wherever *here* is—and hop back before anyone who was tracking you can even think about looking elsewhere. From that point on, they can watch you lift, even get a warrant and board your ship, and they'll have nothing to show for it."

I walked over to the food locker and popped it open. "And if they're hunting you on Popanilla, you just settle in here with your...looks like about three weeks' worth of food and water."

"Or he could go back to Popanilla occasionally if he wanted to hunt for fresh food," Selene pointed out as she came to her own slightly jerky landing. "Those sugarbirds would certainly be easy to catch."

"Didn't look like they had much meat on them, though. Hatch?"

"Yes, I'm on it."

It took less than a minute for her to find the lingering scent of Dent's hand on one of the plates near where he'd left the jewelry case. She tried pressing her hand against it, as Ixil had showed her how to do on the Popanilla hatch, but this time nothing happened.

"You think he's figured out a way to lock it?" I asked, frowning as I gave it a try of my own.

"That wouldn't be very hard to do if it's set to swing outward," Selene pointed out. "A bar across the hatch would do the trick."

"Ixil said you could also set it to swing inward," I reminded her. "We'll ask him how to do that. So what *can* you tell me?"

Her nostrils and eyelashes fluttered, her pupils looking focused and thoughtful. "There's white jasmine and cinnamon," she said. "Quite a lot of the former, less of the latter. Other trees and plants, as well, but I don't know any of them. There's some kind of copper-based metal—brass or bronze, I think—and some worked stone or at least stone-based dust. There's also a hint of woodfire smoke."

"How much?"

She shook her head. "Not very."

So less likely to be some out-of-the-way primitive part of the Spiral and more likely just some open-air cooking. "What else?"

"I smell humans, k'Tra, and Ulkomaals," she said. "Probably proportionally in that order, though it's always difficult with k'Tra."

I nodded as I headed back to the food locker. K'Tra social status was based on a sliding scale of perfumery, and since they'd enthusiastically adopted a lot of other aliens' scent choices over the centuries a wealthy k'Tra could easily be mistaken for an over-aromatic human.

"So a place with humans, k'Tra, Ulkomaals, outdoor cooking, and a mix of fancy nature and decorative metal and stonework,"

I concluded, pulling out some of the food packages and checking their labels. "Also where you can buy Pachli noodles, BCohn tortellini, and—ah!—Paparry Zindiroon Spice packets. That one's *got* to be local. Great."

I took pictures of the three packages, plus several more of everything just for good measure. "Time to head back," I said. "I'll hike over to Trailhead and have the admiral run everything though the computer. Maybe he can figure out what's at the other end of the rabbit hole before we have to go through it."

"Do you want me to come with you?" she asked as we headed toward the launch module.

"No, I'll be fine on my own," I assured her. "I'd rather you stay with Ixil and help him sort through Dent's safe. You might spot something he would miss."

"Or that he doesn't want us to know about?"

"I wouldn't say that," I said.

"But you'd think it?"

I scowled. "Damn right I would."

It was still dark when I set off for Trailhead and whatever passed for civilization here on Shiroyama Island. Ixil insisted on sending Pix along to help me find my way back again, and together he and I trooped our way through the trees and undergrowth, me making a lot more noise than the little outrider despite the fact that I had a light and he didn't.

Ixil had once told us that on the Kalixiri homeworld outriders in the wild were able to hunt and take down large animals. A part of me rather hoped I'd get to see that happen someday.

There were a few early risers on the Trailhead streets, mostly hikers getting breakfast before setting off into the wilderness. The StarrComm center was another fifteen kilometers past the town itself, but fortunately there were plenty of quick-rent runarounds parked along the quiet streets. I helped myself to one, and fifteen minutes later was sitting in a booth facing a slightly bleary-eyed image of Admiral Sir Graym-Barker. Ten minutes after that I'd finished describing the situation and the Icarus Group computers were busy trying to figure out from my clues exactly where the end of Dent's rabbit hole was.

I hadn't expected Graym-Barker to let me stay on the line while the analysts finished their work, not at StarrComm's rates, and I was right. He told me to get some breakfast and call him back in an hour.

Typically, the area around a StarrComm center had one or two all-day diners, and this one was no exception. I treated myself to a nice meal and then, with half an hour to spare, I went into one of the hiking-gear stores and did a bit of shopping. Exactly one hour after Graym-Barker sent me away I was back in the booth.

And rather to my surprise, they'd come up with an answer.

"The admiral thinks Twin B is somewhere in or near the Erymant Temple in Malfatti City on Fidelio," I reported to Selene and Ixil when Pix and I finally made it back. "The temple is a large complex of marker steles and ruined buildings left by some unknown civilization a few thousand years ago, long before humans and k'Tra started colonizing the planet."

"Two hundred forty-three light-years away," Selene murmured, scrolling down the pages on her info pad. "Interesting. We traveled from Draelon on Brandywine to Dent on Gremon and then to Popanilla; and now the portal is taking us right back toward Brandywine again."

"Yes, I noticed," I said. "We would have saved ourselves about eight days and a hell of a lot of trouble if we'd known. Anyway, the admiral said the temple was first dug up about fifty years ago, and for a while was quite the local attraction. There were guided tours, lecture programs, and souvenir shops and restaurants set up right on the grounds. You could even book one of the conference rooms or lecture-hall chambers for your company meetings or parties."

"Doesn't sound like a place that would lend itself to stealthy entrances and exits," Ixil commented.

"Not back then it wasn't," I said. "But it's a lot more sneakable now. Interest in the place has been waning for the past twenty years, and five years ago the company that owned and operated it went under. Right now the temple and grounds are pretty much a ghost town, though a few tourists probably still pick their way through the weeds from time to time."

"And if the portal is within the temple grounds, there seem to be a number of blind corners and visual blockages that would help protect Dent from view as he came and went," Selene said, scrolling through the info pad pictures.

"I guess we'll find out," I said. "As my father used to say, *The best way to be invisible is to just avoid everyone.*" I nodded toward the partially disassembled safe. "So what else did he have in his stash?"

"A few more of the pictures you saw earlier," Ixil said. "A couple each of Dr. Riley, the Patth, and the two Iykams. There was another jewelry case, and a red-edged document in a script I don't recognize that I'm guessing may be part of an extortion or blackmail scheme. He also had a fair number of less-official documents in English that look like coded bills of sale or transfer."

"We're thinking those are connected to his smuggling business," Selene added.

"We can hand them over to ISLE once we're done analyzing them," Ixil said. "Someone there may be able to match the dates and locations to known crimes. There were also two corona guns."

"Matching the two dead Iykams in Dent's pictures," I said wincing. "If it's all the same with you, I'll just hang onto your DubTrub for the moment."

"No problem," Ixil assured me. "Which leads nicely to the last and most interesting items in the safe. Namely, fourteen of these." He pulled a short, thick, black cylinder from a pocket and offered it to me. "Look familiar?"

I frowned as I took it. My first thought was that it looked like a quick-load for the DubTrub, with the four 2mm barrels forming an orderly array inside the outer shell. It was definitely the right size and shape, but the usual connection coupling for that kind of swap-out was gone. Instead, the non-business-end of the cylinder had been replaced by a three-centimeter extension that was in turn mounted on some sort of triple gimbal and a high-strength adhesive pad.

"Selene says it looks like your description of the weapon Dent's brother was firing through the curtain at the Roastmeat Bar on Gremon," Ixil added.

"Well, the front end of it does, anyway," I confirmed, peering down the barrels. The tips of the four tiny missiles were just visible, black against the black of the barrels. I also noted that a *04* had been scratched into the side of the cylinder's extension. "We never saw the back end, so I don't know if it had this same extension. Looks handmade, by the way—there's no serial number or place for one. These numbers etched into the side all different?"

"The way they were laid out started at zero-three on the far left, went to twelve, and then started over at zero-one," Selene said. "The one you're holding was the farthest on the right."

"Any idea what the numbers signify?"

"They identify which cylinder is which, obviously," Ixil said. "Aside from that, I don't know if they have another purpose."

"I guess we'll just have to ask him," I said, putting the cylinder in my pocket. "I think it's time we headed through and checked out the other end. Selene, you coming with me or staying here to help Ixil with his inventory?"

"The inventory's basically done," Ixil said. "If you two want to head to Fidelio, I could go to the Aerie StarrComm center and copy these documents to the admiral."

"Or you could stay here and keep watch in case Dent gets past us," Selene said. "He's surely going to return sometime for the jewels and papers."

"I think it unlikely he'll try to move more than one item at a time," I told her. "Since he's already got the one jewelry case—and hasn't yet delivered its contents—it should be a while before he comes back for more."

"I agree," Ixil said. "Which is why I think I should go to Aerie now, so that I can be back before he returns."

"Seems reasonable," I said. "Oh, and I bought some camping gear to make future stakeouts a bit more comfortable. There's a better collection of packaged food, some woodland tools, and three inflatable mattresses, plus blankets and rain canopies."

"I doubt we're going to be here *that* long," Ixil said.

"You never know." I turned to Selene. "You still don't look happy with all this."

"I'm concerned about Ixil being out of touch if we need backup," she said. "We don't actually *know* Dent won't be coming back soon."

"We'll be all right," I soothed. "Remember, Dent doesn't know we know anything about Icarus or the portals, let alone that we've found Twin A. He won't be expecting us to suddenly show up in Twin B."

"Castor and Pollux," Ixil murmured.

I frowned. "What?"

"Not Twin A and Twin B," he said. "The names in Dr. Riley's journal for his theoretical Gemini portals were *Castor* and *Pollux*."

I opened my mouth to ask a bit snidely if this was the same Dr. Riley who'd caused infinite grief for all of us by playing his cards so close to his chest that we couldn't even find the damn things after he disappeared. But Ixil would probably take exception to the tone of any such question. Even if he didn't, Selene almost certainly would. "Fine," I said. "In that case Dent doesn't know we've found Castor and are planning to pop out of Pollux."

"Maybe," Selene said, her pupils still unconvinced. With her full attention on the problem at hand, she might not even have noticed that I was being snarky. "But there's also his brother to consider, and we don't have *any* idea where he is right now."

"Good point," I agreed. "Ixil?"

"I don't know how Weston Dent could have gotten here from Gremon this quickly," he said. Still, he didn't sound entirely confident. "But we can't just wait for things to happen. We know Easton is on Fidelio, and we have to move on that knowledge before we lose all initiative."

"I have to agree," I said, looking back at Selene. "It'll be all right, Selene. He'll never see us coming. Come on, let's go."

I was right about that, as it turned out. He didn't. But as my father used to say, *Just because you're right doesn't necessarily mean you understand what the hell is going on.*

During the time I was in Aerie, Ixil had shown Selene the launch module control that switched the receiver module hatch from outward-swinging to inward-swinging. He'd also revealed that portals typically had a large number of possible hatches around the receiver rim that could be opened as circumstances and the positioning of the portal required, and showed her how to choose among them.

It was, in retrospect, a fairly obvious design feature, especially given that the majority of the portals the Icarus group had located had been at least partially buried. All the more reason for me to be quietly embarrassed that that possibility of such an option had never even occurred to me.

In this case, the Pollux receiver module hatch that Selene had identified as Dent's turned out to be surprisingly convenient, opening up into a blind corner and situated at right angles to Fidelio's own gravitational field. It also had a snakelike bronze bar wiggling its way across the outside, which explained why we hadn't been able to push it open earlier. Selene confirmed that no one was nearby, I shoved the bar upward out of the way, and we rolled our way outside.

The articles and pictures of the Erymant Temple Selene had showed me had been pretty impressive. The reality of the place, as we moved out into the grounds, was even more so. Narrow passageways lined with carved and decorated stone pillars would suddenly open up into broader avenues or gathering areas set between the various buildings. The walkways were all tiled with dusty, closely fitted flagstones, while the buildings were all curves and arches, their white stone highlighted with more of the serpentine bronze metal trim that meandered across the surfaces like frozen ivy. It was evening in this part of Fidelio, and as I gazed out into the fading light I could imagine vaguely shaped aliens in toga-style outfits strolling serenely along the flagstones, conversing in melodious tones.

But there weren't any such exotic aliens here, or even any of the crowds of tourists that had once come to gaze at the quiet grandeur. Selene and I were alone, staring at the deserted ruins in the fading light.

So what the *hell* was a portal doing here?

Selene touched my arm, jolting me out of my musings. Her nostrils were fluttering, her head moving slowly back and forth as she sampled the air. "Four humans," she murmured, pointing to the textured wall to our left. "That direction."

"Dent?" I murmured back.

"No," she said slowly, her eyelashes joining in the analysis. "But I can smell him. I think they've had recent contact with him."

His buyers? Possibly. But in that case, why were they poking around out here instead of making tracks for the nearest spaceport or runaround rental? "You're sure Dent's not with them?" I asked.

"No, he isn't," Selene said, her pupils suddenly tense. "But I think...Gregory, I can smell blood.

"Dent's blood."

CHAPTER EIGHTEEN

———— ❖❖❖ ————

I had Ixil's DubTrub out in an instant, wishing for about the thousandth time since Huihuang that I still had one of my plasmics. DubTrubs were nicely concealable, but with only four shots per load they weren't exactly designed for protracted combat. Fleetingly, I wished I'd taken the time to strip off whatever the extra length was that Dent had added to the quick-load cylinder in my pocket so I would at least have an additional four shots to play with. Too late now. "Any idea what they're doing?" I muttered.

"They seem to be just be moving around," Selene said. "Not hurrying, just moving slowly around."

From the direction she'd indicated came a soft clatter, followed by an equally soft curse. "Like maybe they're searching for someone?" I suggested.

"I already said Dent's not here."

"But they may not know that," I pointed out. Briefly, I wondered if we could have just missed Dent on our way in, that he might have been sliding up the extension arm in the Pollux launch module right as Selene and I arrived from Popanilla and started drifting toward the receiver module deck. It would take exquisite timing, but given the way the portals were set up we could literally pass in the night without either of us being aware of the other.

But no. If Dent had come into Pollux just before we did Selene would have smelled a fresh infusion of his scent. It also didn't explain the scent of blood she was getting out here.

I scowled. In the meantime, I needed to stop wool-gathering and get on top of the situation. I still had way too many questions for Dent to let someone kill him now. "Are they still searching?" I asked Selene.

"They're still moving around," she said. "I don't know if they're searching."

"Oh, they're searching, all right," I said. Now, suddenly, the whole thing was obvious. "Stay here and keep out of sight. I'll be right back."

Dent's jewelry case was right where I'd left it, a couple of meters from the entry hatch. But whereas it had been mostly full the last time I'd looked into it, now it was half empty. I picked the most distinctive of the remaining gems and headed back to Selene.

She was still where I'd left her, but the scuff marks in the flagstone dust showed she'd done a bit of local exploring in my absence. "Our friends still out there?" I asked.

"Yes, but they've moved on to a different street," she said. "And I think I've found Dent."

"Where?"

She pointed at the top half of a small domed building that was visible beyond a low retaining wall and past a line of decorated steles. "Someone went in or out—you can see the top of the door just over that wall—and a minute later Dent's scent went a little stronger."

"Sounds good," I said. "Any idea what that is?"

"It's one of the buildings the tour guides called lecture halls," she said, keying her info pad to a map of the temple grounds. "There's a podium in the front faced by three tiered rows of seats."

I nodded as she pulled up a floor plan. It looked like a small lecture hall, all right: six seats in the front row, eight in the middle, ten in the back. More like a small-group conversation chamber, in my opinion, but as my father used to say, *The only reason for labels is convenience or obfuscation.*

Though of course just because it was small didn't mean it wasn't packed to the gills with armed goons. "I suppose we *could* just drop in on them," I told Selene. "But I've never liked leaving people with guns behind me. Let's see if we can get ourselves an escort."

"You think they'll just take us to Dent?"

"I think they'll take us to whoever owns this," I said, showing her the gem I'd taken from Dent's case. "Or who thinks he does, anyway. They're this way, right?"

The four humans were right where Selene had said they were, and it was instantly obvious that they were indeed searching for something. They were strung out along one side of the street, peering behind steles and into clumps of vegetation or poking around the flagstones.

As my father used to say, *Always get in the first word when you can, even if that word is just hello.* "You're wasting your time," I called as Selene and I came around the corner.

Of course, as my father also used to say, *The first word probably isn't as important as the first gun.* Before I'd even finished my greeting all four of the thugs had snatched Blago 6mm snubnoses from concealment.

All of which remained pointed at the ground as their owners belatedly spotted the DubTrub I had pointed in their general direction. "Who the hell are you?" one of the men demanded, his eyes shifting from my gun to my face.

"I'm the one who's going to show Easton Dent the error of his ways and get your boss what he wants," I said.

"Really," he said flatly.

"Really," I said. "Meanwhile, you're not getting any closer to the gems, and I doubt Dent's getting any healthier. Shall we go?"

One of the men took a step, stopped at a gesture from the spokesman. "You giving us orders?" the spokesman asked.

"I'm trying to offer a solution where everyone gets what they want," I said. "If you really want to stay out here sifting through rock piles, you're more than welcome to do so. I just thought it would avoid a misunderstanding if you escorted us in to see your boss, instead of us walking in on him by ourselves. But never mind. If you'll all just turn your backs for a minute, we'll be on our way."

"What do you want to see the boss about?" the spokesman asked.

"Like I said: a solution," I told him. "I have what he wants; he has what I want. I just want to make a deal."

For a long moment the spokesman didn't speak. His eyes flicked to Selene, standing silently beside me, and I thought I spotted a flicker of recognition cross his face. "All right," he said at last. "I suppose a smart guy like you already knows where the boss is." He gestured behind me. "After you."

"Better idea," I said, lifting my DubTrub a bit for emphasis. "You four can lead the way. That way I won't have to take your Blagos away from you before we leave."

He gave me a slightly ironic smile and a microscopic inclination of his head. "Yeah, that'd be a trick, anyway," he said. "You a badgeman?"

I shook my head. "Bounty hunter."

"Yeah, I figured," he said, a subtle new edge to his voice. "Who's your target?"

"You got anyone in there except Easton Dent?"

"So it's Dent?"

"Of course it's Dent," I said. "Not to rush you or anything, but I imagine your boss values the time he's currently wasting."

"Yeah, he does," the spokesman agreed. "Fine. You just better not be blowing smoke. You wouldn't be the first bounty hunter the boss has iced."

"I'll remember that," I said, a shiver running up my back. Yet another reminder, if I'd needed one, of why I'd given up that business in the first place. "After you."

The building they led us to was indeed the lecture hall Selene had tagged. Our spokesman gave a hand signal to the two thugs manning the tall door and one of them pulled it open for us. The spokesman gestured; I nodded acknowledgment and Selene and I walked past him and stepped inside.

As we passed the threshold I slipped the DubTrub back into my pocket. The last two times I'd deliberately disarmed myself as a gesture of good faith—first in front of Mottola in the Huihuang tunnel building and then in Gaheen's office—things had worked out reasonably well. Hopefully, I could make it three for three.

It was probably just as well that I hadn't walked in brandishing a weapon. There were three more thugs standing guard at widely spaced positions in the lecture hall, all of them with Blagos drawn and ready. Beyond them, a short, thin man was seated in one of the front-row seats.

Facing him, tied to a chair beside the podium with his arms behind him, was Dent.

The man was a mess. Blood was trickling down his face from both sides of his lip plus a pair of wide cuts over his cheekbones. His shirt was matted with more blood, though whether that was leakage from the facial injuries or whether he'd been knife-poked in the chest a few times I couldn't tell.

The thin man half turned to look over his shoulder as we entered. "These walking corpses have names?" he called in a harsh, grating voice.

"I'm Gregory Roarke, sir," I called back. "Please forgive the interruption, but I have an offer that I hope will be mutually beneficial for the both of us."

"Yeah?" he said, not sounding particularly impressed. "What kind?"

"I believe I have what you're looking for," I said, pulling out the gem I'd taken from the case in Pollux's receiver module. I started toward the steps—

And stopped as every gun in the place was suddenly pointed straight at me.

"Balic?" the boss prompted.

The spokesman from the outside search team held out his hand, and I placed the gem in his palm. He gave me one last speculative look, then turned and headed down the steps to the bottom level. He handed the gem to the boss, and for a few seconds the other studied it. Then he looked up at Balic and nodded. Balic shifted his eyes to us and gestured, and the two thugs who'd been manning the door nudged Selene and me forward. "Go," one of them muttered.

"Thank you," I said. Taking Selene's arm, I started down.

We'd made it four steps when she casually leaned in close to me. "Ceiling," she murmured. "Above the center seats."

I glanced around the room as if scoping things out, idly stroking my left thumbnail as I did so. I lifted that hand to rub the first two fingers on the skin in the center of my forehead, tucking my thumb partway behind them where the mirrored nail was close to my left eye.

In the center of the domed ceiling, spaced a couple of meters apart, were two small, black blotches in the aged but otherwise gleaming white facing of the stone. I frowned, trying to figure out what they might be.

And then, abruptly, the images resolved in my mind. They

weren't defects in the stone, as I'd first thought, but two of Dent's gimmicked DubTrub quick-loads, fastened to the ceiling by their bases' adhesive pads.

I looked around the lecture hall again, all the puzzlement that had surrounded those things finally evaporating. The gimbals and the additional length on the quick-load cylinders—the remote control on the Popanilla safe in place of a standard keypad—the battles in the Roastmeat Bar on Gremon and outside the *Ruth*— and Dent's total lack of concern about any danger the mysterious backup shooter might be in.

Because there hadn't been a backup shooter. Dent's toys were simply four-shot quick-loads modified to be fired by remote control.

So if Dent had them in place, why was he still sitting here bleeding? Had the control been damaged or taken away from him?

That was the obvious answer. But I'd been watching him in the Roastmeat and later as he clambered inside the *Ruth*, and I hadn't seen anything that looked like a control. If it was camouflaged well enough that I hadn't spotted it, there was a good chance the thugs who'd searched him hadn't caught it, either.

The thugs.

I felt my throat tighten. Of course. Each of the quick-loads peeking coyly down from the ceiling had four shots, giving Dent a total of eight to play with. But counting the two men still guarding the outside of the lecture hall, we had a grand total of one boss and nine thugs to deal with. With Dent tied to a chair, killing or incapacitating only eight of the ten would do nothing but earn him a quick and violent death.

Only now that number balance had flipped. He had me and my four-shot DubTrub as backup. Even better, he had me and the other remote currently in my pocket. The trick would be how to introduce one or the other into the conversation without getting myself shot.

Selene and I were halfway to the lower level, and I was still working on that problem, when Balic retraced his steps, meeting us just as we reached the middle level of seats. Setting his right palm on my chest in silent command, he held out his left in equally silent invitation.

Frankly, I was surprised it had taken them this long. Using two fingers, I pulled out my DubTrub and set it on his palm. I started to take another step forward.

And stopped again as Balic's hand briefly increased its pressure against my chest. "And the other one," he said.

I suppressed a grimace. I'd hoped he would miss the small bulge of the quick-load nestled in my other pocket.

But there was nothing for it. I pulled it out and handed it over. His forehead creased a bit as he saw the unusual design, but merely put it away in his own pocket. He ran his eyes over me one final time and then nodded. "He's clean, sir," he announced.

The boss didn't answer, but merely flicked a finger. Balic stepped out of our path, and we continued down to the floor. The boss waited until we arrived, then turned his head and looked up at us. "Gregory Roarke," he said, his grating voice going a little darker. "I've heard of you."

I felt the bottom fall out of my stomach as I finally got a clear look at his face. This wasn't just some random crime boss we'd walked in on, or some local fence Dent had chosen to pass his stolen goods to.

I'd been out of the bounty hunter game for a long time. But I hadn't been out so long that I'd forgotten the name Francisc Pacadacz.

"I'm honored, Mr. Pacadacz," I said, forcing my voice to remain calm. Pacadacz had a violent reputation and a bloody history, but all the stories about him said that he mostly responded to respect and civility in kind.

Which wasn't to say that he might not kill Selene and me where we stood if he decided that would gain him something. It was just that he would respect us the whole time we were bleeding out.

"I've heard of you, too, of course," I continued. "Again, please forgive us for any trouble our arrival may have caused. I had no idea you had your own interest in Mr. Dent. My business with him can certainly wait until you've finished yours."

"You think there's going to be anything left of him after I'm finished?" Pacadacz countered. He held up the gem. "Where did you get this?"

"From Dent's stash," I said. "I hoped I could trade the rest of the gems for him."

"He's a target?"

"Yes, sir."

"Who's your client?"

"I'm sorry, sir, but I can't reveal—"

"Who's your client?" he repeated.

I felt my throat tighten. There were protocols bounty hunters were supposed to adhere to, the biggest of which was confidentiality. But people like Pacadacz didn't care much about other people's rules. "His name's Draelon," I said. "He's one of Luko Varsi's people."

Something that a charitable person might have characterized as a smile touched the corners of Pacadacz's mouth. "Luko Varsi, you say? Haven't heard his splashes for a long time. What does he want with Dent?"

"I'm afraid he didn't share that information with me."

"Convenient," Pacadacz said. The brief smile had vanished now like summer dew in a hot sun. "Varsi usually goes in-house for his hunters. I don't think I ever heard your name connected to his organization."

"I was mostly a contract employee," I said, feeling sweat breaking out on the back of my neck. Dropping names like Draelon and Varsi could be useful in a situation like this, but only if the other party believed you. "And he didn't pick me up until I'd mostly retired from bounty hunter work."

"Also convenient," Pacadacz said. "You know what *I* think, Roarke? *I* think you're Dent's partner. *I* think you're the person he's been trying to threaten us with for the past three hours."

I looked at Dent. After the beating his face had taken there wasn't much room for subtleties of expression, but I could almost imagine I saw a fading of his last bit of hope. We were all squarely under Pacadacz's thumb, and there was no one else who even knew where we were, let alone might be curious enough to come looking for us.

Except that we still had Dent's four-shot wild cards. Unfortunately, one of those cards was currently tucked away in Balic's pocket.

I'd just have to change that.

"Full points for cleverness, anyway," I commented, turning back to Pacadacz. "Dent knows we're on his trail, so he drops vague hints about a mysterious partner who might be sniffing around. We show up, he pretends all is lost—just look at that face—and your men relax their guard. Once that happens, his *real* partner is free to swoop in."

"And who would this *real* partner be?" Pacadacz asked, clearly not believing a single word I'd said.

"His brother, of course," I said, frowning slightly. "Weston Dent. Surely you've heard of him."

A flicker of something crossed Pacadacz's face. Whether he believed in Weston's existence, it was clear he'd heard the stories and rumors. "You think he'll have a better chance of getting in than you did?" he growled.

"With all due respect, Mr. Pacadacz, I don't think you understand what you're up against," I warned. "I presume you've heard the stories. People who try to take out Easton Dent get shot, usually in the back. And up to now no one's figured out how Weston's always been able to invisibly infiltrate the scene before the carnage takes place."

"You telling me you *have* figured it out?"

"I think so, sir, yes," I said. "It comes down to a very special type of sniper weapon, and a very special type of sniper."

I paused, partly for dramatic effect, partly to see if I had everyone's attention. From the utter silence in the room, I gathered I did. Even Pacadacz, who clearly didn't trust me farther than he could spit me, was fully focused on what I was saying "We need to start with the man himself," I went on. "Weston Dent is a master of disguise and stealth. He can find holes in the best security screen and slip through without being spotted."

"He tries that here, he'll get a bullet in the head," Pacadacz said flatly.

"Absolutely," I agreed. "Which is why he'll try something different. A tactic designed for targets inside an enclosed place like this one."

"You seem to know a lot about all this," Pacadacz said, his eyes narrowed. "Makes me wonder why."

"It's part of my job," I said, loading all the sincerity into my tone that I could. "I have to know as much about my target as I can before I go after him." I nodded toward Dent. "Especially when so many people have died while he was delivering or bargaining with them. I don't want to end up on that list."

I pointed back toward the door. "But as you said, Weston will know better than to try a straightforward infiltration. He'll need to go with his backup strategy, which near as I can tell is based on a modified DubTrub 2mm."

"Like yours?" Pacadacz demanded.

So he'd paid close enough attention to Balic's disarming of me to note the kind of gun I'd been carrying. "Yes, sir, only his will be modified for longer-range work," I said. "The standard DubTrub is a close-in weapon, very concealable, with a load of four missile slugs. What most people don't know is that you can elongate the gun's barrel section to handle longer missile slugs that are large enough to carry gas, fog, or breaching explosives. I brought a sample of the extended barrel to show you, one of the Number Four"—I leaned a little on the word—"varieties." I gestured to Balic. "Show them. Be careful you don't pop open one of the tubes and drop out the slug."

Maybe if he'd had a moment to think he'd have wondered what showing the rest of the thugs a plain black cylinder would accomplish. Or maybe if Pacadacz hadn't been focused so hard on finding flaws in my story so he'd have a reason to have me shot he might have countermanded my totally unauthorized order.

But Pacadacz was preoccupied, and Balic was used to delivering instant obedience. He pulled the gimmicked quick-load from his pocket and held it up, gripping it a little gingerly by its adhesive pad. Out of the corner of my eye I saw Dent straighten in his chair, his lips compressing into a determined line—

Abruptly, the quick-load twisted around in Balic's grip, and with a low screech like the shriek of a distant banshee, it fired a shot toward the group of thugs at the door.

"Aaahhh!" I shouted, clutching my chest and collapsing to the floor, grabbing Selene's wrist and pulling her down with me as I fell. One of the best ways to avoid getting shot in a melee, I'd long ago learned, was to pretend it had already happened. Balic was still standing there, his attention frozen somewhere between my unexpected death scene and the inexplicable behavior of the device that had come to life in his hand.

But he had no time for either set of thoughts. The quick-load's next shot took out one of the inside guards, while the third slammed into Pacadacz himself as he bolted from his seat and tried to scramble to the relative safety of the podium.

The fourth shot blasted into the side wall just below the dome of the ceiling as the remaining thugs opened fire on Balic, their trained reflexes targeting the one who was clearly shooting at them. The shriek of DubTrub fire went silent, the response gunfire likewise faltering as Balic collapsed in a bloody mess. Across the room, I could hear someone bawling orders, sending two of the remaining thugs clattering down the stairs to check on Pacadacz while the other two moved to defend the door.

But Pacadacz was beyond saving, and the door wasn't where

the threat was coming from. As the thugs leaped to obey the new commands, one of the DubTrubs in the ceiling opened up with its own deadly fire. It emptied its four shots into the remaining four thugs, leaving the last one poised and ready as the door swung open and the two outside guards charged in.

Five seconds later, it was over.

Cautiously, I eased my head up to the level of the chair backs, doing a quick but systematic check of the room. All nine thugs lay crumpled on the floor, their blood forming rivulets and small pools as it stained the lecture hall's white stone. All of them dead.

All except one. Even as I finished my survey a small movement caught my eye: Balic, struggling weakly to get his Blago free of its holster. Standing up, I walked over to him.

"Out of the way," Dent ordered in a raspy voice. "I've got two shots left."

"It's okay," I said, holding out a warning hand toward Dent. "He's not a threat."

"Roarke—"

"More than that, we need him alive." I reached Balic and squatted down beside him. He was still struggling with his gun; I helped him free it then took it from his weakened fingers and stuffed it into my belt behind my back. From his pocket I retrieved my DubTrub and held it loosely in my hand, not pointed at anything in particular. "How you doing?" I asked.

He looked up at me with an expression that was bouncing between pain, hate, and uncertainty. "How do you *think?*" he grated.

"As long as you can still talk," I said, looking him over. He was wearing body armor under his clothing, I saw now, which had absorbed most of the volley his panicked allies had directed at him. Dent had obviously also expected the armor—I'd already noted that most of the DubTrub rounds he'd remotely fired had been head shots. Probably why he'd set his backup guns in the ceiling in the first place. Balic wouldn't be doing any wind sprints any time soon, but he wasn't likely to shuffle off and die on me, either. "I assume the late Mr. Pacadacz has a ship nearby with other staff aboard?"

Balic's eyes flicked over to Pacadacz's motionless body. "So he *is* dead."

"Afraid so," I said. "Sorry, but there wasn't any way around that. But like my father used to say, *Just because the king is dead doesn't mean the livestock don't have to eat.*"

"What the hell does *that* mean?"

"It means that the king is dead, but the organization lives on," I said. "At least for a while. So here's what you're going to do. You're going to call the ship and get a team here to clean up this mess before the badgemen find it. In return, we're going to let you live. Got that?"

His eyes narrowed as he gazed up at me. "Why?"

I shrugged. "Call it a last act of mercy. I doubt Mr. Pacadacz would want this to be the story of how he died, sucker-punched by an invisible sniper. But once all the bodies are out of here and the blood's been cleaned up, you'll be able to tell whatever tale you want. Hang on a second."

I crossed to Pacadacz's body and did a quick search. One of his pockets yielded a cushioned bag with more of Dent's gems inside, which I tucked away in my own pocket. The gem I'd given him had ended up on the floor a couple of meters away; retrieving it, I took it back to Balic. "This is yours now," I said, holding it out so he could see it and then stuffing it into his pocket. "If you decide to bail on whoever takes over the organization, you'll at least have some traveling money. Either way, you need to get off Fidelio as soon as the cleanup is done. Deal?"

Again, he took a moment to study my face. Then, he gave me a small nod. "Deal."

"Good," I said. "Go ahead and make your call. We'll be out of here in a minute."

By the time I reached Dent Selene had freed him from the chair and was helping support him as he walked shakily toward the steps. "An act of *mercy*?" he croaked. "That bastard doesn't deserve any mercy."

"I know," I agreed. "You want to try to get rid of all these bodies before someone stumbles over them? Or would you rather have the whole temple grounds crawling with badgemen and journalists for the next week?"

He glowered at me. "How did you find me? How are you even *here*?"

"We can talk about that later," I said. "Unless you really want to go into it here and now."

His eyes flicked to Balic, who was working a phone out of his pocket. "I suppose not," he said. "Fine. Lead the way."

CHAPTER NINETEEN

———— ❖◆❖ ————

It was full night by the time we got back to the Pollux portal. We didn't see anyone as we staggered along, but Selene reported that a group of humans and Narchners had arrived. Given the lack of badgeman-style hue and cry accompanying their arrival, I was pretty sure that was Balic's cleanup crew. I got the hatch open and sent Selene inside, and between her pulling and me pushing, we got Dent through the gravity transition with a minimum level of effort on our part and a mostly minimum level of groaning on his.

"Couple of cracked ribs," I told him as I systematically fingered his various bones through his skin, wishing I had a proper medical scanner. "No full breaks, so no risk of a punctured lung. Considering how many times you got hit on the head and face, you also might have a mild concussion. Too many cuts and bruises to count."

"Trust me—I know where they all are," Dent assured me, a ghost of almost-humor peeking through the bottle of painkillers we'd poured down him as he rocked gently in his hammock. I'd reconfigured it on its stand so that he would be lying mostly flat on the mesh, but I doubted even the slight curve the hammock imposed on his body was particularly good for his injuries. Once we had him settled I could go back to Popanilla and bring back one of the camping mattresses I'd brought for Ixil, but for now this would have to do. "You sure that right ankle isn't broken? It feels like it's broken."

"Pretty sure, yeah," I said. "Looks like a strain, maybe a sprain. Did someone kick you there?"

He snorted. "Fell over my own feet trying to run from his thugs."

"Ah," I said. "All things considered, I think you got off pretty easy. What in the name of sanity made you think it was a good idea to get cozy with someone like Francisc Pacadacz?"

"I didn't," Dent said grimly. "I was hired to deliver the gems to someone else. I'm guessing Pacadacz tumbled to the arrangement and decided to cut himself in."

"And it didn't occur to you to just hand over the gems?"

"And get myself in trouble with both ends of my original deal?" Dent countered. "Besides, Pacadacz didn't want the jewelry. Well, not *just* the jewelry. He wanted the name of the supplier."

"Which you chose not to give him?" Selene asked, kneeling down beside Dent's hammock stand and offering him a tall glass of water and a bowl of vegetable twists and roast meat strips she'd put together from his supply cabinet.

"Of course not," Dent said, easing one of the meat strips gingerly between his swollen lips. "No, I never claimed to be a hero. The problem was that once he heard who it was, he got the brilliant idea that he could send me back to him as a warning. You see the kind of shape he wanted that warning to be in."

"Yeah, you wouldn't want a message like that to be misunderstood," I said grimly. "So who is this supplier?"

He rattled off a name I didn't recognize. "I gather he and Pacadacz are rivals or something," he said. "Or maybe they were sometime in the past. Some of these feuds go back decades."

"Easy to let that happen," I said, wincing at the memories of some of my own past failings. "I'm sorry we didn't get there sooner."

"Me, too," Dent said. "I suppose we're lucky you showed up before Pacadacz decided to start cutting off fingers."

Selene winced, and I saw the revulsion in her pupils. "Well, severed body parts *are* sort of a traditional warning to your rivals," I said, frowning. There'd been something else in his tone just then...

I focused on the fingers digging out Selene's meat and veggie pieces. They looked normal...but there was something just a bit off-kilter with the ones on his right hand. I looked back at his face.

To find his eyes steady on me. "So," I said, nodding toward his right hand. "The remote control is in your hand, isn't it? It's the"—I flicked another look at the hand—"first and second fingers and the thumb."

"I'm impressed," Dent said, a hint of reluctance in his eyes. Clearly, this wasn't a secret he shared very often. "Most people can't see the difference even when they know."

"It helps when you have one of your own," I said, lifting my left arm a bit.

"How did it happen?" Selene asked.

"An accident." Dent's throat tightened briefly with memory. "A stupid accident, actually. Lost all but my little finger. Anyway. I'd already been playing the *Weston Dent* card with people, trying to make them think I wasn't working alone, and while I was waiting for my hand to be ready for the prosthetics I realized that if I worked it right I could do more than just talk about him."

"So you had a control system put in and created a bunch of remote DubTrubs as your backup," I said, nodding. "So there never was a Weston Dent?"

He shook his head. "One hundred percent made up. But like I said, it was a card that was worth playing." His eyes narrowed slightly. "Speaking of cards and playing, you two are taking this rabbit hole thing awfully damn well. Not to mention finding it and figuring out how it works." He paused. "Unless you already knew?"

"We'll get to us later," I said. "Right now, let's start with you."

"Or perhaps with Dr. Riley," Selene murmured.

"Who?" Dent asked.

"The dead man in the photo you showed me," I said, letting my gaze harden. "You *do* remember him, don't you?"

A flicker of fresh pain crossed his face. "Way too well," he said quietly. "I just never knew his name."

"Well, now you do," I said. "Tell us about him."

For a moment Dent was silent, as if gathering his thoughts, or maybe trying to decide how much of the story he was going to tell us and how much he was going to conveniently forget.

He was welcome to try. Selene was kneeling right beside him, her eyelashes beating rhythmically as she sampled his scent. The minute he veered off the truth into lies she would know it.

"And before you start," I added, "remember that we just saved your life."

"Yeah, thanks for the reminder," he said. "I wasn't planning to lie, you know."

"That's good to hear," I said. "On the other hand, I've seen a lot of such noble resolutions go off the rails into the weeds. Though I'm sure yours won't. Please; continue."

Again he took a moment, though I suspected this one was mostly to annoy me after my interruption. "I was working on Shiroyama Island as a hiking guide," he said. "I was—well, I guess it's not a secret. I was tagging people to rob."

"Like Dr. Riley?" I asked.

Dent snorted. "Tell you the truth, I barely even noticed him. He was the academic sort, all archaeology or sociology or whatever. That type never has anything worth stealing. No, what caught my eye was the Patth hanging around the lodge."

I pricked up my ears. "This the one in your pictures?"

He twitched. "The—? You got into my *safe?*"

"After a fashion," I said. "We had to take the back off."

For a moment he glared at me. But the sheer expenditure of energy was too much for him. With a sigh he subsided. "Yeah, the one in the picture," he growled. "I wish to hell I'd ignored him. I should have just let them—"

He broke into a coughing fit, each spasm sending a flicker of pain across his face. "When are those painkillers supposed to kick in?" he asked when he was breathing more or less normally again.

"Any time," I promised. "But bear in mind these are just your first-aid kit pills, so don't expect miracles. So you were watching the Patth...?"

"And his two Iykam sidekicks," Dent said. "After it was all over and I was able to think about it, I realized they were always in the lodge because they were trying to stay hidden from your friend Riley. But at the time I just thought they were acting squirrelly because they were sitting on a stack of commarks or valuables and were worried about thieves."

"Which made you watch them even closer."

"Yeah." He gestured with a fumbling hand, and Selene helped

him take a drink. "Then, one day, just as I was finishing up a tour, I spotted the two Iykams hustling Riley into the forest along one of the lesser-used trails. Half leading him, half carrying him. The Patth was bringing up the rear, looking around and behind him like he was making sure no one was following them."

"So, naturally, you did."

"Yeah," Dent said ruefully. "There was another trail that would keep me more or less running parallel to them for the first part of the hike. I got on that one and paced them, wondering if this was a deal gone sour or if something else was going on. They were nearly to one of the turns, and I didn't want to lose them, so I left my trail and moved toward them just in time to see them leave theirs. I followed them the rest of the way..."

He paused again and took another drink. "When they finally stopped, it was at a full-blown campsite that Riley must have set up days or weeks earlier. I guess he'd been working out there all that time, and the Patth and his pals had been right on top of him. They probably headed out to the site at night, after he'd quit for the evening, to check on his progress. Riley was smart, though, and kept all his documents in that monster Brinx-Chakrars safe. You said you took its *back* off?"

"It was a fake," I told him. "Cheap safe rigged to look like a Brinx-Chakrars. Didn't you wonder how Riley could have gotten something that heavy out there by himself?"

From the look on Dent's face it was clear that thought had never even crossed his mind. "Well, *damn*," he muttered. "Clever little flink. Anyway, I watched while the Iykams drugged him with something—with something else, I mean, since they must already have dosed him with something to get him out there. They asked him some questions I wasn't close enough to hear, then the Iykams hauled him to his feet again and they all trooped over to the scree field."

"And when they got there, the Patth pushed on what I thought was a chunk of rock and opened the rabbit hole."

He shook his head, and I could see an echo of the memories flick across his face. "They all went inside. The two Iykams had to shove Riley in, but they managed it. I waited until they were out of sight, then headed over and peeked in. I was just in time to see them climb the last few steps around the big ball and do their rolling entrance thing into the little ball."

"We call them the receiver module and the launch module," I put in. "If you care."

"Who calls it that?" Dent asked, eyeing me closely. "You? Icarus?"

"We're still talking about you," I reminded him.

"Sure," he said. "Well, I have to admit that watching them walk around was a kick in the teeth," he said. "I'd never seen artificial gravity that could change direction that way. I was watching them roll Riley through the hatchway and thinking about maybe it was time to get out of there when the second Iykam in the big ball pulled out a gun before going inside with the others."

Dent's swollen lips pressed themselves into a thin line. "I don't know what the Talariac Drive did to the bounty hunter business. But for everyone else out there, it was like getting hit in the face over and over again. I can't even count all the shippers who went out of business as their customers disappeared. Or how many maintenance yards stripped out eighty percent of their mechanics, or how many cafés and bars around those yards shuttered up. I didn't like the Patth anyway. And now one of them was pulling a *gun* on someone?"

"So you went in?" Selene asked gently.

"I went in," Dent said, giving her a lopsided smile. "Yes, Easton Dent, professional thief and smuggler, suddenly going all brave and noble. And stupid. I rolled inside—not nearly as cleanly as they had—and headed around the inside in the opposite direction they'd taken. I guess I figured that if they came out they'd go back the way they came and might not see me up on what would be the ceiling."

"And it worked," I said.

He seemed to draw back. "How do you know?"

"I saw the pictures you took," I reminded him. "They showed one of the Iykam bodies out in the receiver module, while the other Iykam and the Patth were in the launch module. That means one of them got all the way across the receiver without seeing you."

He huffed out a breath. "You're smarter than you look," he said. "Yes, I'd just gotten to the top of the inside when the Iykam with the gun came rolling back out and headed for the exit. Going to stand guard, I guess, and never even bothered to look up. I had my DubTrub with me—I always carried it out on the trail, just in case. I waited until he'd gone outside and then walked the rest of the way around to the little ball opening.

"The Patth and Iykam were crouched over Riley, the Patth pointing around at the various bits of equipment and asking questions. Riley was in pretty bad shape, but whatever drug they'd given him was working, and he was able to answer. That was how I learned how to run the thing, with the spike and all." He raised his eyebrows. "I suppose you have another name for that, too?"

"The extension arm," I said.

"Right. Anyway, the Patth finished the interrogation and said something to the Iykam, who pulled out his own gun and handed it over. The Patth pointed it down at Riley..."

Dent's eyes seemed to drift to something an infinite distance away. "And I shot him."

For a long moment none of us spoke. I waited, watching Dent's eyes slowly come back to focus. "The Iykam grabbed the gun and turned around to aim it at me. I shot him. I looked back across the big ball, figuring the shots would have drawn the other Iykam's attention. They had. He was already inside and charging toward me. So I shot him, too."

"It was in defense of another person, Easton," Selene said quietly. "It's nothing you should feel guilty about."

"Yeah, that's what I tell myself," Dent said. "Every day."

"What about Dr. Riley?" I asked. I remembered the first time I'd killed, too, and just because it had been legally justified hadn't made it easier to live with. The faster I got Dent out of this memory, the better.

"He was too far gone," Dent said. "I don't know. The drug mix they'd given him, maybe, or some kind of reaction. The way the Patth pulled that gun told me he hadn't figured on Riley living past the interrogation anyway. I went inside, told him he was safe, and asked what I could do to help. He looked at me and said, *Find Gregory Roarke. Find Icarus.* And then he died."

"I wonder how he had your name," Selene said, looking thoughtfully at me. "I wouldn't think a researcher would have heard of you."

"We'll have to ask about that," I said. "Go on, Dent."

"Well, I sat there for a while, trying to figure out what to do," Dent said. "All I knew was that I was sitting in an alien artifact that had weird artificial gravity, and that I'd better find out if there was something more to this thing. If I'd just killed a Patth for nothing... anyway. I'd heard Riley's instructions on how to work it, so I went over to the spike and rode it up. There was this—well, you know what it's like. And I ended up here."

He waved an arm around the Pollux receiver module. "I was about as freaked out as I've ever been in my whole life. First thing I did when I hit the ground was head straight back to the little ball and see if I could get back to Popanilla. I did the round trip three more times, just to be sure, before I tried opening the hatch and seeing where I was. Nothing looked familiar, so I took some pictures and headed back to Popanilla to run everything through image match."

He looked down at his hands. "And while my info pad was chewing on the problem, I buried the bodies."

"In the little open area between the portal and the safe?" I asked.

"Yes," he said. "I didn't want to mark the graves in case someone came looking. But I know where they are. Oh, and before I did that I collected all of Riley's data and notes and buried them with him."

"How did you open the safe?" Selene asked.

"It was already open," Dent said. "The Patth must have done that before I got there. Probably part of his first interrogation was getting the combination. Anyway, you can figure out the rest. I found out this end was in the Erymant Temple on Fidelio, set up a camp of my own on Popanilla, and started using the rabbit hole for smuggling."

He waved a hand at me. "I also started looking for you. In hindsight, that seems to have been a really bad idea. The rest you know. Your turn. Who's Icarus?"

"Icarus isn't a who, it's a what," I said. I didn't know the rest, of course—far from it. But there was a fairly good chance that I now knew most of what Dent could tell me. Time to shoot some information the other direction. "It's a secret group that's been investigating these portals since the first one was found a few years ago. Unfortunately, somewhere along the line the Patth found out about it and have been trying to get their hands on one ever since."

Out of the corner of my eye I saw a frown form in Selene's pupils. That wasn't exactly the way it had all worked, of course. But it was close enough, and there was no point in making the story more complicated than I had to.

As my father used to say, *Dragging someone through the weeds is a good way for both of you to get lost.*

"Yeah, I can see why," Dent said. "Someone figures out this tech, and the Talariac Drive gets left in the dust of history. So where are they?"

I frowned. "Excuse me?"

"Where are the Patth?" Dent repeated patiently. "Why aren't they here? I mean, it's been almost five months since the one I killed found the Popanilla end of the rabbit hole. How come they haven't already swooped in on it?"

I looked at Selene. That was a damn good question. "I have no idea," I said. "You're right—a swarm of Patth should have been on the scene before you'd even finished swapping out the lock on Riley's safe. Someone must have dropped the ball."

"Whoever it was, I hope they shot him," Dent growled. "One less Patth in the universe."

"I'd be careful about saying things like that in public," I warned. "Especially given the glass house you're in at the moment."

"Yeah, I know," Dent said, his words suddenly sounding a little uncertain. "Probably the painkillers."

"Could be," I said, looking questioningly at Selene. She nodded; the meds were indeed running deep enough to alter his scent. "Let's tuck you in and let you get some sleep."

"You're not going to leave me alone, are you?" Dent slurred.

"Don't worry," I soothed him. "I'm going back to Popanilla to get some sleeping gear for Selene and me, but I'll be back."

"What if someone comes in?"

"They'll live just long enough to wish they hadn't," I promised. Pulling the Blago 6mm I'd taken from Balic from my belt, I checked the mag and the safety and handed it to Selene. "Selene will stay on guard until I get back."

"Okay," Dent said. His eyelids fluttered once, and then closed.

"Dent?" I asked softly.

No response.

"He's asleep," Selene confirmed, turning the Blago over in

her hands and testing its balance. "We don't need bedding, you know. It's warm enough in here, and empty food containers make a comfortable enough palliasse."

"After a day like this, I'm interested in a little more than just *comfortable enough*," I told her, levering myself to my feet. "I'll be back as soon as I can."

"You *do* realize it's still at least a two hour hike to Trailhead and back."

"Yes, I should have asked them to move the town farther east when I was there," I said. "Too late now. Anyway, I also want to make a StarrComm call or two."

"You going to bring the admiral up to date?"

"I might," I said. "Or I might leave that job for Ixil."

"Ah," Selene said, her eyes steady on me. "So who *are* you going to call?"

"You heard Dent's question," I reminded her. "Why haven't the Patth swarmed Popanilla in general and Shiroyama Island in particular?"

"And you're going to ask the Patth?"

I pursed my lips. "Actually," I said, "I am."

Ixil was nowhere to be seen when I rolled out through Castor's hatch. I gave a soft call and he emerged into view through the trees at the edge of the scree field. "Did you find Dent?" he asked as I walked over to him.

"Yes," I said. "Unfortunately, someone else found him first."

I gave him a quick rundown of the day's adventures. Aside from Dent's general well-being, he seemed mostly interested in the part about Francisc Pacadacz and the off-shuffling of his mortal coil. Though he didn't say anything, I had the impression that Pacadacz had already been on his personal radar.

I'd never heard what Ixil had been doing before he joined the Icarus Group. Someday I'd have to look into that.

"Anyway, I'm heading into Trailhead for some extra supplies," I finished. "I don't think we want to move Dent right now, which means we're going to have three mouths to feed in there. I'll need one more camping mattress, too, unless you want to donate yours."

"Since a trip to Trailhead is necessary anyway, I hardly think such a sacrifice would be worthwhile," Ixil said, a bit dryly. "But

I'm happy to go instead if you'd like. It sounds like you've already had all the exercise you need for one day."

"Thanks, but with Floyd and his buddies poking around the island I'd rather you stay hidden. As my father used to say, *The best hole cards are the ones no one knows you have.*"

"True enough," he said. "But they won't recognize me or place any significance on my appearance if they see me. They *will* recognize you."

"In which case I'll just have to spin them a new story," I said with a shrug. "Don't worry, I've got several to choose from."

"Very well," Ixil said. He didn't sound convinced, but he could tell I'd made up my mind. "I assume you'll want Pix along to guide you back?"

"That's okay—I know the route now," I said. "I'll be back in a couple of hours."

I was actually a lot less confident about my navigational skills than I'd made it sound. After all, I'd only done the round trip to Trailhead once, and half of that had been in pre-dawn darkness.

But I had a good eye for detail, and maneuvering through the forest turned out to be a lot like finding my way through the warren of twisting streets and alleys of an urban criminal sanctuary. I found the Scree View trail without trouble, and reached Trailhead with every confidence that I would find my way back to Castor with equal ease.

More importantly, I could now make my StarrComm call without the risk of Pix eavesdropping and relaying the details to Ixil when I returned.

The StarrComm center was more crowded now in late afternoon than it had been during my first early morning visit. I checked out the line, then left and did my camp gear shopping, figuring the place would probably clear out some as we approached the mealtime hour. When I returned half an hour later, the wait turned out to be barely three minutes.

It took me another five minutes of hunting through the directories to find the number I needed. I punched it in, and found myself talking to a calm but stiff-faced receptionist. My name got me past him to the next tier's version, and through her to the final stop.

"Name?" the gatekeeper asked.

"Gregory Roarke," I said. "My name should be familiar to—"

"I'm told you wish to leave a message."

"Yes," I confirmed. "A message, and an invitation. I assume you can record?"

"I'm already doing so," she said. "The recipient?"

I braced myself. As my father used to say, *The only time it makes sense to poke the bear is when you're already up against the tiger.* "One of your chiefs," I said. "Sub-Director Nask."

CHAPTER TWENTY

─────── ❖ ───────

We spent the next two days in Pollux with Dent, keeping him fed and hydrated, helping him and his swollen ankle to his chemical toilet when necessary, and in general nursing him back toward health. I expected him to be a rotten patient, but was rather pleasantly surprised that he turned out to be docile and cooperative.

Of course, that could have just been the painkillers.

I went back to Castor twice during that time to check in with Ixil, update him on Dent's recovery, and to see if Floyd's island-wide search for us had wandered anywhere close. So far it hadn't, but Ixil was clearly not going to let his guard down. He'd already rigged up defenses around an impromptu fortress he could retreat to, using the two Iykam corona guns and the blast ribbon I'd left him. He also had Pix and Pax running a continual scout pattern to alert him if anyone came too close. I assured him that once we got Dent mobile again we could contact Graym-Barker, and that I fully expected both Gemini portals to be safely within the Icarus fold within the next two weeks.

Ixil, needless to say, was less optimistic about that. "I trust you haven't forgotten that there are other parties to this venture, none of whom is likely to bow out gracefully," he reminded me.

"I haven't forgotten," I assured him. "But there are ways to deal with them."

251

"Ways you'd care to share with your associates?"

"Sorry, but there's a little more information I need before I can put together a coherent plan," I said. "Speaking of which, can I take a couple of Dent's pictures?"

"Certainly, if you need them," Ixil said, eyeing me closely. "What do you intend to do with them?"

"It occurred to me that it's only an assumption that Dr. Riley started out here at Castor," I pointed out. "It could also be that he found Pollux first and only then found out that Popanilla was the home of its counterpart. I thought I might show his picture around Malfatti City—discreetly, of course—and see if anyone recognized him as poking around the Erymant Temple ruins."

"I don't think that's a wise idea," Ixil warned. "It could attract attention you don't want."

"Like I haven't already had plenty of that," I said sourly. "But yes, I'll be careful. And of course I'll make sure no one follows me back to Pollux. I assume the pictures are still in the safe?"

"Most of them, yes," Ixil said, still looking unconvinced. "I took out a representative sample for safekeeping. Help yourself. Just be careful not to close the door."

"Oh, you got it open?"

"There was an inside latch trigger Pax was able to get to," he explained. "I also reattached the back under the assumption we might need to move the safe at some time in the future, or possibly need to quickly seal it against an intruder."

"I assume you first detached it from the tree. How did you get the back on?"

"I used one of the corona guns to spot-weld the back in place. But again, don't close the door. Right now, Dent's the only one who can open it without a great deal of effort."

"True," I said. "Though he *does* owe us a favor or two, of course. I'll bring you another report tomorrow."

I found the safe door ajar with a sturdy stick wedging it open to make sure the wind or some animal didn't unintentionally close it. I picked out the pictures I needed, then headed back to Castor.

Five minutes later, I was once again in Pollux.

"How's the patient?" I whispered as I crossed to where Selene was watching Dent asleep on his new camping mattress.

"He's better," she said. "Less snoring, which I think means

his nasal cavities are clearing up. Why *do* humans have those, anyway?"

"Lots of theories," I said. "Not sure anyone really knows. I'm heading out—keep an eye on things here."

"You're going outside?" Selene asked, her pupils surprised and uneasy. "What if Balic and his people are still around?"

"I doubt they're still around *here,* on the temple grounds," I said truthfully. "But I'd certainly appreciate you checking for any unwanted company before I commit myself. Come on, it's getting late out there."

I got the hatch open and waited the few seconds it took Selene to confirm that no one was wandering around nearby. I rolled through the hatch, got my bearings, and headed for the edge of the grounds. I saw no one until I reached the low wall marking the temple grounds boundary and crossed into the busy city beyond.

I had to walk three blocks before I found an available runaround. I fed in the bills and drove another ten kilometers to Edgeling Kai, the high-end restaurant in the Malfatti City Center district where I'd reserved an interior private dining room. I was nearly an hour early, so I parked the runaround a couple of blocks away and made a casual walking survey of the area, paying special attention to the exits and the availability of cover and escape options outside each of them.

Edgeling Kai's own parking lot was supplemented by a larger municipal lot beside it, the two open spaces separated by a row of bushy trees that looked like birch but smelled strongly of lemon. It was currently the quiet hour between normal commercial business closing and the time most residents headed out for dinner and both lots were only sparsely occupied. I checked them out from a distance, paying special attention to the four closed vans and other large vehicles.

Finally, as the sky darkened into early evening, I went inside the restaurant and let the receptionist show me to my dining room.

It was laid out exactly as I'd specified: a single six-seat table, draped with an elegant black tablecloth with six place settings that included entrée and salad plates, wine and water glasses, and a full set of flatware that included rather intimidating serrated steak knives. I'd specified that the tablecloth should be large; the Edgeling Kai staff had gone beyond my expectations, the cloth draping all the way to the floor on all sides. Not a setup that would sit well with my guests, I knew, and it took me a few minutes to drape the extra length and width on top of the table, moving the place settings so they wouldn't be covered.

An elegant arrangement that would perfectly complement the dinner I'd ordered. It was a shame that none of us were likely to be around to eat it. Hopefully, the staff would enjoy the treat.

I was seated facing the door from the far end of the table when my guests arrived.

"Good evening, Sub-Director Nask," I greeted him, rising from my seat. A universal gesture of respect, as well as an equally universal proof that I wasn't holding a weapon. Nask himself didn't seem to care much about either, but the three Iykams who crowded into the room behind him definitely did. I also got the sense that they were disappointed not to have an excuse to shoot me down on sight.

"Good evening, Mr. Roarke," Nask said, sending a quick look around the room. "I assume your associates are patrolling outside?"

"I brought no associates, Sub-Director," I said. "I wanted to talk to you in private."

"Really," Nask said, the Patth version of a frown settling onto his face. "That may have been a mistake."

"I suppose we'll find out," I said, feeling a small shiver run up my back. "I invited you here to offer you some information that I think will be of profit to you."

"And to obtain some information for yourself, no doubt?"

"If such an exchange seems reasonable to you, yes," I said. "But let's start by seeing what I can offer."

"Very well," Nask said, a little stiffly. He stepped to the end chair facing me and sat down. As he did so, I noticed his eyes flick to the empty space under the table, confirming there were no surprises there. Just as well that I'd folded over the tablecloth. "Please," he added, gesturing me to also sit.

"Thank you." I resumed my seat. While we'd been talking the three Iykams had spread out to the sides of the room where they could see me and also watch the door. Under the circumstances, I appreciated their thoroughness. "I have a picture here—"

"Before we begin, I have a question," Nask interrupted. "In your message you specifically asked for me. Why?"

"I had information I needed to share with a Patth," I said. "You're the only one I knew I could trust."

"Really," Nask said, gazing intently at me. "Such a statement begs further explanation."

"Allow me then to offer it," I said. "A few weeks ago I was in the Red Poppy taverno on New Kyiv, hoping to meet with someone who'd been messaging with me. A few hours after I left the taverno a human male was found dead with my contact's identification, his face burned off by a couple of plasmic shots. Just for good measure, my wallet was also found at the scene."

"I assume from your phrasing that the victim was *not* your contact?"

"Correct," I said. "It appears that someone else was also looking to connect with this man. Unfortunately, his agents accidentally grabbed an innocent bystander who happened to fit his general description and was wearing similar clothing."

"What does this have to do with me?" Nask asked.

"It struck me afterward that there should have been no reason to kill him," I said. "Assuming it was a group of Iykams who grabbed him—"

"Have you proof that Patthaaunuth or Iykams were involved?"

"No, not at all," I assured him. "Hear me out, please. Assuming it was a group of Iykams who grabbed them, all that their supervising Patth needed to do was check out their prisoner without himself being seen, realize a mistake had been made, and turn him loose. There would be no repercussions—no offense, but I doubt a human could pick a given Iykam out of a lineup even if they were all wearing name tags. But this Patth made the mistake of walking in on the prisoner, probably gloating, and only then realized he had the wrong man."

"You still have no evidence the Patthaaunuth were involved," Nask said stiffly.

"No, but I know the Patth are interested in him," I said. "My contact was Easton Dent. I assume you've heard that name?"

Nask's expression didn't change, but one of the Iykams gave a small twitch. "I have," Nask said calmly. "Again, why me?"

"Because walking in on a prisoner without double-checking his identity was a stupid thing to do," I said. "You're the only Patth I know personally who's not that stupid. Ergo, you're the only Patth I know wasn't involved."

For a long moment Nask just stared. Then, almost unwillingly, the Patth version of a smile touched his expression. "Your logic is hardly solid," he said. "But your conclusion is indeed correct. I was not, in fact, involved in that incident."

"Do you know who was?"

The smile disappeared. "No," he said, his voice going dark. "But we mean to find out. It's unacceptable for a high-ranking Patthaaunuth to be involved in unnecessary killing."

"Glad to hear it," I said. So it *had* been a Patth and his attendant Iykams who'd killed the stranger in the New Kyiv morgue. I'd been pretty sure, but it was nice to have confirmation.

Though having Nask all but admit it was something I hadn't expected. Maybe he was ready to build at least a tentative working relationship with me. More likely he was just playing friendly in hopes of keeping me relaxed and off-balance until I spilled whatever information I'd brought to share.

In that case, I hoped he was ready to be knocked a little off-balance himself. "Now that that's out of the way, I have something less pleasant to discuss," I said, easing my hand into my jacket pocket. "I have a picture here I want to show you."

Nask nodded and gave a small hand signal to the Iykams. Just the same, I kept my movements slow as I pulled out the picture of the Patth Dent had shot and slid it across the table. "Do you know him?"

Nask stared down at the picture, his fingers pressed against the tabletop. "Yes," he said quietly. "Conciliator Yyng. Where did you—?"

He looked up sharply. "This is a *death photo*."

"Sadly, it is," I confirmed. "And no, I didn't kill him. Nor was I there when it happened."

"I find that difficult to believe," Nask bit out. So much for the friendly working relationship. "Conciliator Yyng's mandate should not have brought violence upon him. Furthermore, he was last known to be on Popanilla, from where you sent my invitation to this place."

I winced. I'd forgotten that the Patth probably had a backdoor into StarrComm, just like they did with most other major electronics and security systems in the Spiral. "Conciliator Yyng died five months ago," I said. "I was nowhere near Popanilla at that time. What do you mean, his mandate? His mandate for what?"

"That is internal Patthaaunuth business," he said shortly. "What do you know about his death?"

"Absolutely nothing," I told him, frowning. The Patth internal operations and government were shrouded in fog as far as the rest of the Spiral was concerned. But I'd spent a lot of time with Nask, and I was pretty good at reading his face and vocal tones. Adding in the fact that Dr. Riley had been an Icarus researcher—

"They took the portal mandate away from you, didn't they?" I said. "After Firefall, the Director General took you off search duty and gave that job to Yyng."

If there was a signal I never saw it. But suddenly all three Iykams had their corona guns drawn and leveled. "Who spoke to you of the portal mandate?" Nask asked, his voice almost too low to hear. "Tell me who spoke of that."

"No one spoke of it," I said between stiff lips. "It's all right there. The fact you didn't know Conciliator Yyng had disappeared— you'd have been more in the loop if you were coordinating a portal hunt. The fact that you came here alone to talk to me—if you were still hunting portals you'd have whistled up an army of Iykams, and I'd already be a prisoner aboard your ship. And the fact that it's been two days since my message, and yet that same army of Iykams hasn't descended on Popanilla. So if you aren't going to get credit for whatever Yyng found, you aren't going to lift a finger to help him? Or rather, help whoever now has the mandate?"

For a few thudding heartbeats he just stared at me. This time I *did* see the signal, and the Iykams' weapons disappeared again into their robes. "Again, your logic and conclusions are flawed," he said reluctantly. "Even a sub-director must present cause in order to requisition additional Iykam support. But more than that, you do me a severe injustice if you believe I am motivated by recognition or reward. Patthaaunuth officials are not permitted to expand outside their mandates without the express authorization of the Director General."

I frowned. "Are you saying that if you happened to trip over a portal tomorrow, you couldn't do anything about it?"

"Any Patthaaunuth without a specific mandate cannot act directly," Nask said. "He could only send a report and request expansion or transfer of mandate. But such a decision would require time, and in that interval overt action could not be taken." He paused. "That inaction is precisely what I am doing right now, since I now have proof that there's a portal on Fidelio."

I felt my stomach knot up. "What makes you think there's a portal here?"

"Your presence at this table," Nask said. "You called from Popanilla, yet are on Fidelio two days later. That trip is impossible by normal spacecraft. When it was still possible that I would be meeting a representative instead of you personally, I had no evidence. Now, I do."

"Not necessarily," I said, keeping my voice casual. "There are at least a dozen places within a two-day flight of Fidelio. The other portal could be on one of those."

"True," Nask agreed. "Another reason to delay making a report. Still, I expect your superiors would be upset to learn you'd given the Patthaaunuth such valuable information." He paused expectantly.

I gazed at him as the pause stretched out. Was he actually suggesting...? "Are you trying to *blackmail* me?"

"You said we were here to exchange information," he reminded me. "I merely seek an additional bit of data in exchange for not filing a report on you and Fidelio."

"Ah," I said. "Yes, I suppose that makes sense. All right. Ask me your question, and I'll see if I can answer it."

"I'm certain you can," Nask said. "Tell me where Luko Varsi is."

It was about as off-the-edge question as I could have expected. "I have no idea," I said reflexively. "What in the world do you want Varsi for?"

"If you don't know, there is nothing more to discuss," Nask said, standing up. "Farewell, Mr. Roarke—"

"Wait a second," I said, quickly rising to my feet. The Iykams' guns came out again, but I barely noticed. "I said I don't know where he is. I didn't say I couldn't find him."

Nask eyed me a moment, then resumed his seat. "Continue."

I sat down again, too, my mind spinning as I tried to think this through. "All right," I said. "I assume this pertains to the scheme he had of getting hold of Patth pilot circuitry and feedback systems so they could be implanted into his face and he could then fly Talariac-equipped ships. Is that correct?"

"What my question pertains to is of no importance," Nask said tartly. "Tell me how to find him."

"Ah," I said, eyeing him closely. The question had mostly been a stalling tactic to buy myself a few more seconds to organize my thoughts. But his reaction was clear evidence that I'd hit something sensitive. "I'm sorry, but I thought the Patth settled with him months ago."

"Why would you think that?"

"Because that's what I was told," I said, trying to remember Draelon's exact words. *Tell me, how would you respond to the charge that you betrayed him to the Patth?* "I was accused of betraying him to the Patth. I can't think why the person who said that would have phrased it that way unless the Patth had already caught up with him."

"Who spoke that to you?"

"His name's Draelon," I said. "I don't think I ever heard his first name."

"Manx," Nask said thoughtfully. "Manx Draelon. I assume he learned of that situation from Luko Varsi himself?"

"I don't think so," I said, again searching my memory. "It sounded to me like the piloting gear was a deep, dark secret that Varsi wouldn't have told anyone."

"Even his closest associates?"

"*Especially* his closest associates," I said. "Whatever he was planning, no one else was supposed to be in on it. I assume that whoever the Patth was who confronted Varsi also wouldn't have talked to anyone else?"

"No Patthaaunuth would have been directly involved," Nask said. "The message would have been delivered by an Expediter."

"Of course," I agreed, shivering a little. I'd had enough contact with the Patth's cadre of black-ops agents to last me two or three lifetimes. "As long as we're on the subject, what exactly would the protocol have been for an infraction this serious?"

"There are several options available," Nask said in a tone that suggested this wasn't the sort of thing the Patth usually discussed with outsiders. "A warning could be issued under circumstances that would show that a second, more lethal confrontation couldn't be defended against."

I nodded. That would fit with Varsi disappearing so deeply underground that even Selene hadn't been able to sniff out a trace of him. The Expediter had shown he could get to him at any time, and Varsi had exercised the proverbial better part of valor.

"A physical or electronic attack against possessions or business assets would be another possibility," Nask continued. "The underlying purpose of such a demonstration is to show the target the error of his actions, remind him that a more crushing punishment can be administered, and offer the chance for restitution."

I felt myself sit up a little straighter. "Restitution?"

"Of course," Nask said. "The Patthaaunuth are at heart businessmen. We would prefer to regain our losses, or at least to minimize further outlay of time and resources."

"Yes, the scorched ground approach seldom accomplishes very much," I murmured.

"Unless a highly visible warning is necessary," Nask said. "Even then, there are usually less expensive ways to achieve that purpose."

"Yes. Interesting," I said. "So what's the message you're trying to deliver to Manx Draelon?"

"I have no message for him," Nask said. "I merely seek to locate Luko Varsi through him."

"But you *do* have a mission on Brandywine," I persisted. "Something included in your new mandate, I assume."

Nask himself didn't react. But once again, that same Iykam gave a little twitch. "You're mistaken," Nask said. "I haven't been on Brandywine. Nor does my current mandate require me to be there."

"Come now, Sub-Director," I admonished gently. "Lying doesn't become you." I pointed to the Iykam. "And he really needs to work on his inscrutability. Come on—what can it hurt to tell me what's going on? There's a good chance that I can help you with it, in fact."

"I doubt that, Mr. Roarke," Nask said, his official expression coming down across his face like a heavy curtain. "Nor can I conceive of a situation where you would even make such an offer."

"It's not *that* outlandish," I objected. "As long as you're not actively hunting portals there's no reason we can't work together. Or, you know, as long as you're not trying to kill Selene or me."

He inclined his head politely. "Farewell, Mr. Roarke."

"And speaking of killing," I said as he started to turn around, "I believe there are a number of people outside the restaurant whose goal is to kill me. Along, probably, with everyone else in this room."

CHAPTER TWENTY-ONE

———— ◆◆◆ ————

Slowly, ominously, Nask turned back to face me. "What did you speak?" he demanded quietly.

"Sorry—I suppose I should have mentioned that earlier," I said. "They're the remnants of a gang headed by the late Francisc Pacadacz. I had a run-in with him a few days ago. I suggested they leave the planet, but it looks like they decided to stick around and try for some vengeance."

"And you did indeed come alone?"

"I did."

Some of the tension seemed to fade from Nask's stance. "A quarrel with you should not impact upon me," he concluded. "I wish you luck in finding an escape from them."

"Thank you," I said. "But I'm afraid it's not that easy. They know I booked a private room, from which they'll infer I'm meeting with someone, who they'll probably assume is either a friend or someone to whom I've passed useful information."

Nask's eyes narrowed. "In which event they are not interested only in revenge against you."

"It's a possibility," I said. "More importantly, you still need me alive, because in eight days I'm going to give you information that will resolve your mandate."

"You speak nonsense," he bit out. "You lay out an incentive in hopes that I will help your escape."

"Not at all," I assured him. "It's just that I need to bring other participants to Fidelio in order to confirm the information I'm promising, and they can't arrive for another eight days. Don't worry, I really don't need your help in escaping this place—I just thought you should know people with guns might try to interfere with you on your way out."

"You do not need my assistance? You, a lone human?"

"Well, a bit of a diversion would be nice," I conceded. "But really, all you have to do is walk out the front door and head to whatever vehicle you came in. The thugs will provide the rest of it. Oh, and you can shoot anyone with a gun who tries to give you trouble."

For a moment Nask stared at me in silence. "They will not dare to stop a Patthaaunuth," he said at last. "Very well. Eight days. In this same place?"

"It'll be a slightly different venue," I said. "But close to here. I'll message you the location." I lifted a finger. "One other thing, if I may. I know the Patth have a backdoor access code for Everlock vehicle security systems. Would you mind giving that to me? I promise to use it only once and then erase it."

"You ask a great deal of me, Mr. Roarke," Nask said, his voice going even more ominous. "We are not allies. We are not friends. Yet you presume upon me as if we were both."

"Yes, I do," I admitted. "But that's because I know what your mandate is, and I'm as anxious as you are to see it resolved."

"I doubt that strongly."

"Nevertheless, I assure you it's true," I said. "May I have the code?"

Nask looked at one of the Iykams. "Feed this number into your phone," he said reluctantly. "Activate when within ten meters of your target vehicle."

I got out my phone. "Go ahead."

He rattled off a string of twenty numbers. I punched them in, double-checked the list, and nodded. "Thank you," I said, putting the phone away. "I'll erase it within the hour."

"No need," he said. "It will erase itself after a single use."

"Of course," I said. "No problem—I really do only need it once. Now, the east side door, the one away from the parking lot, has the best cover if you're planning to make a dash for it. The west door will take you straight into the lot, where I presume your vehicle is parked."

Nask drew himself up. "I shall leave via the main entrance," he said firmly. "A Patthaaunuth does not run or hide like a frightened prey animal."

"Main entrance it is," I said, nodding. Which was the door I'd hoped he would take in the first place. "I'll need a couple of minutes, then I'll be ready to back you up."

"Backup is unnecessary," Nask said, turning toward the doorway. Two of the Iykams moved quickly to get there ahead of him, setting up as a vanguard, while the third moved into rearguard position. "I shall await your message," he added over his shoulder. "*If* you survive this night."

"Good luck to you, too," I called after him.

I waited until the last Iykam closed the door behind them. Then, I gathered the six dinner plates, four of the steak knives, and the long tablecloth and hurried for the door. It really was a shame that I couldn't stay for dinner.

Thirty seconds later, slipping through the stream of waitstaff moving briskly back and forth between the kitchen and the main dining areas, I was on the roof.

Bounty hunters in general don't like rooftops. The enhanced visibility can be useful, but given that sight lines run both directions it also means the observer is at heightened risk of being spotted. Add in the fact that most roofs have little cover and limited exit capability, and it's easy to see why hunters prefer to keep their feet solidly on the ground.

Me, I love rooftops. They offer options that a lot of people never think of.

I kept bent over as I hurried north, heading toward the awning over Edgeling Kai's main entrance. I got there and crouched down behind the roof's half-meter-high parapet just as Nask and his three bodyguards came striding into view past the edge of the awning. As they headed toward the street three men detached themselves from a couple of shadows on either side of the walkway and angled casually to intercept.

I didn't know what the Patth rules of engagement were regarding threats or perceived threats, but I knew I could comfortably get through the rest of my life without ever again having to see someone get blasted by an Iykam corona gun. Fortunately, I was in position to at least blunt a little of whatever the thugs had planned.

Half rising from my crouch, I took one of the dinner plates in hand and Frisbeed it at the nearest thug.

I'd been aiming for the center of his back, but I was seriously out of practice with low-tech combat and the plate instead slammed into the back of his right knee. But the end result was the same. The thug went down like a dropped bag of laundry, his hand hitting the pavement hard as he broke his fall, the impact shaking loose the nasty-looking gun he'd just drawn.

The two nearest Iykams spun around as the weapon bounced its way along the ground, their own corona guns leveled. But the attackers' focus had been wrenched away from Nask to the more immediate task of finding and dealing with this unanticipated attack.

Unfortunately for them, I was already crouched down again, my head presenting only a small and easily missed bump in the otherwise smooth line of the parapet. I watched their eyes swing past Edgeling Kai's entrance to the parking lot.

And with their attention once again elsewhere, I half rose and threw another plate.

My aim was better this time, the plate slamming edge-first into the second thug's abdomen. He went down alongside his companion, gasping for air. Two more thugs were hurrying in from the side as backup, and this pair had enough presence of mind to add the nearby rooftops into their visual search pattern.

But once again there was nothing for them to see. I was already headed back toward the center of the roof, crouched as far over as I could while still keeping up a good pace. Once I was completely out of sight, I turned to my right and headed for the west side of the building, which overlooked the twin parking lots. I reached the parapet on that side and carefully looked over it.

There were two more thugs below me, presumably the ones who'd been watching the exit on that side of the restaurant. They were hurrying toward the front of the building, their eyes darting back and forth as they watched for another of the sneak attacks that had already taken out two of their companions. I headed south along the edge, moving toward the rear of the building, watching the thugs as they loped away in the opposite direction. Another few seconds, and this entire side of the building would be deserted.

And then, in perfect unison, both thugs skidded to a halt and spun around, their necks craned to look up at the roof. They spotted me and raised their guns—

A second later both dodged to the sides as I sent two more dinner plates whistling in their direction.

I ducked down again, pausing to take a good look at the parking lots. Just visible through the line of trees separating the two sections I could see one of the four vans I'd spotted earlier in the municipal lot.

I smiled tightly. Sight lines worked both ways, and whoever was directing the attack had apparently just at that moment spotted me through the trees as I moved around on the roof.

As my father used to say, *When you're the mouse part of a cat-and-mouse game, spotting the cat is a good half of the job.*

A distant, crackling noise wafted across the night breeze, and I felt my smile turn into a wince. One of the Iykams had apparently felt the need to open fire.

Which now offered the remaining thugs a choice between massing for a counterattack, running for their lives, or shifting their focus exclusively to me. Whichever way that decision fell, it was well past time to get off this roof.

Once again, I headed toward the center to get clear of their view, as well as to suggest that I was going for the stairs. With the thugs' command station to the west and the main battle to the north, the south and east were my best exit choices.

So instead, I made an about-face and headed back to the west.

But to the southwest this time, toward a spot where I knew the sight line from the van would again be blocked by one of the trees. I reached the parapet, confirmed that no one was beneath me or in sight, and got to work.

The ground was about seven meters below me, an intimidating drop for anyone who wanted to keep their knees and ankles intact. Luckily, I had three meters' worth of Edgeling Kai tablecloth slung over my shoulder. I laid it out with its edge at the base of the parapet, anchored it solidly to the roof with the steak knives, and tossed the rest of it off the edge. I rolled off the parapet and slid down the cloth toward the ground, my skin itching with the knowledge that for the next few seconds I would be a perfect target for anyone who decided to take a shot.

But everyone was apparently busy elsewhere. I reached the

end of the tablecloth and safely dropped the rest of the way to the ground.

I turned and headed south, jogging a hundred meters to the next street, which defined the edge of the municipal parking lot. There I turned west, and another hundred meters later curved into a big circle that would take me back into the municipal lot.

The van was still dark and quiet as I slipped through the other parked vehicles and came up behind it. Most criminal gangs I'd gone up against had been smart enough to invest in the allegedly pickproof Everlock security protocol on their buildings and vehicles. Hopefully, Pacadacz hadn't been the exception.

I'd find out soon enough. Pulling out my phone, I triggered Nask's code. Then, DubTrub in hand, I stepped up to the van's rear doors and pulled the handle.

Pacadacz was indeed not the exception. The door swung open without resistance, revealing the backs of three heads, two in the front seats and one more behind them. "Don't turn around," I said.

The rear-seat head started to turn, stopped as I tapped the DubTrub's metal barrel warningly against the van's metal ceiling. I climbed inside, pulled the door closed behind me, and frog-walked my way forward until I was behind the rear seat. "Correct me if I'm wrong, Balic," I said, pressing my gun barrel gently against the back of his head, "but didn't I tell you to get off the planet?"

"Roarke?" he asked, a frown in his voice.

"Like there's anyone else on Fidelio who gives a flying leap about you," I countered. "I asked you a question."

"What do you want me to say?" Balic growled. "You killed our boss. We can't just run away after something like that. Besides, you still had all those gems."

"Oh, come on," I scoffed. "I wasn't born last month, let alone yesterday. A gang with your resources and interests isn't going to risk stirring up a city's worth of badgemen for a measly half-million commarks' worth of jewelry. Why are you *really* here?"

"I don't know what you're talking about."

"Fine—have it your way," I said. "I suppose I can't have you talking about me to anyone afterward, so I guess it's time to say good-bye." I pressed the muzzle of the DubTrub a little harder against his head. "Good-bye, Balic."

"No, no, wait—wait," Balic said hurriedly. "Fine. We were hired to do a job."

"Which was...?"

He muttered something under his breath. "We were supposed to pick up Easton Dent," he said reluctantly. "He said Dent was supposed to be here to make a handoff to a local fence. We got to the fence, found out where Dent was meeting him, and went there instead."

"What happened to the fence?"

Balic snorted. "What do you think?"

"Right," I muttered. Really, what *had* I thought? "So why are you still here?"

"We didn't finish the job," Balic said. "We got a message saying you hadn't left Fidelio, and then another saying you'd booked a room at Edgeling Kai. We thought Dent might be with you, so we came out."

"I gather you weren't expecting a Patth?"

A small twitch went through him. "No. We were just told to grab Dent if he showed up."

"And me?"

He snorted again. "You were just a bonus."

"Like the Patth."

"Yeah." He huffed out a grunt. "Who *were* those things, anyway? And what the *hell* were they shooting?"

"People and things you don't ever want to mess with again," I said. "That's all you need to know. How did your client know I hadn't left the planet?"

"He said you weren't on any of the ship passenger lists."

"Astute of him," I said. "This genius have a name?"

"I never talked to him. It all came as texts."

Not unexpected, but also not very useful. "All right then. Fact number one: Dent was never here. Fact number two: he's gone, permanently and forever beyond your reach."

"Nothing is forever."

"You can count this one as close enough," I said. "Whatever your client wanted with him, it's not going to happen. Ditto for whatever he might have wanted with me. Double ditto for whatever he might have wanted with the Patth who just left. I trust that the bodies of your men are all the underlining that you need?"

Balic hissed out a breath. "I suppose you want me to clean those up, too?"

"You're the reason they're there," I reminded him. "But if you want to leave bodies with enough undamaged DNA left for the badgemen to trace them back to you, be my guest. Either way, it's time for you to fade into the sunset. Clear?"

"It was clear when you put that gun to my head," Balic growled. "You don't need to beat it into the ground."

"That's what I thought the last time we had a conversation," I said. "But you proved to be something of a slow learner. Now, I'm guessing that after our last interaction you're still not too mobile, so you probably aren't going to follow or otherwise try to inconvenience me. Do I need to shoot your driver and spotter to make sure they also aren't a problem?"

The two men in the front seat visibly stiffened. "No, we're good," Balic said grimly. "Don't know what the client will say."

"Tell him you fulfilled as much of the job as you could, and that you're done," I said. "If he still wants Dent he can find someone else to take another crack at him. Whether you offer him a refund is up to you."

I tapped the side of his cheek with my free hand. "One other thing. The next time I see you I *will* shoot first, and I'll shoot to kill. That goes for each and every one of your thugs, too."

Balic snorted. "Most bounty hunters would have done that already. With a *lot* less talking."

"Oh, I've killed plenty of times," I assured him. "I just hate sitting around badgeman stations filling out paperwork. Have a pleasant evening."

Keeping my gun trained on them, I backed up to the rear doors and popped them open. A quick look to make sure a crowd of unfriendlies hadn't gathered behind the van, and I was once again walking briskly through the night air.

Maybe Balic had finally had enough, or maybe he was just leery of trying to come up with a new plan on the fly, especially now that a Patth was involved. Either way, I made it down the block without trouble to a parked runaround, and a minute later was once again cruising along the streets of Malfatti City.

But not toward Erymant Temple and Pollux. I wouldn't have gone directly anyway, not with Nask on the loose. Protocol or not, mandates or not, I could imagine him even now licking whatever the Patth used for lips in anticipation of having a brand-new portal to wave under his Director General's nose. But before I could weave a trail-shaking route home, I had some calls to make.

With the business day over and the evening mealtime winding to a close, the local StarrComm center was getting busy again as city residents lined up to make more personal calls across the Spiral. I added my name to the list and found a seat where I could watch both the door and the entrance to the booth area. For once I wasn't in a hurry, and in fact had some serious thinking to do. By the time my name was called, I was confident that I finally had all the pieces.

Only time would tell whether I knew how to fit all those pieces together.

Dent was asleep again when I finally rolled over the threshold into Pollux's receiver module and sealed the hatch behind me. Selene was sitting in one of the two camp chairs I'd brought from Popanilla, the Blago I'd left her lying ready in her lap. "How did it go?" she asked softly.

"About as expected," I said, walking around the module hull toward her. "Nask identified the Patth Dent shot, made some noises about how his mandate wouldn't let him do anything about a portal even if he bumped into one, and left without threatening me."

"And Balic's men *did* show up?"

"With Balic even personally running the operation from inside a van," I said, easing down into the chair beside her. Suddenly, I was feeling immensely weary. "He must have been swimming in pain meds."

"Yes, I can smell them," Selene said. "A wonder he could talk straight."

"Oh, he talked just fine," I assured her. "I just hope he remembers this evening clearly enough to take some life-lessons from it."

"One can always hope," Selene said. "I assume Nask's lack of threats means he didn't suspect you were planning to play Balic off him if he gave you trouble?"

"Not as far as I know," I said. "And really, it was always a toss-up as to whether I'd need Balic to run interference against Nask or Nask to run interference against Balic. Just depended on which side decided to play rough."

"Yes," Selene murmured, her nostrils sniffing hard. "Gregory... am I smelling...?"

"Burned flesh, yes," I confirmed, my stomach tightening. "It was a ways away, but I imagine that smell gets everywhere. Let me rest a minute, then I'll grab a change of clothes and head over to Castor to clean up."

"There's no hurry," she said. "Like you said, it was distant. Before we go to sleep, though, it would be good. Balic's thugs?"

"I heard at least two shots," I said. "Don't know if there were more—I was sort of focused on other things—or whether one might have been a warning shot."

"Yes." Selene shivered. "That was one of the life-lessons you mentioned?"

"Probably the biggest," I said. "Hopefully, even if Balic doesn't learn it, the rest of his men will. The man may be stubborn, but he won't get far alone."

I stood up and walked over to the stack of supplies I'd brought. "Oh, and I went to StarrComm and sent out the invitations," I added over my shoulder. "I figure everyone will be able to get here in eight days."

"Whether they actually come would be another question," Selene pointed out.

"Oh, they'll come," I promised. "All of them. Dent's presence pretty much guarantees that."

The eight days passed slowly. Dent mostly spent the time recovering and mending in Pollux's receiver module, while Ixil spent most of his time in his camp outside Castor or else tramping through the woods to Trailhead and Aerie on the various errands I gave him. Neither he nor Dent was exactly thrilled by my plan, but between my logic and Selene's far better persuasive skills we were able to get them to grudgingly go along with it.

Those same skills also came in handy when I had her call Malfatti City's Historical Preservation Department and tell them about the damage to the lecture hall wall that had been caused by the misfire of Dent's remote DubTrub quick-load. Given the sheer number of buildings and artifacts on the Erymant Temple grounds they were reluctant to spend any of their limited budget on a building that maybe one in a thousand tourists even bothered to step into. Despite their protestations, though, when I checked out the hall the day before the meeting I found a tall scaffold in place against the wall, both the scaffold and the chairs around it covered by large loose drop cloths to protect against whatever they were putting on the stone up there to repair or at least disguise the damage.

The ceramic, glue, glaze, or whatever had also left a lingering hint of exotic aroma in the air. I hoped it wouldn't interfere with Selene's sense of smell, and made a mental note to stop by the hall a couple of hours before our guests were due to arrive and prop open the door.

And when everything was finally ready, there was nothing to do but wait. To wait, and to run over the details of the plan a few more times.

And to hope like hell that we all lived through it.

CHAPTER TWENTY-TWO

———— ❖ ————

Selene and I were waiting at the temple grounds' low border wall when the first of the invited guests arrived.

And they were not at all happy to see me.

"Hello, Roarke," Floyd said coldly as he, Cole, Mottola, and Fulbright climbed out of the first of the three dark-windowed vans that pulled up to the side of the street. "You get lost?"

"Yeah, sorry about that," I apologized as they strode across the narrow strip of textured grass and stepped over the wall. "But we were getting shot at, and all we could do was run."

"All the way to Popanilla," Floyd said, his eyes flicking around the grounds behind us. "Never occurred to you to leave me a message?"

"I didn't have your number," I reminded him. "Or anyone else's," I added, nodding in turn to the other three. "And once we had to ditch the *Ruth*, getting to a StarrComm center got a little tricky."

"You managed it okay a few days ago with this little invite."

"That's because as of a few days ago Dent stopped being in position to keep a gun pointed at my back," I said. "Anyway, what are you complaining about? You found Popanilla pretty quickly on your own. Mind telling me how you managed that?"

"Ask *him*," Floyd said, jerking a thumb at Fulbright. "He's the one who pointed us to Shiroyama Island."

"I'm impressed," I said, shifting my attention to Fulbright. "You're better connected than I would have guessed."

"Or I'm just smarter than you are," Fulbright said, glowering at me. "You said Dent would be here."

"He is," I assured him. "Well, he's close. We'll be heading out to meet him soon enough."

"How about we head out to meet him *now?*" Floyd countered.

"Patience, Floyd, patience," I soothed. "We have some things to discuss first. I've got a nice little place all ready for us out of the public eye."

I gestured toward the other vans that had arrived in Floyd's convoy. "So if Mr. Draelon would be kind enough to join us we can get things moving."

For a moment Floyd just gazed at me. Then, he gave a small hand signal. Behind him, the first and third vans' side doors opened and fourteen guards climbed out briskly, their hands resting on holstered guns. They formed a semicircle around the middle van and paused as if in anticipation. Out of the corner of my eye I saw Selene's head tilt slightly—

"Hello, Roarke," Draelon's voice came from behind me.

I turned around. Draelon was striding toward us, a self-satisfied smile on his face. Marching alongside him was Jordan McKell, still in his Algernon Niles bounty hunter disguise, with another two large thugs rounding out the foursome. "Hello, Mr. Draelon," I greeted him. "I trust you enjoyed your stroll across the Erymant Temple grounds."

"I'm enjoying finally catching up with you," Draelon said coolly. "You've wasted a great deal of Mr. Floyd's time with your shenanigans. The results had better be worth it."

"I think you'll find everything you were hoping for, and more," I assured him, glancing back over my shoulder at the array of thugs still waiting by the vans. "I'm afraid the venue for our conversation was chosen for privacy instead—"

"What conversation?" Draelon cut me off. "You said you were going to take us to Dent and the object."

"There are a few subjects we need to discuss first," I said. "Compensation, guarantees—that sort of thing. It shouldn't take long, and then we'll be on our way. As I was saying, the venue was chosen for privacy, not size, but it should be able to accommodate your entourage."

"Yeah," Draelon said suspiciously. "So we should all just leave the vans here, hey?"

"Well, your men would have trouble getting them over this wall," I pointed out. "But I doubt we'll be gone long enough for anyone to steal them, if that's what you're worried about."

He gave me a thin smile. "You know, Roarke, I learned a long time ago that when someone goes out of their way to point you in some direction, you'd better keep an eye on all the others. You're worried about local car thieves, are you?"

"It was just a thought," I said mildly.

"Right. Just a thought." Draelon gestured to one of the men by the vans. "Stay here and watch the vans," he ordered. "Keep a special eye out for any of Roarke's friends who might try to make trouble. Floyd, you and your group will come with us. That's eight of us and two of you, Roarke, and I can see from here that you're not armed. Do I need to make it clearer?"

"Not at all," I said. "I assure you, Selene and I are just here to talk."

"Good," Draelon said. "Let's get on with it."

I nodded and set off across the temple grounds, suppressing a smile. Draelon's cynical comment about diversionary tactics was *exactly* like something my father would have said.

The lecture hall was a two-minute walk from the vans. I'd left the door propped open a few centimeters, and we were about twenty steps away when Selene casually reached over and gave my hand a small squeeze. I acknowledged with a microscopic nod, wondering whether our other guests would be waiting for us inside or stay skulking around outside a little longer. I reached the door, pulled it the rest of the way open, and peered inside.

Skulking around outside, apparently. The domed room was just as I'd left it: its chairs unoccupied, its floor empty, showing no signs of life at all.

As my father used to say, *The best way to handle unexpected company is to not open the door for them in the first place.* Unfortunately, today that wasn't going to be an option. "Mr. Draelon; gentlemen," I said briskly, stepping out of the way and gesturing them inside. "Please; make yourselves comfortable."

Silently, they filed in and headed down toward the floor and the podium. Fulbright and McKell gave me speculative looks as they passed, the others ignored me completely. The two bodyguards

Draelon had brought took up flanking positions just inside the door. I ushered Selene in, again leaving the door ajar.

One of the bodyguards reached back to close it. I put a warning hand out to stop him. "They've been doing work in here," I murmured, nodding toward the draped scaffolding and the damaged wall. "Whatever they're using is pretty stinky."

He sniffed, made a face, and gave a reluctant nod, leaving the door open. I nodded silent thanks, then headed down to join the others.

Draelon had taken the seat directly in front of the podium, with Floyd on one side, McKell on the other, and Cole, Mottola, and Fulbright in the row behind them. Selene took the seat at the far end of the front row as I stepped to the podium.

"This won't take long," I assured them, noting to my mild surprise that my voice filled the room better than I'd expected. I hadn't realized the podium had a built-in sound system the last time we were here, let alone that it was functional. Still, a bit of amplification certainly couldn't hurt. "But there are some things we have to clear up before we visit the object that you've all come so far to see and put in so much effort to possess."

"Your share of the prize, I assume?" Floyd said.

"Actually, there's another topic we need to deal with first," I said, looking him straight in the eye. "A small matter of betrayal."

For a moment I held his gaze. Then, deliberately, I turned to Fulbright. "So, Fulbright," I said. "You want to tell them about it? Or should I?"

A deathly silence filled the hall. Fulbright glared at me, but remained silent. "I guess it's me, then," I said after a few seconds. "First, I have three questions for Selene."

The surprised, angry, or speculative looks everyone had been giving me turned magically to Selene, sitting quietly in her chair. "Selene: question one."

"Yes," she answered.

"Question two."

"No."

"Question three."

"Yes."

I nodded. "Thank you. Well. The story starts a few months ago—"

"Wait a minute," Draelon cut in. "What the hell was *that* about?"

"I had three questions for Selene," I told him. "She answered them. The story begins—"

"What the hell were the questions?" Draelon demanded.

"We'll get to that, Mr. Draelon," I said. "The story—"

"Like hell we will." Draelon lifted a hand and gestured—

And suddenly the two bodyguards at the door were pointing their Skripka 4mms at me. "You've got ten seconds to take us to the object," Draelon said, his voice almost calm. "Then you start losing body parts."

"I'm sorry, sir," I said mildly. "I assumed you'd first want the details of how Fulbright betrayed you."

Draelon's eyes narrowed. His eyes flicked over his shoulder to Fulbright, then back to me. "What the hell are you talking about?"

"Fulbright. Betrayal," I said. "Do you still want to go see Dent, or shall I continue?"

Again, Draelon looked back at Fulbright. "Yeah," he said. "Sure. Continue."

"Thank you," I said. "The story starts about six months ago. Mr. Varsi had recently been in Havershem City, supervising an operation. He left Pinnkus and—I assume—returned to Xathru.

"Unfortunately, the operation had left behind some fallout. Specifically, the Patth very much wanted to talk to him and sent an Expediter to deliver a message. Mr. Varsi was therefore forced to go into hiding."

"Mr. Varsi is never *forced* to do anything," Draelon growled.

"Went into hiding of his own free will, then," I said. "Meanwhile, an entirely different Patth was very interested in talking to *me*. Unfortunately for him, my job as a Trailblazer routinely takes me off the edge of the map—often quite literally—and he was unable to find me. The reports from Pinnkus had mentioned our friend Fulbright here, so the Patth in question got in touch with him and hired him to track me down.

"There was just one slight problem. This particular Patth didn't have a mandate for anything concerning me, which meant he had no funds or resources to draw on. That left Fulbright with a job but essentially no budget."

I looked at Fulbright. His face was rigid, trying not to give anything away and not really succeeding. "Mind you, at first he didn't mind that," I went on. "He had personal reasons for wanting me to take a fall, and getting any funding at all beat the hell out of chasing me on his own. But once he started thinking about it he realized he could search the Spiral for months and still come up dry.

"So he came up with a rather audacious plan to make life a little easier. He knew I'd been working for Mr. Varsi on Pinnkus, and he'd heard that Mr. Varsi had disappeared. So he went to Mr. Draelon, hinted broadly that I had something to do with Mr. Varsi's troubles, and suggested Mr. Draelon hire him to track me down."

I raised my eyebrows at Draelon. "That *is* how Fulbright pitched it, isn't it?"

"Mostly," Draelon said. His eyes were steady on me, his face far more unreadable than Fulbright's.

"Mr. Draelon, of course, already knew where Mr. Varsi was, so that approach gained Fulbright exactly nothing," I continued. "Fortunately for him, there was something else Mr. Draelon wanted that I might be able to help him with. Mr. Varsi had taken one of the sporetes Selene and I had brought back from one of our crockett trips and developed it into a drug. Curiously enough, the drug had two wildly divergent capabilities: medicinal for the Najiki, but more of a street-level drug for Narchners. The drug was already on Huihuang and about to be tested on a Najik subject under the auspices of the local boss, Mr. Gaheen."

I looked at Floyd. "That was the test we inadvertently walked in on in Mr. Gaheen's house."

"Yeah, I figured," Floyd said, his face as stone-carved as his boss's.

"Anyway, at that point, everything was roses," I said. "At least from Fulbright's point of view. Mr. Draelon assigned him three of his top enforcers, gave him a ship and presumably a bunch of intel resources to draw on, and sent him off on an expedition to find me so that he could hopefully get his hands on the drug. And not, I presume, for its medicinal value."

"We were also to grab anything else that you came up with," Floyd added.

"Hence, following the *Ruth* and snatching our bioprobe," I said. "I imagine Fulbright wasn't happy with you on that one."

"He said we were wasting time," Floyd said, eyeing Fulbright. "Said we should just grab you and be done with it."

"Yes, I'm sure he did," I said, nodding. "Though snatching

a Trailblazer ship from mid-atmosphere would be a pretty iffy maneuver. But I digress.

"Because while you were searching, the Patth who'd originally hired Fulbright stumbled on something else. A thief and smuggler named Easton Dent had been doing his own search for me. Our mystery Patth jumped on this new possibility, and eventually was able to track Dent to New Kyiv, where he'd arranged to meet up with me.

"What neither the Patth nor Fulbright realized was that they'd both ended up in the same place: Floyd and Fulbright tracking me, the Patth tracking Dent. Once they figured that out, Fulbright sent Floyd and the others out into the city to look for me while he and the Patth held a private meeting aboard Fulbright's ship."

I paused, waiting for someone to disagree. But the room remained silent. "And then the Patth did something stupid," I continued. "His Iykams had a line on Dent, even hired a pickpocket to lift his wallet for confirmation. The Patth or one of the Iykams must have spotted the two of us talking, so they had my wallet lifted as well. Armed with all this proof, the Iykams charged into the crowd...and managed to grab the wrong man."

"And then, what, just killed him?" Floyd asked, frowning.

"He had reasons," I told him. "We'll get to that. Anyway, the Patth decided he could still pull something useful out of the fiasco. He left the body and my wallet in plain sight, figuring he could let the badgemen find me and haul me in and that he could break in and grab me back later. Unfortunately for him, someone else got to me first. That left Fulbright and Floyd free to track the *Ruth* to Marjolaine and finally reel us in.

"But somewhere on our way back to Brandywine, something changed. By the time you brought us to Mr. Draelon, Floyd, he no longer cared if I was alive. In fact, from the way he was talking, he was halfway to buying into Fulbright's accusation that I'd betrayed Mr. Varsi."

"Because you had," Draelon said, a fresh edge to his voice.

I shook my head. "No, but kudos on the attempt at diversion. No, actually, there were two things that had changed. The first was that you'd been able to suborn the Najiki doctor on the Huihuang drug test, Physician Livicby, into stealing a sample of the drug for you. The second—"

"Wait a minute," Floyd put in. "That doesn't make any sense.

We already had the drug. Why would Mr. Draelon need to steal a sample?"

"Actually, the only thing that makes sense is if it *was* for Mr. Draelon," I said. "The sample couldn't be for Mr. Gaheen or the Najiki—they already had the drug. More telling, Livicby was willing to stick his neck out for me after he found out I'd come from Brandywine. Who else would he be willing to do that for except Mr. Draelon?"

"How about Mr. Varsi?" Draelon countered. "Livicby would stick his neck out for him."

"Except that Mr. Varsi was the one who developed it," Floyd said, his voice gone quiet. "What are you suggesting, Roarke?"

I braced myself. This was where it was going to get dicey. "You know, Floyd, all the way to Huihuang I had the nagging feeling that something didn't add up. Why send three high-level managers, even ones who'd once been ground-level enforcers, to deal with a supposed traitor like Mr. Gaheen?"

"There's no *supposed* about it," Draelon bit out.

"And then I saw Gaheen's house and security setup, and I wondered if maybe Mr. Draelon was trying to kill four birds with one stone." I looked at Draelon. "Literally."

"You're looking to get yourself shot right now, Roarke," Draelon said in a low, vicious voice.

"Maybe," I said. "What do you think, Floyd?"

"Wait a minute," Cole put in, sounding bewildered. "This doesn't make any sense. Mr. Draelon wanted us to find Dent and bring him back, remember?"

"Only we weren't supposed to deal with Gaheen until *after* we delivered Dent," Floyd said quietly. His eyes were focused on Draelon now. "You told me Gaheen was loyal, Roarke. How sure are you about that?"

"Very sure," I said. "As sure as I am that you, Cole, and Mottola are, too. At least, to Mr. Varsi."

Abruptly, Draelon lunged out of his seat, spinning to face Floyd, his hand darting beneath his jacket. The hand froze in place, Draelon's back unnaturally stiff, his eyes on the plasmic that had magically appeared in McKell's hand. "Floyd?" McKell prompted.

For a long moment, Floyd just sat there, staring up at his boss. "What are you saying, Roarke?"

"I'm saying," I said quietly, "that Mr. Varsi is dead. And that

Mr. Draelon figured his best way out of any responsibility for it was to dump all the blame on me."

Floyd held his pose another couple of heartbeats. Then he stood up, reached past Draelon's hand into his jacket, and relieved him of his Skripka. "How?" he asked in the same voice.

"It was the Patth," Draelon said, spitting out the word. "They tracked him down, tore him up—"

"I don't think so," I said.

Draelon spun to face me, fury and hatred steaming from his face. "Shut up!" he snarled. "What the hell do you know? Were you there?"

"No, I wasn't there," I agreed. "But I know a little about Patth procedure when they're mad at someone. They deliver a warning"—I raised my eyebrows—"and then they demand restitution."

"As in taking over part of the organization?" Floyd asked.

"That would be my guess," I said. "We'd have to find the Expediter who delivered the message to be absolutely sure. The thing is, since the crime was Mr. Varsi's the punishment would also be his. If he was no longer in charge of the organization...?"

"So he killed him," Floyd said flatly.

"No," Draelon bit out. The fury was still there, but the steel was rapidly draining from it. "I hid him, protected him, tried to find a way out of the mess he'd put us in. But then he got sick, and the doctors couldn't do anything, and he died."

He spun around to face Floyd. "I didn't kill him. He *died*."

"Maybe," Floyd said. The gun he'd taken from Draelon was now pointed at his boss's stomach. "Doesn't explain you trying to kill Cole and Mottola and me. And Mr. Gaheen."

"Kill him!" Draelon snapped. "What are you waiting for? *Kill him!*"

He jabbed a finger at Floyd as he looked up at the top of the lecture hall. The two guards he'd left flanking the door—

Were standing stiff and motionless, a pair of Iykams behind them, a pair of Iykam corona guns pressed into their sides.

Draelon froze, his finger still pointed. Floyd was looking up at the guards now, too, and Cole, Mottola, and Fulbright had swiveled in their seats to do likewise.

And the look on Fulbright's face was one of pure gloating.

I cleared my throat. "I was wondering when you'd show yourself, Sub-Director," I called. "Please; come join us."

For a moment nothing happened. Then, at an unheard order, the two Iykams gave their prisoners a nudge toward the steps and the four of them started down toward us. Behind them, a Patth I'd never seen before stepped through the doorway and followed.

And behind him, ten more Iykams flowed silently into the room, fanning out to both sides along the upper level.

"It's been a long road, Gregory Roarke," the Patth called back as he descended the steps. He made a sharp gesture to Floyd; reluctantly, Floyd set his gun down on the floor. "I'm pleased to finally meet you."

"Likewise," I said. "Fulbright, would you care to make the introductions?"

"This is Sub-Director Surn," Fulbright said. "Soon to be Director Surn."

"Very soon," Surn added. "Director Surn, who will personally deliver Dent's alien portal to the Patthaaunuth."

CHAPTER TWENTY-THREE

———— ◆◆◆ ————

"Well, technically, it's not Dent's," I pointed out as the group continued down the steps. The two Iykams paused at the middle level to shove their prisoners into two of the middle-row seats, then stepped around behind Cole and Mottola and relieved them of their Skripkas. Tucking the weapons away in their belts, the Iykams rejoined Surn, the three of them continuing the rest of the way down to where Draelon and I were standing. One of the Iykams stepped over to McKell, took his plasmic, and rejoined Surn.

Meanwhile, Fulbright had stood up and moved off to the side, away from Cole and Mottola, the same self-satisfied smile still plastered across his face. "And it's not going to be *Director Surn*," I continued as Surn stopped in front of me. "It'll be whatever is a step or two below sub-director. Assuming he doesn't banish you from the leadership hierarchy entirely."

Surn smiled thinly. "Because I don't have an official mandate? Surely you don't believe the Director General will be ensnared by such rigidity."

"No, it won't be because of any mandate protocols," I said. "It'll be because you've screwed up so often and so badly on this whole fiasco that he'll have no choice."

The smile vanished. "You know nothing about the Patthaaunuth."

"Maybe not," I said. "But I know a lot about screwups. Would you like a list?"

"No," Surn said flatly.

"You really ought to hear the list," I pressed. "How else will you know how much you need Mr. Draelon here?"

Draelon's gaze had been fixed on the Patth. Now, he turned toward me, his eyes narrowed. "What are you talking about?"

"Why else do you think I asked you all to come here today?" I allowed some puzzlement into my voice. "You two each have half the solution. Unfortunately, both halves are wrapped up in a whole lot of trouble. I'm just going to show you how to put the pieces together, clear out the trouble, and make this work."

"What the hell game are you playing at?" Draelon demanded.

"You did not invite me anywhere," Surn added.

"Of course I did," I said with exaggerated patience. "I invited Floyd, knowing that Floyd would tell Fulbright, knowing that Fulbright would tell you. Are we all going to stand here arguing, or shall we figure out how to get you both the immense profit that you came here for?"

Draelon and Surn eyed each other. "Fine," Draelon said stiffly. "You already spilled open my dirty laundry to Floyd. I guess it's our glorious sub-director's turn."

"I guess it is." I turned to Surn. "I assume you were outside listening this whole time, so we don't need to go over the deal you made with Fulbright and the scam he then turned around and played on Mr. Draelon. We'll also skip over the mess you made trying to grab Dent on New Kyiv and your murder of the wrong man. I frankly doubt the Director General will care much about that.

"No, where you really messed up was in the Roastmeat Bar on Gremon. Like all sub-directors you'd been assigned three Iykams, so you already had some muscle to take along with you." I was guessing on that one, but having seen the Iykam count on New Kyiv, plus my meeting with Nask a few days ago, it seemed a reasonable assumption. The fact that Surn didn't contradict me was also a good indication. "But you knew they could never cover a facility that big by themselves. So you called the Patth freighters that happened to be in port—there were two of them; I checked—and commandeered all their Iykams."

I cocked my head thoughtfully. "Or at least you grabbed all

they were willing to give you. I know Patth pilots are supposed to have an Iykam escort when they leave their ships, so some of them might already have been unavailable. At any rate, you collected your troops, stashed a few of them near the *Ruth* in case we got past you, and sent the rest into the Roastmeat.

"Unfortunately, you hadn't counted on Weston Dent handling backup for his brother." Out of the corners of my eyes I watched for reactions. But there weren't any. The truth about Dent's secret weapon was apparently still intact. Hopefully, Dent would appreciate that when this was over. "When the dust settled you'd lost three Iykams. I don't know if they were yours or the ships', but it didn't really matter. However many you'd borrowed, that same number had to be returned. Which now left you completely alone."

"He still had us," Fulbright pointed out.

And instantly winced away from the withering looks he got from Floyd, Cole, and Mottola. "I suppose unwilling and unaware allies still count as allies," I agreed. Fulbright winced again, which was the reaction I'd been going for in the first place. The madder I could make Floyd at Fulbright, the easier it would be to get him on my side if and when I needed him. "Tell me, Sub-Director: how good a friend was Conciliator Yyng?"

"We weren't close," Surn said darkly. "But we shared ambitions and information. Did you kill him?"

I shook my head. "No."

"Yet you carried his picture in your wallet."

"It was a gift," I said.

"From whom?"

"From someone else," I said. "Do you want to wallow in your past, or look to your future? Fine. You knew Yyng had been poking around Shiroyama Island, so after Dent, Selene, and I escaped from Gremon you had Fulbright pretend he'd had a revelation or something and sent them to Popanilla. Finding the *Ruth* confirmed that deduction, and you kicked the hunt up to full power. Meanwhile, you used the Patth backdoors into StarrComm and the official badgeman comm nets to see if you could narrow the search.

"And then, Dent threw you a curve ball. He contacted a fence on Fidelio and arranged to deliver some stolen gems.

"And with that, you were well and truly jammed up. You'd hoped against hope that the portal wasn't on the island, or that it might have failed, or that Dent might not really know how to use it. All of that was now down the tubes. He was heading for Fidelio, you couldn't get there in time, there were no Patth freighters there you might bully out of their Iykams, and without a mandate on either Dent or the portal you had zero authority to call any Patth operations centers for reinforcements. And so, in desperation, you launched yourself straight into your major screwup: You contacted the crime boss Francisc Pacadacz and hired him to get a team to Fidelio and hunt down Dent for you."

I paused, doing another quick assessment. Draelon looked interested in a sort of malevolent way, probably the way he looked at every negotiation where the other side was starting in a pre-dug hole. Floyd was back to his stone face, taking it all in but keeping his thoughts to himself. McKell was doing similarly, though with his altered face I wasn't sure I'd be able to read his emotions even if he was showing them.

And Surn was gazing at me with a look that was equal parts quiet fury and quiet desperation. He knew what he'd done, but hadn't realized until now that anyone else had put all the pieces together. He was in serious trouble, and he knew it.

"Which about wraps things up," I continued. "I see from your entourage that you've been commandeering from Patth ships again, which will be one more strike against you when the Director General gets wind of it. Anyway. Now that you both know how deep in the muck you are, are you ready to talk deal?"

Surn looked at Draelon, then back at me. "You speak well, Roarke," the Patth said. "But your words are useless. You have no proof, and the Director General will never accept your word above mine."

"What about all these witnesses?" I asked, waving a hand around the room.

"Are they Patthaaunuth?" he countered. "If not, the number does not matter."

"But if they *were* Patth?" I asked.

"That question is meaningless."

"I don't think so," I said. "Mr. Draelon, you wondered earlier about the questions I asked Selene. Question one was whether Sub-Director Surn was the Patth who we knew had visited Fulbright's ship on New Kyiv. Question two—well, we'll get back to that. But question three was the big one. That question was whether our last guest had arrived. And the answer to that was also yes."

I filled my lungs. "I believe the tale has been sufficiently told," I called. "If you agree, we would be honored if you would join us."

And from behind the cloth covering the scaffold a familiar figure stepped into view. "Yes," Sub-Director Nask said quietly. "The tale has indeed been told."

For a fistful of heartbeats no one moved. No one talked. I couldn't even swear that anyone breathed. The two Patth stared at each other, the air between them all but crackling with energy and a subtle struggle for dominance. Three Iykams came out from behind the cloth and took up defensive positions behind Nask and to his sides.

And with that, the spell was suddenly broken. Surn's eyes flicked to the twelve Iykams in his own array; and when he turned back to Nask I could see a small smile on his face. "Greetings, Sub-Director Nask," he said calmly. "Do you now collaborate openly with humans?"

"I cooperate with all in the seeking of truth," Nask said in a matching tone. "Do you then dishonor the Patthaaunuth with broken protocols and needless killing?"

Surn made a rude-sounding noise. "Your narrow vision of protocol is of no consequence. And my conversation is not with you."

Deliberately, he turned to me. "You say Draelon and I can together bring success to this day," he said. "Explain."

"Certainly," I said, avoiding Nask's eyes. "You, Sub-Director, cannot bring the portal to the attention of the Director General without running afoul of Patth mandate protocols. Mr. Draelon, on the other hand, is under threat of Patth economic reprisals for Mr. Varsi's actions. I therefore propose that Mr. Draelon be the one to find the portal, and that he then contact you in order to offer it to the Director General, and that part of his price is to withdraw the Patth demand for restitution from his organization. You won't have violated the mandate protocols, he'll get out from under the Expediters' threat, and the Patth will finally have a portal to call their own."

"Yet you are human," Surn said suspiciously. "Why would you offer this to us?"

"For a great deal of money, of course," I said. "Plus, to be honest, I think you're going to be disappointed. This portal is different from all the others we've found up to now. It's a dyad: two portals that are linked together and don't go anywhere but back and forth between them. We call that version a *Gemini*."

"That seems... unuseful," Surn said, throwing a hooded look at Nask. Nask, for his part, just stood there silently.

"It does, doesn't it?" I agreed, putting some regret into my voice. "But you could at least set up one corridor for yourselves."

"Such a portal would also be useful for study purposes," Nask added quietly.

"Yes—study purposes," I agreed, jumping on the comment. "And I only want thirty percent of the final purchase price."

"You said *twenty* percent back on Brandywine," Draelon growled.

"That was to find Dent," I reminded him. "This is to deliver you a set of Gemini portals."

Another silence, a thoughtful one this time, descended on the room. I risked a glance at Selene, sitting quietly and continuing to sample the air, then one at McKell, who was just sitting quietly. I'd expected him to be looking at me, but instead his eyes were going back and forth between Surn and Draelon. He still had no idea what was going on, but he seemed willing to let me carry this to whatever end I had in mind.

"What about us?" Floyd asked into the silence.

Both Draelon and Surn turned to him. "What's that supposed to mean?" Draelon asked.

"You killed Mr. Varsi," Floyd said, his voice sending a shiver up my back. "You sent Cole and Mottola and me—"

"I already said Varsi died of natural causes."

"—Cole and Mottola and me to kill Mr. Gaheen," Floyd continued stolidly. "Or maybe for him to kill us, or maybe all of us to kill each other. Trying to get rid of those who were most loyal to Mr. Varsi."

"If you wish these three dead, that can be part of the purchase price," Surn offered.

"Yeah, I appreciate that," Draelon said. Stooping down, he picked up the Skripka that Floyd had taken from him. "But I can handle that myself."

"Whoa," I said quickly, holding up a hand. "No, no, no. No shooting in here. Not with Selene and me in the room. You want to kill them, do it somewhere else and *after* we've got our money and some alibis. I'm not going to get hauled in by badgemen looking for someone to charge with multiple murders."

"Fine," Draelon said, an edge of contempt in his voice. For him, apparently, murder charges were no big deal. "You want this, Surn?"

"I believe it will work for both of us," Surn said. "Yes, I accept the terms. *If* Roarke is telling the truth about the portals."

"I'm just waiting on you two before I bring out the goods," I said. "*And* on my advance."

"You said thirty percent," Draelon said, his eyes narrowing.

"And I want an advance against that," I said. "As my father used to say, *Five percent cash is better than fifty percent promise.* It's not like I can take you to claims court if you renege. Come on, come on—cash or certified bank checks; I'm not picky."

Draelon sent me a look that could have blistered paint, but he pulled out his wallet and extracted three ten-thousand-commark bank checks. I raised my eyebrows questioningly at Surn, who grudgingly handed me two more. "Excellent," I said, putting them away. They really didn't have to be so grumpy about it, I reflected, given that they almost certainly planned to kill Selene and me as soon as they had the portals anyway.

Along with Floyd, Cole, Mottola, maybe McKell, and probably Nask. At this point Fulbright was a toss-up, but I wouldn't have bet pocket change on his surviving the day, either. "If you'll follow Selene and me?" I invited. "It'll only be a short walk."

Selene stood up and walked over to join me, and together we started up the steps. "Wait a minute," Draelon called after us, sounding confused. "The thing is *here?* On the Erymant grounds?"

"The Erymant Temple is ancient; the portals are ancient," I pointed out. "It really should have been an easy connection. If you want to send someone to go fetch the group at the vans, we can wait." I nodded toward McKell. "Though I'm thinking that Niles is probably the only one you can trust at this point."

"No need," Surn said before Draelon could answer. "My Iykams will provide sufficient security."

"Yeah," Draelon said slowly, his gaze sweeping around to take in the silent aliens, suddenly realizing how completely outgunned he was right now. I held my breath . . .

"We cannot do this deal without both of us," Surn reminded him. "There is no danger of betrayal."

"*Further* betrayal, anyway," I said under my breath.

If Draelon heard me, he didn't show it. "Fine," he said. He hunched his shoulders once, then gave a brisk nod. "Fine. Okay, Roarke. And remember that we only need one of you to show the way. Try anything cute and your partner dies."

"I'm not likely to forget," I said, starting to breathe again. "Can we go now? As my father used to say, *Time is money you can't make change for.*"

We would have made a bemusing procession as we made our way across the temple grounds, had there been anyone out there to see it. Selene and I walked up front, with Draelon and Surn close behind: Draelon with his two apparently still trustworthy bodyguards, Surn with two of his borrowed Iykams in close attendance. The rest of Surn's Iykams followed a few paces behind us, guarding McKell, Floyd, Cole, Nask, and Nask's three Iykams. Between the two groups, looking rather like an afterthought, was Fulbright.

"All right," I said as we came up to the Pollux hatch. "Now, there's limited space in there—"

"Just open it," Draelon growled.

"All right." I turned back to the smooth surface and keyed the hatch. A quiet murmur went through the assembled group as the hatch swung inward and melted into the hull on that side. "The entrance is a little tricky, too—there's an artificial gravity inside that points outward from the center. Watch Selene and me, and do as we do."

"We'll watch *you*," Draelon corrected, taking Selene's arm and pulling her to his side. "She stays out here until we have a few more guns inside."

I rolled my eyes. "Really, there's no one in here to be afraid of. But fine. Watch me."

I got a grip on the edges of the hatchway, swung my legs up, and rolled inside. I gave my inner ear a couple of seconds to acclimate, then stuck my head out the hatchway. "See? Okay—next?"

I'd expected a couple of the Iykams to be next. But Surn had clearly been obsessing over this thing too long let someone else get in front of him.

Still, as my father used to say, *Enthusiasm is no substitute for knowing what you're doing.* He failed to make it far enough inside on his first attempt and dropped back, only a firm grip on the edge keeping him from ending up flat on the ground. He muttered something in the Patth language and resettled his hands on the edges.

And as he braced himself for his next try, I looked casually around the receiver module.

Dent was there, of course, lying on his camping mattress, his expression tense. His supply pantry door was open, showing that there was nothing inside but sealed food and water packages. The hammock Dent had slept in before his run-in with Pacadacz's thugs was back on Popanilla, eliminating any suspicions that the mesh or the stand could be used as a weapon. Through the interface into the launch module I could see the glow of the status lights.

And a quarter of the way around the receiver module was the safe from Popanilla, its door closed and its back sealed, just the way I'd asked for it to be delivered.

There was a grunt and a sort of thud, and I turned back to see Surn picking himself up off the deck. He again murmured something under his breath as he looked around.

"I didn't catch that," I said.

"I was remarking on the unassuming splendor of this device," he said.

"We like it," I said. "I assume you're also going to want a demonstration."

"Yes," he said. He walked a few experimental steps, watching first the hull curving up in front of him, then focusing on his feet. He stopped, and his eyes flicked around the module again, pausing briefly on Dent and somewhat longer on the safe. "Conciliator Yyng's reports spoke of a Brink-Chakra safe," he said.

"That's the one," I confirmed, nodding toward it. "All of Dr. Riley's notes are in there."

"I presume they're part of the deal?"

"Or can be negotiated separately," I offered.

"Like hell," Draelon growled.

I looked back to see him rolling his way into the module. He made it on the first try, though to be fair he'd gotten to see both Surn and me do it first. "It's part of the deal, period."

"Okay, fine," I said. "Just thinking out loud."

"Don't think," he said, standing up and looking around. "It's not healthy for you. So you're Dent?"

"Yes," Dent said. His face was still pale, but his voice was calm enough.

"Nice to finally meet you," Draelon said. "Where's your brother?"

Dent's eyes flicked to me, then back to Draelon. "He'll be here if and when I need him. He always is."

"Sure he is," Draelon said, craning his neck to look above us. "I wonder how ricochets work in here. I'll bet you can do some fancy bank shots, too."

"I'm not going to make trouble," Dent said. Again, he looked at me. "Roarke says this is the only way to end it."

"Sometimes Roarke knows what he's talking about," Draelon said, turning back to watch the Iykams and then Nask roll into the module. The Iykams were pretty good, as were Floyd and his friends. Selene was as good as they were, and a lot more graceful.

McKell and Nask, not surprisingly, were better even than I was.

A few minutes later we were all together again: Draelon and his two guards, Surn and his twelve Iykams, Nask and his three, Selene, Floyd, Cole, Mottola, Fulbright, McKell, Dent, and me. Even if Floyd and some of the others could be persuaded to remain neutral, I reflected, we were still facing rotten odds. I'd thought Surn might leave a couple of his guards outside on sentry duty, but he was clearly expecting a last-minute surprise and wanted his whole borrowed army there in case they had to shoot back. At me, if I had something up my sleeve, or at Weston Dent, should he make a sudden appearance.

It was almost a shame that Selene, Dent, and I were the only ones who could appreciate the irony of that thought.

"All right," I said briskly. "Now that we're all here, we'll head into the launch module. That's the opening over there, and I'll warn you that the transition is even trickier than the one you just did. The portal can transport up to eight people at a time, so for twenty-seven of us—Dent's still too injured to move—that adds up to three full loads plus a partial. Who's going first?"

"I am," Surn said. "You will of course accompany me."

"Wouldn't miss it for the world," I assured him. "Mr. Draelon?"

"Yeah, I'll go," he said, his eyes narrowed as he looked at Surn. Despite Surn's assurances—not to mention the basic logic of the situation—the lopsided balance of firepower was still clearly bothering him. "Turlow and Perf will go, too."

"There is no need to take your bodyguards," Surn said. "They would be put to better use watching Dent."

"Since when do we need Dent anymore?" Draelon retorted. "You know what's waiting at the other end of this transport thing?"

Surn looked at me. "No."

"Exactly," Draelon growled. "Neither do I. Turlow and Perf are going."

"You make an excellent point," Surn said. He didn't look worried, exactly, but suddenly he was looking at an imbalance of power going the other direction. He looked around, pointed to three of his Iykams. "You three, with me."

"Maybe Sub-Director Nask would like to go, too," I suggested. "We could leave one of the Iykams behind to make room."

Draelon snorted. "Forget it."

"Agreed," Surn said, eyeing me suspiciously. "Why do you make such a suggestion?"

"I just thought it would be a nice gesture," I said with a shrug. "He held the portal mandate for a long time. Just seems fair."

"Fair for me to share the glory with him?" Surn said contemptuously. "You truly do not understand the Patthaaunuth."

"I guess I don't," I said. "Anyway. Sub-Director Nask—everyone else—make yourselves comfortable. I'll be back in a couple of minutes for the next group."

Once again, my long practice with portal transitions stood me in good stead, allowing me to roll into the launch module with precision and a certain degree of grace. Once again, everyone else had a rougher time of it, with frustration and embarrassment the order of the day. But finally all seven of them were inside and grouped around me.

"That spike thing is the trigger," I said, leading the way around the curved surface toward the extension arm. "We all hold onto it, the gravity field around it shifts and takes us up to the center of the sphere, and in about three seconds we'll be in Castor."

"Where are the destination settings?" Surn asked, looking around.

"There aren't any," I told him. "Like I said before, this is a Gemini. It only links to one other portal, and vice versa. Come on, come on, let's get this over with."

I got a grip on the extension arm with my left hand. "You can hold it loosely or tightly," I said as the others gathered around the arm and tentatively took hold of it. One of the Iykams moved in behind me; Draelon elbowed him aside and shoved himself between us, pressing his chest against my back as the others maneuvered for position. "It's not pulling you up—the grav field does that—so you don't have to worry about falling," I went on, wondering what Draelon was up to. "Just hold it loosely and enjoy the ride."

"Sure," Draelon said softly, his breath tickling my left ear. He let go of the arm and shifted his left hand so that it was resting on top of mine, his first two fingers curved around the extension arm itself, the last two fingers and his thumb wrapped around and pressing against my fingers and thumb. "Just in case you thought about cutting out early."

"Right, because there are so many places to go from here," I muttered back. "But fine. Whatever." The last Iykam got his hand on the arm, and with the shift in gravity that I'd become far too familiar with, we all started drifting upward.

And as we rose toward the center of the module, I reached up across my chest to my left elbow, and pressed my thumb and fingers into the quick-release points hidden under the skin, squeezing and twisting to free the artificial limb. I held onto the now detached forearm with my right hand, holding it in position as I watched our progress upward. With a single second left before the portal activated, I pulled my upper arm out of my now flopping sleeve and shoved against the extension arm, pushing myself away. Draelon's eyes and mouth had just enough time to open wide—

And then they were gone, all seven of them, with Draelon presumably still holding onto my arm. The launch module's gravity shifted back to normal, and I dropped gently back toward the deck. In my mind's eye I could imagine the explosion of consternation and anger as the travelers realized what had happened and tried to prepare themselves for whatever was about to come at them.

I smiled tightly. Little did they know.

I landed on the deck and hurriedly returned to the interface. A quick glance showed that the remaining Iykams had spread out a bit, their corona guns held loosely in their hands, their full attention on their prisoners. I dropped flat beside the opening and rolled over into the receiver module. "As you were, everyone," I called.

It was like a magic trick, possibly the best one any of them had ever seen. Every head snapped around at the sound of my voice, every eye goggling at my completely unanticipated appearance.

And with every eye on me, no one noticed Dent's fingers moving subtly with their own magic. No one saw the safe door pop open in response to his signal.

But everyone saw the explosive flurry of sugarbirds as they boiled out through the open safe door and fluttered off madly in all directions.

"Don't shoot!" I shouted. "They're harmless."

The assurance came too late for two of the Iykams. Their corona guns were already up and tracking, and for a second the module crackled with the familiar sizzle and acrid blue-white electrical discharge. Fortunately for the sugarbirds, they were lousy targets, twirling and flapping and jinking back and forth, and neither of the Iykams' shots connected.

"What the hell is *this*?" Fulbright demanded, staring open-mouthed at the frenetic midair ballet taking place above him.

"They're birds," I told him. "Sugarbirds, to be exact. Really, they're completely harmless."

"Where is Sub-Director Surn?" Nask demanded.

"He's fine," I assured him. "He and the others are in the Castor receiver module, exactly as I said. Probably thinking and saying furious things about me."

"What then is this?" Nask persisted, pointing at the birds.

"Ah. Yes. That," I said. "See, I thought you and I needed a little time alone, and this seemed the most convenient way to do it."

I looked up at the birds. They were still trying to get higher from the ground, no doubt so that they could find the trees and forest scenery they were used to.

Unfortunately, the minute each crossed the center point, the definition of "down" suddenly reversed, sparking a mad course reversal. With twenty or more of them doing the same thing, their usual graceful dance had degenerated into a bewildering free-for-all.

"I see," Nask said, sounding a little calmer. "Yes. The center of the receiver module must be clear for the launch module to transport anyone there. With the birds keeping the center occupied, Sub-Director Surn and the others cannot return."

"But they can still get out through one of the Castor receiver module's hatches," McKell pointed out.

"Not anymore," I said. "See, I have a friend there who has—who *had*—a nice piece of blast ribbon with him. Yes, *your* blast ribbon," I added as sudden understanding flickered across Floyd's face. "We found it under the door of Mr. Gaheen's home on Huihuang and thought it might come in handy down the line. Anyway, between the friend and the blast ribbon Castor has been completely buried, the entire surface of the receiver module covered. That means the only way out is via Pollux. Which, as you pointed out, isn't happening."

"You will release Sub-Director Surn at once," one of the Iykams grated, leveling his corona gun at me.

"Certainly," I soothed him. "But before I do, I need a word with Sub-Director Nask. You recall, Sub-Director, that a few days ago I told you I would help you solve your mandate?"

"I do," Nask said.

"Back in the lecture hall, you'll remember that I asked Selene three questions. The first was about the unknown Patth in Fulbright's ship. She said yes, which told me Sub-Director Surn was indeed Fulbright's contact and silent boss. The third question was whether you were in the room. Again, she said yes."

"And the second question?"

"The second question," I said quietly, "was whether the Patth in Draelon's manufacturing facility outside West Pontus on Brandywine was here."

Nask's expression seemed to tighten. "She said no."

"She said no," I confirmed. "The Patth who was there wasn't Surn, and it wasn't you." I braced myself. "I believe, Sub-Director Nask, that you were mandated to find a kidnapped Patth pilot. I believe we've found him."

For a long moment Nask was silent. He looked at Selene, at McKell, back at me. "How did you know?" he asked at last.

"I didn't," I conceded. "But Varsi had also been playing games with Patth pilot equipment, and either he told Draelon about it or Draelon was listening in when the Expediter came to call. However it worked, Draelon apparently thought getting access to Talariac Drive ships could come in handy, and so he decided to finish what Varsi started."

"Or else Varsi handed the operation off to him," Floyd said.

"Or didn't have a choice," Cole added grimly. "Maybe he's right. Maybe Varsi died of natural causes. Or maybe Draelon just got greedy and didn't want to share."

I winced. *Varsi. Draelon.* No longer *Mr. Varsi* and *Mr. Draelon.*

As my father used to say, *Losing an ally's loyalty is like losing a live grenade under your chair.*

"So what now?" McKell said.

"I assume Sub-Director Nask has ways of getting a team to Brandywine," I said. I looked at the Iykams. "Can I also assume that when Iykams are commandeered by someone and then abandoned, that another Patth of equal rank can eventually assume command of them?"

"Yes," Nask said. "That period being six hours."

"Ah," I said. "I was hoping it would be shorter. I wish now that I'd brought a deck of cards."

One of the Iykams growled something in the Patth language. Nask answered, and the Iykam said something else.

And then, to my amazement he stepped up to Nask and handed him his corona gun.

"Sub-Director?" I asked carefully.

"He waives the transfer period," Nask said, his eyes still on the Iykam. "He gives me full authority."

I nodded. Of course he did. He knew now how badly Surn had messed up, and how some of the blowback might come against him and the others Surn had commandeered.

But more importantly, I suspected, was that a Patth pilot was in danger...and the Iykams' chief service to the Patth was the protection of those valuable and vulnerable people.

"So?" I prompted.

Nask hesitated, his eyes tracing the smooth walls of the Pollux receiver module. He had all the Iykams, he had all the guns, and there was nothing that stood in the way of his taking the portals. Nothing except his mandate, and the protocols of his people.

And the life of a single kidnapped Patth pilot.

Nask stirred, speaking again in his own language. "We travel to the StarrComm center," he translated as the Iykams hurried toward the receiver module exit. He held my gaze a moment, then briefly inclined his head to me. "There is a Patthaaunuth pilot on Brandywine who needs our assistance."

CHAPTER TWENTY-FOUR

————— ❖ —————

"You realize of course," McKell was saying from one of the fold-down seats as I walked into the *Ruth*'s dayroom, "that absolutely none of that should have worked."

"What shouldn't have worked?" I asked, heading toward Selene and the foldout couch as I ran a critical eye over McKell's face. He'd gotten rid of the Algernon Niles prosthetics hours ago, but his skin was still red and blotchy in places.

"Your plan to get Draelon and Surn to cooperate and then trap them inside Castor," he said. "By all rights one of them should have shot the other right there in the lecture hall and then tortured Gemini's location out of you."

"Or they should have been careful enough to send in surrogates instead of going in themselves," Ixil added from the fold-down seat beside McKell. At his feet, Pix and Pax were curled up on the deck, enthusiastically demolishing a pair of nut bars.

"You underestimate the power of ego," I said, sitting down beside Selene. "As my father used to say, *Ego, greed, and stubbornness are ninety percent of the levers you'll ever need.* Surn was hell-bent on staking a psychological claim by taking the first trip to Castor, and Draelon was equally determined not to take a back seat to anyone, especially a Patth."

"And of course, neither trusted the other," Selene said. "That was why they both wanted to take as many guards across to Castor as they could."

"Which helped clear some of the guns out of Pollux," I said. "And yes, they certainly would have killed us as soon as they'd secured the portal. But I figured they'd want to take a ride first." I spread my hands. "Actually, given the personalities involved, I'd say there was no possible way it *couldn't* have succeeded."

"I do so appreciate confidence in a person," Ixil said dryly. "I trust all the *Ruth*'s systems read out to your satisfaction?"

"Yes, everything looks good," I confirmed. Ostensibly, I'd just been on the bridge to confirm that the Malfatti City Spaceport fuelers were on the job, but of course I'd also taken the opportunity to run a quick diagnostic. "Thanks for getting the glitterpaint scrubbed and flying it here, by the way. Hitchhiking back to Popanilla would have been tricky."

"Not a problem," Ixil said. "Freeing it from impound was faster than waiting for the admiral to find me other transportation. And after everything you've done, you certainly deserved to get your ship back."

"I appreciate it," I said. "Does this newfound gratitude translate into additional money?"

"That will require additional conversations," McKell said. "But I'm sure the admiral will at least spring for the two bioprobes you asked for." His eyes flicked down to my left elbow. "And a new arm, of course," he added.

"Thanks," I said, looking down at my stump. The note Ixil had left inside Castor had convinced Draelon and Surn that neither had betrayed the other, circumventing the seven-way shoot-out and mass slaughter I'd been half expecting from them. That hadn't prevented them from venting their fury on my artificial arm, of course, which they very much had.

"Until then, we're paying for this fuel load, plus you've got those bank checks from Draelon and Surn to tide you over," McKell continued.

Beside me, Selene stirred. "Tera is here."

"We're in the dayroom, Tera," McKell called toward the hatchway.

A minute later, Tera appeared. "Hello, everyone," she said. She looked tired, but there was a definite air of satisfaction about her. "Jordan, you look almost human again."

"Thank you," McKell said dryly as he stood up and gestured her to his seat. "How's the excavation going?"

"All finished," she said, dropping gratefully onto the fold-down and nodding silent thanks as McKell took up a standing position beside her. "By sunrise this morning Pollux was on its way to the traditional undisclosed location."

"Did you really get permission that quickly?" Selene asked, her pupils showing surprise.

"Hardly," Tera said. "As Gregory's father probably used to say, it's easier to ask forgiveness than permission."

"Actually, what he used to say was *You don't need forgiveness* or *permission if you can convince them someone else did it*," I corrected her. "Don't suppose that really applies in this case."

Though now that I thought about it, that saying might indeed come into play. Possibly very soon. "I assume the Patth are furious?"

"Strangely enough, we haven't heard a peep out of them," Tera said. "Must be some interesting goings-on in their government right now."

I felt my throat tighten. In their government, or somewhere else entirely.

Yes. My father's saying was definitely going to apply.

"Actually, all the heat we're getting is coming from the Malfatti City Historical Preservation Department," she continued. "They're furious that we've demolished one of the Erymant Temple's most interesting structures."

"A structure no one could actually enter," Ixil pointed out.

"Because as we now know it was mostly full of Pollux," Tera said, nodding. "But it was beautiful and historically significant, et cetera, et cetera, and they're still furious."

"Luckily, cash on the counter is amazingly good at soothing such righteous indignation," McKell said. "I trust the admiral gave you an adequate budget to work with?"

"So far, yes," Tera said. "It helps that the main Fidelio government really doesn't care all that much, given their current preoccupation with having a major criminal boss found and detained on their soil. I have the sense they're not sure whether they're more pleased or more embarrassed."

"Speaking of Draelon, any idea what happened to Floyd and his fellow enforcers?" McKell asked. "Between dealing with ISLE and trying not to get run over at the speed Nask was getting Surn off-planet, I lost track of them."

"Oh, they're long gone," I said absently, my thoughts on other matters. If I said something now, maybe there was still a chance...?

No. There was no chance. There had never been a chance. "He told me they were probably going to Huihuang to join up with Gaheen and his branch of the organization."

"Wonderful," Tera murmured. "Like the old hydra myth: cut off one head and two more grow back."

"This might not be so bad," Selene said. "As Gregory told you earlier, Gaheen was using the drug from our sporete for Najiki medical purposes, not as a Narchner street drug. He may be trying to move his part of the organization into a more legitimate business."

"Or is waiting until later to exploit the Narchners," Ixil pointed out.

"I guess we'll find out," I said. "But after Floyd talked down the crew Draelon had left at his vans I figured we owed them at least a quiet exit."

"Speaking of exits, what happened on Brandywine?" Ixil asked. "The *Ruth* and I were in transit at the time and I never heard the final report."

"It went about the way everyone expected," Tera said grimly. "The Expediters who raided Draelon's factory killed everyone guarding the place and then burned it to the ground."

"The Patth pilot was in pretty bad shape," McKell added. "I gather Draelon's people had been doing a *lot* of work trying to get the implants out without destroying them. But from what the admiral said it looks like he'll make it."

"That's what Nask said, too," I confirmed.

"*Nask* said?" Tera asked, frowning. "You *talked* to him?"

"He sent me a message," I said. "During our restaurant meeting I told him I cared as much about resolving that issue as he did. I guess he decided to take me at my word."

"I thought you didn't like him," McKell said.

"I don't," I said. "What does disliking Nask have to do with hating kidnappers and torture?"

"Point," McKell conceded. "So how exactly did you know he was looking for a missing pilot?"

"Simple deduction," I said, feeling the growing tension of knowing we were standing on the edge of disaster while recognizing there was still nothing anyone could do to stop it. "Tera, you said Pollux was on its way back to Icarus?"

"Yes."

"And all the work crews and guards have gone with it?"

"Everyone's gone except me," she said, her eyes narrowing. "Why?"

"Just wondering," I said. So it could be any time now. "We start with two facts: McKell and Ixil had a highly classified job on Brandywine, and Selene had smelled a Patth in Draelon's factory. The logical lineup was that you were shadowing Nask and Nask was hunting a missing Patth—"

"Hold it," Tera interrupted. "Back up a step. What made you think Jordan and Ixil were following Nask?"

"Because sometimes McKell is just a little too good at his job," I said. "For his first in-the-flesh appearance as Bounty Hunter Algernon Niles he changed everything about himself, from his face and his voice to his gait and his stance. Even the shape of his ears and the pattern of his beard hairs were different."

"Those last two were the admiral's idea," McKell said, rubbing his cheek gingerly.

"Which makes the admiral smarter than most people," I said. "See, there's no need to go to all that effort to hide your identity from other humans. We *know* how humans recognize each other—eyes, facial shape, lips, voice. The only reason to change *everything* is if you're hiding from aliens."

"Because we *don't* necessarily know what cues they use to distinguish one human from another," McKell said, nodding as he finally got it.

"Exactly," I said. "And the only alien I know who's worth a Jordan McKell stalking *and* who would instantly recognize you on sight...?"

"Nask," McKell said ruefully.

"Nask," I agreed. "Actually, he more or less confirmed it at our restaurant meeting. I'd given him just two days to meet me on Fidelio, and he had no problem making that appointment. Granted, there are other systems within range of a Talariac drive besides Brandywine, but adding in your presence there made the conclusion solid enough for me to put some weight on it."

"Nicely reasoned," McKell said. He scowled. "He *could* have told me, you know."

"He could also have told us where he's spirited Dent off to," Tera said, her eyes flashing a little. Clearly, she wasn't any happier than McKell at having been left out of that particular loop. "You should know by now the admiral likes to keep a few secrets up his sleeves." She pulled out her phone, frowned at the display, and held it to her ear. "Tera."

I braced myself. This was probably it.

It was. Five seconds later her face went rigid. "Where?" she asked sharply. "Do we have...? What about Fidelio Patrol? Can they—? No, no, absolutely not. It absolutely wasn't us...because I just *said* it wasn't. Where—?" She broke off, and for another handful of seconds listened in silence. Then, she seemed to slump a little in her seat. "I understand. Thank you."

"What's happened?" McKell demanded as she lowered the phone. His back was stiff, his hand gripping his holstered plasmic. "Pollux?"

"No," Tera said quietly. "No, it was—" She paused and took a deep breath. "I was just informed that a large structure on the eastern edge of the Erymant Temple grounds was just blasted to rubble." Her eyes turned onto me. "And a large object that appeared through the smoke to be a double sphere was pulled out of the ground by four heavy lifters."

"The *hell?*" McKell bit out, hauling out his own phone as he headed for the hatch.

"Don't bother," Tera called after him. "The lifters are already clear of the atmosphere. It'll be in hyperspace in six minutes."

"We can still—"

"No, we can't," Tera said bitterly. "It's over. Leave it. It's over."

Reluctantly, McKell stopped in the dayroom hatchway and turned back to face the rest of us. His expression, I noted uneasily, was a mix of disbelief and growing anger. "How in hell did anyone—?" He broke off, turning suddenly toward me. "There were *two* of them hidden in Erymant?"

"So it seems," Tera said, her eyes going hard as she also shifted her gaze to me. "I notice, Roarke, that you don't seem surprised. How long have you known?"

"I've never actually *known*," I told her, forcing myself to meet the glares trying their best to pin me to my seat. "There were indications that there was another portal on Fidelio, that's all."

"What indications?" Ixil asked. Of the three of them he seemed the least furious. Or maybe I just wasn't as good at reading Kalixiri expressions.

"Nask abandoning his hunt for the missing Patth pilot to come talk to me instead of sending an Expediter or other representative," I said. "Nask not making any moves against me after our conversation. The Patth in general not raising a fuss about you digging Pollux out of the temple and letting it go without trying to interfere."

I felt my stomach tighten with the memory. "And Nask looking around Pollux's receiver module before heading to call Brandywine about the pilot. At the time I thought he was wondering if he should try to take it. Now, I realize he was just memorizing the view so he'd be able to tell later if there were any differences between it and the one they'd already found."

"Why didn't you tell us?" Tera demanded, her voice low and dark. "Why didn't you *say* something?"

"Like what?" I retorted. "I thought there might be a portal on Fidelio, but I had no idea where it might be. Were you going to patrol the whole planet? Demand the government chase the Patth off and never let them back?"

"You must have suspected it was part of the Erymant Temple complex," McKell said. He was still angry, but I could sense that some of the surge of emotion was fading. Slowly, reluctantly, he was coming to the same conclusion I already had, that there had been nothing anyone could have done to stop it. "We could have cordoned off the place."

"For how long?" I asked. "The thing had gone undetected for decades, and that wasn't likely to change any time soon. The Patth would have just sat back and waited until Fidelio got tired or bored with the fuss and kicked you out."

"We have Selene," Tera said tartly. But she, too, seemed to be heading toward unenthusiastic acceptance.

"No," I said. "The exposed part of Pollux's hull had already contaminated the whole area. She would never have been able to pick out the other portal's scent from the background."

McKell muttered another curse. "You still should have told us."

"Maybe," I conceded. "But bear in mind one other thing. Nask knew all about Pollux. He'd been inside, knew where the entrance was, and in the hours while we were processing Draelon and watching the Iykams haul Surn aboard Nask's ship there was ample time for him to have sent someone to sabotage it. But he didn't."

McKell snorted. "What, he's suddenly decided to be a sportsman about all this?"

"Or he decided he owed us for finding his missing pilot," I said. "Take your pick."

For a moment McKell, Tera, and Ixil all looked at each other. I waited, feeling the tension in the room slowly fading away. "You still should have said something," McKell said.

"Next time," I promised. "Okay, so we ended up with a draw. Let's take what we got and move on. Now that we know what Shiroyama Island was for, we should have a better shot at figuring out where the other end of Nask's Gemini is."

"I thought Shiroyama was the scene of a battle," Tera said, frowning.

"Actually, it's more the aftermath of one," I said, gesturing to Selene. "Selene's been doing some research, and she came up with a couple of interesting facts."

"There have been a number of alien bodies found over the years," Selene said, sounding a little uncertain. Maybe McKell and the others weren't quite as over their anger as I'd thought. "Along with many military-style armbands. But there's only *one* species of alien, not the two or more you'd expect if there'd been a major battle."

"Maybe the winning side went in and removed their fallen," McKell said. "Or maybe it was a civil war."

"No," Selene said. "Because despite all the soldiers who supposedly died there, no one's ever found any weapons. Or armor, or communications systems, or any of the other things armies use."

There was a pause as that sank in. Then Ixil stirred. "It was a prisoner-of-war camp," he said quietly.

"That's what we think," I said, nodding. "With Erymant the site of the military base and tribunal that decided the cases and sent them there."

"But why *two* Gemini portals?" Tera asked. "Two different camps? Officers and enlisted?"

"Or ordinary soldiers and war criminals," I said. "Or people who were expected to behave themselves and people who weren't. All I know is that if you want to send prisoners somewhere you want them bottlenecked so there's only one exit."

"Unless Shiroyama was the only camp," McKell said, his face gone suddenly grim. "Unless Nask's new portal was how they funneled prisoners from multiple worlds into Erymant for processing."

Tera shot a look at me, then looked back at McKell. "Are you saying Nask could actually have uncovered another Icarus?"

"I'm saying we need to get some pictures of the heist as fast as we can," McKell said. "Someone has to have *something*. We know Geminis are significantly smaller—if we can get a handle on the dimensions, we may be able to tell what it is he just made off with."

"We need to get this to the admiral right away," Tera said, standing up.

"Agreed," McKell said. "Ixil, you stay here and get the *Ruth* ready to fly—right now it's our fastest way off Fidelio. Tera and I are heading to the StarrComm center. We'll be back as soon as we can."

Together they disappeared out the hatchway and headed aft. "You heard him, Gregory," Ixil said, getting to his feet. "Let's see how the fueling is going."

"It's not done," I told him. "I can still hear the pumps."

"We can at least begin the checklist," he said, crossing the dayroom toward the hatchway.

"In a minute," I said, making no effort to stand up. "First, we need to talk."

"Can it wait?"

"It could," I said. "But it's not going to."

Reluctantly, he came to a halt. "What's it about?"

"Selene and me," I said. "If we're going to keep getting tangled up in Icarus business, we need to have all the pieces. All of them. *And* we need to get them the same time you do."

"I understand your concerns," Ixil said. "But you're still on probation."

"Then get us *off* probation," I said. "This isn't a matter of ego or of feeling like we're stuck at the children's table, Ixil. We were hired to find you new portals. Now, instead, we've been dropped headfirst into a pit with one group who wants us dead and another group who wants to take over the Spiral. Without timely information we're sitting ducks; and I submit that we're way too valuable to be wasted as cannon fodder." I ran out of breath and stopped.

"You make some valid points," Ixil said, a bit grudgingly. "And I can certainly speak to the admiral on your behalf." He held up a warning finger. "Just be sure you understand what you're asking. If the admiral agrees to bring you in, you'll be routinely thrown into missions like this. When things are quiet enough you might be able to continue searching for new portals. But you could be recalled to action on a moment's notice."

He looked at Selene. "Or at least *you* could. Given Selene's unique abilities and value, the admiral may choose to pair her with a different partner for the portal searches."

Beside me, Selene stirred. "No," she said quietly. "I stay with Gregory."

"You may not have a choice," Ixil warned.

She straightened up, determination in her pupils. "Of course I have a choice. I stay with Gregory."

Ixil looked like he wanted to say something, hesitated. "I'll speak to the admiral," he said instead.

"Good," I said, listening closely. The pumps had stopped. "Sounds like the fueling is finished. Go ahead and start the checklist—I'll meet you there in a minute."

Ixil nodded and snapped his fingers twice. Abandoning their snack, Pix and Pax scampered across the dayroom, climbed up his boots, trousers, and shirt and settled themselves on his shoulders. Patting each one on the head, he disappeared out into the corridor.

"He's right, you know," I said to Selene. "I can handle the nasty stuff by myself. There's no reason you have to come along."

"Of course I do," she said, a knowing look in her pupils. "Now, are you going to tell me what that was *really* about?"

I craned my neck. Ixil and his outriders should be comfortably out of earshot by now. "The sound you hear is me jumping backward from a couple of bad conclusions I jumped to earlier," I told her, lowering my voice. "The restaurant conversation I had with Nask. Remember me telling you Conciliator Yyng had the Patth portal-hunting mandate?"

"Yes."

"I was wrong," I said. "Nask said himself that Yyng's mandate shouldn't have brought violence. My guess now is that it was something wholly innocuous, like monitoring the StarrComm systems in that area or something. Whatever it was, he somehow tagged Dr. Riley, probably purely by accident, realized he worked with Icarus, and decided to follow up on him."

"Couldn't he have then asked the Director General for the portal mandate?"

"He could have," I said. "But if he did, he didn't get it, Remember, he tackled Riley with just two Iykams, which I gather are a conciliator's usual quota. If he'd had the portal mandate he would surely have brought a lot more to the party. Yyng playing his cards under the table also meshes with Dent's question about why the Patth didn't raid Popanilla after Yyng's death. They didn't come running because Yyng hadn't told anyone what he was doing."

"Except Surn."

"Right," I agreed. "I'm guessing Yyng brought him in under the assumption that a sub-director had a better shot at getting the Director General's attention than a conciliator once he was ready to make his pitch for the mandate. But even there he was cagey about what he was sharing, and Dent got to him before he could feed Surn enough information to pinpoint Castor. At that point, the whole thing died on the vine."

"Until Surn picked up on Dent's search for you and Icarus."

I nodded. "Exactly."

"All right," Selene said, her pupils now showing puzzlement. "But I don't see how this helps us."

"It helps us," I said quietly, "because if Yyng didn't have the portal mandate, who did?"

Her pupils went suddenly wide. "*Nask?*"

"Has to be," I said. "You saw how fast he got their portal out of Erymant and off Fidelio. There was barely enough time to pull together the necessary people and equipment, not to mention those heavy lifters and whatever supersized freighter they're probably going to stash it in. There's simply no way he could have also gone through the process of getting the mandate swapped over to him."

"But then—" She broke off, looking confused.

"Exactly," I said quietly. "But then what was he doing on Brandywine looking for a missing pilot? It sounded like a sub-director only gets one mandate at a time. Even if sometimes they get two, the Director General *certainly* wouldn't want to sidetrack someone away from portal-hunting duty."

"Or sidetrack him from the hunt for a kidnapped pilot." She turned to look across the dayroom. "Nask's hunt for the pilot wasn't business. It was personal."

"That's the only conclusion that makes sense," I agreed soberly.

"The pilot was a friend, or a relative, or the friend or relative of someone close to him. That's why he only had the three Iykams when he met me at the restaurant—he was off his mandate and didn't dare call attention to himself by requisitioning more to bring with him."

"But once he was on Fidelio, he *didn't* have to worry about his Iykams killing those thugs outside after your meeting," Selene said. "He could argue that with a known portal here he was within his mandate to look in on it."

"Especially since they apparently hadn't yet figured out how to extract it without bringing all sorts of grief down on themselves," I said. "Icarus moving on Pollux was the perfect cover. As my father used to say...?"

"*You don't need forgiveness or permission if you can convince them someone else did it,*" she murmured.

"Exactly," I said. "The point is that we know something about Nask that no one else does. We can either keep it to ourselves and hope he'll cut us some slack in any future encounters, or let him know we know and use it as a lever. Either way, we have a handle on him that no one else in Icarus does."

"Or even knows about," she said, nodding. "But in order to fully exploit it, we need access to more of their resources and intel."

"Exactly," I said. "So. You still in?"

"Of course," she said. "I'm sure your father used to say something about situations like this."

"Probably something like, *Never join a noble cause unless large payments or self-preservation are included.*"

"Very deep," she said. "I assume we're going for self-preservation, since I don't see much money coming our way."

"Self-preservation it is," I said, standing up and offering her my single hand. "Let's go see if Ixil's messed up anything yet."

Of course there was something else my father used to say, I remembered as we headed into the corridor: *Never assume the other guy knows what he's doing.*

I could only hope that in this case the other guy wasn't me.

The End